Witching and Scheming

A Huckleberry Hollow Witchy RomCom

BY: NOELLE RIDER
COVER ART: KACI KEYSER

Copyrights

Copyright © 2024 by Perry Dog Publishing

All rights reserved.

No part of this publication may be reproduced, distributed, or transmitted in any form or by any means, including photocopying, recording, or other electronic or mechanical methods, without the prior written permission of the publisher, except as permitted by US copyright law. For permission requests, please go to : .

This is a work of fiction. All characters and places are a product of the author's imagination or used fictitiously. The story, all names, characters, and incidents portrayed in this production are fictitious. No identification with actual persons (living or deceased), places, buildings, and products is intended or should be inferred.

Book Cover by Kaci Keyser @spooki_sheets

First Edition, Hardcover Published 2025

ISBN: 978-1-957539-20-1

 Formatted with Vellum

CONTENT WARNING

Note for Readers: This book contains talk of bullying, physical harm, thoughts of suicide, mentions of vigilante murder, magic, violence and sexually explicit scenes.
There is also a bare-assed Scotsman and the use of politicians / the alt-right as boner-killers.

Fuck the Patriarchy, we will not apologize.

To my husband, dogs and coffee, this wouldn't have happened without your love and support.

Shout out to my mom / editor. Thanks for not making it weirder than it needed to be.

PROLOGUE

PENELOPE

Artemis paced behind me, filling up too much of my tiny bedroom. The two feet he traveled generated enough heat that mixed with his voice and his anger in a suffocating chokehold, stealing any words I might have to send him away.

Even as my heart begged to crawl into the safety of our connection and hide there from the world.

Friendship was one of the cruelest paradoxes of life.

Instead of dwelling, I threw books over my shoulder into the bag on the floor beside my bed. It was haphazard, but magic sent every item sailing into the bag with precision and ease.

"Three days, Artie. I said I would stay three days after graduation and my 18th birthday until the new moon and then I was out. It's not my fault you were too busy to spend any of those days with me. It's not your fault either. You're a popular, well-liked being. But I can't stay." Random clothes flew behind the books. Every movement rubbed the lace inset of my shirt against the angry pink flesh of my arm.

The town's last gift to its least favorite person.

"Wait for the full moon, then! What's two more weeks? If you're going to make major life choices by the cycles of the moon, pick a different phase! They're all the same as long as you don't sprout fur!"

Scrubbing his face with his hands, Artie kept course between my bed and my dresser. It was the smallest in the house, a choice I'd made at seven when I was allowed to choose any room in the house and saw this one looked out at the forest behind our house and the Canadian border two miles away.

My favorite place in the world: anywhere but here.

Through the open window, a breeze carried the scent of strawberries and burning driftwood from the Litha festival below. Eighteen years of memories joined the smell, all of them as rotten as the strawberries smashed on the soles of my sneakers. Everything worked together, pushing against my forced calm to release a wave of magical revenge that would level this town.

Midsummer was a curse.

Like the child it brought into this world and the unrelenting heat that scorched tender flesh, midsummer sought to burn out anything beautiful.

Turning all that lived into a delicate tinder that could ignite at any moment.

I rubbed the fresh burn stinging through my shirt and felt another fiber of my sanity fray.

"I need to get out of here," I whispered in a strangled gasp.

"No, you don't. You need to stop holding back and show them who they're messing with. Also, you need to show me your latest injury and tell me who needs to die." His joking tone belied the growing rage that spilled out on an invisible cloud of ash and soot. His own emotional turmoil with the scent of my own past, a simmering cauldron bubbling over, pulling me under.

Burying me alive.

Tugging my shirt off, I thrust my arm at him, matching his anger with a wave of my own that charged the air in an electric current, setting his already gelled-up hair crackling at the tips.

"Fine. Here! Are you happy now? Is this what you wanted?" I shouted, voice too high-pitched. I was losing my edge, crumbling.

"What the fuck, Penny!"

His voice rattled the windows, shaking the wooden beams above us. A hand too fast to track appeared around my arm and dragged me against him, pulling me close in a death grip that I knew wouldn't bruise.

Even enraged, Artie would never hurt me.

"I cut through the festival field to get home from school. It's not easily accessible by car, and you know how Yasmin and her stiletto sisters hate to walk. She... or her mom... Someone spelled it. As I approached the perimeter, a searing pain shot through my arm. The closer I got, the worse the pain until I reached the center of the field and a small fire ripped through my flesh, leaving the shirt and the surrounding area untouched. Apparently, now that I'm 18, whatever code of ethics that kept bullies from crossing the line into permanent disfigurement has expired. We are officially in...," Artie stroked my arm and my voice caught on a sob.

So much for anger...

He dragged a single finger around the outer edge of the tarot card, relief following the gentle caress until my whole body shuddered. When I realized my eyes were closed, I snapped them open to see the burn still fresh on my arm.

A Knight of Swords.

"This is a threat," he whispered.

"Obviously." I took my arm back, pulling on the softest shirt I owned. "I'm the one who taught you about tarot."

A weird design that spelled out "Fuck Off" in a pattern of squiggles that concealed the message. It also glowed in the dark, which would be beneficial at 10PM when the sun finally went down, not that it had seen enough light to be much use for very long.

"New moon, new me. Whoever said I suck at listening and following instructions can kiss my ass."

"I'll be first in line to do so, and the last. But fuck, Peep, you can't leave! Physically, witches can't..."

"Leave a 300-mile radius of the forest like felons out on bond? Yeah, I know. But Idaho has a lot of places that aren't here. The magical bond will be taut, but it won't kill me to stretch it."

Artemis resumed his pacing, setting an alternative course between the nightstand and the hamper. A real feat in the 8 by 10 bedroom with too much furniture.

"So, you're just going to leave and let them win?"

"I was always leaving, and they were always going to win, Artie. Since the day I was born, I knew I didn't belong."

"You didn't *know* the day you were born. That's when everyone else decided because of that stupid old crone... Just..." He shoved his hands through his hair, the crunching hair gel catching on his fingers. He somehow avoided catching his shit-kicker boots on my faded rug, dancing amongst the contents of my room like he'd been there a million times and would be a million more. "Wait two weeks, please?"

His tone pulled me up short, and I stopped throwing things into my luggage to study his face.

The usual smirk and self-assurance had melted into pain. His pacing took on a small quiver, and the golden flecked brown eyes I'd grown to adore were too wide and bouncing around the room. Everything about him screamed agitated, unsettled, and... *something*... Something malicious.

Dangerous.

Possessive.

When he'd hit puberty, Artemis's demon half had turned out to be a succubus, needing to feed on the pleasure and lust of others. He'd fed on well over half the student body of our high school, feeding their lust for him and taking every ounce of pleasure in return. Just not me. Never me.

But none of the hungers and cravings written on his face compared to the pure dominion he commanded I grant him.

"Artemis, why do you look like that? You'll never get the lusty coeds to feed your beast if your face freezes that way. They'll think you want me." I tried to smile and sell the joke, but the man bit back a sigh before he whirled around to stare with a pleading stare.

"That's not funny. You know I need you... you're the only one who doesn't treat me like a fuck toy."

"You'll be fine, Artie. Just because you can't control the need doesn't mean you are nothing more than their toy. And you know the New Moon is the safest time to travel."

"It would be safer if you stayed," he muttered, and I waved my arm in annoyance.

"It might not be life threatening, but this isn't safe. I'd rather take my chances with strangers and dragons who might want me dead than stay here with the assholes who are actively working toward the cause."

"What about shifters?" He demanded, but it was a useless argument.

"What about them? You, of all people, know that shifters aren't really dangerous until the Full Moon. Another reason to go now. Your dad hates me as much as the rest of this town. He wouldn't lift an alpha command to save my life. Treaty between the Pacific Northwest Pack and The Coven be damned. Hell, it might earn him and the Kootenai people better land from the white man if they kill the fat witch everyone hates."

"My dad doesn't hate you and he can't let anyone kill you. He's just mad that I... that we..." the words strangled against a sudden pressure, marring his youthful face.

"That we what?" I looked around for an answer, baffled even as he squashed his head between both palms and let out a snarl of pain. "I ... I can't. Not yet. Penny..."

"Then don't! It's fine. He can't be mad if I'm not here. Write it in a letter, instead? When you can..." I offered, willing him quiet with a soothing burst of sweet sleep magic. It left a lingering taste of lavender on my tongue, every light just a little cooler, a little softer.

I inched closer, pulling his palms from his face and cupping his jaw as I focused on sending the tranquil force into his rigid frame.

Mind spells, anything with the brain, really, was like breathing.

Easy to accomplish with little to no effort and minimal consequences.

Ahh, brains... the most easily manipulated organ in the entire human flesh suit.

Beneath my palm, he went slack, allowing every muscle to relax into my touch. His arm snaked around my waist and he buried his head into my hair, taking a long deep inhale while his breath tickled my neck, warming the skin and sending little pinpricks of awareness traveling down my arm.

"Stay. For me?" He whispered, and I pulled him as close to me as I could.

Channeling every drop of love I had for my best friend, I mouthed a spell silently before I pressed a kiss against his temple.

You will find more joy in my absence than in my presence.

May you find my memory fleeting and impermanent.

May you let go of this bond, but remember it fondly.

Love will keep us connected, conquering all doubt.

"I can't Artie. I love you and am forever grateful for our friendship, but it's not safe."

When I let go, his eyes clouded over before a smile graced his lips once more.

"Safe travels, PenPen. Maybe one day..." he shook off the incomplete thought and shuffled toward the door before my next tear could fall.

"I'll miss you."

You won't, I thought with a swipe of my cheek as he left the room. *But you'll be happy.*

His happiness would be enough.

It had to be.

Goddess knew he deserved a better friend than a cursed witch with no future.

ONE

PENELOPE - FIFTEEN YEARS LATER

Death was the only card laid on the day Penelope was born.

Studiously, I looked anywhere but at the hideous blue dress hanging off the bookshelf in my office. My fingers worked the black pen between my fingers, bouncing it up and down on the blotter covering my desktop to the same rhythm of my left leg bouncing under the desk. In my mind, the James Earl Jones voice continued.

She was a curse. Delivered to the Earth by an innocent witch marked by the devil himself.

The pen and my foot bounced faster, and I put the thumb of my other hand into my mouth, chewing on the nail I'd already gnawed to the quick. Removing my hand from my mouth, I gripped the black coffee mug on my desk and took a long chug of modified life force elixir. My chest felt tight, but the words kept going.

She will end us all to serve her dark master. Only the devil benefits from death.

"The devil and mushrooms..." I grumbled.

But no one could hear me. Me or the narrator who'd plagued my internal dialogue since I was told of my tarot card draw at three years old when grown men crossed the street to get away from me. Oddly, it was the same age I'd learned about mushrooms and the two were now inextricably linked forever.

Though I was mostly against evil, petty vengeance was my jam, and I personally thought mushrooms were the absolute worst.

Last scoop of coffee on a Sunday night kind of bad.

Seriously, who saw a squishy sponge popping out of the ground like an erection and thought, *yes, I would like to put that in my mouth.*

That it was probably a man was a given. It seemed unlikely he was the leader of any hunter gatherer society if he was stupid enough to stick foreign objects in his mouth... But what would his name be?

I feel like Fred...

Fred would have to be skinny... and probably easily manipulated by peer pressure... Trying to picture it, really trying to put myself in that mindset, quickly lost its appeal when an email pinged to my inbox letting me know my credit card bill was due in fourteen days.

I hit refresh on my appointment book.

Nothing.

I hit refresh on my FedLoan account.

Still owed one hundred fifty thousand dollars.

"Hex me sideways..." I muttered, facing the blue dress. It held the memories of my cursed fate and more than one *Girl, Interrupted* life moment. Death, change, anarchy... massive student loan debt. There was nothing foretold in my future worth hanging onto.

Yet here I was, making it work like a contestant in RuPaul's *Drag Race* who forgot his shoes and only added half his fake lashes.

So... tragically.

"Why can't I pay off loans magically? Just magically lower the account balance to zero and..." The thought ended with an email from the magical detection branch of the financial wellness initiative. A secret branch of the US government, they kept all magical beings from stealing money or under-reporting their magical gains.

This message was from a subset related to taxation and debt, Interagency Resource and Security. Just thinking about using magic to alter human financial issues was grounds for a warning email with a Splenda sweet reminder that *magic is a privilege.* "Now you're thought policing. Stupid other IRS..."

A new email came in with a single line: *We heard that.*

I stuck my tongue out at the machine and looked around for another solution. There was always death, but I was a little harder to kill than the standard mortal.

Agitated and desperate, I ripped the awful blue garment off its hanger and stuffed myself into it.

"If anyone in the hospital room the day I was born was a curse, it was my damn mother," I grumbled to my familiar, though he remained passed out in his dog bed while I stomped out into the hallway, through the front door and up the road. "She could've told that old lady to stick it where the sun doesn't shine and keep her tarot cards to herself."

I continued my tantrum up the street, sensible heels sending pebbles and small lizards scattering across the walk.

"She could have moved after the first attack," I muttered to no one while reliving the pudding pants incident. There was no magic to get chocolate pudding out of pale pink pants when a mean kid wants to make it look like you had diarrhea.

"She could have magicked Madame Fortuna to the top of a mountain and left her there until she figured her shit out and stopped wielding tarot cards like weapons, like *Doctor Strange*. Hell, she could have sent the bullies there too, not that she'd have needed to because…"

Rounding another corner, I stomped past some defunct shops and foul-smelling trash cans. Several raccoons looked up, feasting on the garbage with glowing eyes and a general appearance of rabid starvation.

"And I…" My brain came up short as I got my bearings and discovered I'd made a wrong turn and had to go back.

"And I need to get my shit together," I muttered, redirecting myself toward the medical center and all the horrors it contained.

⁘ ✦ ⁘

HUCKLEBERRY HOLLOW HOSPITAL and Hellscape remained unchanged in the 33 years since my birth.

Well, except the fact that someone had magically graffitied the word "hellscape" onto the sign.

Someone who may or may not have been me when I was 12 and less mature. Though I still wasn't mature enough to remove it, so perhaps I stopped evolving at 12.

Now I'm lurking in a stairwell like a perverted fugitive, so I might have gone backward in the maturity department, I thought with an eye roll that threatened to register on the Richter scale.

Being in this town made me feel childish, inadequate, and unwelcome.

Staring out across the hospital floor, I was reminded that my immaturity wasn't the only thing predictable with clockwork certainty.

Doctors, mostly human and female, wore the same pale blue shift dress I had on. Males sported powder blue suits, all of them partially concealed under white lab coats. Though most were witches, none could cast a spell that made the hospital floor look like anything more than a 1950s prom in hell. Circling the doctors were nurses, all female because this place was *that* backwards, wearing red and white striped pinafores and white caps with the red cross in the center.

Though aside from all female, species ranged from winged through fanged and any manner of shifter in between.

Which left the milk man white clad orderlies, lumbering on the periphery in ill cut white pants and button-down shirts with their name sewn onto a patch at the left breast. All of them large, all of them ogres, all of them positively ridiculous in the straight legged pants and chest hugging starched collared shirt.

The entire floor was sporting a fake smile beneath eyes that practically screamed, "Save Me!"

A Voldemort-esque reminder that all other magical creatures served witches and wizards adoringly.

Gag me.

Frankly, with how they ran this town, it was surprising that I didn't have a line of patients circling the Canadian border for psychiatric services.

Sure, Canada was only two miles away, but you can fit many people in two miles, and I could fit a lot of people in my schedule book. Magic or not, the town of Huckleberry Hollow, Idaho, stayed trapped in a time capsule that everyone insisted was "for the best".

The same people who insisted that excluding me from solstice celebrations, quarter solstice gatherings, and the high holidays were "for the best".

I let my gaze travel the sea of hospital workers. Mixed in with the humans bustling about was hospital equipment older than dirt. Serving as a disquieting reminder that little had changed since my birth, there was still a cart of glass rectal thermometers being pushed down the hall with zero irony.

Because Goddess forbid we evolve to technology that would save an anus.

It seemed unlikely that this trip was going to change anything, for me or the other misfit residents of this town. Not because it doesn't need to, but because the people of this town have shunned and beaten down every person who might try to make that happen.

Deep breath, Penny. You are a highly educated professional now and...

My pep talk trailed off as I looked at the stack of business cards in my pocket. I was here because I was a highly educated professional without any profession to speak of until I got at least one patient in my appointment book. "If this fails, you have to start chasing ambulances. Running means chaffing and exercise. We hate both of those, so this has to work," I chastised myself, and then sucked in a breath.

A fae nurse passed by, close enough to hear my mutterings. The nurse's eyes studied me with suspicion, but ultimately kept moving.

Note to self: Don't have prolonged conversations with yourself in a stairwell.

My hand went to my hair bun, pushing against the magic that reflected an alternative image into the mind of any observer. The magic layer was a firm, blonde illusion firmly fixed over my own auburn hair. Smoothing my blue dress and lab coat, I took another pointless breath and let it out.

Everything was in order.

Picture the patient belonging bags, I coached myself.

The more difficult magic is moving matter.

Concentrate on the bags. Putting your card in the bags next to the patients' socks.

Work on convincing hospitals to let patients wear their own socks.

I nodded to myself, feeling the sweat pooling between my thick thighs and in the seam beneath my boobs. Being fat in the fall was usually fine, but something about being in this hospital had me sweating like a witch on a Roomba in a lightning storm.

A hazard to my disguise, since the witch I was impersonating didn't have touching thighs and mine sounded like a slip and slide just after the hose turned off.

Hex it all, woman-up Dr. Odenberry!

It was impossible to be a woman or give yourself a pep talk as an adult that didn't end in *because you're too healthy to fall over dead and make it look like an accident;* but it wasn't impossible to own the same confidence in my magic that you'd see in a mediocre white man for a 200-yard walk through a Psych ward.

Fake it 'til you make it... literally.

I took my first step out onto the floor and felt every other thought evaporate.

What I lacked in personal confidence, I had in spades for my magic. Illusion charms, memory charms... if it involved manipulating the mind, I was unstoppable. Getting a medical degree in psychology was like a native German speaker getting a doctorate in German.

Borderline cheating and still perfectly legal.

With clipped strides, I ate up the hallway with single-minded purpose. Simultaneously checking room flags, connecting with the object of interest, and putting my card smoothly beside the socks.

Pink, difficulty learning and socializing–card.

Orange, depression and anxiety–card.

Blue, backfiring hex turned trauma–card.

Purple...

I froze at the sight of the purple plastic flag over the door to my left.

Puberty transformation.

The words felt like lead in my gut.

Teenagers.

But worse than teenagers.

Teenagers with bodily modifications and potentially weaponized hands, teeth or... genitalia.

Frozen in place too long, my body jolted at the blood-curdling scream on the other side of the door. Stumbling over the mandatory heels, I fell backward, colliding with a passing laundry cart and landing hard on my ass.

"Watch it!" An ogre grumbled, heavily browed face contorted in disapproval. Whether his disapproval was over my sudden collision with the floor or the idea of hazardous footwear, I couldn't say.

I also couldn't resist an internal eye roll that someone made people on their feet all day wear heeled shoes.

"S-s-sorry," I whispered, backing away from the purple door on all fours. My back connected with the wall as the scream transitioned into a hollow, piercing sound that shattered my concentration.

"What?" The ogre's eyes bored into mine and I froze, trying to remember etiquette. But... ogres didn't have any apology etiquette. "Did you just *apologize*?"

"Yes?" I asked, my confusion matching his outrage. It had been a few years since I lived amongst the magical, but certainly such a major change would have appeared in an email blast.

"You're not Miss Misty!" He shouted, grabbing my hair and shoving through the illusion. His fingers hooked into my hair tie and the band snapped, releasing the waves of red hair that shattered the magic. Misty Marino's thin, medium stature evaporated, and I was looking down at my own extra-large and extra-tall frame in the too-tight blue dress.

"It's Death!" a three-foot pixie candy striper squeaked, fainting where she stood.

Then all hell broke loose.

CHAPTER

TWO

PENELOPE

"Death ate Dr. Marino!"

"She's not a doctor, damn it!" I shouted after the last one, but no one heard me over the din.

"Abandon the nut jobs and run! I'm not dying for these assholes!" The last was a doctor I recognized from junior high, a weaselly blonde man who was more suited to a nineties boy band than being a witch doctor in northern Idaho. He'd been less than average academically, and I was willing to bet he didn't actually have a medical degree.

Or a brain.

It was impossible to resist. I threw magic at his back. The spell exploded, and every visible inch of the man's skin erupted in neon yellow warts. He screamed at his own reflection, tripping over his own feet into an elven elder checking in on her son. With a gentle shake of silver blonde hair, the elf sent the spotted man careening toward an open window.

Bouncy butt, I thought, just as he tumbled out into the daylight.

His scream lasted a moment, then a bark of concern, and his face reappeared in the window before continuing up, up and up... then gliding back down.

17

"Penelope Ophelia Odenberry!"

The sharp feminine bark was as familiar as my face. I glanced behind me to watch the slender, blonde woman in a skirt suit of deep maroon eating up linoleum on toothpick heels.

Anywhere but here, as long as it's safe, I begged the universe, drawing a finger circle on the floor that widened beneath my body to pull me through until my body was falling through space and time. Everything had dulled, the bleach scented sage of medical and spiritual cleansing replaced by jasmine, pine and Palo Santo musk...

My eyes snapped open, only to clench shut again at the bright autumn sun.

"Sadistic sunshine, hex off!" I muttered, but a tippy tapping of thunder punctuated by the metal rattle of tags drowned out the sound.

"No!" I whispered, opening my eyes to dodge the incoming missile.

It was too late.

His momentum transferred, and I fell off the black heels, toppling over under the efforts of 90 pounds of Pitbull Husky mix. My body landed with a punctuated thud beneath the unfinished sign in front of my newly opened medical practice.

Dr. Penelope Odenberry, Psycho

"That bastard better be dead or he's getting herpes the size of golf balls," I swore to Grim, who was actively bathing my face with a sandpaper tongue. "Big, pus oozing herpes on his ball sack that will never go away because I'm a vindictive hexer and if he wants to see psycho..."

"Should I be concerned that this town suddenly needs a professional psycho, or are they cracking down on truth in labeling laws?" A deep, sensual voice drifted to my ears from somewhere beyond the great black dog and heat flooded my body. "Or did you run out of coffee and decide to watch the world burn instead of just buying more?"

Taking Grim's head between both my palms, I tilted it over and away to look up at the owner of the hottest voice I had heard in half a decade. It was a raspy baritone with treble amped up into nerve tickling euphoria.

The owner made me salivate openly.

If his voice was euphoria, the man himself was a Norse God wrapped in caramel. As an independent medical professional with a deep appreciation of art, it seemed very important to study the specimen before me.

And what was in front of me was the best kind of anatomically correct art.

Not to mention the potential for deep...

Appreciating. Deep appreciation.

Black combat boots, battered jeans, green flannel, russet complexion. The man had serious hipster energy with none of the pretense. Everything about him was designed to make a woman, or man, fall over in a spontaneous orgasm. He wore his jet-black hair pulled into a lazy bun at the crown of his head above shaved sides that showed off multiple ear piercings. Beneath pushed up shirt sleeves, he sported an artistic web of impossibly complex tattoos snaking around taut forearms from a wet dream come to life.

Emphasis on *wet*.

"Artie."

His name slipped out like a moan, breathy and a little too dreamy for talking to your once best friend.

"Penny," he smirked down at me and took a deep, slow inhale that reminded me shifters, even half shifters, could smell everything... EVERYTHING.

I snapped my legs closed, feeling my face burn. Cowering back behind Grim's head, I tried to think of the least sexy things my brain could imagine.

Racists. Anger bubbled up, and I had a powerful urge to hit something... anger and lust were too similar.

Sexist politicians with no regard for women. Anger bubbling into rage, I was ready to screw him and then go on a killing spree.

Trump supporters. The rage took on a frosty edge that polar bears might enjoy. You can't fight stupid, and you certainly couldn't talk to it.

Trump.

The last one did the trick, and every happy thought vanished from my mind. In its place was a weight that made me both nauseous and desperate for wine with a side of chocolate.

Joining it, a strong sense of regret that I'd never learned to be a sharpshooter or knife throwing assassin... Considering I was Death, it felt like a missed opportunity.

"I know that face. Whose murder are you plotting?"

"No one's..."

"Former president?"

"Yeah."

"Supreme Court?"

"Parts of it," I conceded. "What brings you to-"

"How dare you, Penelope!"

I was interrupted by the woman from the hospital, her tone a shrill screech, reminding me of a hen being strangled in barbed wire. Grim winced above me, ears flattening as he slunk down beside me, shoving his colossal head under my back and propping me up so he could cower behind me.

"Baby!" I whisper-hissed in his direction, knowing that if the threat were real, I'd have put him there myself. But the woman marching toward us on toothpick heels in her skirt suit wasn't dangerous to anyone who wasn't spawned from her womb.

I'd ruined her body and reputation to live as the world's biggest disappointment in all the areas that counted.

Occupational success.

Being thin and beautiful.

Having a rich or good-looking husband, preferably both.

My sister had managed to accomplish being nearly everything my mother wanted. A small, somewhat vindictive, part of me had hoped that it meant I was off the hook and could burn down villagers and sleep with the husbands of the hanging committee.

The larger, people-pleasing part of me couldn't let go of the need to make her happy.

"Penelope Ophelia Odenberry!" She shouted again, and I flinched against the reminder that my mother had thoughtfully named me with the initials POO.

"Yes?" I asked hesitantly, sending a mental curse at Artie when he snickered into his hand. The sound turned into a cough, a brilliant butterfly bursting from his lips, half obsidian black and half an opalescent rainbow.

Huh... not what I was going for.

"What the hell were you doing at the hospital impersonating me?"

I sucked in a breath, preparing some sort of defense, but the air came with the butterfly I'd plucked from Artie. It went straight to the back of my throat, tickling the soft red flesh of my tonsils while I prepared to cough.

Except there was no need to cough.

The butterfly slipped, smooth as honey, into my throat. A warmth started in my chest, spreading out until a fulfilling light stretched from the top of my head to the tips of my toes, being pinched by hideous hospital heels. Everything was brighter, more vibrant and, for the first time, not overwhelming.

Until a pointed insult killed the light and every positive feeling inside of me.

"You could have at least tried to lose weight before pretending to be me, Penelope," my mother said, looking down on me critically. My eyes met hers and much like the entirety of my childhood, teens and every day until I turned 18 and ran away, I prayed the devil would open the ground beneath me and suck me into the underworld.

After all, I was used to being burned.

THREE

PENELOPE

As a child, I always puzzled at the portrayal of prisoners being marched to the electric chair. They always trudged, as though walking slower and more morosely would overturn their conviction... or do anything other than annoy the sad sack who was being forced to walk them there.

Life, after all, was just a slow march to a death you didn't choose... at least as long as they frowned on doctor assisted suicide.

But escorting my mom through the closet that served as a patient waiting area, past the empty reception desk and two dust coated chairs, it was starting to make sense.

The destination might not change, but I was fairly certain if I moved slow enough, I could die before I arrived at my office.

If I didn't, my mother was certainly going to kill me with "constructive criticism".

Hand gripping the brass knob beside the plastic placard bearing my name, I prayed silently that my childhood bullies had returned.

That they had returned, electrified the door handle and I would die a quiet death without ever having to hear...

"Penelope! Your office is a disaster! You need to clean this place up before your next patient comes!"

That, I mentally shuddered.

It's too late.

I'm dead and this is hell.

"I don't have a next patient, mom. I don't have any patients," I sighed, ruffling Grim's ears before he flopped into the over-sized dog bed beside my wooden desk. A worn leather chair sat behind it, facing the new-to-me CPU that held nothing more than reminders of my debt, failure, and nasty letters from the magical IRS.

The rest of the space had a couch, an armchair and a very large bookcase that was one rolling ladder away from fulfilling a childhood dream of being a Disney princess. It held not only the leather-bound tomes of magical history, but the informational texts about psychology, neurobiology and paranormal development.

Not to mention a few shamefully filthy paperbacks that had gotten me through some dry spells during my residency. Those were enjoying a cloaking spell in the upper left-hand corner and I considered removing the spell to see if the covers alone might send my mother to an early grave and spare me.

Unlike the books, which I'd carefully collected over three decades, the furniture had come with the office. The practice and all its contents were an acquisition from the town's former psychiatrist, who lacked personal skills and a respect for patient privacy.

Or personal privacy, if the rumors of her penchant for nudity were even partially true.

"Do you even own a vacuum?" Miss Misty, aka my mother who'd kept her maiden name Marino, asked. I tried not to look at the office space too closely, validating her judgment was worse than death. I knew it was clean, knew that she was just expressing excess frustration in a manner deemed socially acceptable, but knowing didn't stop it from hurting.

Or making me wish I'd tried harder.

"What does she need a vacuum for? It's spotless! Holy hell PenPen, did you become a germaphobe?" Artemis Daemon Nita-nusi shouted from the doorway and I startled.

I'd known he was with us, but the booming shout was at direct odds with the sensual declarations from outdoors and I had no idea why he'd decided to become a human megaphone. Our eyes met, and he braced his palms on either side of the open doorway, slowly scraping the painted white metal with the calloused skin of his hands as he held my gaze captive.

"Indoor voice, dude," I admonished, and he quirked an eyebrow as he leaned against the door frame and studied my outfit, the room, and the dog with interest. He'd definitely shouted on purpose.

He did not, however, come inside.

Maybe he was bitten by a vampire and needs to be invited?

Do we want him to come inside?

Hehe... come inside...

I slapped my palm against my forehead and tried to shake it off. Pacing nervously and eyeing him as I moved in small increments toward my desk and then away from it.

His large frame filled the door and then some, dwarfing me by a few inches and a lot of muscles I could name if I'd paid better attention in anatomy. Larger still was the rolling testosterone wave that pummeled me with the force of a tsunami, drowning me in a craving as new as it was unwelcome.

He is your friend.

Was your friend...

Is your friend?

We hadn't seen each other in five years. On my last attempt at familial fraternization, he'd somehow also been home at the same time. Though the family portion had ended the way it always does: tears, headaches and coffee, seeing Artemis had been a rare bright spot.

We'd caught each other in passing, his face curiously blank whenever he tried to remember anything about me. But like always, he'd remembered how much love and joy we shared, which was enough to share an afternoon. There'd been no plans made for the future, no talk of the past, just a quick chat over coffee that had left me anxious and longing.

Like I'd chosen to cut off my arm to save it from the trauma of being attached to the rest of me.

Would he have remembered if we had made plans?

He remembered you're addicted to coffee...

That might have been smell related.

My mind was whirling, and I couldn't seem to form a coherent thought. His magnificent scent was invading my personal space, making my brain and nether regions feel possessed. A heated need started in my scrambled brain, coursing through my bloodstream with every beat of my heart until my whole body craved his touch, his words, his everything.

Like a slutty poltergeist.

"Why is it so quiet in here?" He yelled again, and I winced.

His low rumbling timbre, even at an obnoxious volume, was doing wicked things to my lady parts.

None of which I'd had any desire for before...

Liar.

It was a small acknowledgement, but I had always loved Artie. Not in a sexual rip off my clothes and grind against him kind of way. His hugs and soothing voice had been enough to bring me peace.

And now his mere presence was threatening to force me into spontaneous combustion.

Waving my hand, I activated a hidden sound system that piped calming music into the room. It was something soft: pan flutes and hand drums with running streams.

Sounds that did nothing to calm the raging heat between my legs that pulsed in time with my pounding heart.

Maybe this is what a panic attack coupled with a complete mental breakdown feels like?

It was a sound hypothesis if not for my very damp undies.

"I need to change," I declared, scooping up the sweater and leggings I'd abandoned earlier and moving toward the very full door frame. Mortified and overwhelmed, I kept my gaze on the industrial carpet, the faux leather green couch, anywhere but on the man who was giving me hot flashes with his warm scent of pine and ash. "Could you... I mean... excuse me."

Artie remained motionless, daring me in silence to look up from his shit kicker boots.

Hooded lids sat above dilated pupils and a sumptuous grin. It didn't promise forever, but it promised enough pleasure and relief. I could forget my name, my life, and every grudge I'd held so dearly to keep a safe buffer between me and the world.

I could forget everything but his name.

That I would be screaming until I had a simultaneous aneurysm heart attack and exploded into a pile of human organic matter.

Orgasmic matter, I snickered.

"Running away?" He whispered, somehow mastering the quiet he refused to give me earlier. "Or is that dress not the only thing that needs to be replaced with something... fresher?"

His sentence was punctuated by a long deliberate sniff that burned through my whole body and smoldered near my ears.

"I was in a hospital," I hissed. His knowing smirk spoke volumes.

"If you'll excuse me," I slid under his arm and somehow avoided physical contact.

Ten points to Hufflepuff, I rewarded myself. Escaping cost me, my skin itching with a need to either be closer to the object of its desire or ripped off and dropped at his feet like an offering.

Not happening, I told myself, even as my vagina and heart screamed in protest.

I need a skank exorcism. This is so wrong.

Locking the bathroom door, I waved my hand again and created a barrier between the space and the rest of the office. Dingy industrial grey-flecked yellowed tile surrounded me, clean but depressing. The three metal stall doors, a similar shade of not quite yellow, gave off the scent of fresh bleaching and I wondered again how much energy I should put into bringing this office into the 21st century.

My thoughts halted when Artie's booming chuckle shook every bone in my body. The waves of pleasure it carried were strong enough to send me to the brink of orgasm faster than any battery-operated boyfriend ever could.

"What the fuck is happening?" I grumbled at myself, dumping my clothes onto the floor of the bathroom to splash cool water on my over-heated face and ears. Rubbing repeatedly, I waited until the water beneath my face ran clear of make-up, wet strands of hair clinging to my cheeks and trailing through the water pooling in the basin. Shaking my face, I looked up and into the mirror.

Errant droplets of water clung to my nose, chunks of wet hair adhering to the freckles that coated my skin and black smudges under my eyes from not-quite waterproof mascara.

Emerald-green eyes blinking back at me, I shouted again.

"What the fuck?"

None of my body parts answered, least of all my brain, who was supposed to be in charge.

"We aren't doing this. We aren't getting involved or invested in Artie or anyone else. Yes, we took over this practice to help out the town and because my mom said she needed me here, but this is just temporary. I'm not helping anyone if no one will be my patient, so there's no reason to stay and Artie is probably gone in a couple days tops. We can help my mom with whatever rich white lady magical emergency she's manifested and then get the hell out, blaming money and the town that hates me. Is everyone clear on the plan?" I looked specifically at my crotch, knowing of all my body parts, the needy little slut between my legs was the most likely to ruin the plan.

She remained throbbing and hot, a clear defiance of my request.

"This is crazier than talking to yourself in a stairwell," I told my reflection. The woman staring back at me was miserable and psychotic, a near replica of who I'd been when I packed up and left the first time. Turning away, I stripped off the blue dress and replaced it with my version of armor.

Efficiently, I pulled on my black leggings and super soft orange sweater, ignoring the scar on my arm and my nipples poking out through the fabric of my bra. Staring down, down at my feet, I saw I was still wearing the stupid heels, and I'd forgotten to bring replacement shoes with me.

"Fuck it."

With a paper towel, I swiped at the make-up on my cheek and cleaned it into a respectable semblance of neat while finger combing my hair back into a new ponytail holder, hiding in the pocket of my legging and ready to take the place of the one that snapped. Bunching all my hair at the base of my skull, I bound it into a low pony/bun and huffed out a breath.

I was antsy, but unwilling to leave the bathroom and face the world outside. Bouncing my weight from foot to foot, I studied the bathroom for anything else that might need my attention.

Any reason to stay here until either my mom left or Artie spontaneously shifted into a bear like his father and ate her.

Just because he hadn't shifted before doesn't mean he couldn't now, I thought, still searching the bathroom.

All the stalls had toilet paper.

Paper towel dispensers were full.

Trash cans were empty.

Nothing.

Flinging the blue dress into the trash can, I gave myself one last look. Still red.

Still not sporting a visible lady boner because our traditionally high maintenance anatomy had that one thing going for it: visually neutral arousal as long as you didn't know about nipples.

"I'll just tell everyone I'm cold."

Opening the bathroom door, I paused at the words drifting from my office.

"I'd heard you were performing hockey with side gigs in modeling and less than reputable acting jobs. I mean, your skin tone alone, but adding in the shifter build and reflexes... the supernatural league must be hurting without you, no? Don't they pay well? Surely you don't need to sell..."

Storming up the hallway, I shoved past Artie to stare at my mother in horror.

"Mom! Do not behave inappropriately in my workplace. Everyone has a right to share and be who they are without judgment. In this space and every other. If you cannot respect that, you will have to leave." I crossed my arms over my chest, glaring at her until she removed the manicured claw from the corner of her mouth and placed that same hand on her hip.

"I was only attempting to get reacquainted with Artemis. It always surprised me you two became such good friends and yet he did not know you were leaving," she fished while I swallowed a lump in my throat. "It makes me wonder if perhaps he was the reason and you were more than friends while he was off being a..."

I held up a horrified hand to stop her from talking, vehemently shaking my head no.

Artie, however, was wearing a smile that matched the semi-vacant expression on his face.

"Hey Penny! Do you work here?"

My mom opened her mouth, but I spoke over whatever damning comment was about to come out.

"Yep. I'm the psycho on the sign." I shrugged, scrambling away only to catch the pointed toe of the stupid pump on a misaligned bit of carpet. My shoe stayed behind while my foot went forward, stepping on the cord of my ten-pound relic phone just where it angled from flat on the floor to its upward trajectory.

The ancient technology quivered on the edge of the desk before toppling over, the receiver banging my shin while the heavy base narrowly avoided amputating my pinkie toe.

"Son of witch's tit!" I shouted, grabbing for my shin, only to find another hand already there.

A darker, bigger, warmer hand that was caressing my leg like it was made of fine china . He stroked the spot in a gentle circle, the same way he'd traced the tarot card on my arm all those years ago and butterflies fluttered low in my belly. Artemis leaned in and placed a gentle kiss on the spot, lifting his gaze to study my face, his racing pulse thumping from his palm into my leg in time with my own rapidly beating heart.

"Are you ok?" Artie asked from the general vicinity of *between my legs* and reality crashed into me.

I panicked and did what all truly badass heroines do- let every thought in my head tumble out of my mouth in a single breath.

"Of course, I'm fine. I'm always fine. You don't get bullied as much as I did and not learn to manage minor pains. You're the one taking headshots in the supernatural league... sometimes out of it. Are you OK? Do you need to see a shrink? Not for your head, especially not the lower one, but for the..."

Artemis chuckled, the rumble traveling from his chest into his arms and through my leg straight to my...

"You think about my head?" He whispered.

"Stop laughing! Stop laughing and tell my..." He finger-walked upward, hands barely separated from my skin by the ultra-thin fabric of my leggings while I floundered to end a sentence. "Ya... you..."

Our eyes locked, and for a moment, the entire office faded away. Where his hand sat on my upper thigh, fingers splayed to cover a decent portion of its surface area, became the center of my universe. The entire rest of my being was anchored to that single point, held captive in his eyes while the rest of me fell away, and for the second time, I felt our hearts beating as one. This time, however, it felt like his pulse was thrusting into me, edging me higher.

Wicked, dangerous, exciting.

An abrupt *ahem* from the depths of reality pulled me back, and I scooted away from the man on the floor to stare at my mom.

"Yes?" I squeaked, but only Grim seemed to hear me, his paw swiping at an ear in discomfort. Clearing my throat, I started again while using the edge of my desk to haul myself up from the floor.

"Mom, you were saying something about me being unclean and Artie is a slut?"

The man rose slowly, smirking like the Big Bad Wolf just before he gobbled up Granny . He lumbered like the half bear that he is over to the couch, flopping down on it to recline with his boots on the arm rest opposite from his head.

Artie wasn't the Big Bad Wolf, he was the bear who devoured Goldilocks... hopefully after she discovers his porridge was juuuust right.

And now I've perverted children's stories.

"Penelope, are you listening to me?" I snapped back to the room and eyed my mom. Despite being my polar opposite physically, mentally and socially, her eyes showed the same explosive anger that occasionally got away from me.

With it came a wave of minor magic that tickled my nose, and I sneezed.

"Godzilla," Artie answered, head tilted to the side like Grim.

"Thanks..." I added, while my mom sent off another wave.

"What did you call me?"

"He didn't call you anything. Crack a meme, mom," I sneezed again and searched my office for a tissue. The only box was on the small table between the green leather-ish couch and the armchair in a color that was comparable to either mud or snot.

Both existing squarely on the other side of Artie.

"Could you..." He nodded and reached out for the box, flannel shirt and black tee riding up to reveal perfectly smooth skin with black tattoo ink and... an Adonis belt.

Goddess, help me, the man had the cut muscle on his hips that promised he knew how to thrust, deep and hard...

"PenPen?" He cleared his throat with a very pointed inhale that blew his pupils so wide, the only parts of his iris visible were the smallest of golden flecks. "Tissue?"

"Huh?" I blinked at him.

Instead of answering, he undulated from the couch and closed the space between us. Plucking two tissues from the box, he pressed the soft paper sheet against my face. His pinkie brushed my chin, and my skin pebbled from my neck down to my toes. Moving impossibly closer, he lined up our bodies from knee to... *holy hell, is that a bulge?*

My heart rate broke the sound barrier. Everything was going bright hot white at the edges...

A heated, damp caress touched my ear, the word barely audible as I fought to stay upright and clothed.

"Blow."

Standing alone in the summer solstice clearing, the woman in black was a stark contrast to the glistening snow. The towering pines did not impose on her waif-like frame, her pale skin and hair making the dress look like a floating shadow in the woods.

Gasping for air, I kept running toward her. Alone, the trees bent to her will. Roots elongated in clawed fingers to rip at my flesh, stinging reminders I wasn't meant to be here.

Bursting through the trees, the woman finally spotted me.

She laughed, a cold, cruel sound of disdain and disbelief.

"How could you possibly be so foolish as to come for him?" Her voice was a caress with a biting edge that crossed the line between pleasure and agony.

Crumpled before her, head in his hands, was Artie.

Or what I knew to be Artie, despite his enormous paws and elongated snout. Thick black fur covered the colossal bear, sitting on his knees in the most human expression of despair.

"Artie!" I shouted at the bear, but his blinking eyes didn't register a sound.

"You can't save him," the haunting voice drew me back, and I gave her a hard glare, feeling my magic rise into my fingertips. "Ah ah ah.."

Her scold came with a howling roar, the bear a mask of agony clawing at the ground. Rampage and revenge flitted across eyes I'd come to know so well.

Eyes that I loved more than life itself.

"You can't save him," she said again, and I felt the first tear of many trail down my face. "Unless you're willing to make a deal."

"Come on, PenPen, wake up," the bear was talking, but he wasn't *looking at me. "Penny."*

The whipping wind died down, the trees no longer hovered. The sun and moon were swallowed by the trees. Warm... hard...

My eyes snapped open, too bright light spilled in through the office windows.

My office windows.

Blinking repeatedly, my eyes drifted closed again as I focused on my breathing.

"Don't go back to sleep, PenPen." Artemis was hovering over me. I could sense him and his heat. On my opposite side, a smaller person hovered. Smelling of jasmine, amber and Chanel No. 5, I'd know the smell of my mother anywhere.

"Mistletonia" by Calvin Klein... if they could afford to buy Chanel.

It felt like being a child again, when she read me bedtime stories and brushed my hair. When life was simpler and I didn't yet know that no one could forgive the cursed child marked as death.

Back before you were the world's biggest disappointment.

"Why am I on the floor?" I croaked, trying and failing to re-wet my dry mouth.

"You..." Artie seemed to struggle for words, but my pragmatic mother completed the thought.

"You passed out, dear. Have you eaten today?"

My eyelids fluttered open, and I studied the two faces looking down at me. Both concerned and a little anxious. Above my head, Grim panted his hot doggy breath into my face.

Cautiously, I reached for him first.

His shiny black fur was smooth and familiar.

Leaning into the comfort and familiarity, my arms wrapping tightly around his shoulders. I buried my face into his fur, trying to get it into the soft white undercoat he kept year-round. Thick black strands tickled my nose, and I wriggled in deeper against the urge to scratch it. The smells of grass and a hint of skunk clung to the fur, but the sensation cleared the fog and brought me back.

Brought me home.

"Not sure... what time is it?" I asked them, nuzzling Grim's fur. My mind reached into the mini fridge behind my desk, picturing the cold plastic water bottle inside. Every indentation and groove, the perfectly still meniscus of liquid at the top, was clear in my mind before I switched from viewing it in the fridge to viewing it in my hand.

When the cold weight appeared in my palm, I opened my eyes again.

"I could have brought you that," my mom huffed, and I gave her a single raised brow. Cracking the lid on my bottle, I took a long drink. In five gulps, the bottle was empty, but I still felt dry. "Now, food?"

"Right..." Glancing at the clock, I saw the little hand sitting at 11. "I guess I could go for some lunch."

Following my gaze, the woman who birthed me pursed her lips.

"Unfortunately, I won't be able to join you. But I would like you to come to dinner tomorrow," her tone held an edge of foreboding that poked a hole in my slowly inflating thought bubble. "It'll be something healthy, lots of veggies from the garden. Perhaps you should mirror those choices in your other meal plans."

Her eyes dipped to my waistline.

"Right..." A damp paper towel draped itself across my forehead and I smelled Artemis around the hot doggy breath facial Grim was offering. In contrast to Grim's grass and salmon oil, the man was crisp, cool pine with a smokey undertone.

A forest fire in the dead of winter that only burned me, a sharp contrast to the cooling cloth he draped on my forehead. Gently lifting my head, I was now draped across his lap like the images of fainting women in Renaissance paintings.

Way to set back feminism, I thought, but was far too comfortable to move and they always said to play dead when faced with a bear.

"Veggies are great, but they aren't a complete meal, you know?" Artemis beamed with a sunshine voice that could compel the Trojan army to return Helen of Troy. "What time would you like us there and can I bring anything?"

"If you do bring something, it will be for seven. Your father and his beta will also be there, in addition to Penelope's brother. Though I'd recommend checking if the alpha is comfortable with you being in on this discussion," Artemis tensed above me, and my jaw clenched in apprehension. "Be sure to check with him. Now, I really need to go. See you both at seven tomorrow, and Penelope-"

Her gaze skimmed my body. Despite the recent blackout and still cooling puddles of sweat behind my knees and under my arms, she was without sympathy.

"Try to wear something appropriate. You are representing the whole of the Marino-Odenberry line." She gave a very dignified sniff and floated out of the room.

Like the ghost of childhood trauma come to pass.

Beneath me, Artie shuddered like he'd had a run in with the ice queen. Not that it did anything to lessen the waves of volcanic heat he gave off as both a non-shifting shifter and a non-soul dealing demon, but it did make me wonder if he *could* get cold. Listening for the front door to close, I waited to lock the door and felt something off in the office. A flicker of something... My head still nestled in Artie's lap, I reached out into the room.

There was the small glamor at work on the upper corner of my bookcase. A lingering tickle of weak spell craft that threatened to make me sneeze and...

A warm fire burst beneath me, a powerful magic of ancient origins that stung the back of my throat and started my eyes watering. Its metallic edge and sinewy coils held secrets, promises of violence and pleasure if only I gave in.

The power was everywhere and nowhere, a vice around my chest that had no graspable edges.

"Peep?" Artie had a firm grip on my chin, our faces angled toward each other *just so*. With startling clarity, the sharp objects in the room came into focus.

A desk corner.

The edge of my bookcase.

A thumbtack lost beneath my desk.

Just a little jab, a little blood, to bind you for eternity.

"Penny!" Jostling my shoulders, Artemis stole the sudden clarity in my vision. With it, I came back to his lap, his face, those eyes. "What just happened?"

"I'm..." I looked at the once tantalizing objects that begged for my hemoglobin. They'd returned to simple office furniture and supplies. When I reached out into the room again, the magic was gone. All trace of it swallowed into another calm fall afternoon. "I'm not really sure... Probably just hunger."

Artemis remained tense beneath me, and I looked at him again.

"Did you feel it too? The..." I couldn't find the words, but the sweat droplets on his brow said maybe I didn't need to know the words just now. Taking the cool cloth off my forehead, I used it to swipe at his, holding it there when he leaned into my touch.

Together, we breathed.

"No idea. Maybe..." He reluctantly returned my hand back to its resting place on my belly. "Maybe we should get some food. I heard about this place..."

I was on my feet, head shaking, before he could finish the sentence.

"No way! We are not going anywhere you pick!"

"What? What's wrong with the places I pick?" He climbed gracefully to his feet, somehow maintaining at least one point of contact between our bodies.

A hand, a leg, a hip. Carefully, I extricated myself from his force field and stood a few feet away.

"You always pick the weirdest place in town, and I have to play *Food or Fungus*!"

I walked over to my desk, grabbing a slightly oversized purse from my desk drawer. Without Artie's body heat, I felt cold... empty...

Confused.

Grabbing Grim's lead, I avoided eye contact with him and waited for my brain to catch up with my feet. We were going to have a friend lunch. None of this touching and lust meant anything.

"How would you know? When have we ever gone to lunch together?" Reality slammed into my chest and I stared at him in wide-eyed panic. He'd turned away, missing my impersonation of a deer in head-lights, and had already moved on from my faux pas. "Besides, fungus is food. Ask any forest creature. You need to at least try it and you'll see. A portobello burger with a side of-"

Crisis averted.

"It is not food! It's a by-product of decay," I interrupted, trying to move the conversation and food acquisition along. The sooner we lunched, the sooner he could go back to his life in the supernatural league not having a clue who I was and I could... My stomach let out an audile rumble.

"Come on, the place I know is nearby and the servers all-"

Though I hadn't been hungry in Artie's lap, I was suddenly starving.

"Not a chance, Bear Man. I don't troll the graveyard for dates. I'm not going to troll it for lunch."

"First off, a by-product of decay is still alive. There are zero similari-ties between corpses and mushrooms. Second, you can't date a corpse, but you can eat a mushroom. If you can eat it, it's food."

I lead him through the door and down my vacant, slightly dusty office hallway. All around me, the faded paint and thumbtack holes served as a reminder I was a visitor here. All the weirdness was happening because I didn't belong.

"Just because you put it in your mouth doesn't mean its food, Artie," I tossed over my shoulder while shoving open the exterior door. A cooling breeze hit me with a welcoming embrace, returning my mind to my body and making me whole. It suddenly didn't matter where we ate, but I hated the idea of conceding, so I angled my head down at Grim.

"He eats poop, and that is the literal opposite of food. And if *you* ate everything you put in your mouth, not only would you be a cannibal, but Thanos wouldn't have needed to snap away half the population. You'd have already taken care of it!"

His footsteps faltered beside me, and I gave myself a mental gut punch for the asshole comment. I knew better than everyone else how much he hated the urges. Hated how much time and energy he spent wringing pleasure from people who didn't know his name, or that his favorite color was the pure green of an emerald.

"Are you trying to slut shame me, doctor?" His smirk held so much sadness and I was looking at the almost nineteen-year-old boy in my room, begging me to stay.

For him.

The memory slipped in unbidden, and I let out a frustrated sigh. I couldn't keep him and I couldn't protect him from me anymore now than I could fifteen years ago. Turning on my heel, I placed a hand on his shoulder and brushed a finger across his cheek, trying not to read into the way he leaned into the touch.

"Nope. That was a douche thing to say and I'm sorry. Sex is supposed to be great and you should definitely enjoy it as a consenting adult with other consenting adults. Just... you know... use protection and don't confuse dick and mushrooms. Only one of those is clean enough to put in your body. You on board with sandwiches?"

"Sandwiches are fine. As far as protection, shifters heal. We can't catch anything." His weird sulk morphed into a swagger, and I fought an eye roll while lowering my hand and continuing on toward Main Street. His whiplash was as bad as mine, fighting emotional upheaval and sexual arousal in the same breath. Whether his was a practiced air of want to feed his inner need or he actually wanted me was barely a question.

I wasn't on his radar, not that way.

A saving grace since until today, he hadn't been on mine either.

This too shall pass... hopefully.

"Right, well, be sure to remind Naomi of that before you ask her nicely to make you something with mushrooms."

His sudden panic pulled a cackle from my throat, dispelling the weighty emotions that hung over us a second before.

"Does she still work at Gnomewich?"

"Owns it now. Though the Council wouldn't let her change anything- menu, façade, décor... And from what I heard, she tried and was almost railroaded out of town by a warlock older than Merlin."

It was an interesting tidbit, but probably not as important as what he really wanted to know.

"Do you think she's still mad about the crabs?"

I offered him a smirk of my own.

"Only one way to find out... can you identify poisonous mushrooms?"

"No! Can you?" His eyes were on the precipice of leaping out of his sockets and the sadist in me reveled in the opportunity to see him flustered and squirming. He'd always been so confident, so sure, so... easygoing.

I needed to see him sweat for some reason that probably had to do with my mother.

"Nope."

I lied.

"Then what am I supposed to eat?" His voice sounded on the verge of tears, but I knew crocodile antics when I saw them.

"Crow, I imagine," I snickered and led the way down the block with a ball of masculine anxiety bouncing after me.

CHAPTER

FIVE

PENELOPE

CROW LOOKED A LOT LIKE GRILLED CHEESE WITH TOMATO and pesto.

"Are you sure she didn't poison it?" Artemis asked, lifting a corner of the bread and sniffing. Naomi had insisted on making the sandwich personally, a fact that sent the entire shop's staff atwitter with delight. In defiance of her own layout, Naomi made Artie's sandwich completely out of sight from the entire rest of the room.

"Anything is possible," I qualified, accepting a sly wink from the woman in charge.

At three-feet tall, the woman still seemed to tower over everyone who came inside. A fact that was emphasized when she shortened most of the furniture, replaced the check-out counter with selenite and turned one wall into a mural the day she closed escrow on her purchase of the shop. It let her survey everyone and everything, giving everyone in the room a clear view behind the counter at the food prep area in return.

Like Subway for short, supernatural creatures, but with better food.

In a concession to the court of elders, she'd left all the gnome centric artwork, exposed log sides and a 40-foot bearded gnome that could feed 12 generations of termites and stake a vampire with his conical hat, assuming incredibly pointy hats fit in with the staking lore. If conces-

45

sion could be used to describe a contractual clause that literally bound her hands if she tried to go against it.

As soon as she discovered what they'd done, she painted the gnome's hat a glossy red that looked perpetually wet and pierced a sandwich on the top. Where the traditional fillings would rest, she had a black-robed humanoid sprinkled in rainbow glitter.

The most beautiful threat I'd ever seen.

If that wasn't enough to keep them out, the chairs were only about 6 inches off the ground. A whole five and a half feet lower than the top of every Council member's head, forcing every single one of them to either look up at her from the ground or eat their lunch somewhere else.

And she didn't offer to-go orders.

It was both brilliant and simple, like Naomi Awinita herself.

Though she was generally pleasant, her expression of shrewd calculation and vengeance was at odds with the black button nose and graceful sweeps of dark brown fur across high cheekbones any model would kill for. Even less congruous were her doe's ears poking up from ultra fine chestnut hair, each sporting at least ten piercings.

Naomi was also constantly moving at a speed that sent the metal rings clinking against one another like a tambourine player who just did a line of coke after chugging two Red Bulls.

Both things I'd seen the woman do... the cocaine and Red Bulls. She'd *never* play the tambourine.

Woman was clearly a drummer.

"Maybe you should trade me. She'd stop you from eating it if it was poison!"

Artie was completely comfortable in the miniscule chairs, despite being six feet of muscle. At five foot ten, I was only comfortable because I was floating on a cushion of magic.

He probably does yoga...

"Nope. But you've done riskier things than eat a sandwich from an itchy ex-lover, so suck it up, Bear Boy," I said between bites of my steak fajita quesadilla. Naomi couldn't officially change the menu, but she'd been covertly serving a secret menu. Unlike the overrated California burger chain, her secret menu was a legitimate secret, not just sticking cheese and onions on your fries "animal style".

Like any animal should eat onions.

Not only did Naomi's secret menu cross cuisine styles, but the food was enchanted to look like a PB and J sandwich to any *persona non grata* around town.

"How did you get that?" Artie asked, eyeing the steak poking out of my cheesy tortilla and scenting so hard I thought he might turn into a vacuum cleaner.

"Magic," I offered with a shrug, noticing that Naomi was headed over. The wood nymph and I had become friends in secret over the years. She knew better than to be seen with me as a child, but apparently, old age and vengeance had made her brazen.

Also, whenever I was in town, she and her wife could con me into babysitting because I was a sucker.

"What's wrong? Don't like your sandwich?" She leaned in close, lips and breasts nearly brushing against Artie's ear and shoulder. A wave of violent jealousy ripped through me, rattling my teeth and burning through my skin. Grim lurched to his feet beside me, nearly toppling our whole table, pulling my attention away to keep the plates on top. I took a long deep breath, listening to her whisper, "Afraid it might bite and leave an itchy... itchy rash?"

Get it together, Penny! She's been closer. This is not a big deal.

But my pulse pounded in my ears, and I had to stroke Grim's fur to keep my hands down. My one-ish friend was still toying with my once best friend, and neither of them seemed to know that I was about to go on a murderous rampage.

For Artie.

"C'mon, Nay. High School was almost two decades ago, and you know you are way better off now..." I gestured to the image on the wall beside the register. It featured her hugging Leila, her water sprite wife, and a small army of children in a Rembrandt worthy painting Nay had created in a mixed media mural of paint, glass and fur.

I somehow sounded normal around the thunder of blood crashing through my veins. The wood nymph's ears turned first, then her nose, both working and watching before her eyes studied me. They bounced from the death grip my fingers had weaved into Grim's fur, to the pulse point at my throat and my gently bouncing leg.

She took a step away from Artie, and sixteen muscles in my body relaxed. With a single lifted eyebrow, she asked a thousand questions.

My panic fueled swallow seemed to answer them all. She took another step back, and I picked up my quesadilla while Grim stretched out across my feet under the table.

"I know... but you know what they say about pixies and vengeance."

"Except you're a nymph," I challenged, grateful she was willing to move on, but not so grateful I wouldn't call her on her bullshit. We hadn't become friends by telling the other what she wanted to hear.

"Still, small creatures, we like to keep our emotions and grudges. They're simple and eternal. But fine," she let out a long-suffering sigh that moved her farther away from Artemis. "I'll stop poking the bear."

"The bear pokes back, you know..." Artemis growled, still staring at his sandwich. "And he needs food."

"It's fine, you giant ass man baby. Now," her attention was back on me. Bright brown eyes peeking just barely above the table, I could see her tail twitching slightly as she scented. "Georgie! You're burning the bark again!"

A goblin hobbled over to a standard oven and pulled out a tray of wood chips without using an oven mitt. He let out a slurry of grumbles that could have been words, tossing the whole aluminum tray on a wooden butcher block. Some of the wooden pellets bounced off, scattering across the concrete floor while he lumbered back to the register, eyes lasered in on a blonde elemental who was pretending to flirt with him while stealing ice under the counter.

Naomi extended a branch from the plant beside the counter and smacked the thieving princess, who stormed out in a huff.

"Good help is so hard to find," she sighed and then brightened again, as though she hadn't just thwarted a shoplifter. "Now that you're back, and I've given you the regulatory three-day timeframe of reacquaintance with the area, I think it's time you started getting out. First, you'll need a coven. Sue's is meeting Thursday. She's my neighbor, and I've already let her know you're coming! Second-"

"Nay, I..."

"Second," she continued, steamrolling my objections with the same merciless energy she put into everything her light touched. "You'll need a place to live. I know this really cute..."

"You don't have a place to live?" Artie interrupted the proprietor, causing the woman to shoot daggers at him that promised laxatives in his next cup of coffee. "Where have you been sleeping for the last three days?"

"In her office, dummy. Now shut up and eat your fries. No one is talking to you."

Naomi continued glaring at him until he tucked into his fries like a wise man who knew when to keep his mouth shut.

Ten points to... what house was Artie in? Had we talked about it? I don't think he'd be Slytherin. He was almost always over-sharing.

Maybe a Gryffindor? They were brave and kind of dumb with life choices. Not at my level of dumb, but that was more personal failure than actual group psychology.

Naomi cleared her throat.

I blinked in her direction; vaguely aware I'd been staring at Artie with my mouth hanging open.

"What house are you?" I shouted. Both Nay and Artie pulled back, looking between each other.

"Gryffindor," Artie answered while Nay replied.

"Fuck Harry Potter."

I nodded at their answers, not sure what asking or knowing accomplished. Artie was already eating again, but my sandwich friend was still looking at me, assessing.

Swallowing a few morsels of bell pepper, I put on my best sane and competent adult face.

After a few considering head tilts, Nay carried on listing the steps in Project Penny, deciding I may have had a minor stroke and that was no reason not to continue fixing my life. Her primed fingers indicated it was going to be way more than two, a not-so-subtle reminder that of everyone at the table, and Grim underneath, my shit was the least together.

"There's a cute townhouse around the corner from me that's always available for lease. The owner is some sort of vagabond who's never home, so you'll only have a roommate occasionally and I hear when he does come to town, it's never more than a couple of days at a time. I've already left a message with the property manager, and you're scheduled to see it tomorrow at noon."

"That's really sweet, but I don't..."

"Then we'll need to redecorate your office because when I walk by, it gives me the willies. It's like something out of the shining. I expect creepy twins and clowns in sewer pipes. There's no way people are going to trust you to assist with their mental health if you look like the psycho on the sign who broke it. I'm not saying we couldn't use a town psycho-"

"Nay, breathe. For the love of all that is good in this world, breathe!" She humored me and took a breath so shallow I was certain she'd hyperventilate if I asked her to take another. "I don't need a fixer. I'm not even sure if I'll be here all that long, it's...."

"Nay oh meee, what the hell!" A high pitched nasally voice rattled the windows and my magic bubble burst. I fell past the chair, landing on Grim's tail, who didn't notice as he pawed at his ears in agony. "I thought you were told to always have my soy macchiato and mixed spring salad ready at exactly noon as part of our weekly business owner get together. Instead, you're over there, talking to some insignificant... Artie?"

Jet-black smoke shot out of my palms. It singed the already scarred wood flooring and table legs on its way toward the glitter red fuck-me pumps on the feet of my nemesis.

Feet attached to legs, attached to a perfectly flat belly, impressive breasts, thin arms and a hand. A hand that was reaching out to brush a strand of hair from Artie's face.

Heat surged from the tip of my nose, through my torso and rode waves of violence out to the tips of my fingers. The smoke went from jet black to neon green, solidifying around her shoes in a churning chaos of thick wet tentacles, writhing and slithering up her naked calves.

Confused, entranced, I could only stare at the living embodiment of my jealousy sliding up her legs. Waiting, watching, both scared and obsessed, wondering when she'd realize it was her time to die.

A soft breeze of merlot floated through the air. It carried away the green and black magic, leaving a fuzzy grasp of reality and the tranquil scent of eucalyptus in its wake. The balm smoothing down the vindictive fire and leaving guilt in its place.

Nay jingled her piercings at someone in the corner and I let out the breath. Taking in another, I weighed my options and there was only one —RUN!

Seizing my advantage, I crawled on all fours, away from the table and toward the far wall. Behind me, I could feel Grim following suit, confused as to why he had to crawl.

You don't need to crawl, I thought at him. Dodging people's purses, shopping bags, coats and shoes, it was like an obstacle course to get away from the table... and Yasmin. Behind us, I could hear her whinny of a laugh at something Artemis muttered.

No one seemed to notice me, but I couldn't stop hearing all of them.

"They'd be so cute together."

"Imagine if he were her husband instead of that pretty boy?"

"I hear he has a rubber ass now."

Naomi appeared at the wall just as I got there, tapping twice on a pine knot at eye level. Her expression hung on the precipice between concern and amusement. No matter how much she'd seen or understood, I was pretty sure Project Penny just got a few more bullet points.

"I'll see you at Sue's meeting Thursday," she spoke in a low voice that offered violence if met with resistance. "Maybe someone there can help."

My head bobbed, and I kept crawling through the narrow opening in the wall. It was roughly the same size and shape as a dog door, a fact that was proven when Grim barged through first. Following his large, fur tufted paws, I burst into the bright autumnal afternoon and took my first deep breath. Holding it until my lungs ached, and I was certain no bronchus had been left constricted, I blew it out and flopped onto my back beside a grassy patched lot.

Grim flopped over beside me and we stared at the overcast sky. I counted darker grey patches in blocks of ten, trying to match my heart rate to the slowly roving masses sliding by above my head. Listening, I held my breath to see if anyone was going to come arrest me for almost attacking the town darling.

Bland sounds of everyday life swirled around me, no more concerned with what had happened than they were with whether or not it would rain.

"What in Lilith's name are we doing here?" I asked no one in particular. Grim's response was to shake his paws out, and switch to facing me. With a wide yawn, I enjoyed an unobstructed view of every tooth in his mouth and a curly Q tongue that stayed flopping on the concrete. "What are we supposed to do now?"

He didn't twitch a single muscle. Full on dead dog mode activated.

"Yeah, I guess we could take a nap."

CHAPTER
SIX

PENELOPE

THE SOUND OF KNOCKING STARTLED ME AWAKE, AND I jumped off my couch, groggy and uncoordinated. A tangle of blankets captured my foot, and I toppled over, narrowly avoiding the end table with the side of my head as I tumbled onto the industrial grade carpet.

"Herlo?"

From my vantage point, face down on the ground, I couldn't see anyone. A quick glance around my general vicinity, aka the floor, showed Grim wouldn't be able to see anyone... from his vantage point of snoring, with his tongue lolling out of the side of his mouth.

Clearly, if we were in danger, I'd have to sound the alarm.

"Hello?" I tried again, a huge chunk of hair sticking to my tongue. Spitting and trying to clear the sensation, a large, warm hand slid under my forearm and somehow arranged me into an upright position. In the process, he also cleared my hair from my face, extricated my legs from the blanket, and returned my sleep tank to the upright and non-exhibi-tionist position.

I.E. my boob was no longer half hanging out of the sleeve.

His scent gave him away before I could figure out which direction to look for his face.

"Artie?" I asked, and his chin dipped to meet my gaze. We didn't have much of a height difference, but his boots compared to my bare feet gave him a leverage that encouraged the pulse in my throat to leap and stutter. I reached up and brushed an escaped strand of hair from his face, wondering if I was still dreaming.

The dim light of my office made his eyes glow golden, and I trailed a finger down his cheek, every bit of stubble catching on my fingertips. Every angle of his face was shadowed, and he was so damn beautiful that I couldn't stop exploring, even if it was a dream.

Just at this moment, he was my dream.

"Hey PenPen," his deep rumbling voice traveled through his body and into mine from the arm he'd somehow kept around my waist. My hand drifted down his neck to his chest, his arm... "I was told you work here."

Reality spat in my face, and I let my hand drop to the side. Inching away from him, guilt scratched against my chest. I wanted to sigh, scream the truth into the sky, and take the spell back to have him with me.

To have him look at me like who he really was, the only man who'd ever seen beyond the walls built to save people from the curse of being me.

That would be selfish. Just take the moments you have and let him go.

I tried to hold in a tear that I was blaming on just having woken up and not yet having had coffee.

"Sign didn't give it away?" I asked, eyebrow raised as I attempted to get some breathing room. He was real, and he was here.

For now.

It would have to be enough.

"You mean the 'Psycho' part? Nah, everyone knows you're only psycho when they don't let you have coffee before math class," he sighed, wrapping his other arm around me and stealing back all the space I'd put between us. Artie burrowed his nose into my hair, inhaling my scent while his large hands kneaded the soft rolls at my waist. "You smell so good."

It came out like a partial growl and the sound did things to me. Combine that with his hands and I needed to cross my legs and pray to the goddess my hair was the only thing he wanted to put his face in.

Or not...

"What time is it?" I asked, because it was the coolest, least *rip off my pants and ride him into the afterlife* thing I could think of to say. Moving away from him was proving difficult, either because of his impressive mass or my own weak-willed lady parts that throbbed in time to the waves of liquid heat that poured off him and the rhythmic circles of his hands massaging my waist.

"A little after six. I thought you were working..."

His response was joined by a growing awareness that he'd found me in my pajamas, midday, clearly having been asleep for more than an hour.

"It's kind of dark, let me just..."

Without any grounds for objection, he moved one hand to my lower back and escorted me to the window. With the other, he flipped open the blinds, letting in the hideous light of the day star.

"Hsskkk!"

My arms flapped around, trying to bat away the excessive and, in my opinion, unnecessarily bright sunlight he'd allowed into my personal space.

"It's too bright! I thought it was nighttime," I whined, batting useless hands at the non-substantive substance that was threatening to singe my sun averse flesh. "It burns! IT BURNS!"

I started wilting toward the floor, placing more and more of my weight on Artie's body until he either had to let me go or fall over.

Instead, he threw me over his shoulder like a sack of potatoes and carried me out of the direct beam of light.

"You're so dramatic, PenPen," his laughter held an undertow of eye roll I did not appreciate.

"I am not! I'm Scottish! We're petty and we've never seen the sun," I quipped to his ass, which was very nearly at my eye level. It had a curvature that defied gravity and my brain warred with my teeth that wanted desperately to sink into the flesh while I...

Artie froze in place, interrupting my thoughts.

"Wha-" I started, just as his chest rose with a long deep inhale that pressed me closer to him.

Close enough that I felt the growl in his chest before it slipped through his lips.

"Penny..."

Another wave of heat sloshed against the thin fabric of my undies beneath the thinner fabric of my sleep shorts.

Hex me sideways...

"Maybe you should..."

I was sliding down his body, legs spreading to rest on his hips. I was now eye to eye with Artie's dilated pupils while his oversized hands diffused heat into my ass, massaging the soft flesh there in the same pattern he'd used on my waist. His fervor grew, the languid affection growing rough with heat and need. Each motion of his hands dragged my core against the ridge of his cock just behind the zipper of his pants and I gasped against the sensation. Fighting to finish my sentence.

"... put me down," I finished on a half moan that brought back Artie's bear, the gold flecks barely showing, but I felt him beneath the surface.

Struggling to get out.

Get to me.

"Artie?" I breathed, wanting him and knowing why I couldn't have him.

Eyelids sliding closed, Artie appeared to count slowly from ten. With each breath, he loosened his grip on me until I was resting back on my makeshift bed. The loss of his heat hit with a punch, the single step he placed between us as cold and wide as the Grand Canyon.

When his eyes opened, they were chocolate brown, but no less heated.

Scrubbing his hands over his face, I watched the man fight with himself until he took another step backward and gave me his familiar lopsided smile.

"Maybe we should go get some coffee," he offered, and I salivated, impersonating Pavlov's dog.

All feelings of loss replaced by a new need, one that wouldn't ruin both of us to fulfill.

"Yes, please, always..." I was practically vibrating with desire and there was no need to send my nether regions to the frozen tundra of polar bear town this time. Hopping off the couch, I stuffed my feet into the nearest pair of shoes and grabbed my phone off the charger. "Let's go!"

I was halfway through the door when he caught my arm.

"PenPen!"

"Hmm?" I asked over my shoulder, baffled by his sudden lack of momentum.

"Pants."

FOR A MAN who played professional sports, he was strangely attached to the idea of me wearing clothes.

After I'd pulled on leggings, he'd insisted they also needed to be worn with a sweater of some kind. Then he made me go back and add a bra. Afterward, it was deemed better if I took off my boots and added socks.

By the time we actually left, I was practically wearing floor length robes and a habit.

"You suck," I said again. Still pissed I'd had to waste another 20 minutes not having coffee.

"I was trying to make sure you didn't get sick!"

"It's not that cold. You're just ashamed of my nudity," I grumbled as he angled us toward the main drag of Main Street. "I could have worn my PJs out here if you weren't so against seeing me nearly naked."

Grim was ambling beside us, clearly not happy to be leaving the safety and comfort of bedtime to be outside in the sadistic sunlight.

"No, you couldn't have," he scoffed, angling me around a group of girls who giggled and whispered when they saw him. Something curdled in my stomach, locking onto another group of young women who were trying to sneak pictures of Artie. He leaned into me, stubble grazing my neck and sending blips of desire running through me. "It's way too distracting. Because I definitely want to see you naked."

"Mmmhmm... yeah, sure..." I moaned, but he moved away from a pole and I spotted yet another group with their eyes locked on him. Glaring between the young women and girls who were still ogling Artie, my pulse quickened and anger burned at my cheeks. *My Artie*, I snarled internally as my arm took on a life of its own and moved to point their direction.

Grim cut off my stride and I stumbled into a group of men easily thirty-plus years my senior. My arm went down as I attempted to steady myself without actually touching any of them. Their sudden presence was a bucket of ice to freeze-out the anger I felt and replace it with a cold wariness.

"Penelope," Council Member Halibut croaked, and I blinked several times until he came into focus. Shadows seemed to dance between them, a quasi-darkness that bounced around and linked them together. It kept them blurred in a mass even as they stood separately and I swiped at my eyes.

Beside him were the remaining six men who made up the Huckle-berry Hollow Town Council, a group of wizened witches who made Dumbledore look youthfully obtuse. They were all named Chad or Brad... and hadn't taken off the mortuary black robes since before I was born. Standing side by side, they reminded me of a foosball table. All the same size, moving as a single unit.

"Council member," I tried not to sound like I was insulting him, spitting out member like it was made of black licorice and star anise. Based on the arched caterpillar working overtime as Chad/Brad number one's eyebrow, I didn't try hard enough.

Or at all.

Dishonesty isn't one of my skills, and I put very little effort into improving.

"What brings you back this way?" His casual question was under-lined with a serious interest that reflected in the bearded faces of his counterparts. A breeze came by, carrying the scent of sweat and sulfur, a combination that clung to the back of my tongue.

Fear.

Shame.

I could nearly pluck both out of the air and I studied each man in turn, waiting for each to squirm. Though none of them was unique, they all had the same pinched expression as they stood with their hands at their sides, obscured in gloom.

Secrets.

"She's home with me, obviously." Artie threw an arm around me and dragged me closer to him. "Well, me and family... we're thinking of really settling somewhere and it's been a while since either of us was here, you know."

"With you, Artemis?" Commissioner Dillitant spoke up, and I thought a puff of dust and cobwebs came with the words. I also wasn't sure how I knew who had spoken, since none of them appeared to move.

Crusty old witch, my anger burned the back of my throat. It singed like swallowing a box of Red Hots and choosing between spitting them out and certain death. I waited for Artemis to tell them about grabbing a coffee while I tried to make even one of them look like a whole person. Leaving me completely unprepared for his declaration.

"Yeah, she's my girlfriend... well, fiancée as of today, right?"

"What the hell was that, Artemis?" I hissed, my palms sweating pools on the tile floor of the coffee shop. I kept swiping them up and down my leggings, but the fake engagement ring he'd pulled out of nowhere weighed a million pounds. "Why did you..."

"Because they were waiting for you," he whispered. He'd angled me into the coffee queue and there was a pretty hefty crowd for this time of day.

Grim was panting beside me, a silent mockery of my ill-ease. He was acting like he knew the whole time I was going to end up engaged to a man who wouldn't remember me tomorrow.

"Of course I could smell it, and taste it, they were practically..." I paused, lost for a metaphor. There was a stink that wafted off them that hadn't quite lined up with their position in the town. "That still doesn't explain this!"

I waved the ring in his face, wishing I could give it back. My hair had escaped its bun and was back inside my mouth. Artie absently traced my jaw with his fingers, the warm tips sending chills down my spine as he tucked my hair behind my ear. The delicate touch lingered there as the line crawled forward and time stood still between us.

"It's just something I had lying around," he whispered, middle finger massaging my jaw. "It looks good on you."

I swallowed hard and slid the ring off, pressing it back into his hand. "I'm sure it has a real owner you bought it for. Can't ruin her jewelry by pre-wearing it." I shifted slightly to face him, forcing Artie to move his hand to my shoulder. "What do you think it was about?"

He stared at the ring in his hand, contemplating its weight with a myriad of expressions on his face. I couldn't tell if he was confused about who he'd purchased it for or hurt I'd given it back, but I already wished it was still on my hand. The damn thing had fit perfectly, and I was irrationally angry that another man or woman would someday be photographed wearing it.

"I don't know, but something's off." He slid the ring back into his jeans pocket. The arm around my shoulders guided me forward while his gaze remained off in the distance. My palms itched it stroke his cheek, but I forced them to stay at my sides while he thought.

"Since I've been back in the Hollow, I've been losing time. The Council has been seen out more, lurking and being weird... I can't explain it." He shook his head, dropping the arm from my shoulder and slipping it around my waist, pulling me against him as the queue narrowed.

He fit perfectly. All of his hard muscle created the perfect valleys for my curves to rest.

It felt like he was made to hold me against him, the same way it felt like his friendship held me together for years. *But I'm the reason he's losing time...* I swallowed hard and opened my mouth to confess. The pressure in my chest was getting heavier, and I wasn't sure if telling him was worse than letting him think the council was sabotaging him.

"How does pretending to be with me help with that?" The question defied my heart, once again stuffing down the truth in favor of a few more moments in a beautiful lie. His touch settled something deep inside me, not counting the parts of me that wanted him deep inside me, giving the impression for the first time everything might turn out alright. "Aside from the fact you scare the bajeebus out of people and it gets me a little breathing room?"

We were getting closer to the counter and Artie was working his way beside me at an angle, mouth very close to my ear. His scent circled me, an intoxicating and heady reminder that my body didn't think this was fake.

"Yeah, besides that."

"I..." His cheeks were tinted red in my peripheral vison. He brought his hand up to rub the back of his head, squirming slightly. "I'm feeling unsteady... but with you... I feel grounded. You... your touch makes me feel safe. Like everything is in focus and I might not need to be running nonstop to the next thing all the time. Like I can just be."

Guilt bubbled in my belly. His words had just mirrored my own thoughts, and I was lying to him.

"You make me feel the same way. But we *are* friends, Artie. You don't need to lie to spend time with me."

"Funny thing about that claim," he said, angling us to the next in line spot. "You never seem surprised to see me, but I don't really remember us spending time together. Before or after you left... but I remember we were friends. How does that happen?"

The knowing smirk danced on his lips and his eyes dared me to lie to him... again.

"How does-" I gulped and was saved when the barista waved us over.

We reached the counter, the man asking for our order. The barista looked between Artie's hand at my waist and the handsome face with a slightly off-center nose, then less appreciatively scanning my wide middle and dog drool flecked leggings, furrowed his blonde eyebrows. The all-black outfit under the teal apron showcased a haughty frame. Then he wrinkled his nose at the pair of us.

All he needed to convey the obvious juxtaposition of a gorgeous man with the red-headed death card.

"Two pumpkin spice breves with quad shots and a pup cup. You need a snack, babe?"

Babe? The fluff... My thoughts were cut short by a spreading heat in my abdomen.

Artie's thumb was moving in little circles at my hip, pulling a more approving look from... Erich, if one believed name tags. It sent my world tilting on its edge, an intoxicating wave of something possessive beating in time to my racing heart, that kicked up a beat with every swipe of his thumb under my sweater.

"N-n-no, thanks," I answered, realizing both men were waiting for me to say something. The butterflies in my belly had taken up Irish dancing, stomping out a driving beat with my heart thudding in my chest.

"No? Have you eaten?" I blinked at Artie, trying to figure out why he was working overtime to sell the doting boyfriend routine to a man who'd immediately forget us both. Nothing but sincere affection and concern... none of this was fake to him and I was about to have a stroke. "Babe?"

I forgot how to breathe, and he squeezed me a little tighter, pinching the extra padding of my abdomen and letting his fingers linger at the waistband of my pants. When words continued to elude me, he turned back to the coffee keeper.

"What have you got with cheese?"

"Ham and cheese croissant and potato haystacks," Erich said, staring at the hand under my sweater. It was the only surety I had that this whole thing was really happening, and I wasn't blissed out on a porn fantasy in a coffeehouse.

"Give her one of each."

"That's not-" Artie cut me off with a hand over my mouth, pinching my muffin top with the other. It was a little too close to a hand necklace, and I suddenly wanted to know what that felt like more than coffee.

More than coffee? Shit... something is seriously wrong.

"That'll be $23," Erich announced and Artie removed his hand from my waist to do some sorcery, where he waved his phone at the electronic box. It beeped, money mysteriously changed hands, and Artie returned his hand to my waist, shuffling me sideways toward the pickup counter with a casual nod of thanks to the man behind the counter.

"Since when can you do magic?" I asked, looking between him and his phone. It may have been a wand of sorts, but I didn't sense any sort of magical camouflage altering my perception. The only "wand" I was certain he had was still safely in his pants, the same location his phone had just disappeared into.

"Magic?" He looked at me with a very slight head tilt. Below us, Grim mirrored the movement, and I felt like they both might be pranking me in a bro before hoe solidarity nonsense.

"Yeah…" I watched the next customer do the same thing and looked around at everyone with wonder. I knew the woman who'd just purchased coffee was a magical vacuum, a Faraday bag for supernatural transmissions. Crystal would not have been able to do magic and yet… she moved to the pickup counter area without any fear that her order wouldn't arrive.

"It's a digital wallet, PenPen," Artie laughed as two more people tapped their phones and were granted the magic bean water. The entire system seemed startlingly efficient, and I wondered when and how such non-sorcery came to pass.

"What's a digital wallet?"

Two coffees, a paper pouch and a small cup of whipped cream were placed on the counter, the barista shouting for Artemis. Artie steered me to the counter, refusing to take his hand off of my waist. With his free hand, he grabbed one coffee and the pup cup, leaving me to grab the second and the cheesy snacks I hadn't wanted but would definitely eat.

We paused to look around and found all the nearby tables occupied. Two patrons narrowly missed Grim's paws and the surge of people in line placing their orders hadn't yet dwindled.

"Let's walk, yeah?" Artie inclined his head to the street. Steering my leashed canine and clutching my sustenance, I let Artemis take charge of the rest, smoothly leading our crew outside.

Standing amid the patio tables, I took my first drink of pumpkin-y goodness while Artie dropped to a crouch and gave Grim his whipped cream. The sugary spices burst on my tongue and my eyes drooped closed, a perfect moment made better by the cool breeze carrying the rustle of leaves and scent of wood-burning fireplaces.

And the tightening grip of Artie's hand on my love handles.

"Wha-" I started, opening my eyes and holding still at the predatory need rolling off him.

"Don't make that sound, Peep," he rumbled, the heat underscored by the tap of the paper cup against the concrete patio. "If you do it again, you really will be naked in public."

My throat closed, and I tried to swallow around the sticky dryness. Grim's cup continued to click against the ground, and giggling girls tittered just beyond, but he was the only thing I could see.

The entire world zoomed into a fisheye of just Artemis.

A light trick made him glow like an opal bursting around us, my shadow broke into pieces around it and for a second I thought we'd merged together. His fingers slid down my temple, index tracing the cupid's bow of my top lip, and I held my breath while his face inched closer.

Grim's tail brushed my leg, and I moved backward slightly, the colors gone in the slowly fading light of day.

Just a light trick, I breathed to myself. Turning away, I took a long drink of coffee and counted to ten. We hadn't almost kissed; he had probably just been swiping the pumpkin off my lip.

Too scared to open my eyes, I kept counting until I reached thirty and could no longer hear Grim. Glancing down, the familiar was staring at me with amber eyes and upright, pointed ears that were a little too accusatory for a casual coffee date.

"You done?" I asked, and he blew out a sigh that toppled the empty cup.

Collecting his trash and exercising extreme cowardice, I pulled away from Artemis and tossed his cup and mine into the bin. Instead of going back toward Artie, I opened the metal gate to the street and gestured for him to exit the patio.

He blinked rapidly, trying to replay the tapes that ended with him standing empty-handed and me several feet away.

"Where do you want to go?" I asked, careful not to meet his gaze. Artemis took a few steps forward, passing me and pausing on the other side, arm outstretched for me to link his elbow.

I pretended not to see it and moved to the far side of him. Grim tried in vain to loop me closer, but I sidestepped the familiar as well, angling out onto the sidewalk while stuffing pastry into my mouth as I went.

"Anywhere is fine, you lead the way," he sighed at me, somewhere between hurt and annoyed.

Not to worry, I told myself, *he won't remember tomorrow.*

Pointing us toward the older parts of town, I kept to the outside of the sidewalk. The move intentionally kept trees, streetlights and fire hydrants between us, leaving only room for me to walk the curb like a balance beam.

"I know what you're doing," Artie rumbled, grabbing my biceps and pulling me to the main part of the sidewalk. He moved himself between me and the roadway, with Grim in between us.

"What am I doing?" I feigned innocence, but it was as poor an acting job as my effort to not insult the Chads.

"Look, I promise to let you keep your bullshit buffer and not ask you why you're suddenly being a Panicky Penelope. But you can't walk on the street side." He held up his hand to stop my interjection before my mouth even opened. "This isn't some chivalry bullshit, PenPen. You are a walking gravitational nightmare and you are not allowed to fall down into the street. I can pick you up off a sidewalk, but I'd need a shovel to pick you up if you fell into traffic."

Skeptical, I looked up and down the street before crossing my arms and giving him my best *you're an idiot* look.

"Just because there aren't any cars *now*, doesn't mean you wouldn't manage to fall in front of one. Remember that time you fell off a parade float and were almost run over by a giant caldron on wheels?"

I turned pink despite myself.

"That's not fair. You know Jessica was driving and I wouldn't put it past Yasmin to 'arrange' for me to have an accident... and Jessica is a shit driver," I shrugged, laughing despite myself at the memory. "What about the time you fell off the bench in the cafeteria and landed in the Fly Team Captain's lap? What was his name... Eddy? Freddy? Pineapple? Whatever. Then the two of you hooked up in the janitor's closet and you came back to class with a cleaning rag of window cleaner stuck to your pants."

Artie gave me an odd look.

"How do you know about that?" He asked, guiding us smoothly around a group of witch tourists whose accents screamed midwestern.

"What do you mean? I was there," I waved him off as we moved further up the street. Unknowingly, I'd lead us toward the hospital, and we were now at the mouth of an alleyway that linked our street to the mysteriously deserted area I'd wandered into before. "I mean not *there*, there, but I was in the class you had after."

Two steps down the alley, Artie grabbed my arm and pulled me back toward a neighboring business.

"Penny, why did you leave?" His gaze traveled from the building on the left to the one on the right and back to me. "Why were you just suddenly gone from my life? Why don't I remember being in class together?"

His searching gaze made me squirm, his grip right over the scar tissue from the very night in question. My sweater became itchy, and I scratched at my leg, trying to clear the discomfort in my skin.

This wasn't the first time he'd asked. Normally, I saw it coming, but I'd been too distracted by our weird connection. Too distracted by the need to confess.

Too desperate to hold on to the only person who'd made living here bearable.

It wouldn't be fair to him, my rational brain held fast. All the reasons from fifteen years ago were still true, but we were both here.

For now.

"You know why, Artie," I whispered, gently pulling my arm away to keep going down the alley. Two more steps in and he pulled me back again.

"No, I don't. Everything feels right when we're together and you just... keep leaving. And you take everything with you."

"I needed to go somewhere I wasn't Death," I answered, and tried for a third time to make it to the neighboring street. Once again, Artie pulled me back and this time he led me down the road and across the street. I looked down at Grim and then back at the alley. The dog looked at me and then toward the alley, his gaze traveling between the buildings as though the gap didn't exist.

The same way Artie had.

"Do you want some ice cream, Penny?" Artie asked, and I turned back to him, surprised by his sudden change of topic.

"You... what?" I paused, staring back at the alley.

"Ice cream? You want some?" It was like he'd completely forgotten what we were talking about.

"Yeah, sure," I answered, following along. Whatever his reason, this iteration of "the talk" was over.

At least for now.

EIGHT

No way was that a normal animal.

The low snarl had come from between the bank and an unoccupied law office. It grew louder every time Penelope drifted toward the buildings. Her lack of personal safety, and the seeming indifferent attitude of the beast beside her, was infuriating. It was like he couldn't even sense the danger.

Whether or not Penny could was a fucking mystery. Her erratic heartbeat had been pounding since I placed that ring on her finger. It had looked perfect there, like it belonged there.

Because I knew in my gut it belonged there.

Instead, she'd given it back, and I'd let her.

Fucking smooth, Nita-Nusi.

There was no way to explain the ring to her without making everything worse. It was a truth I knew with no facts or evidence I could point to that her scientist brain would demand, but I knew the ring was hers and she was mine. Sadly, there was no way to explain any of this without sending her off the deep end... the one she was standing on the edge of at every second, ready to dive.

The whole town was on edge, had been since I'd arrived, but there was something about Penny's behavior that was suspect. We'd only been together a few hours and the smell of her desire to fuck me was driving me absolutely nuts, but she didn't seem the least bit surprised by this reaction. Jealous, angry and scared... but not surprised.

To me, it was new and alluring. To her, it was old news, and that shit grated against my bear. I may not shift, but he paced beneath the surface, begging to claim her as though he thought half breeds were worthy of a mate.

Worthy of her.

We *so* weren't worthy, but damn if a taste wasn't the one thing we needed before Callisto called us home to live with the other bear shifters in the sky. My demon didn't give a shit about being worthy. He would feast on her until every drop of pleasure was wrung from her body like a wet rag in the southern sun.

Those tiny ass pajamas she was wearing were like a wet dream come to life. A dream I'd had before, with her. Only when I woke up, I didn't know her anymore. It was like the most aggravating torture, a boner that wouldn't go down no matter how many times you jacked off.

Forgetting her was terrifying to me, and yet I knew in my gut it would happen again. I also knew that someone in this damn town had the answer of why, but I couldn't form a clear thought around the scent of Penny's fear.

What the hell is she so afraid of?

I looked at the woman beside me, prepared to ask, but she was a thousand miles away, staring behind her at the buildings that hid danger. Instead of looking scared, she was curious. Something about that place intrigued her and there was no sense of danger. Whether because the woman refused to have a sense of self fucking preservation or because she thought her magic could save her from anything was anyone's guess.

But it would probably get her killed, and that wasn't on my list of acceptable outcomes.

I slipped my hand into hers, lacing our fingers together until she stopped looking back at the buildings. She stared at our joined fingers and looked like a deer in headlights. It was fucking adorable, and I leaned in to kiss the tip of her nose, holding tight so she couldn't pull away.

"The council is watching," I lied, pulling her in closer. Her head turned, and I guided her toward a wall to avoid a group of teenagers that weren't anywhere near us. "Don't look. They'll think you're hiding something."

She tried to look again, more discreetly, and I pressed her into a wall. Using my whole body, I surrounded her with my scent until her breath hitched and the sweet scent of her arousal hit my nose. Her body squirmed against mine, sending every drop of blood straight to my dick.

I couldn't help it. I breathed deep to take in every last drop.

A memory slid into place, of when we were younger and I'd held her against a wall like this in our high school. Yasmin and her friends were taunting Peep about her weight, making obscene parallels and throwing plastic food at her.

I'd been in the closet with someone and I shoved them out, pulling her in. She'd tried to hit me, angry, confused, and hurt. Until she inhaled my scent and every muscle slowly relaxed against me. Instead of feeding the beast, I'd held my best friend until she stopped shaking, her face pressed into my neck while the chaos outside grew louder and then faded into silence.

It wasn't a tactic my beast would allow twice.

This time, we were having a taste of her.

"You're being naughty, PenPen," I whispered into her ear, feeling my cock twitch at the soft mewl that slipped through her lips. Her pink tongue darted out to wet them again, and I considered pulling it into my mouth so she couldn't say anything to ruin this. If she refused, we'd have to step away. I could smell what she wanted, but the woman had a bad habit of lying to herself... and me.

"You're being a pain in the ass, Artie," she huffed, but the nipples poking through her shirt said she wasn't all that mad about it. I ran my nose along her neck as a group of girls from our high school bickered across the street. The sound carried, but I couldn't catch any of the words around the steady pulse of Penny's heart thrumming in her chest.

"As long as it's your ass, Peep," I breathed against her collarbone. My demon pressed against my insides, feeding on her desire. He slipped my knee between her legs, pressing it against her heated core and devouring the rush of pleasure that crashed against me. "Do you want me to stop?"

Penny's pupils were fully dilated and my eyes locked on her lips, drawing me in. I leaned in, mouth brushing against her while the sound of angry voices crowded in. Her lips parted, and I smiled, ready to feast on every inch of her.

Finally! I was going to get a second chance at that first kiss.

"Get away from him!"

Thick claws ripped at my shoulder, dragging me away from Peep.

My bear snapped, snarling and putting my pitiful human shape between my Penny and... Yasmin. The fucking twat stood there with her small army of dumb followers: Ditzy, Handsy, and Satan-ie. The same group who'd tortured her for over half a decade were still fucking trying to make her life hell. If the four of them had been nuked from the planet, the smoldering remains would still have been too much of them left. They were the only pieces of ass even my demon wouldn't sink low enough to fuck.

And he'd once had an orgy with the Blue Man Group.

"She's put a spell on you, Artie! You need to get away from her so we can try to break the curse," Ditzy whined, though her name might have been Jessica. Where Yasmin's arm touched me felt like a barrel of slithering serpents and I pulled it roughly back, setting her off balance.

The witch wavered on her toothpicks but didn't fall over, because gravity wasn't anymore my friend than luck.

"Don't touch me," I snarled, letting my bear and my demon surface, both fighting to rip her apart and then feast on Penny's flesh while the nasty woman lies bleeding to death beside us.

Whoa, dude, graphic... tough not an unappealing visual. I could feel Penny shaking behind me. Priorities said to get her the hell away from them and worry about the rest later.

"But Artie," she simpered, and I tucked Peep into my side, trapping her arms to prevent escape and potential curses. "She's not good enough for you."

"Get out of the way," I ordered, using the closest approximation I had to an Alpha command. "We need ice cream."

"You won't be able to get any," she snapped, straightening her spine again. Whatever I thought of my authority as an alpha, she thought more highly of herself. "I own this town, Artemis. As long as you're under her spell, no one will serve you!"

"We'll see about that."

CHAPTER

NINE

PENELOPE

 in a horrified silence.

The sun had finally gone down at some point during our search for a place to purchase ice cream that wasn't owned by Yasmin's stupid family. Despite not being directly related to any council members, her family had an unhealthy attachment to "the way things were" that suggested they'd gladly reimplement the Witch Trials of Salem if it meant progress was halted.

This viewpoint had curried quite a bit of favor with the Board of Economic Development, which was still the Council but with a new name, and Yasmin's family had been given the opportunity to purchase businesses before they were available on the open market.

As a result, those fuckers owned almost everything.

Every business they owned had a picture of me inside a red circle, a giant line slashed through. It was an awful picture, one I would replace if they hadn't charmed the doors with an incredibly unoriginal spell that stopped me from entering. While being banned from businesses was inconvenient, I deserved to at least be entertained for my suffering.

Like a spell that gave me a rubber ass to bounce down the roadway after being forcefully pushed out of the business... or the building

79

suddenly turned into larvae that squirmed away when I touched it... not that I'd given this much thought.

In the end, we'd ended up back at Gnomewich, where Naomi had given me sidelong glances and extra large scoops amid the twittering judgment of the town's residents.

Behind Artie, the door slammed closed, interrupting my thoughts. The room was instantly black, and I felt a surge of anxiety at losing my vision. The windowless lobby had been a real positive when I inherited the business, patient privacy being a huge concern in a small town. But without patients and nowhere else to live, it felt like an OSHA violation against gravitationally challenged employees.

A category I occupied unilaterally in all aspects, but still...

"Where's the light switch?" Artie whispered, his ice cream cooled breath carrying the smell of cherry and chocolate as it brushed against my cheek. A shiver crept down my spine that had nothing to do with the chill.

"I don't know."

I whispered back, fighting to dispel the butterfly swarm that took flight in my belly. The visions of us pressed together on the street warring with common sense that said I should stay far away from those thoughts. We couldn't be anything more than friends, if that, unless I wanted to subject him to nights like this forever.

"Also, why are we whispering?" I said in my normal voice. Nothing takes the intimacy out of darkness better than firm reminders you are not being intimate, you just can't see. Without that sense, I was overwhelmed by the smell of coffee grounds and dog. Not a terrible smell, but the office might need a wall plug if anyone who wasn't me ever came in here.

It was also extremely un-sexy, so I figured it was conveying the correct mood for my suddenly amorous fixation on my childhood friend.

"Because..." Artie whispered, moving around me. He passed close to me but didn't touch, like he knew I was picturing our tryst in the street and fighting to prevent it from happening again. It was both an acknowledgement and a subtle mockery of its premise, the same way he'd hold my hand every chance he got and claim the Council was watching, even though my magic knew for a fact the crusty old farts were nowhere near me.

But I wanted to hold his hand too, so I pretended.

Pretended we were two people on a date. Holding hands and getting ice cream, never mind that whole getting physically barred from businesses, I felt normal for the first time in my life. The walls I'd built around my heart and around the idea of Artie cracked just enough for me to see a different future, one where we could be more than ships passing in the night and part-time friends.

I saw forever with him and it filled my heart with light.

And absolute terror.

An angry mob with pitchforks and torches had nothing on the traumatic realization that I was not mentally capable of forming a functioning adult relationship with a man. I knew I loved Artie... but was I in love with him? The traitorous hammering of my heart said I might have a stroke standing here in the dark with him before I ever had to find out.

With his shifter vision, Artemis had no trouble navigating the unused lobby furniture and fake plants. Before my sweaty palms could dislodge my ice cream cup and create another trip and slip hazard, Artie reached the correct wall as the click of Grim's nails announced he was abandoning me.

Artie, however, declined to announce when he found the switch.

"Baa!" I squealed, squeezing my lids shut to watch the neon light show reflecting from the lens onto my retina. "Warn a woman, would you?"

"Sorry... why didn't you use magic? Just *Lumos* it up like Harry Potter?"

He'd stopped whispering, and I flinched. Between his volume and the sudden light, I was in sensory overload. Added to it, the glorious scent of Artie still clung to my clothes and swirled around me-a confusing mix of heaven and hell.

"Well, I don't have a wand or anything for the light to come out of unless I crack my spine like a glow stick... or use my boobs like radioactive Care Bear headlights, so it seemed like the most reasonable choice was to let the man who can see in the dark handle the situation."

Scooping the last of my ice cream into my mouth, I walked behind the reception counter to toss it in the black plastic trash can. A layer of dust covered the surface of the desk and the counter, a small collection of cobwebs between the multi-line phone and a black wire cup filled with Bic pens. Where a monitor should sit was just a handful of cords coming out of a CPU, a moving accident I hadn't had the time, money, or mental fortitude to rectify.

"What's wrong?" Artie was beside me, sliding an arm around my shoulder and tossing his cup into the can with mine. I fought back the urge to spill all my fears and frustrations into his ears. He'd stood by me through the encounter with the Stiletto Sisters, supported my exile from business after business with a joking shrug... should I really let him know the rest of my problems?

A selfish person would dump it in his lap, hope the memory spell held, and feel unburdened. I was selfish, but I couldn't handle my own guilt over what I'd already put him through. No way could I give him even more.

Even if my memory spell held forever and he never remembered, everyone else would. No amount of time or space would make the town's most influential people forget what I was.

Death.

Change.

An unwelcome reminder that not everyone could be coerced to fall in line.

Though they still managed to use me. A warning of what it meant to be different.

Bitterness burned like bile in the back of my throat and my eyes brimmed with unshed tears.

"Penny?" He asked again, pulling me closer. His embrace held love, care and genuine affection–all having the unfortunate effect of making the urge to cry stronger.

He doesn't deserve your burdens.

"Nothing. So, how long are you in town for?" I asked, leaving the reception area filled with reminders of my failure. "What brought you back?"

Adjusting his arm onto my lower back, he came with me.

"It's a harvest moon following a full moon in the same month as a blood moon," he shrugged, like that on its own, was an adequate answer. Not quite as rare as a blue moon, blood moons were rarely the color suggested in their name, but when the stars... or moon, as the case may be, aligned–it was magic.

Real magic, that many practitioners without power tried to bottle, empowering themselves with varying degrees of success. A harvest moon, on the other hand, was nothing more than an angle of incidence between the sun and the moon that happened in the optical region of the earth.

While it was cool, it wasn't magic.

"No idea what that means," I prompted when he just kept walking with me to my office, which was also my bedroom.

"It's a shifter thing, *when the moon children walk among man the same as night*. My dad wants me to give up the league and take my place in the pack. The easiest way to accomplish that is by having me here at a time when a mate bond, no matter how tenuous, will force the issue. He seemed extremely confident that I have one and now is the time to get them." He shrugged as he finished his sentence and then dropped into the armchair. Stretching his legs out, I noticed the same jeans and boots from this morning, still highlighting how long and muscular they are.

Long, muscular and tempting... the man was a glass of water for a parched woman and I had to swallow back a lewd suggestion we pretend for a night I wasn't socially and emotionally incompetent. That for one night we pretend I was his mate and play house in my office... which was also my house.

Ugh... I don't even have a house to play house in. The tragic reminder moved me squarely back into the friend mindset of suggestions to improve his life with an actual mate.

Someone worthy of him.

"Do you want to quit the league? Couldn't you just take your mate on the road?"

He slouched low in the seat, leaning his head back with his hands clasped on his abdomen. Eyes at half mast, he looked as tired as I felt. Lurking in the corners was a worry he hadn't voiced. My eyes drifted to the pocket he'd tucked the ring into earlier.

My ring, Gollum-Penny insisted. But if he was here to meet his mate... my stomach dropped.

He had bought it for her... or him. Whoever his mate was, that ring would be theirs.

As long as he's happy, I reminded myself. The whole point of the distance, the separation... I just wanted him to be happy. If his mate wearing that ring would make Artie happy, then I was excited to see it.

I could also shit rainbows and ride unicorns, because delusions were better with company.

"You know I only joined the league to feed the beast," he paused and seemed to study me. Whatever he saw there didn't comfort him. "Maybe you don't. I just needed a ready supply of men and women willing to feed me their pleasure without any real attachment or reason for them to force one. I'm not sure I even enjoy the sport anymore, or if I ever enjoyed it beyond the physical exertion and the challenge. No challenge anymore when my demon can sense their weaknesses and exploit it."

"Can you do that to everyone?" I tried not to panic as I put my wallet on my desk, attaching my cell phone to the charger and grabbing a bottle of water. I offered one to Artie by pointing the bottle at him, but his eyes were closed, so I walked over and dropped it in his lap, not necessarily avoiding his junk.

"Not everyone... but in your case, I don't need my demon to tell me what you're afraid of. And you can drop shit on my cock, Peep, but just know I like it... Remember when I stole your first kiss?"

I ignored the memory, staring at his hand and watching it massage whatever residual pain a 14 oz water bottle could deliver to his inner thigh. Probably less than the knee I'd given him at fourteen, but I was too freaked out to appreciate the aftercare then. Now, when he pulled his hand away to crack the seal on his water bottle, I wanted to take over rubbing his... inner thigh.

Make sure the pain is really gone... he doesn't look like he finished.

"Have you considered trying out for football? You have a nice ass. You could probably be a tight end... like that guy on the red and gold team?" I babbled, as my brain continued to fantasize about finishing him. I was out of energy to fight the need. I could only hope he didn't smell the pure lust from miles away when I took care of myself later.

"First off, thank you. Second, you are such a fucking Swiftie," he chuckled a little, and I tried not to let the sound give me a lady boner. Glancing down at my nipples, the peaks threatening to take out my bra and sweater, it wasn't going well.

Note to self: buy hard cup bras.

"She's a billionaire boss babe with the lyrical genius of a tortured poet. I'm a broke witch with a doctorate and psychological issues who has to engage in modern day ambulance chasing. I dressed as my mother to infiltrate a psych ward! Why wouldn't I idolize a woman with her shit together who can make trauma poetry?"

"Dressing like your mom to get into a psych ward makes zero sense. I know she's on the hospital board, but you're batshit crazy. I'd think they'd leave you a trail of books and tacos straight to a bed with railings."

His smirk did funny things to me, even as my brain flashed back to a time they'd tried to do just that. *Hallucinations, memory impairment, paranoia... She accused Yasmin of dark magic–like the daughter of our town's model family would ever set a pile of books on fire without cause. We need to take Penelope in for her own safety.*

I shuddered against the memory, one I'd repressed for so long it might have actually been a dream. Everything was feeling surreal under the weight of energy I'd spent today. Even with the nap, I'd done a lot of magic and a lot exercise...ing of my self-control.

It was a damn workout *not* to jump Artie's bones. I could only imagine how tired I would be if I actually did it.

"Hardy harhar, fucker. Are you excited?" I asked instead, flopping onto my couch and pulling the blanket from earlier into my lap. Cracking my bottle open, I took a long drink and waited for him to answer. When he didn't move, I replayed my words and clarified my question.

"To meet your mate?"

He shrugged; eyes still closed, with his secrets safely on the other side. In another life, I thought we'd shared everything, but in retrospect, his life in the pack was something he'd always kept to himself.

"If I haven't met them yet, I probably don't have one. No matter what my dad implied," he sighed into the silence. "Which is good, I guess. Being a half shifter in the pack, none of them..."

He trailed off, and I studied his angular profile, wondering if asking for more would pick at old wounds. For all that we'd been friends, we'd mostly hung out at my house or in the woods. We'd shared stories and scars, but most of his had been from living in the deep south. Strangled by the bible belt that seemed only to hold up the white and human. Even before shifters had been discovered, he'd suffered for looking different.

The one time I'd been to the pack lands was two days before I left. The plan was to drop off something for Artie's nineteenth birthday and leave, knowing I wouldn't be around for the party on his actual day two weeks later.

Alpha Kuruk had turned me away at the door, so I waited for Artie to get home and fell asleep.

Waking up, I heard his voice fighting with his dad about a girl. One who was ill suited and inappropriate... I'd thought it was one of his hook-ups and I'd been prepared to jump in and yell at the alpha that his son was in this situation because his demon half sustained itself on pleasure and the alpha was the one who hooked up with a demon to birth him in the first place.

Until I'd heard my own name shouted during the fight.

Then I'd run away as fast as possible, still holding the gift I'd never given him. The gift held an ancient magic that linked us together, holding part of him and part of me in an object that would have meant we were together forever. But the alpha's shouts about all the harm I would cause him had me second-guessing whether I should have done it.

That night in the woods solidified that he was better off without that little piece of us.

Now I was lucky to get a few hours with him twice a decade and the necklace sat in a drawer, gathering dust with the rest of my shattered emotions under a blanket of sarcasm and flat humor.

"Tell me a story, Peep," he said on a yawn, and I smiled at the old line that shaped our friendship. Two kids in the middle of the forest, building each other worlds out of nothing more than words and hope.

None of which had ever come true... at least not for me.

"Maybe another time, Artie," I let out a yawn of my own and snuggled down into the blankets. "I think it's bedtime."

"Can I come by tomorrow? Maybe help out at the reception desk until you get someone to work there for real?"

"Yeah, sure," I answered, kicking off my boots and thinking really hard about replacing my leggings with shorts and sweater with the tank top hanging on the back of my office chair. The outfits traded spaces, the payment to make it happen, a forfeit of the last bit of energy I had left. "I open at 8."

My eyes drifted closed, and I felt the couch shift under Grim's weight as he joined me. Large head resting on my thigh, his radiating heat and pressure pushed back my anxiety, the lavender tinge of sleep taking on a softer edge that caressed me as smoothly as the cresting sunrise.

The last thing I remembered was a pair of warm lips against my forehead and the whispered words.

"I'll be here."

TEN

PENELOPE

T HE TOWERING PINES WERE WEARING A BLANKET OF SNOW, the chill seeping into my bones where I stood, listening at the window of the pack house.

Shadows were moving inside the window, Artemis shouting.

"What have you done? You can't possibly believe that!"

"All I know is what is written in her history!" His father bellowed back, the alpha's voice echoing like he was in a rock cave and not a log manor.

"And you believe that demon? She's hiding something, you can smell it!" Artie shouted.

"She is your mother's sister! You can't just dismiss her for being a demon. You are a half demon, and she knows what's best," the other man admonished, a tired sound that showed he was as tired of this argument as he was of Artemis bringing it up. "She's been in consult with the Council..."

"You can't trust the Council! They're gaslighting the whole town and have been since the 90s. I told you what I overheard at Penny's!"

"And I told you, Artemis, that whatever lies they told — the history is real. What happened cannot be born for repetition. Under the light of the *harvest moon, the only way to save the pack is for death to befall the daughter of the moon. Her sacrifice will restore the balance, but only bound to her love could she return."*

"So you think we should just kidnap her and hand her over to them? Or find her a lover, then hand her over."

"No! We can't hand her over... but she will go. The love part... that's really up to her. But I strongly doubt she'll find anyone to love her."

The twigs crunched beside me and my head whipped to the side in time to see a black clothed shadow disappearing in the woods. Two steps into following her, the front door of the pack house slammed shut and Artie's hunched figure stomped into the woods, moving quickly in the same direction the other figure disappeared.

"Artie!" I called out, a brilliant light cutting through the clouds.

"Artie!" I shouted again, blankets trapping my legs together as I thrashed onto the floor of my office. Dog fur flew into my mouth, and I coughed spittle onto the carpet while the dog it came from looked on in disinterest from his bed.

"What the hell, Grim! Why do I keep having..." His loud snore ended on a sneeze that shot slobber and snot at me. "Great, now I need a shower."

I sighed at the thought of another shower in the decontamination suite left over from when this place was an actual general medicine practice with an in-house phlebotomy lab. It had existed before the hospital had been built, and though I don't think they were into bloodletting and leeches, the water didn't heat in less than 20 minutes from the faucet and the decon shower was never meant to heat at all.

Something about hot water and making potential burns worse and pain.

"I could use magic..." I thought, mentally scrolling through the day's to-dos.

Every magic had a cost, one you could give willingly to help the world, or one that would be taken from you later.

The least costly magic was one that paid for itself. Drying your hair by giving the water to a plant outdoors–two gold stars in the balancing ledger.

Redistributing water to a tree or plant was easy. The Goddess, as much a conservationist as she was the mother of all life, was always happy when her children did the right thing on their own. Moving small things like clothing and water bottles drew from my energy. Like spoon theory for mental illness, I lost a spoon every time I completed minor magic. Nothing that food and rest couldn't restore, but I had to be careful. Heating water shouldn't cost me too much energy, but I didn't have a lot to start with today.

My scene in Naomi's shop yesterday left a bone-weary exhaustion that neither sleep nor coffee had fixed, at least not entirely. Digging myself that deep, on accident or on purpose, was stupid and short-sighted.

Do better, Odenberry.

The curtains Artie had thrown open were still letting in the rays of the gaseous ball of death. Its assault was unimpeded, and I was considering the possibilities of global de-warming when a face appeared in it.

"The fuck!" I shouted, throwing a privacy spell on the window that ricocheted off the one already in place. The magic pinged around the room until it smashed into my face, and I fell back in a daze.

"Penny?"

I blinked rapidly until my vision cleared and Naomi was in the doorway holding a paper cup of coffee and a paper bag of what smelled like bagels.

"Yeah?"

Grim's tail started thumping against the side of my desk. The smell of food managing what nearly knocking myself out had not - catching his interest.

"What are you doing?" She sounded concerned. Most people sounded concerned when they talked to me, but this was more than smacking myself in the face with a spell warranted. I checked that my tatas were still in my shirt, I was wearing shorts, and there was no dried blood on my palms from possible nighttime sleepwalking slaughter.

"I meant on the floor..."

"Oh..." I stood up and listened to the snap, crackle, pop of my joints that gave me a small head rush. "Woah... oxygen..."

Eyesight clear of magical face planting, I saw Grim beside me. His furry head was just beneath my hand and I scrunched his ears in appreciation for the stability.

"I fell off the couch... I've been having this... recurring dream except I'm not always asleep and..." Naomi's nose was twitching, and I stopped talking.

"When was the last time you had a shower?"

"There isn't a shower here besides the decontamination shower and there isn't hot water. So, I've been doing the whore bath thing... why? Is it bad?" I sniffed my pits and down my tank top, not noticing anything too funky, but I just had a human nose.

"It smells like..." her eyes widened, and her nose stopped working overtime. "Never mind. My shop has a shower, grab some stuff and we can eat and talk on the way."

It took a couple of minutes to pack a bag of post shower necessities: clothes, deodorant, toothbrush, and eyeliner.

Eyeliner was like armor, especially if you "draw the cat eye sharp enough to kill a man".

Artie's right, you are such a Swiftie.

It was torturously bright outside; the sun slicing through my sleep fog and straight into my retinas to cause permanent damage. I slipped my wide sunglasses over my eyes and let out a hiss of relief at the artificial darkness.

"Sometimes I think you're a vampire," Nay joked, and I shrugged as the town center came into view.

"I'm not a vampire, I'm Scottish," I said back. "But yeah, sometimes I wonder that, too. Then shark week hits, and I decide I'm probably just Scottish."

Nay snorted at my euphemism for menstruation and kept walking.

In the bright morning light, Huckleberry Hollow looked more like a pass-through town in the middle of nowhere. The faded red brick walls needed to be cleaned or brightened, and the roads looked dusty. Instead of charming fairy lights in every tree, there was a heavy weight of stagnation.

Like the earth itself was holding its breath.

"But either way, Scottish or vampire, none of us are equipped to spend time in the sun." I drank the coffee she brought and scooted the bagel up in the wrapper to take a bite. "So, what's the word, woodland nerd?"

Nay shot me a scathing look and I raised my hands in defense.

"Sorry, just making a rhyme. I won't quit my day job to be Dr. Suess."

My friend snorted and opened the back door of her shop. I froze in the doorframe, looking over my shoulder. The sign declaring me a psycho clearly readable from this distance...

"Have we always been this close?" I asked, looking back and forth between my building and the main street running through town, which was conveniently named Main Street. We entered the kitchen and prep areas, all shiny stainless steel with a strong scent of lemon cleaner.

"In the three days since you took over that building?"

She locked the door behind us and dropped her empty bagel wrapper in the trash can beside the door.

"Yeah... that," I said, following suit and then standing by for her to take the lead through the kitchen. "It's only been three days..."

Nay led me past an industrial oven baking a rack of bread, heat from the appliance not yet permeating the space, but in an hour this kitchen could double as a sauna. The smell right beside it was rosemary and sage, tempting me to stand and inhale until I either melted or caught fire.

"Come on, stinky, I don't want your stench near my bread," the wood nymph called over her shoulder. Sticking my tongue out at her back, I followed grudgingly as we left the kitchen area to a concrete corridor that led past fridges and freezers. At the T-point she went right, and we entered an employee locker room with a bank of dust coated lockers.

"I'm still confused why the old owner had a locker room... he had one employee. What did they keep in here?" she queried. I sat down on the wooden bench, looking around to avoid meeting her eyes and failing. Seated, we were at eye level, bringing into relief the concern creasing the corners of her eyes as she tried to make idle small talk.

"Maybe he was hoping to get a sweaty soccer team to change in here while he watched?" I offered, but she barely cracked a smile. "What's up, Nay?"

"What did you do to Artemis?" She asked, looking steadily down her nose at me.

"Hmmm... not as much as you, am I right?" I waggled my eyebrows at her, but she didn't take the bait. "I didn't do anything to him. We went to lunch and then later had ice cream and a stroll around town."

"Penny, why did he need to know where you were yesterday? After you left, he seemed to forget completely that you had lunch together or had seen each other at all. I sent him to your office, but... what the fuck, Penny? Didn't you guys come in together?"

I put on my most innocent face.

"He plays hockey... they get hit in the head a lot. Did you ask him if he's seen a doctor?" I made a concentrated effort to furrow my brow and look concerned about his safety and well-being, but her face called my bluff. "Fine, it's... before I left after graduation... we..."

The building shook and Naomi raised an ear, the collection of piercings adorning the appendage jingling like wind chimes in an autumn breeze. After listening for a moment, she rolled her eyes.

"Guess who that is? Take a shower stinky. We'll finish our conversation later," she started walking out, and I fought the urge to breathe a sigh of relief. "Oh!"

She turned back and my breath caught, wondering how to avoid this conversation for just a little longer.

"Your showing of the townhouse has been canceled. The owner is back in town and the rental agency needs to confirm his timeline before they can show the house." Nay shrugged. "I'll keep looking for a place you can sleep that has a bed."

I nodded, relief flooding me that I wouldn't have to explain to an agency I was too poor and unwelcome to make rent of any variety. Kicking off my shoes and then shucking the hoodie I'd pulled on over my PJs, I walked into the tiled shower and turned the handle, adjusting the temperature to extra hot.

Within moments, the water was steaming and my cheeks cramped with a wide smile. Heading back to the locker bench, I tossed off the rest of my clothes and grabbed my soap, shampoo, conditioner and loofah.

Stepping into the hot water was an unexpected pleasure that only people who haven't showered in nearly a week could appreciate. The warm water caressed my skin and warmed stiff muscles that were too old to sleep on a couch, another reminder of my juxtaposed age and lifestyle.

It's going to be a good day, I told myself, lathering my scrubber. My eyes slid closed as I embraced the idea of being relaxed and clean.

I'm going to be clean, someone I gave my card to yesterday will call... it's all going to be OK.

ELEVEN

PENELOPE

"Well, if it isn't my girlfriend," Artie drawled as I walked into the room. His words pinning me in place as I searched the kitchen for an answer.

He and Naomi were the only people in the room, the bread from the oven now cooling off to the side. No other food had been prepped or placed on the counters, nothing to distract the dual looks of disappointment impaling my perceived safety.

"You... what?" I asked, not quite looking either of them in the eye, but trying hard enough that I might appear innocent.

This was the most Artemis and I had seen of each other in 15 years, and I didn't know what effect that would have on the desperate spellcasting of an 18-year-old. It was impossible to determine what he was remembering and whether or not enough time had passed between our outing and this moment for him to have forgotten.

Really should have written down that damn spell for future reference...

"My girlfriend. We came back to the Hollow to be together after years of making it work long distance. Don't you remember?" He asked, holding up his phone while Naomi was angrily scrolling through her own. Between the two of them was a montage of flannel and unruly red hair in fast forward doom scrolling. "Because I sure as hell don't, and I'm starting to think I know why."

"Well... you see..." I started, rubbing at the scar on my forearm as though it were a magic eight ball with answers. I'd dressed in work clothes, slacks and a soft blouse, but it was suddenly too warm in the back of Nay's shop. The tongue in my mouth grew weighty, all moisture evaporating, gluing it to the roof of my mouth. Something heavy lodged in my throat, blocking out all words and air until lights burst behind my eyes and I gasped.

"What the fuck, Penny!" Naomi took over for Artemis. The four-foot-tall woodland nymph seemed to grow exponentially with rage as she held out a smartphone filled with a social media feed filled with text and images.

Just based on the color scheme, I was guessing Bookfaces.

Inching closer, I squinted at the text above the pictures of me and the half-demon shifter in the coffee shop, wearing his ring.

Us getting ice cream.

Us getting kicked out of every establishment owned by Yasmin.

Artie walking out of my practice in the late evening, looking tired but smiling.

The captions screamed, "Witchcraft! The Supernatural Leagues hottest star would never be with that tub of lard!"

"Council confirms dating rumors, and they aren't launching an investigation!"

"Caught practically fornicating on the street! Won't someone please think of the children!"

Not daring to touch the phone, I assumed the whole feed was inundated with accusations, insults and calls for an intervention to prevent corruption of such an important and prominent man. Barring that, a solid tar and feathering of the accused, aka me, followed by a trial where I was beheaded or burned at the stake.

"Oh, that..." I shifted out of arm's reach and walked toward the coffeemaker at the far end of the kitchen. My hands were trembling as I fought back panic at having to explain... anything. Though being accused of nefarious witchcraft wasn't new for me, there was something about the salacious comments toward Artie and the implication that I would harm him that left me frazzled and on edge. "I would never hurt Artemis."

The ceramic mug I picked up was an off-white, coated in grey dots, the tapping of pottery on stainless steel the only sound in an otherwise silent kitchen.

I stared into the mug, wondering if I could ask to be swallowed by it. Simply sucked into a vessel for coffee, like a permanent resident of the Twilight Zone, but I could steal drinks of other people's coffee for the rest of my days.

"Penelope," Nay warned, and I finally let go of the cup to pour coffee into it. The carafe shook as I poured and before I could slosh it everywhere, a warm large hand took the pot from me and filled the mug.

My eyes traveled upward to meet Artie's. He didn't have pity or anger in his eyes, just a genuine curiosity.

A reminder of the love we'd shared when we both felt unlovable.

"I'm sorry," I whispered, and he nodded once. Holding the filled cup out to me, I wrapped both hands around it and let him guide me to the small kitchen table in the corner he and Naomi had been seated at when I arrived. Nay looked less accepting but held her silence, waiting for an explanation.

"Last night, you said the Council stank of fear and told them we were dating... engaged technically and you had a ring in your pocket. You were worried about me... being too much on their radar. Something about being here with you, the town's playboy and most underestimated resident... it made me less threatening. Like if I was with you, everything was fine."

He gestured for me to keep talking.

"You also said you felt like you were losing your memory and wanted to force me to spend all our time together. Which was sweet, but it freaked me out. I wasn't actually planning on telling you why you couldn't remember me and also... well, guilt."

"Why would you feel guilty?" He asked, at the same time Naomi chimed in.

"You should feel fucking guilty!"

Ignoring Naomi's justifiable rage, I turned to Artie instead.

"Because when I left fifteen years ago, you didn't want me to leave.

You were in my room, pacing and agitated with this all-consuming energy. Threatening to go after the people who hurt me, encouraging me to join you on the hunt for vengeance. I didn't want you to follow me into the night, even though you were begging me to stay. Didn't want you to get hurt or worse because of my... existence. I thought you deserved better, but you weren't going to get better if you were saddled with being my friend."

Taking a long drink of coffee, my brain working to piece together the memory, I waited for him to yell. To demand I make this right and then vow to never speak to him again.

Instead, the air took on the scent of sulfur and ash.

"What do you mean *hurt you*?" He growled, nostrils flaring as he inhaled and exhaled labored breaths. It was the precursor to a charging bull in matador sketches, terrifying to anyone in his path. I let out an exasperated sigh that of all the parts of the story he could have zeroed in on, he'd choose the relevant.

"It's not a big deal," I said, not looking at him as I set my mug down. There was no way to explain this, not without ruining years of carefully constructed protections. Tracing the scar through my sleeve, I pressed on digging the grave of our friendship. "It's also not really the point. The point is that I put a spell on you and you should hate me and demand that I make reparations for using magic on you against your will."

Eyeing my exposed wrist, noticing the tiniest edge of the scar peeking out of the three-quarter sleeve top, the nymph was the first to catch on.

Naomi missed nothing.

Her tiny fingers curling around my wrist, she dragged my arm away from me. Shoving up the sleeve, she let out a hiss at the Knight of Swords-shaped scar that sat unchanged by time, just beneath the crease of my elbow.

"I'll kill them!" Artemis roared, surging to his feet.

"No," I snapped, taking his hand and trying to pull him back to me. "No, you won't. Because we don't know who did it and you still AREN'T LISTENING!"

My shouts fell on deaf ears.

"Can't you find out? This is bullshit, Penny. You can't just burn a…"

His voice trailing off when I raised an eyebrow at him. His brain and mouth finally catching on. A sheepish look crossed his face before he had the good sense to shut his mouth.

"That, that right there is why you can't remember me, Artie. It was too dangerous. You have a concept of me, a sense that you have a best friend who loves you, but you were too impulsive, unpredictable, and honestly… too important to me. I couldn't let you do something that you'd regret, not for me. But I was also too selfish to make you forget me completely, so now… It's like…" I searched for a metaphor and came up blank. "It's like…"

"Like watching a flashback clip show," he supplied, Naomi looking between us in surprise. "When you're around, I get images and feelings, but nothing specific to hold on to. When we spend time together, I get back flashes of the past. Like that time, you 'accidentally' gave Heather a wart for grabbing my ass when I didn't want her to touch me. It's all disconnected. Everything to do with this town is disconnected… because it's connected to you."

"Certainly not all of it. You did things without me," I reminded him, not intentionally looking at Naomi but letting my eyes drift toward her, anyway.

Naomi kicked the leg of my chair, her eyebrow collided with her hairline, toppling the mountain of anxiety clawing its way out of my throat in a strangled laugh.

The sound ricocheted off the steel, the demented hysterics of a woman who's losing it.

"It's not *that* funny, Penelope," she snipped, but I couldn't control it anymore. All of the stress of keeping this stupid secret for almost half my life burst out. I kept laughing until the tears streaming down my face fell into my mouth, like they were trying to drown me.

"Oh Goddess, what a mess," I coughed out around long breaths. My forehead thunking against the table, I waited in silence for my breathing to level off.

"So… what are we going to do about it?" Naomi asked, and I flopped my head to the side to look at her without expending the energy to lift it.

"I have no idea. I don't even remember the spell," my shoulders shaking in a laughing sob, I turned away from her to stare at the wood-grain of the table. The ashy scent of pine invaded the cave around my face, fingers sliding into my hair in slow, calming strokes.

With every pass his fingers made, my resistance faded until only my biggest fear lay bare on the tip of my tongue.

"We'll figure it out," Artie said, rubbing my scalp gently. "I'm sure there's a way…"

"What if we can't?" I asked him, turning my head in his direction. I needed him to know, needed his reassurance that if I couldn't reverse the spell, he'd still love me. "What if this is our relationship now? Maybe you don't need to remember me."

His grip tightened in my hair, pulling my face up from the table to look into his melted chocolate eyes that simmered with an unhinged longing that threatened to swallow us both. Our noses were nearly brushing when he finally spoke in a chilling voice that sent heat flooding to every one of my good spots.

"I'm not letting you go, Penny."

Somewhere outside, I heard raised voices and stood up, losing his fingers in the process. With the voices came a building anxiety that, at its core, had the blind, bitter scorch of hate. Whatever was happening outside, it wasn't a peaceful assembly.

And I had a bad feeling it had something to do with me.

"I need to get to Grim. We'll have to finish this another time."

Artie stood up, grabbing my hand and pulling me toward the door.

"Let's go… "

The anxiety building in my gut replicated itself on his face when we burst into the too-bright light and encountered pandemonium.

Two large groups gathered on either side of my walkway. Large signs declaring "Justice for Artemis" stood on one side facing off against "Love Knows No Dress Size"

Both offensive in very different ways.

"There she is!"

A woman shouted. Pointing her finger at me beneath a fluffed-up pixie cut, long emo bangs and bleach blonde highlights, I reflexively covered my face with my arms. "She is an abomination! Leading away the wealthy and accomplished with dark magic!"

Artie pulled me tight against his side, gluing us together as the red-faced humanoids yelled at one another. His scent surrounded me, and I pressed my face into his shoulder, dampening the sound of people shouting from either end about whether my life or his was ours to choose.

"Dark magic? You think the only way a woman like *that* could get love is by cursing him? Why can't he just be into *that*?"

Something about being *that* was more insulting than being accused of cursing my best friend. I was prepared to be attacked for dating the most eligible bachelor in the Supernatural world.

I was not prepared to be negged by strangers who thought they were helping.

"No! No man that hot wants *that*!"

Getting more insulting... and louder.

"You don't get to decide who other people love! You don't get to decide what other people want! If *that's* what he wants..."

The voices were right beside me now. Their hot breaths pummeled me from both sides, keeping me from getting safely to Grim. A tremble had started in my hands and was now working its way up my arms. Needing to stop whatever it was, I wrapped my arms around Artie's waist and squeezed until every muscle ached with the strain.

"Get off him!"

Talon-like claws ripped into my forearm. Scraping and scratching until I released my grip and stumbled, colliding with the cement. My hands and knees scraped against the texture, bright droplets of blood beading on my palms and legs.

A voice from somewhere inside began to beg.

Give me blood.

I demand my payment.

Around me, the sharp corners of the picket signs came into focus. The edges, an appealing invitation to draw more blood. My mind searched the crowd for a spinning wheel, craving the sharp point of a needle... a knife.

Your blood for their lives.

Sacrifice yourself or they all pay.

Artie was being held back, each of his arms prisoner to one of Yasmin's posse. Their nails tinted red with polish that matched the rivulets of blood dripping from the scratch marks along my arms. In their grip, Artie's teeth gnashed, making words I couldn't hear through the shouting crowds. If he broke free, he'd hurt them.

If he hurt them, they'd call for my head.

Around us, the two sides had blurred together in a violent clash, fighting to prove what freedom *really* means.

Behind me, a window smashed in muted chaos. The shattered glass skittering on the ground with gleaming edges beside Yasmin and Heather, her most vicious stiletto sister, each clutching a brick in startled delight.

Through the window, crouched low beside the couch, was Grim.

Hauling myself up, I shoved through two women screaming about the validity of psychiatric care. Beyond them was yet another pair, and another, all blocking me from what I really needed.

Grim.

His whimper was the only thing that could penetrate the noise.

"You hexing pains in the ass..." I screamed, feeling the build-up of anger climbing higher as it spread throughout my body. It started with a tingle at the tip of my nose, numbing my lips while traveling to the tips of my fingers.

The women before me moved, and I turned on the rest, Artemis' shirt in tatters from being ripped apart by the not-so-grown-up versions of the girls who tortured me. Their lipstick prints smeared on his neck and chest.

It was too much.

Candy apple red shimmered around my palms, radioactive hands heating and displacing the air around me. My shirt swirled, the magic whipping my hair behind me. An unimpeded view of my familiar, scared and confused, because of two witches with the magical and mental capacity of protoplasm, sent my magic into a fever pitch of cinnamon and ash.

"Enough!"

My shout cut through the noise as a red ring of energy expanded around me and mowed down the crowd. Everyone fell backwards, my mind conjuring soft clouds of magic for their landing. Magically silenced, their moving mouths made no sound.

"You are all self-righteous assholes!" I shouted, stomping over to Artemis and yanking him up from the ground. Yvonne and Vivian screamed silently, vehemently opposed to the removal of their prize.

"Artemis is my friend. What we do beyond that is none of your business! Get the hell off my property and if any one of you set foot on my walkway again, and it's not for the psychiatric services you all so desperately need, I will give all of you hooked noses and boils."

Artemis and I were at my door, and I turned the handle, knowing the lock would only give to my touch. Once I'd shoved the half-shifter through the door where he was safely out of their reach, my power levels dipped, and the first stirrings of sound escaped the lips and throats of the "activists" who only cared about themselves.

"She..."

"How did she do that?"

"No one has that kind of power but the council..."

Ignoring them, I checked the street. Naomi was standing beside her shop, arms crossed and head shaking with anger. There were no words she could offer, but I knew at the end of this, she'd stand with me.

Beside her, across the street, was the Council.

A breeze crossed the street, and the inorganic taste of burnt rubber coated the back of my throat.

The Brads and Chads were terrified.

TWELVE

IT TOOK FIFTEEN MINUTES OF HAVING MY ARMS WRAPPED around Grim to stop trembling.

Artemis had sprung into action, patrolling the interior and locking every door he encountered while keeping the masses from the broken window. It was an unnecessary measure, his handsome face scowling out at them even as the spell took effect. There were sounds of confusion and loud cries of outrage from the recovering group as magic forced them away from my building.

Hooked noses and boils only really worked for Alan Rickman, not the Lululemon soccer moms who just happened to be witches.

All of them had been witches, my brain registered as I mentally catalogued the group who'd assembled. There were no other magical beings or creatures who'd concerned themselves with the love lives and choices of two strangers who barely even lived here.

"You OK?" Artie asked, sinking beside me and gathering both Grim and I against him. Grim almost immediately squirmed away to lay down beside us, his head in my lap. Artie filled the gap he left behind with warm sulfur, a hot spring in a winter snow storm of panic. "Can I get you anything?"

The moment his arms connected with my body, everything settled.

Every jittery nerve ending quieted, and a peace folded over me with a calm I had only felt with Xanax. Even Grim hadn't managed to relax me so completely, and I wondered if I could bottle Artemis and prescribe him to patients as a cure-all.

"Yeah…" I sighed, the phone clanging loudly from my office. Ignoring it, I turned my face into Artie's chest, inhaling him again. My nostrils flared, trying to capture every last molecule of his essence and absorb it into me. "Yeah."

My voice was muffled against him, the vibrations of my words mixing with his very masculine chuckle.

"Do you need me to put one of my shirts on a bag of rice for you to cuddle?"

His tone was joking, but I bristled and pulled away. Feeling my cheeks flame that I'd pushed the boundaries of his proffered comfort, I angled away. Jostling Grim slightly, I looked for a place to leverage myself upright without smushing his tail.

"Sorry, I didn't mean…"

I started climbing up from the floor, confused how I'd ended up in his lap in the first place. Before I made it upright, warm arms snaked around my waist and pulled me back down.

"I'm just teasing you, Peep. You're always so awkward with affection… Which, I guess means I should have known better than to mess with you when you give it freely," he tightened his grip when I tried to squirm away again. "Please? Just… sit with me?"

His fingers stroked my hair, sliding through the strands and rubbing the soft skin below my ears. Quiet settled around us, our hearts beating softly against the other in the darkened front room of my office. Each lap of his fingers through my hair releasing another coil of tension in my body. Surrendering, I relaxed into his embrace and listened to the hum of the town outside, coming back to life.

Inhaling again, my bones melted and I turned into a puddle of goo in his arms. Beside me, Grim let out a soft snore and I giggled slightly.

"Remember our first kiss?"

I startled slightly. Artie's words were spoken near my ear, the warm air sending a shiver of want straight to my core. His lips grazed the shell of my ear and the peaceful waves collided with the jagged rocks of lust.

"You mean my first kiss?" I sighed, trying not to let on how easily he lit my whole body on fire. "Because you were way ahead of me on that front."

Dropping his nose to the base of my neck, he scented along the soft flesh until goosebumps peppered every inch of my skin. I shuddered again, waves of liquid heat flooding my core.

So much for that...

Artie tightened his grip, keeping me close with one hand while his other trailed up the thin trousers I had on. Creeping closer and closer to the V between my legs, I stopped breathing.

"That's not true, Peep. You were my first, too." His thumb started tracing circles on my inner thigh and the sudden waves of arousal threatened to knock me on my ass... except my ass was sitting squarely on his... thigh.

Yes, definitely thigh and that's a tube of mini-M&M's in his pocket...

It was the least believable lie I'd ever told myself, but it allowed me to choke out a breath.

"I can't have been," I gasped out. "You were already with Timmy."

"He and I didn't kiss, Peep. Other stuff, but we didn't kiss..."

"Why didn't you..."

"Because it didn't feel right. After what an asshole he was to you... I needed the pleasure, but he didn't deserve kisses. You, on the other hand..."

Artemis rubbed his lips up my neck while his hand kept getting higher until it rested comfortably on top of my mound. His tongue flicked out against my neck, and I screamed in surprise while his fingers cupped my entrance and pressed the outer flesh against my clit in a sudden burst of pleasurable friction.

"Goddess!" I moaned when his middle finger kept up the pressure. He switched from just pressing to making small circles that coaxed me higher and sent my legs involuntarily farther apart to make room for him.

Without hesitation, he took the invitation to loosen his grip on my waist and toy with the top of my pants. Giving me all the time in the world to object, his hand slid under my blouse and against the soft flesh of my belly, massaging it in his hand. The heat radiating from his palm sank into the depths of cold that clung to me, chasing back everything but liquid hot need.

Angling my chin to him, I brushed the tip of my nose against his, cupping his jaw in my hand. Nudging just a little closer so I could brush my lips against his.

Just like that first time... I thought, closing my eyes as he brought his mouth closer and deepened our kiss. Nipping my lower lip, he slid his tongue inside when I gasped, and his finger worked faster against my core through the pants. His other hand slipped under my bra to cup my boob, fingers inching toward the stiff peaks.

"Penny! Open up!" A hand slammed angrily against the door, and I jumped.

Off balance, I flung a hand to stop myself from falling.

It landed squarely on Artie's manhood, and he howled when I crushed his junk.

"Sorry, I..." Jerking my hand back, I tried to get up and moved my head backward.

The crown of my head smashed into his face, the sickening crunch of nose bones following another exclamation of pain.

"Fuck!" He roared and moved both hands, cupping his nose to catch the blood. Dropping to all fours, I crawled away from him with my elbows tucked, terrified of hurting him again. I made it to the reception counter just in time for the door to fly open as I hauled myself to standing.

Standing on the stoop was my sister, Ali, sporting a hooked nose and boils.

"Ali, what? Oh my goddess," I pulled at the magical features marring her face and returned the spell into the air for someone else. "What are you..."

Her eyes had landed on Artie, pinching the bridge of his nose to stymie the flow of blood while he huddled over his cock protectively. He looked like he'd gone a couple of rounds with a prizefighter, and I blushed hard when he gave me a crooked smile.

"Just like the first time," he snickered, and my burning cheeks flamed hotter.

"I'm so sorry, oh goddess, I'm so sorry," I backed away from him until I tripped over the trashcan by the unused secretary desk. I crashed to the floor and simply lay there, wishing for the ground to open up and swallow me whole. For once though, my brain was too preoccupied with panic to remember the spell that would bury me alive.

"Was that from the mob?" Ali asked sharply, and I begged harder for the earth to just suck me back in before he could rat me out. I wasn't one to kiss and tell, but getting caught with your pants on near a bloodied man with an erection was only good news in dark alleys and bar bathrooms.

In the privacy of my not-quite home, it looked like exactly what it was: the curse of being me.

Instead of shouting, Artie started to laugh from the other side of the counter.

"Not exactly. This is what happens when you're near an extremely uncoordinated person when their sympathetic nervous system kicks in."

Ali joined his laughter and peeked over the counter at me, smiling down at me.

"You went for the nuts, huh?"

My sister favored our mom. She had blonde hair and a slim figure that had never met a snack who could defeat her metabolism. As girls, I'd always been jealous of her, of the approval she received everywhere, despite being related to death and the graceful way her skin tanned instead of turning into a freckle festival. As women, I was still a little jealous, but mostly I loved her sarcastic, quick-witted personality.

"They were there," I joked weakly, and she howled with laughter.

"Mindy is sending Chester over to see about your window," she said, referencing her sister-in-law and Mindy's husband, who worked as a general contractor. "I can't believe you waited this many years to blast all those asshats to kingdom come. Seriously, they should have been put in their place years ago."

Using the chair for leverage, I pushed up to standing and attempted to straighten my clothing. Avoiding eye contact, I started brushing off the dust that had accumulated behind the desk that now clung to my clothes.

Add vacuum to the list of things I need if I ever get money or patients, I thought on a long sigh.

"You'll get some patients soon," Ali said softly, and I nodded like it was even remotely possible. "I'm serious, Pen. You know I work outside of town, but I hear things. People need psychiatric care. Mom might be on the hospital board, but I don't think she believes they are providing adequate care any more than she believes you can cure cancer with graham crackers."

"It's fine. If I don't get any patients, I can just leave again. Mom can't want me here forever," I tried to sound upbeat, but my throat caught at the end. An adrenaline let down that gave me access to the emotions I'd pushed down to ensure Grim's safety.

"You know I can have her disappeared?" Ali whispered, and I looked at her in confusion.

"I thought you liked mom. I mean.... She's extra, but we don't need a hit put out on her. Also, I'm Death... talk about being the number one suspect."

"Not mom, dummy. Yasmin and her posse. You kept all the shit to yourself and after you left, suddenly everyone at school was speculating she killed you and the truth finally came out. I thought the spirit world got cell service the first time you called me... two years later," she glared at me, and I held up my hands in defense. She was perpetually reminding me that I'd left her and Dylan, not contacting them for two years until they too forsook the Council and went to do their own thing.

Unlike me, however, they hadn't gone far.

They'd also not been summoned home from the short distance they had gone.

"Do you know what mom's whole thing is about?" I asked her, walking down the hall to the office. Artie had swept up the broken glass and placed Grim's bed on top of my desk. He'd also picked up the dog dishes and other toys within the spray area, a safety measure that caused my chest to tighten with emotion.

"No. Only that Dylan and I weren't requested. Though there's plans to make a sibling movie night mandatory as soon as possible. We need you to watch the Harry Potter series with us and explain why you elder millennials like it," she snickered at my eye roll and I felt a real smile stretch across my face.

"Mom said Dylan would be at dinner tonight, so he was kind of requested..." I informed her, but she just shook her head.

"No, he was invited. But he's not coming tonight, partly because he doesn't want to and partly because he thinks Alpha Kuruk is an asshat tool, no offense to your bestie. So, you better answer our group text to set up a Harry Potter movie night. You can even bring Artie. I'm sure between the two of you I'll get to see someone cry when a fictional character dies," she cackled, and I narrowed my eyebrows in warning.

"Do not bring up Dobby and Hedwig. It's too soon. But fine, you neophytes and your TikTok have no sense of literature," I teased her, wondering what my sibling's tarot card would have been if they hadn't been home birthed 5 and 6 years after me. Probably something cool... like the Goddess and Knave of something... Dylan was totally a knave.

"Mindy said Chester is busy and sending his idiot cousin to fix your window," Ali declared after her phone chimed a weird tone that made me want to scream about the bells of Notre Dame. "She said he's an absolute tool and you'll have to stand over him, wearing a scowl and holding a tape measure. I met him once, and I'd think a whip or some sort of leather crop may be more appropriate."

Artemis had entered the room and wrapped his arms around my chest, chasing off a chill I hadn't noticed until it was gone. Instinctively, I reached my hands up to grip his forearm, leaning into him and the easy affection. Grim padded in beside us and sat on my foot, the perfect pairing of anti-anxiety bliss.

My sister stopped talking mid-sentence, and I refocused on her.

"I don't own a whip. Or a crop... Can I show him my teeth?" I bared them at her in my best snarl.

"I think I might have at least one of those things, but they're only for fun times," Artemis snickered and I elbowed him in the gut.

Instead of horror or astonishment, Ali was staring at us with excitement. Bouncing on the balls of her feet, Ali clapped excitedly, and I swallowed the urge to run away.

"What? Are you... impressed?"

"No! It's just... Oh, my goddess! It's true!" She gestured between us.

Wincing, I offered a noncommittal shrug. Not willing to lie to my sister, but scared that after the morning we just had, telling her the truth would do more harm than good.

"Of course it's true," Artie purred, and I closed my eyelids to hide my annoyance at how easily he lied. "So, when is the idiot cousin coming?"

"Oh! Right..." She checked her phone before answering. "In about an hour. Your snarl is not scary enough, maybe let Artie do it. Oh shit... One of the students just bit another student and I need to get back to the school. See you guys later and good luck with mom!"

Ali practically skipped out of the office and down the hall, letting the door slam shut behind her.

"Should we pick up where we left off?" Artie asked against my ear and I shook my head, stepping out of his arms to the not-so-subtle protest of my throbbing lady parts.

"We need to finish cleaning this up," I sighed as the phone started ringing again and I reflexively answered.

"Dr. Odenberry, psychiatrist," I said into the line, a brief pause preceding the sudden screams.

"You psychotic bitch! How dare you..."

I hung up the phone and looked at Artie, who was already snickering as he reached for the broom.

"Wrong number?" He joked.

I sighed as it rang again and grudgingly reached for it.

"Wrong time of day... I need tequila."

THIRTEEN

ARTEMIS

After the thirteenth call, I unplugged Penny's phone.

She likely hadn't noticed, her eyes trained in unblinking horror at the "idiot cousin".

Chester wasn't someone you'd mistake for a ballerina, but the man had to have been part giant somewhere along the way. After toppling her desk, her couch and the sitting chair, I dragged the couch into the lobby and stacked the chairs that were already lying on their side when I heard my Peep scream.

"Stop moving! Just... stop!"

The idiot cousin had toppled Peep's bookcase.

Paperbacks and textbooks scattered across the floor, cracked spines and dog eared pages.

"Family or not, I'll kill you! You book murdering..." I picked up my best friend and started carrying her away. "Put me down, I have to avenge the books!"

Setting her down on the relocated couch, I squatted between her legs. Gripping her chin, I gently redirect her face to mine and studied her eyes. Exhaustion creased the edges, fear and anxiety swirling around her like it had been since her sister had left an hour ago.

"I'll rescue the books and move all the furniture. You should rest."

"I can't rest! He needs to be murdered!" She snapped. I stroked her cheek, rubbing the crease between her eyes until they drooped lower. Muttering under her breath, I heard a startled shout from the other room and then nothing.

"Penny!" I shot up and ran down the hall. Chester was still working, easily moving through the desk, chair and bookcase. The books on the floor were neatly stacked and against the wall.

"Put window in now," Chester grunted and I nodded once, walking back out to Penny where she was slumped on the couch, stroking the large black dog absently.

"Semi-permeable furniture?" I asked her, squeezing in on the opposite side from the dog. Lifting up my witch, I silently cheered when she curled up against my chest, burnt out from the oversized magic. My finger instinctively threaded into her hair, stroking the soft hair and massaging her scalp.

"Yeah... It seemed easier than murder." She yawned widely and burrowed in deeper. "Also easier to clean up than blood and guts."

"Blood can get messy..." I agreed, though I wasn't really paying attention as she fought sleep in my arms.

Another memory surfaced, one from junior high.

It was probably a few months after I moved here, she was finally starting to trust that I actually wanted to be her friend. After school, I'd followed her home, trying to avoid going back to the pack land. Her mom had immediately started in on her for trying to snack on something and before I could knock, she was climbing out a window, down a tree and into the woods beside her house. Running after her, I found her crying on a fallen tree and scooped her into my arms.

Just like this.

She'd tried to fight me then, but eventually she gave in.

It made me think I was the first person to ever hug her and mean it.

"You should rest, little Peep."

"I can't. What if they come back? I have to protect you. And Grim. There's a huge ass hole in the wall and broken glass everywhere!" She struggled against me and I held her tighter.

"First, we took care of the broken glass. That is definitely gone. I think between the giant, my beast, and your boil, boil, hook nose and trouble spell, we can manage to keep the office standing long enough for you to recover," I murmured, kissing her temple. I let my hands slide out of her hair and down her neck, rubbing a knot in her shoulder with my thumb.

My demon flashed in my mind, taking control of my other hand. Sliding it under her shirt and rubbing her soft flesh. Salty cinnamon hit my nose and I watched her legs press together, my demon smiling inside while my bear hummed with approval.

"Be my good girl and go to sleep, Peep." I felt her core tighten and her legs press tighter. My little Peep had a praise kink. "Don't you want to be good?"

I stroked the underside of her breast and she shuddered.

"Yes."

"Then relax, PenPen," I whispered against her, sliding my hand back out of her shirt to the annoyed protests of my other halves. I rubbed her back and rocked gently back and forth. "Good girls get a treat when they follow directions."

She shuddered against us, but she didn't have enough energy for desire. My inner turmoil settled, wanting what's best for her more than their own pleasure.

"We've got you. I've always got you."

Penny's legs went still and her breathing evened, her body finally surrendering to the weight of her fatigue.

We stayed like that, me watching her sleep. There were so many memories that flooded back. Watching Cool Runnings, over and over again because it gave her hope. Every cheesy 90s and early 2000s RomCom, going to the bookstore and watching her tap the spines of books she'd read like giving the main characters high fives... I'd missed so much about her.

"Please don't let me lose you again," I whispered, kissing the crease between her eyes.

***

"It's crooked," she declared, glaring at the window.

Penelope had slept for exactly forty three minutes.

It was the most relaxing, peaceful forty three minutes we'd shared until Idiot Cousin Chester tripped through the lobby, upended our couch, and disappeared into the Hollow beyond.

"It can't be crooked. The window is in the same frame it sat in before. Also its made of glass," I reminded her, cursing the fucker waking her up.

"If the glass was misshapen, he could have reshaped the frame and made the whole thing crooked. Which he obviously did, because this is crooked!" I wandered away, heading back out into the lobby to grab her couch. It wasn't especially heavy, so I lifted one side and dragged it up the hall, tilting it sideways and moving it in to the sight of Penny's ass in the air, bent over her mini fridge for bottled water.

"What are you doing?" I asked, my voice catching at the peeks of her underwear through the somewhat sheer work pants. Pants I'd be stealing and throwing the fuck away so she could never wear them for other people again.

Throw all her pants and clothes away, my bear suggested and my demon agreed. *Then never let anyone else see her because she's ours.*

Except she probably wasn't ready to hear that yet.

Penny stood up and walked to the coffee maker, dumping water inside and adding coffee. Flipping the switch, she turned and gave me her most obvious *you're an idiot* look while I tried to adjust myself discreetly. Images of her naked and wandering around my house flashed in my mind. The filthy montage had her bent over my kitchen table, drinking her coffee. Sitting on my couch, with legs wrapped around my head. Spread out on my bed...

"Did you unplug my phone?" She snapped and I tried to re-enter the room. Penny was holding her phone cord and glaring at me with narrowed eyes.

"Nope. Must have been Chester tripping over shit," I lied, taking an empty cup and pouring coffee into it. Adding milk and sugar so her stomach had something besides coffee sloshing around, I passed it over as she plugged the phone cord back in.

"You're a crappy liar," she muttered, taking a long drink of coffee. Almost immediately the phone clanged to life on her desk and she reached for it. I got there first, picking it up and setting it back in the receiver. Her mouth flopped open at me and I smirked. "That could have been a patient!"

"You know it wasn't."

I went over to the coffee maker and made my own cup. My woman liked her coffee brewed to wake the dead and the smell was stirring something in my memories. A date last night at the coffee shop, one where I'd given her a ring.

"It could have been, though! I need patients, Artemis!" She slammed her mug on the counter and I took it gently, refilling it at the coffee maker. "And what the hell was with lying to my sister? Should we really be pretending to our families?"

Something heavy sank in my chest. Though I'd been the one to say we were together without actually asking her, I'd never said we were fucking pretending. It felt like she needed the lie and I hated every last asshole in this town that kept her from seeing that what we had was real.

"If you need patients, why don't I be your patient?" I reached down and unplugged her phone again, directing her to the couch next to me and placing my coffee on the table beside me. "Actually, let's do a role-playing game where I'm the psychiatrist and you're the patient."

"That sounds stupid," she muttered into her coffee and I smiled.

"And how does that make you feel?"

"Like I want to punch you."

"Mm... I love it when you talk dirty."

She slugged me in the arm and I made a fake orgasm sound like I'd cum in my pants.

"Now that I've gotten mine, let's start with our session. Why are you so afraid when we're together, Peep?" I asked, trying to be gentle with her. When her muscles tensed, I rubbed at her neck and used my best fuck me face to lure her into relaxing. "Come on, if you're a good girl, I'll give you a lolly."

"There aren't any lollipops in this office." She crossed her arms and sulked. I wiggled my eyebrows at her suggestively and she hit me again.

"If I say harder..."

My best friend rolled her eyes and I smiled at her.

"See? Nothing to be scared of. Talk to me, Peep."

She clamped her mouth shut and I was torn between wanting to kiss her adorable face and carrying on with my mission of breaking down het fucking walls.

She has to let us in.

"Penny," I warned. But she wouldn't budge, so I did what had to be done. Diving in, I dug my fingers into her sides. Tickling her stomach and her ribs while she squirmed underneath me, rubbing our scents together. With our bodies pressed together, I felt myself get hard inside my jeans, noting how easy it would be to rip off her pants and take her on this damn couch.

Not until she admits it's real.

"Are you going to tell me what you're afraid of?"

I tickled her harder, picking up the spike in her scent.

"Come on, Peep..."

"Because being with me could get you hurt. Now that everyone thinks we're together, I don't know if we should keep pretending to protect you or tell the truth so people will leave you alone."

I let her go, watching as she tried to sit up. Breathless and with her clothes disheveled, she looked even hotter than she had before. My gaze raked up her body as I made a mental list of all the ways I could make her look that freshly fucked in the future.

"You're staring."

"You're beautiful."

Rolling her eyes, Peep started chewing on the edge of her finger. Her scent said she didn't believe me and I pulled it out of her mouth, sucking it into mine until her breath caught on a moan. Pulling it back out, I placed her finger on the exposed skin of her belly, tracing my name across the skin.

"How does that make you feel, Peep?" I whispered.

"G-good."

"Do you like it when I make you feel good?" I asked her, leaning in to pull an earlobe into my mouth and kiss along her jaw.

"Yes," she moaned, my hands moving against her skin.

"Then why would you want to push me away?"

"Because... It's not safe," she hissed out and I scraped my teeth along her neck. My demon and bear in agreement that she needed to submit.

It wasn't her job to protect us, or anyone else. If she managed to not actively put herself in danger we'd consider it a huge fucking win.

"Don't you think I can decide what's best for me?" I asked her, dipping my hand into her pants and back out. I gave in and slid my mouth over to hers, kissing her hard. Coffee swirled with the taste of her and I didn't stop running my tongue along the inside of her mouth until her panting breaths threatened to give out.

"Well?" I asked again and she nodded. "Good girl."

I felt her skin pebble beneath my touch and I smirked at her. Taking the coffee mug from her hand, I got up and refilled it.

"Then what I want," I told her, holding the refilled coffee mug just out of her reach. "Is you, beautiful. Do you understand?"

She looked up at me with a mix of desire, defiance and overtired acceptance.

I handed the coffee mug over and let her drink.

"When you finish that, you're going to take a nap."

"But-" She started and I held up a finger in warning. When she pouted, I threatened to take away her coffee. "You're a pain the fucking ass."

"I'll keep in mind that you like ass fucking," I said, dropping a kiss on her head and taking the now empty cup from her. I set it on the counter with mine and put a blanket over her. "If you behave yourself, I'll see if I can have a lollipop for you when you wake up."

As breathing evened out, I headed into her lobby and started a list of all the things she'd need to make her practice a success.

FOURTEEN

Bright pink nail polish sparkled up from the damp earth, filling the space between my toes. I took a deep breath, inhaling the scent of pine and sagebrush from the vast forest before me. Above, the late afternoon sun had begun its lazy descent toward the horizon and I was delighted by the promise of night.

Towering conifers rustled with the autumn breeze, squirrels and birds scattering pine needles as they hopped from branch to branch. Somewhere just beyond the thick trunks was another world and with a few steps, I'd be free of the town behind me.

"Are we going into the woods?" Artemis asked, his hand sliding around my waist. The touch was warm, safe, and released a swarm of butterflies into my stomach.

His touch was making me feel things, deeply uncomfortable things that I didn't know how to process. Like being called beautiful or being taken care of and lured into sleeping for four hours.

"I am," I told him, trying to shift away from his possessive touch. Instead, he moved around so that he could retain physical contact with me while appearing to move out of the way.

If I weren't completely overstimulated and overwhelmed, it might have been sweet.

Instead, it poked at a raw nerve I hadn't known was fraying until it snapped. His touch was gentle, full of affection and kindness, and never once demanding anything in return. Just like it had been the several hundred other times he'd done it throughout the day. Like his kiss and his magical fingers, his every lingering caress had carried a promise of more, whenever I was ready.

And I wasn't sure I'd ever be ready.

It's just pretend, I reminded myself again and again.

But it doesn't feel like I'm pretending, which was part of why I needed to go deep into the woods and never come back out. Because I was starting to think he wasn't pretending either.

"Should we go to the spot?"

His thumb rubbed small circles on my back, sending a shiver through me that lodged somewhere between my heart and whatever organ wanted me to jump his bones. Affection and lust were urging me to lean into his touch while my sanity screamed to run the hell away before we did something I couldn't take back.

I pushed him away gently.

"I need some alone time, Artie," I said, forcing myself away from him. His presence was intoxicating, and I wasn't ready to admit just yet that when he forgot me again, I would be crushed. Wasn't ready to admit that I wanted to be with him every second of the day and it scared the shit out of me because I already had to leave him once.

If we got any closer and I had to do it again, it would kill me.

It's already going to hurt as bad as it did the first time.

"Penny, I…"

He stood frozen, looking down at the hand still held out for me.

"It'll be fine. I'll see you at dinner tonight," I backed away, nodding at him with false assurance while Grim whimpered his disapproval. "It's all going to be fine…"

"What about the spell?" he asked and I flinched. "What if… Shouldn't we stay together?"

"Artemis…" I sighed, looking around me. "This is really hard for me. I'm hoping that spending this much time together today will keep you from forgetting. I just… need some time."

When I was a few feet from him, Grim gave one last grunt and joined me as I walked deeper into the woods. Pretending not to hear Artemis protesting behind me, I picked up speed—magic spurning me forward with a strength and stamina I hadn't personally built. Knowing my familiar could, and would, keep up, I let the shimmering power carry me deeper into the forest.

Please don't let him forget, I whispered to myself.

But I also wasn't sure I meant it.

The light changed first. The steady increase in the canopy above us obscured the bright autumn light until the moisture rich dirt sank beneath each footfall. In the shade of the towering trees, the temperature plummeted. No longer was my light sweater sufficient to ward off the gathering chill as I pushed myself harder to get farther and farther from the perimeter.

We were moving too quickly for me to pinpoint the exact moment we left the boundary of Huckleberry Hollow, but I took my first full breath at a jagged rock beside a gap in tree groupings. Following another breath, I waited for the anxiety jitters to fade while Grim flopped on his side, panting. Each of us tasted the air and reveled in the freedom and wonder of what it felt like to be outside of the town.

Ancient, rooted in nature, it was the type of magic the Council claimed no longer existed. It existed without intention, an untapped energy that could not be bent to the will of man but carried man through its will.

Nothing was more powerful than the land spread out before me.

"Excuse me, but… could you ask him to move?"

My eyes whipped to a neighboring rock where a two-foot-high woman stood half-obscured by the trees. Her piercing voice sent shivers down my spine, but it was the nature of being a banshee.

At my feet, I looked under Grim's hulking form and saw a light Robin's egg blue swath of fabric sticking out beneath his belly.

"Dang it, sorry!" I called, louder than necessary in the still air. Crouching low, I nudged my familiar until he rolled onto his back, four paws in the air with his canines visible. Furry vampire mode fully activated. Grabbing the blue shirt, I pulled the moisture from it and gave it to the trees, doing the same with the soil before willing the air beside the banshee to become the shirt in my hand.

She caught it and pulled it over her head, stepping out from behind the rocks, fully attired.

The shirt was a dress... if you were two feet tall.

"I know you," she remarked, and I squinted toward her face. The white hair on her head and light wrinkles gave her an aged appearance, but as I unknowingly took a few steps closer, I could see the young woman underneath.

"Aoife?" I asked, crouching low in confusion. When I'd seen her last, she hadn't appeared so small.

Though I'd been eight, so the math on that probably tracked

"You got so big!" she screeched, and I laughed as she bounded over and wrapped me in a hug. Though she had at least a century on me, I felt like we were children in kindergarten.

"Human problems," I laughed, and she released me to give Grim some ear scrunches. He wasn't bothered by her piercing voice, dogs are not affected by the banshee call, but he rolled back and forth in delight when her claws extended to give his thick fur deep, raking pets. "How are you?"

Her gaze swung to me, maternal assessment fully underway and completed in a nanosecond.

"Better than you, it would seem. The last time magic brought you here, you hadn't been invited to a birthday party. Every kid in town, including your siblings, had been invited to. While everyone was at the party, you tried to run away," she spoke from beside Grim. My knees and ankles were tired of crouching, so I just sat down beside them. My legs crossed in front of me, stretching deeper than I had in ages.

"They were two and three years old. What were they even going to do at that party?" I muttered, but she didn't take the bait.

"Are you running away from something now?"

I offered a noncommittal shrug in lieu of an answer. When Aoife continued to look at me, sharp red eyes daring me to withhold secrets, I flopped on my back and answered.

"I wasn't supposed to have to come back to Huckleberry Hollow," I spoke to the shifting light above my head. The sun peeked through trees whispering their secrets on the soft breeze tickling their branches. "I left at 18 when this..."

I shoved up my sleeve to show her the Knight of Sword scar and she studied it in silence. The trees themselves seemed to join her in urging me to continue.

"But my mom called me back to help with a 'problem'. She hasn't told me what it is yet, making me wait until dinner tonight, which will also be attended by Alpha Kuruk and his son, who was my best friend and now, he's making me feel uncomfortable things. Emotional and sexual things. Whenever I'm here... I feel trapped. Like I'm a child again but worse because the one friend I had when I was younger doesn't really remember me and when I see him I feel like a horny teenager fresh on the hormone bandwagon which would be easier to ignore if it weren't for all the other feelings. Other than that, though, nothing has changed... the people, the town... hell, even the hospital is exactly as it was. It all feels..."

"Unnatural?"

"Yeah..."

"Including your more friendly than normal feelings toward the man?"

I scrunched my face, thinking of how Artie's every touch soothed and warmed me.

"No... that feels like..."

"Home?"

Her knowing tone brought me up short, and I studied her face.

"You know something... about the town?" I was guessing on the last. Aoife knew lots about a lot of things, but she seemed disinclined to share. When I was a child, she'd distract me with the small wonders of nature. Reaching out into the clearing, I felt the old magic sitting expectantly.

"I know many things, Penelope. About this town and about your young man. I can say for certain that the second is part of the natural course. The first... is much more complex."

The trees stood still, all chittering and scurrying among the branches ceased as energy gathered between the earth and the wind. A flicker of sunlight danced like a flame between the gaps of the trees and water beaded on the blades of grass at my feet.

The elements have gathered here... but who brought them?

I studied each element in turn, following their movement to an impenetrable shadow that lay in the direction of the town.

I turned back to Aoife.

"Are we no longer part of the whole?" I asked her and she stood sentry with her silence. Exasperated and exhausted, I flopped back down and studied the elements. The water droplets on the grass flooded onto my feet, droplets magnifying in the light that sought to blind me through closed eyelids. My hair battered my face, catching the moisture beaded on my lips and sticking it to my cheeks and nose. The tickle grew to an itch, and I sneezed.

Then sneezed again as Grim butted his head against my arm and I reached to scratch his ears.

"There's so much power out here..." I whispered, shaking off the water and trying to untangle my hair from my face. When I sat up again, Aoife was no longer studying me but gazing in awe and wonder.

"So, it is true..." she whispered, and I looked around. "You are the one who can right the imbalance."

"What's true?" I asked, looking around. "What imbalance?"

She shook her head, dissolving the expression of wonder into a mask of false cheer and secrets. Following her sudden change, the air grew cooler, and I shivered against the light sweater that had been too warm most of the day.

"You should head back to town," Aoife said kindly, and I cocked my head to the side. "You should go to your mom's dinner."

"What about..." I gestured to the forest as she started to walk away.

"When it is time, you will know. Until then, stop fighting the world, Penelope. There is love in it for you," her sage advice sounded both terrifying and perfunctory. Like she had to say it to keep me from falling apart.

"And I'm not just saying that, silly woman. You need to let go of the past," her voice fading as she was slowly swallowed by the trees and carried away in the breeze.

I blinked at the unexpected moisture on my cheeks.

"How do I let go of a past that doesn't want to let go of me?" I asked the trees, but they simply waved away the question as irrelevant.

Trees were stoic like that.

Grim let out a wide yawn and nudged his head against my leg. Following his lead, we walked back to the tree line with growing lethargy that weighed heavier the closer we got. By the time we exited into the outer edge of town, the canine and I could barely stand.

"Ugh," I groaned, mentally calculating the distance to my building. "Forget it, we're napping anyway."

Kneeling beside him, eyes closed, my arms wrapped around Grim. Picturing my office, couch and pajamas, I willed us into my office and we were almost immediately asleep.

FIFTEEN

Napping was a mistake.

Four coffees in, I was still groggy. As we stood in front of my parents' house, I felt like a petulant child again, screaming about how she didn't want to go inside for dinner. My neck tilted up and up until the very tips of the castle spires came into view and I needed armor to reach the peak.

Magical armor.

Medieval armor.

A neck brace... armor.

Anything to protect me from what lay on the other side... and looking at this side.

"All it needs is a dragon, a blonde-haired maiden in the tower, and a moat..."

A sharp cramp ripped through my neck, pulling a squeal of pain with it. Gripping my head holder, I massaged the stiff tendons and looked at the other parts of my childhood home.

Driveway that used to be littered with chalk threats from the other children in pre-K to banish the cursed one.

Shrubs, useful for hiding when puberty hit and I was banned from anything resembling comfort food. They were the perfect place to scarf chocolate during menstruation where my mom couldn't take it away.

The Crabapple tree, my ladder to freedom out of my second-floor bedroom. I'd used it a few times after I met Artie... meeting up in the woods to snack and tell each other stories. The first time he'd followed me there, but all the rest we'd met there on purpose.

"Is it too late to run?" I asked the oversized familiar beside me. His gently wagging tail and lopsided tongue declined to comment. "You know they'll judge us in there, right?"

A short muzzle prodded the back of my leg, urging me closer.

"This isn't fair. My parents bribe you with snacks."

The dog resorted to delivering a headbutt against my upper thigh/lower ass that nearly spilled coffee number five, which was currently staying toasty in a metal mug with vampire teeth declaring *I Bite*.

"OK! OK! You win, geez! Stop threatening the coffee."

We made it another ten steps toward the ornate wooden door before I needed another fortifying sip of Columbian roast brewed dark like my soul.

Then sweetened with cream and sugar, like the candy sprinkles that live inside that soul, trying to pretend they're unpredictable and dangerous while wishing they were unicorns.

Every house in The Hollow had a different vibe. The more natural beings chose homes that incorporated the surroundings, seamlessly blending in with the woods and banks of the nearby lake. Ostentatious and gaudy new money had McMansions on small lots that pushed the boundaries of what it meant to be a bad neighbor. Despite a large collection of them festooning the eastern border of the town, McMansions weren't the majority, and not just because unimpeded views of your neighbors' personal bits were more likely than not.

Most people occupied duplex townhomes and modest single-story houses built in the 1980s with wood-burning fireplaces, slightly above average backyards, and picture windows at the front that showcased seasonal filigree of every variety. It was eclectic but cohesive in a Brooklyn meets a San Francisco suburb planted in the middle of the Pacific Northwest woodlands.

Then, there was my parent's house.

If Dracula were alive, and not retired to Florida, even he'd say they should lighten up. Many buildings in Boise had retained a neo-gothic brick façade that was easier to appreciate with rainbow flags and neon signs.

My parents' house skipped the neo part and went straight to Gothic.

Gargoyles on faux parapets, a wooden front door with an uncanny resemblance to a drawbridge that touched on a plank walkway over a water feature. Large hedges obscured a magically groomed lawn, the perfect vantage to stare up and gawk when dragons roosted above the west wing.

OK, there weren't any dragons above the west wing... and probably we didn't have a west wing.

Either way, it was large, drafty, and unwelcoming.

"Seriously, I can buy you snacks. We don't need the ones my parents control," I said to Grim, catching a glimpse of a large figure cloaked in shadow at the edge of the drive.

"Normally in these parts, speaking to an animal means it's a human at least part time," the deep male voice was slightly rough with age. His southern twang had settled some, though the oracle beside the campfire demeanor had not, and when I turned around to look at him fully, his immediate recoil was somehow more prominent.

"That, however, is just a dog and couldn't possibly be listening to you ramble."

"Alpha Kuruk," I said with a slight incline of my head, wondering how a human as open and accepting as Artemis spawned from such a total tool. My sister was right, he totally sucked. "Long time no see."

Not that I was complaining.

His gaze traveled from my beat-up sneakers to the orange, thin strapped maxi-dress I covered with a cardigan to achieve "dinner appropriate". The gaze was judgmental, and it didn't take a jury of my peers to render the verdict that I still failed to measure up.

Especially when compared to himself.

The older Nita-Nusi had chosen to wear a black button-down shirt and black slacks with glistening black shoes that reflected the quarter moon above us. His long hair, held in a leather strap at his neck, was perfectly straight in a tapered tail that defied physics by staying exactly where he laid it.

"This is Grim," I gestured beside me to my familiar, who narrowed his eyes at the alpha.

Daring the human to say something demeaning about his being "just a dog".

"Charmed, I'm sure," he said with an eye roll.

My familiar looked at me, irritated and choosing violence.

I shook my head, trying to prevent a war between my best furry friend and the Northwest Pack alpha. We both knew who would win, my beastly bestie was way too cute to lose to a middle-aged man who thought he was superior, but it wasn't worth the energy and conflict to prove us both right. Grim conceded, letting out a sneeze in the man's direction, his version of a stiff middle finger.

The alpha frowned, considering the canine again. He let a wave of alpha command roll our direction, setting on edge the hairs at the back of my neck. Grim yawned and showed the man all of his teeth before turning around and giving the man his erect tail. Kicking the air behind him.

Hiding my smirk behind another sip of coffee, I fought the urge to laugh when Grim farted and fanned the air with his tail toward Alpha Kuruk.

"That insolent..." The alpha started, but his words faded from my consciousness. The sudden heat that instantly stole my breath and sanity was the only precursor to the waves of anxiety and lust that rose from my core.

Behind him, rising from a shiny black sedan, was Artemis.

"Artie," I whispered, once again breathy and damp with need. He was wearing a sport coat over jeans and a T-shirt, a look that screamed professional man meat. Before I could say hello, Artie's face snapped in my direction, his nose working. Despite the darkness of night, I could see his dilated pupils as he prowled toward me.

The night air simmered over into a boil as he got closer, threatening to cook me alive.

Apparently napping and hiding in the woods was not the cure to my suddenly persistent lady boner, I lamented even as my pulse sank lower and gave my clit her own slutty pulse.

"Hello Penny. Surprised to see you here," He moved to give me a hug, confusion and hurt, fighting for top billing on his flawlessly chiseled face. Part of him felt the pain I caused him earlier, but he couldn't remember the conversation. "I seem to miss you every time you're in town and it still feels like we were just together... I had a dream about you."

Wincing slightly, I nodded with a half-hearted smile as his arms wrapped awkwardly around my shoulders in an embrace void of the same easy affection we'd had earlier. We'd spent more hours together today than we had in the past 15 years, but it wasn't enough to keep more than a vague notion of our relationship after five hours apart.

My usual relief at having once again dodged the bullet of attachment was marred by sticky guilt and regret. The small moments of affection from earlier, the kind gestures toward Grim... all of them had faded from his mind like sand in an hourglass, and I had no idea if he'd get them back.

Which brought another uncomfortable truth to the forefront of my mind.

Does his dad know about the dating rumors? What does my mom know?

I looked back at the Northwest Pack alpha's expression and found him looking back at me with a frown that could mean anything. Neither of us spoke until Artie's words cut through the tense silence.

"In my dream, you were advertising yourself as a psycho. We were talking about dating and then we were under attack, ending up on the couch in your office with my hands about to make you scream and the smells..."

My underwear flooded with arousal and panic took control of my mouth.

"Happens to me a lot. The psycho part... the other part would imply I'd have or had seen patients or men or... Should we go inside?" I stammered, my face burning redder than the hair on my head. Taking Grim's leash and gesturing for the Alpha to go first, I held my breath and prayed to the goddess that Artie didn't keep talking.

The alpha studied me, seeing through my uncomposed ramblings to the heart of the problem: I wanted his son and he knew that I was a travesty to witches and the community of Huckleberry Hollow.

"Alpha?" I prompted, attempting to get his thoughts to the logical conclusion that this conversation was better had indoors.

Or never.

"Kuruk, Artemis, Penelope," my mom called from the lowered drawbridge...formally known as an open front door, but that was just semantics.

"What are you standing out here for? You'll catch your death! Dinner is almost ready. Where's the Beta?"

There was a moment of silence where the shifters processed my mom's rapid-fire questions while I struggled to not roll my eyes at the supposition that dinner would be served any time in the next hour. I kept my gaze on Grim's furry head as we fell in behind the two shifters, who still hadn't answered. Both radiated enough body heat to keep both Grim and I warm in subzero temps, even without his fur and my extra insulation, but sure... we could freeze.

"Apologies, Mistletonia. Beta Onca recently had a cub and with Artemis here, it would have been rude to disrupt the panther family bonding," Alpha Kuruk spoke diplomatically, but he had an undertone that suggested he wasn't really sorry.

That or I'm projecting... It was so easy to see the man who'd discounted and diminished my place in his son's life as the villain. My anxiety reaching new heights every moment I was reminded that my unresolved childhood issues made dining here with a precarious spell situation a ticking time bomb.

There was no way to know for sure when everything would blow up in my face, but it was a mathematical certainty.

"Of course! Family first," my mom's brittle voice suggested she'd heard the intonation as well, and I felt slightly validated that I wasn't the only one annoyed with the bear shifter.

"Please, come in."

She stepped out of the doorway, making room for a parade that was progressively less enthusiastic the farther back it went. By the time I'd crossed the threshold into the entryway, fake niceties had already filled the air in what I imagined a cotillion in the afterlife looked like.

Boring, uninspired, and terminal.

Trooping into the foyer, I strained my neck again, looking up... and up... to the mural on the ceiling. Matte colors portrayed my much younger mother luring my Scottish farmer father from his sheep amid a cloud of siren song that was threatening to swallow the lot.

It was as historically accurate as the image of Nessie rising from the cursed Loch, but the subtle bits of magic woven into the metallic paint shimmered and I loved watching the interplay. It was a mesmerizing dance of magic and light that served to make the viewer forget the painting's occupants were standing there- watching.

"What's Nessie doing in the Loch?" Artie asked, his chest plastered against my back while his fingers played with my hair. "Didn't she open a Scot bar in Ireland where talking shit about the Brits gets you a euro off a pint?"

"Nessie is the least problematic part of that. You know my dad is the siren," I said back, keeping my voice low and expecting his hearing to make up the difference. "The only thing my dad has ever farmed is chips from a bag of crisps."

"Can your mom sing?"

"Only if you want the neighbors to think we're murdering cats," I snickered and he stroked a finger down my neck with his own raspy chuckle.

Remember where he had that finger earlier... My brain was a cruel bitch and she was toying with my lady parts.

"It is art, you two. Artists are permitted certain liberties, and you would do well not to criticize things you yourself have never tried," my mother barked, and I attempted to mask my laugh as a cough that conveniently moved my neck away from the half-demon's roving fingers. "I heard that, Penelope."

Her sharp tone failed to do more than make me laugh harder until a small trickle of saliva tried to slide down my trachea. A once fake cough became a juicy attempt to keep my airway fluid free. Folded in half, I braced my palms against my knees, hacking and sucking air through my nose.

Lack of oxygen and acidic spit burned through my chest and I had a moment to be horrified that of all the people wanting to do me in, my own spit would be what kills me.

A warm hand slid under my sweater, touching the uncovered skin between my shoulder blades. The calloused tips worked in a small circle, spiraling outward and then slowly back in until my breathing mellowed. My face was still red, the tears on my cheeks still damp, but the heat permeating my near-death experience told me exactly who that hand belonged to... and more importantly, where his second one was.

Gripping my hip, just below my belly, my folded torso was creased around his hand while also pushing my ass out... into Artie's waist, because he was still pressed against me.

Except it wasn't his waist that was softly probing my dress in line with my opening.

Nope, that was his... *Hex me sideways that can't be his... oh Hecate, save me before he splits me in half.*

Even through his jeans, that cock was massive. A tube of mini-M&M's had been a massive understatement, because no way was this anaconda the same thing I sat on earlier. His cock pressing against the seam of my ass and pointing toward the space his fingers had been stroking earlier ensured the tear stains on my cheeks were no longer the only thing damp.

The hand fisted at my hip gripped tighter and he slammed my hips back against him, bringing little Artie even closer to...

His hand on my back slid to my neck, wrapping around to the front and pulling my whole torso roughly up against his own. Not releasing his grip on my neck or my hip, his nose burrowed into my hair to whisper against the tender flesh just beneath my ear.

"If our parents weren't watching, I'd take you right here, Peep. Remember that next time you forget how to swallow." The sentence ended with a graze of his teeth against my neck and a firm kiss before he let me go and took a full step back, removing his arm from my sweater as he went.

And taking all the oxygen with him.

"I think we should probably eat now," Alpha Kuruk declared after a very pointed throat clear that barely made it through the ruby fire tinting the edges of my vision.

"Yes, of course," someone who sounded like my mother said from the great beyond. "Before Penny dry humps any more of our guests."

Artie smirked, and raised a suggestive eyebrow that promised unlimited orgasms, not just the two he'd almost given me today. It was too much of a head trip to consolidate what he could remember with this moment, and I snapped under the pressure.

Ambling just a smidge closer, I raised my left hand as though to touch Artie's cheek, throwing a gut punch into his solar plexus with my right. With a grunt, he folded in half, arms wrapped protectively around his center. Satisfied, I stomped gracefully into the dining room, grabbed a bottle of wine from the table, and started chugging.

In the foyer, Arties laugh carried to me ears.

"**Penelope, have you been listening to me?**" My mom asked, but from where I couldn't tell.

Composing the wall surrounding my face were two empty wine bottles, courtesy of yours truly, a partially empty one that the rest of the party had been sipping on like responsible adults, and a whole plate of food I wasn't eating.

Because eating might make me sober, and we were *soooo* not being sober right now.

"Hmmm... yeah. Neighbor copied your Yule decorations, and you retaliated by hexing her hedges to claw runs into all of her panty hose."

I sneezed at a ticklish wave that drifted from my left, revealing the location of my mother, staring at me with furious eyes from her seat at the head of the table. To her right sat my father, a short ruddy Scot perpetually in a kilt and red faced from the wind blown off a loch he hadn't seen for more than a fortnight in years. Though my mother had come from a long line of very tall witches and stopped just shy of six feet, my dad was hardly able to reach either of our chins in the stacked heel dress shoes he insisted were cultural and not a desperate attempt to be taller.

To the left of the head was the alpha, seated beside a still smirking

Artie. Though his smile usually did wicked things to me, just this moment, all I had was guilt. The reason we were in this situation was because I'd once again put my own needs ahead of his and ruined everything.

You're a shitty friend... and fake girlfriend.

I finished the partial bottle and added another to my fortress of starvation and poor decisions. Defensive and embarrassed, I kept attempting to distract the room.

And my mom, Goddess help her, commits more acts of petty vengeance in a month than I've done since I left the Hollow.

"That's not what I said, Penelope."

"Were you telling the story about the time you brought flesh eating tentacular bulbs to the garden fair when they rejected your entry and slipped them into the judges quarters to bite them?" I asked, watching her face swim around. "Or when you replaced the neighbors' sleepy time tea with colon cleanse tea?"

She gave me a dark look.

"What? You did!"

Instead of looking embarrassed, my mom looked pissed and unlikely to be derailed.

Damn.

I opened my mouth to try again but was cut off by the only man at the table not wearing pants. He was also one of only two people, gender nonspecific, who could predict the sheer amount of stupidity that would come out of my mouth.

"Penny," my dad chided, his thick Scottish accent making it sound like *pen, eh?*

With a single raised eyebrow and pointed look, he reminded me that my skeletons weren't buried that deep. My dad, the merman who traded his tail for a woman, visited the loch annual to maintain his siren magic.

With one puff of mer-magic, I'd be telling my mother what really happened to her prize-winning Azaleas.

"Sorry. What were you saying, mom?" I asked, giving in to the tempting aroma of ratatouille while performing my most convincing dutiful daughter face. A single bite and I nearly moaned at the burst of flavor and contrasting textures that exploded in my mouth. The crisped edges of the squash with smooth tomato base, sprinkled with dried basil and non-traditional inclusion of sausage, was heaven. Nostalgia hit hard as I remembered a childhood filled with fresh veggies and watching my mom bibbity bobbity her plants into almost comedic displays of photo-synthetic prowess.

She was one with the garden and all that dwelled within.

"I was asking what you had noticed since you'd been back," she took a prolonged sip of wine. It was a measured activity, a way of making sure she didn't lead or influence the answer. "Assuming your social life hasn't become too distracting."

I had her undivided attention… and the attention of everyone else at the table if Artie's sharp inhale at the mention of my "social life" was any indication.

With a forkful of squash, I thought about the past few days. Weighing what parts of it were weird-normal, weird for me, or legitimately odd in this context. Aoife's words rattled around my head.

Unnatural.

What had made the town feel unnatural?

The hospital had seemed the same. Depressing, fake… with an undercurrent of malice.

Had that always been there?

It was a question for someone who didn't consider the place cursed and I made a mental memo to find someone who knew more about the place with less baggage… Though Ali had hinted at something wrong there as well.

Reliving my walk to the hospital, I considered that street I'd gotten lost on… the memory merged with another one, where Artie kept preventing me from making a trip down the alley that would lead me back to that street.

Neither he nor Grim could see it….

I tried to pull forward the memory, bringing different parts into focus to read the signs and search for clues against my childhood memories. Trying and failing to find memories of the street, the businesses or anyone whose names matched the establishments, I had my first inkling of dread.

Where were those people?

Backing my mind toward the exit, I could only remember times I'd nearly gone down that alley and then suddenly remembered something or somewhere that I needed to be. A magical pull drawing me away and then erasing whatever I may have glimpsed on the other side.

So how did I end up there today?

"There's a street just beyond an alley off of Main Street," I started, looking up and meeting my mom's flabbergasted expression. Though I was occasionally a pain in the ass, that was no reason to be astonished I could take something seriously.

I switched to look at my dad, then the alpha, but they were both staring with open-mouthed expressions of wonder and confusion.

Except... they weren't looking at me.

They were looking *in front* of me.

Floating in the center of the table, just above my wine bottles, was a 3-D rendering of the street and the alley I'd tried so hard to find words for. The size of a dinner plate, the image interacted with me the same as if we were standing in it.

A VR experience plucked from my mind.

Across the table, Artie was smiling with a knowing look.

Instead of a smart-ass comment, his leg brushed against my calf. The hem of his pants tugged up the bottom of my dress, and our skin came into contact. The heat exploding through the image until it expanded to the size of the room. Our dinner table became the road, everyone seated living my memory in a video recreation that stacked each one to complete an area only I'd seen before.

When I got to the memory of Artie and me last night, the man himself split.

Superimposed over his face was a black bear and a horned being, facing off against each other above his narrow-eyed determination. No one else noticed as I watched each facet of him fight and attack the other.

Slowly, nostrils twitching, they both turned to me. The bear's piercing cognac eyes locking with mine, a low growl that sent my libido into overdrive and multiplied itself tenfold in the sparkling hunter clawing his way from Artemis to be closer.

Need, hunger, want, the bear was screaming into the mystified room that continued to study a memory. The murmurs of their analysis were completely oblivious to my bear who couldn't get closer.

Mine, he screamed without words.

Mine, I shouted back, chest arching in a scream that shattered the illusion and returned the room to normal.

But I'd seen something that was not normal. Shoving back from the table, I grabbed an unopened bottle and stumbled backward, fighting alcohol, confusion, and the sudden stares of every "real" adult in the room.

Artie was now a single person, his inner turmoil where it belonged, wearing a hooded gaze and an expression that promised vengeance for the memory he didn't share. A low, growly voice broke through the haze.

"Where are you going, Peep?"

"Bathroom," I announced, too loud and squeaky. Bolting down the hall while unscrewing the top of my wine bottle, my heart thudding in my chest, I narrowly avoided running face-first into three walls to the barrage of jumbled thoughts colliding in my head. Tossing the cap to the floor, I paused to take a long pull from the bottle and tried not to hear the murmured condemnation floating out of the room behind me.

I had bigger problems than being rude, and all of them were named Artemis.

SEVENTEEN

THE BATHROOM, DECORATED IN SOOTHING WHITES AND greens, was too warm.

Sweating, desperate, I shoved open the miniscule window above the tub and stuck my head out into the night. The soft click of claws on tile announced Grim's arrival before his large head nudged the door open. The dog wisely turned around and used his head to push the door closed again with his head, making sure it clicked securely before lying down in front of it, head resting on crossed paws while amber eyes stared at me with concern.

All around us, seafoam green towels and white tiled lilacs reflected a calm environment supplemented by lavender pot-pourri sitting in a large seashell on the counter.

None of it put a dent in the rising panic that built in my chest, attempting to explode out of my meat suit and paint the room red.

This was the second display of powerful magic that I'd performed today. But this time, no one's life had been in danger. There were no extenuating circumstances, just... Artemis's touch. But I'd somehow projected the contents of my mind onto the table the same way I'd delivered an ass kicking to the ladies of the Hollow even before he touched me.

"I shouldn't have been able to do that," I said to Grim, pulling my head back inside the house and taking another slug of wine from the bottle. Small droplets of the deep red merlot dribbling down the shimmering label *Love Potion on the Vine*, until they splattered onto the white fiberglass bathtub and pooled into the crevices. "I shouldn't be able to do any of this. How am I doing it? Magic requires intention. I didn't plan to do any of that."

Grim let out a soft whine and I looked at him again.

"What's happening to me?"

He let out another sigh and lifted his colossal head to incline toward the mirror.

Staring into it, my bright red cheeks had taken on an almost holographic glow. Every turn of my face changed the color and depth of the image reflected, making me nearly unrecognizable to my own eyes.

"Is this a mental breakdown? It feels like a mental breakdown." I looked away from the mirror and slid to the floor, taking another long drink from the wine bottle until the room tilted a little and I let out a small giggle.

"Drinking in my parent's bathroom after doing something weird... this is so my twenties all over again," I laughed, wrapping my lips around the bottle only to discover it was empty. Pressing a single eye to the opening, I stared into the brown bottle to see if any more wine was hiding inside, but it was definitely empty.

Which left me with two choices: process my feelings without alcohol or leave this bathroom and sneak out without anyone noticing.

"Damn..."

Grim let out another whimper, crawling over on his belly to put his head in my lap. Setting down my empty bottle, I stroked the fur along his head, brushing against the grain to reveal the brown and then white undercoats beneath. Mesmerized, I slowly let it drift from white to brown, then back to black, over and over, until my panic ebbed, and I took my first deep breath since the scene in the foyer.

Turning, I peaked over the rim of the tile counter to look at the mirror above the sink. Reflected was me, unfocused and intoxicated emerald eyes, unruly red hair that was somehow also drunk, and more freckles than anyone could count.

No hologram.

No projected memories.

Just me, on the floor, peeking over a countertop.

"OK…" I drew out the letters and slouched back down, staring into the golden eyes of Grim. "Do we go back out now? And is it reasonable to claim we feel unwell and leave? Do we have to claim anything at all? Irish goodbye out the front door?"

Grim let out a soft sneeze and I decided that meant yes.

"Let's do it then."

Using the wine bottle as a cane, I gripped the neck to start the upward process, turning on my knees toward the counter. Placing my hand flat on the marble, I pushed myself up and set the bottle on the counter. The room quivered, a reminder that I was fat but still a lightweight.

All of this wine would be coming back later.

With a last look in the mirror, I confirmed once again that I looked normal.

You look drunk, I thought, but that was pretty normal in this house.

You need a better trauma coping mechanism, my inner psychiatrist criticized. But what did she know, anyway? She only had a doctorate and medical training. My inner slut bunny had an unhealthy resting hard-on for the shifter across the table, and I wasn't listening to her either. In terms of poor decisions, I was squarely in the middle of the road. Exactly where I wanted to be…

Especially if a bus was coming.

"Let's do this," I said to Grim again. The dog wisely stood where my hand could rest on his head. We made it to the bathroom door, and I opened it to the scent of tomato, basil and garlic drifting in from the grand dining room. Voices engaged in normal, non-freak-explaining, conversation drifted in with the sweet smell of apple pie and I took another steadying breath.

Leading us slowly, Grim escorted me to the dining room, which unfortunately blocked my route to the front door.

Foiled by architectural design.

As soon as I walked in, all conversation ceased. Alpha Kuruk, my mom and my dad all looked at me, a variety of looks painting their faces while I set the empty wine bottle beside its brethren. The collection made me reconsider the notion I was a lightweight... that was a lot of wine.

Opening my mouth to apologize and excuse myself, an enthusiastic voice brought me up short.

"Penny! When did you get here? It's been so long!" Artie cooed and I froze in place, scared to look at the man who'd brought out the most powerful magic I'd ever seen... twice. "Did your mom tell you we'd be here?"

Turning slowly with my shoulders against my ears, I glanced slowly along the table and landed on the easy-going blank expression on Artie's face. He wasn't concerned or horrified at the magical projection, didn't look in the least bit aware he'd briefly split into the man, the bear, and the demon living inside him.

He looked...

I watched him go from elated to confused, while he took in my place setting of half-eaten food. Then he studied my face, the now wine-stained dress, empty bottles and Grim seated beside me as a sentry against toppling over.

"Penny?" my mom asked, my dad sending off a silent warning not to lie.

"It's a long story," I sighed and hunched over my plate, hand resting on the back of the chair. I whispered quietly, willing the plate to trade places with a glass container from my mother's kitchen. When the plate relocated, clean and sterile, to its cabinet and a lidded dish sat with the remainder of my dinner and an extra helping from the pot, I plucked it off the table and looked above each person's left ear instead of making awkwardly drunken eye contact. "But, long-story short, he's under a memory charm... spell... curse? Labels, am I right? Anyway, when I'm away from him for some time, he forgets me. That felt like a really short time to be away though and I reeeallly hope you last longer in other aspects. Anyway, if you know we've been dating, he actually doesn't know anymore... he doesn't know a lot of things we've been doing because I didn't want to hurt his feelings..."

Spittle landed on the table with my attempt at making words sound sober, but the general sense of anger and disappointment let me know I had said enough words correctly to get the point across.

"Penny!" my dad scolded while the alpha zeroed in on his son with renewed interest.

"Well, I didn't think it would last forever. We did it fifteen years ago," I slurred and watched the room waver slightly. "Not it, it, though that almost happened earlier. You were there!"

I pointed at the alpha, closing one eye to keep in focus. "Once I'm out of sight, none of the memories of me stick. It's like a magic dealy thing but for brains. I told him all about it earlier, but then I blew up a street full of people. We made out and almost... you know, and then I panicked and ran away into the woods. I didn't think after spending hours together he'd forget me. Or that I couldn't go get drunk in the bathroom without him forgetting me. I'm just forgettable."

A small hiccup escaped and I shrugged, sending me listing toward Grim. The dog used his immense size to shove me back upright, but I wasn't stable enough not to keep going. When that tilted me back toward the table, I reached out to stop myself from face planting into the centerpiece and knocked over a few empty bottles.

"Penelope," my mother said, standing up to gather the bottles and square off with me, her nose inches from my own. "You don't think all of this was prudent to mention earlier?"

Another hiccup bubbled up, and I jolted with muscle spasms while my squeaky *hic* brought an eye roll from the blonde-haired beauty I was somehow descended from.

"Hehe... you said prude!"

"Maybe we should revisit this another time," she sighed, placing a second container of pie on top of my ratatouille. I stared at it, confused where it came from until I saw the heels of a maid slipping back into the kitchen. "I'm busy tomorrow, but I'll see you at dinner on Saturday. There will be no alcohol at that meal."

She walked away, leaving the scent of night blooming jasmine and vanilla in her wake.

"Ye need any help gettin' home?" my dad asked, standing up and tilting his head back to look me in the eye.

"I've got her," Artie responded, appearing beside me. Taking my containers, he wrapped my arm around his waist and draped his own across my shoulders, leaving my secondhand dangling to get support from Grim, who knew better than to let me walk alone. My head dropped onto Artie's shoulder, and I waited for the room to stop spinning before looking up at him through the fog of wine.

"You're pretty," I whispered, small droplets of spit landing on the collar of his sport coat while he moved us from behind my chair to the entryway of the dining room. It felt like magic to manage it without running into anything, and I gawked at the half shifter. "You're a graceful bear bear, bear... papa bear... no baby bear! Cuz juuussst right!"

Ignoring my drunken babble, he gave my dad and his own a nod. Both older men returned the gesture in a very masculine goodnight that would have made me want to barf, but since I already wanted to, I took it as an invitation to put two fingers to my temple and salute them. Artie kept leading me out of the dining area, back into the foyer, and out the front door into the cool night air.

Juniper, cinnamon, and damp earth greeted me as we made our way up the drive toward the black sedan.

Sedans.

There were two identical cars sitting side by side.

"Where did the second car come from? You were a passenger," I slurred accusingly, though I was fairly certain the words sounded more like "were-car pather grr" since he ignored me entirely to open the passenger door and glide me into the leather seat, being mindful of my head and dress.

Setting the food containers on the floorboard, his face was millimeters away from mine while he secured the seatbelt. His breath tickled the tiny hairs coating my face, smelling like Italian spice and apple pie.

I leaned in, running my tongue up his stubbled jawline to get a taste. Breath hitching, his hand faltered and missed the plastic belt receiver, knuckles white around the insertion tab.

"Yummy," I whispered while he made a second pass with the seatbelt and let out a deep throaty growl.

"Stop it, PenPen," his low snarl went straight to my core, and I arched my back into his torso, needing to feel more of him against me as the adrenaline let down from my panic faded into a primal need for release.

"I need…" The belt snapped into place and his warm weight disappeared from above me. The door slammed shut and the door behind me opened, the whole car shifting under Grim's added weight. A look at my familiar in the rearview mirror suggested I'd screwed up big time and needed to put the kibosh on my unsolicited advances.

That door slammed and Artemis appeared beside me in the driver's seat, hands shaking as they gripped the steering wheel. Angry Artie would be absolutely terrifying, but I could taste that under all of the door slamming, he was scared and still aroused.

A hint of citrus in the salty sea of fear and regret.

"I'm sorry this is all new to you… again. But I can't change the past, Artie. You don't have to want to be with me, but being pissed about it now is too late."

"I'm not mad that I'm attracted to you, Penny. I'm mad this is still a fucking problem. I'm mad that my dad, the town and everyone knows more about my life than I do. What the fuck happened today? And yesterday? Why didn't you tell me if you walked away from me earlier, I'd forget everything? Including that we… that we almost…"

A sickening bubble of dread filled my stomach.

If he doesn't remember you basically took advantage of him… but he knew what he was doing at the time. He had his full faculties…

But did that make it any less horrifying to find out you'd almost hooked up with someone and have no recollection of it?

Hex me sideways. I'm a jackass.

"I'm sorry. I didn't know. I thought after the whole day together, a few hours would be fine. And we didn't almost, I almost. At your hand's bidding, but you didn't… You don't have anything to be worried about. I didn't violate… I mean… Maybe we should just stay away from each other and then I won't… I'm sorry. Fifteen years ago, it seemed like the right thing to do."

My voice trailed off, and he turned the engine over, reversing the car out of its slot.

"Don't. Don't say shit like that, PenPen. I'm… shit, I'm hard as a rock and have been for hours. Now I know it's because of you. Because of us and I hate not remembering, because for a while earlier... I was so fucking happy. That was you, wasn't it? It was getting to be with you that gave me genuine joy for the first time in years, and I don't even get to have the memories to hold onto."

Guilt glued my mouth shut, and I let the silence grow while he navigated out of my mom's neighborhood. He took one hand off the steering wheel and squeezed mine.

"We need to figure this out," he repeated himself. Even quieter, his small whispers carried through the otherwise silent car. "I can't lose you. Not again."

By the time he had the nose of the car pointed toward town, my eyelids were too heavy to keep open and I settled into the seat. The ride was smooth, the car hardly registering the loose dirt road beneath its tires. With my ear trained to the rhythm of the car, I settled into the deep even breaths of both Grim and Artie, listening to their synchronized rhythm of inhales and exhales until my mind quieted and I was out.

EIGHTEEN

PENELOPE

THE WIND WHIPPED MY HAIR IN EVERY DIRECTION, TOO warm for the autumn snowfall resting on the ground. All of it making my bones rattle with cold.

I was once again standing in the summer solstice clearing, the woman in black smirking, her existence an unnatural blight on the woods. I looked around, searching for Artie and the bear he had been before.

Instead, a curved horn demon curled into himself. Clutching his middle, the man resembled both the woman in the woods and Artie—a pale version swathed in black clothing trembling on the ground beneath a distorted sky of stars fighting the sun for a chance to shine.

Below the demon was the bear, and then the man. All three shifting under the haunting cackle of the shadowed monster lurking amid the trees.

"What do you say, witch? Are you willing to make a deal for his life?" Her voice raked across my skin, threatening to rip me apart. "What does little Artemis mean to you?"

Everything, my heart screamed over the hesitation on my tongue. The truth, the undeniable truth, was too much to admit, too much to share. It was safer to hold back, safer to play it close to the chest so no one could get hurt.

"Just let him go! How can you do this to your own blood?" I shouted, *watching a ripple of pain overtake Artie as he lay on the ground.*

"He is an abomination. Even you can't love him. Facing death, you can't declare to the world that you love him," her voice snared on the *jagged edges of my feelings, my heart, my sanity. "Your fear will be his undoing. If you deny him again, he will perish. Tell me now, Penelope, do you love this man?"*

"I..."

The wind hammered against the trees, beating a rhythmic curse in my chest.

"I..."

The hammering grew louder, more insistent, the trees whispering...

"No, it's not available for rent. I'll be in residence for a while, and I have a lot of work to do while I'm in town. I also already have a house guest."

The trees sound like Artie.

A softer voice muttered a response, the tone nervous and distressed.

"It doesn't matter what you promised, Naomi... yes, I know she can be terrify..."

A knife slammed into my frontal lobe, and I squeezed my eyes against the pain. Around me was soft fabric, warm and smelling of pine, ash and just a tinge of citrus. Against my better judgment, I stuck my nose deep into the blanket and inhaled deeply.

His voice filled my ears, promising something to whoever still had the faculty to speak.

Matching my breathing to the pulse hammering behind my eyes, I convinced both my eyes and my brain to do something besides be stupid. Cracking open my eyes, I saw daylight, navy sheets, metal and glass modern nightstands and a large window framing a flaming red tree slowly spilling its leaves onto the ground. I watched the two descend, floating gently on an autumn breeze that scattered its ground-dwelling friends in a skittered whisper that failed to penetrate the room, but I heard them nevertheless.

Two more weeks to Mabon, I thought, wondering if this year I'd be welcomed or offered a new scar to join the tarot card singed permanently into my arm.

And maybe unicorns really are real...

A shadow edged in from one side and my head followed the elongation to its apex.

Grey sweatpants, elastic holding them above naked feet, rested low enough to show off the hip cut Adonis belt and the most glorious collection of abs I refused to count with anything but my tongue. Firm pecs flexed beneath a tribal tattoo resembling a black bear threatening to eat another shape on the left, something with graceful swooping horns. Broad shoulders stacked on top, dangling more delectable, tattooed flesh on sinewy arms that looked equally capable of comfort and violence. Hands hanging just below the waistband of his pants with long fingers I knew firsthand were magic. My eyes went back to his hips, licking my lips at the apex of his sweatpants, where a thick piece of man meat pushed against the grey fabric, showing the sloped curve of his thick head and the stiff rod that would tear me apart while I begged for more.

A sound of longing filled the room, mournful and wanting, bringing Grim's head up from the foot of the bed. His left eyebrow moved, a sneeze and then a subtle shake of his head in disapproval.

Shit, that was me.

"If you make that sound again, Peep, I'm not responsible for what happens to you. Don't tease the beast," the masculine perfection above me growled. "You did enough of that yesterday."

"What sound?" I asked in my most innocent voice, my eyes still glued to the tent in his pants.

"Penny..." He warned, toeing around a blanket and a couple pillows on the floor. I looked up, the question dying on my lips at the sight before me. The man brought out a monster inside of me, a craving that pummeled me with a tidal wave of lust. It was involuntary, overwhelming, and all-consuming.

Meeting his deep brown, cognac flecked eyes, I tried to look irresistible and sexy. Fists clenching open and closed at his sides, I watched the easy-going playboy fight for control while the beast within fought to take over.

To take me.

Swallowing my drool, I watched with my pulse pounding in my throat, rooting for the beast. When watching became too much, I squeezed my legs together, trying to keep in my scent and get some much-needed friction. His gaze trailed down the outline of my legs, watching with interest the pumping of my knees to press against *that spot*. Opening and closing my mouth, I struggled between begging him to do every wicked thing playing out in the shadows of his eyes and fleeing this room, this man, and this life forever.

Living like a hermit in the Canadian wilderness with a thrusting vibrator and these memories to fulfill every aching need.

He remained steadfast, refusing to join me in bed. Refusing me, the same way he had the night before.

Cheeks burning, I yielded to the silence.

"Where am I?" I yawned, trying to keep my eyes on his face before turning toward the nightstand and finding an extra-large cup of water beside an only slightly smaller cup of coffee and two little blue pain pills that looked as appetizing as what Grim deposited in my mother's garden last night.

"My townhouse... which is now also your townhouse," he said, moving around to the other side of the bed while I tried to figure out which beverage to shotgun first. "Start with coffee, please."

"Why is it also mine?" Wiggling toward the far side of the bed, I disturbed Grim who let out a grumble of annoyance.

"Drink the coffee."

"Why did you sleep on the floor?" I asked, throwing off the blanket and, grabbing the two tiny blue pills and dropping them into the back of my throat and swallowing.

"Drink the coffee."

"Is that the only thing you know how to say?" I asked, rolling my eyes. Two fisting both cups, I started with the right hand and put the glazed ceramic rim to my lips, delighted by the smell of sweetened coffee with cinnamon and nutmeg.

My favorite.

Which he shouldn't remember.

"I know how to say you're a pain in the fucking ass."

"Old news. Also, I've never fucked anyone's ass. Now... the townhouse and the floor?"

"I wasn't sure if I'd remember last night today. I thought it would be safer to wake up on the floor than next to you... just in case I..."

He gestured to the erection jutting out of his sweatpants.

"Sure... No one wants to be unwittingly probed... I take it you remember yesterday?" He nodded. "If you aren't interested in probing me... What happens if you need to feed?"

"Hopefully we don't have to find out."

Rejection ripped through my chest harder than the hangover that renewed its percussive assault inside my head. I might not have been blind-sided by the sudden animalistic arousal, but Artie's beast needed to feed.

Just not from me.

"Got it. I'll just go... get dressed. Maybe take a shower... Buy a muumuu..."

I stood up, being careful not to spill the liquid from either cup. *Two Girls One Cup* step aside. I was one woman, two cups and three dozen trip hazards. Though I'd never actually watched the viral video from my pre-teen years, I'd heard enough to know there was no walking involved.

Just a high probability of intestinal parasites from fecal coliforms.

"You can't leave the room; we need to talk!" Artie grabbed the pillow off the floor and threw it onto the bed behind me. He grabbed the blanket and balled it into a tight spool of fleece and tossed it into the hamper across the room.

"I have to pee! Do you want me to get a bladder infection?" I lied, though now that the words were out there, I did kind of need to pee.

"Ugh.... No. Bathroom is there." He pointed at a door in his bedroom, and I shook my head.

"I need a bathroom, not in this room. Women do not like strangers hearing them pee." Taking a long drink of coffee that burned my tongue, I tried not to show weakness and blow on my beverage. Stepping through the chaos on the floor, I kept the cup pressed to my mouth and navigated myself into the hall.

"We're not strangers, Penelope!" He called after me, but that seemed like semantics at the moment. "Stop pretending you aren't as frustrated and horny as I am. I saw the damn looks!"

As if.

Drinking and walking, I used intuition and basic deductive reasoning to point my body toward a bathroom. No matter how many levels a townhouse possessed, there was always a bathroom on the ground floor.

Based on the tree outside the bedroom window, we were probably on the ground floor.

Or Artie only planted *really* short trees.

Grim followed, nudging me back to the center when I strayed too close to a wall. We made two left turns, and I wandered into the first open door on the right. It smelled like eucalyptus spearmint and my bare toes were greeted by freezing tiled floors. Taking the last few gulps of my coffee, I moved into the room until my hip collided with a hard surface and I could take my last drink without fear of falling.

When I finally lowered the cup, Grim and I were alone, and I was out of coffee. Starting in on the water, I used the facilities and studied the room. A scented air freshener was plugged in below a modest mirror that doubled as a medicine cabinet. There was soap and a wrapped toothbrush on the counter, hand towels folded into perfect thirds on the metal bar beside the tub, a deep green contrasting with the grey bath towels that lived underneath. The sink had exposed shelving under-neath, a few cubes with essentials like shampoo, conditioner, a hairdryer and tampons. Everything looked professionally staged, laundered and prepped for guests.

"Do you think he rents this place out?" I asked Grim, trying to remember the conversation I'd had earlier about someone renting... someone who was scared of Naomi.

"Shit! I need to call Naomi. What time is it?" I panicked, reaching for the pocket on my left hip and jolting it back at the foreign texture I encountered. "How did I get...?"

Looking down, I stared at a plain white T-shirt and black basketball shorts that not only weren't mine, but were skin tight and showcasing my traitorous nipples. Offended, and a little confused how I'd gone to the bathroom without realizing I was wearing someone else's clothes, I pictured my sweater and leggings in my office. The olive green sweater and brown leggings, embroidered with an autumnal pattern up the side, laying in the box beside my makeshift bed. The brown pants were a perfect match to Artie's eyes, the man with a package too big to contain in sweatpants.

My hand unwittingly drifted lower, wandering to the needy heat between my legs while imagining it was Artie. Long, thick fingers moving toward the waistband of my leggings...

"What the fuck!" I heard shouted from down the hall, stopping the descent of my hand into madness. I let out a frustrated sigh, making a mental note to buy batteries because this sexual frustration was getting out of hand. Reaching for the spot I'd manifested my clothing, I frowned when the counter remained empty. "Penny!"

I exited the bathroom and ran directly into Artie, his broad chest no match for my much softer one. My momentum reversed, and I bounced off his no longer bare chest, landing flat on my ass, just below the man.

"Ow!" I shouted at the same time Grim yelped and scuttled out of the way. My gaze traveled up the man in front of me and my gaping mouth was likely going to attract flies because...

"What the hell? Why are you wearing my clothes?!?!"

The sweater was roomy on my robust belly and breasts, so it was hanging off his smaller frame, straining at the biceps but otherwise comfortable if slightly revealing in the deep V of the neckline. My leggings, however, were not designed for muscular hockey player legs, nor the David Bowie bulge that would make even the Goblin King blush.

"I was going to ask you that very question, Penny... what were you doing in the bathroom?" He inched closer to where I'd fallen, a predatory gleam in his eyes. His nostrils were flared, eyes blown wide, and I knew he could smell what I'd almost done.

"N-nothing..." I scuttled backwards, crab walking toward the bathroom door but ending up flat backed against a wall. "I was looking for my phone and I wanted my clothes so I could shower..."

"Did you shower? You look very... dirty. Like maybe... maybe you got a different kind of wet. And maybe... you were thinking about me and maybe you're going to keep being a pain in the ass until I teach you how to be a good girl. Am I getting... warmer, Peep?" He was directly above me, gazing with unfiltered lust and sinful desire in hooded eyes that flashed from his erection to my mouth. "Do you need me to teach you how to be a good girl?"

"N-no…" I stammered, reaching for Grim to lower my rapidly rising heart rate. Whatever had been on my mind in the bathroom was nothing compared to the traitorous need that was practically dripping down my leg. "I would never let my mind wander during a spell."

But I will lie through my teeth to avoid admitting I was about to rub one out thinking about my childhood friend like a perverted nut job who can't keep it in her pants.

Now if he'd stop staring at my lips like they belong wrapped around his…

"Uh huh…" He slipped his arms under my shoulders and hauled me up against the wall, leaving just my tip toes touching the ground while he pressed himself against my core. Using one leg for leverage, he pushed a knee between my thighs to make just enough space to spread me open. Braced against the wall, my aching clit touching the top of his thigh, his hands ran down my ribs, over my belly, to dig into the fleshy meat at my hips. Dragging them forward and shoving me back, Artie worked me back into a frenzy before falling completely still while I mewled in protest.

"Artie," I whined, trying to move my own hips and finish what he started, but he kept me pinned to the wall.

"Hmmm?" He said, forehead dropping to my collar bone and angling to allow tiny nips on the front of my neck that stung just before he licked away the pain on a wave of lust. Unlike his kisses yesterday, there was no underlying meaning or emotions. "Are you frustrated and horny, Penny?"

We were in the territory of pure animalistic want. If Artemis had been Dr. Jekyll yesterday, this was Mr. Hyde, his beast of pleasure and destruction.

And I would suck both of them off if he'd just put his fingers right…

"Please," I pushed against his hands while he maintained perfect control over both of us.

"Please what, Penny? What were you doing in the bathroom?" His mouth was now at my jaw, hard firm kisses replacing the nibbles until our mouths crashed against each other. He pulled back slightly. "Good girls tell the truth."

I shuddered at the implied praise.

He took the invitation and dove back in.

There was no gentle teasing, a brush of his lips before he planted them firmly against mine, sucking slightly until I gasped, and his tongue dipped inside my mouth.

He tasted like heaven.

Sliding against each other, teeth forgotten, his tongue explored my mouth with the fervor of a treasure hunter. I plundered his right back, tasting every inch I could reach without swallowing him whole.

Breaking away, gasping for air, and staring intently into each other's eyes, we waited out a half dozen heart beats. His hand had moved and was now toying with the elastic of my basketball shorts. My own hand had dug my nails into his round ass that felt like sculpted clay just ready to be baked.

"Are you going to tell me the truth, Penny?" His husky voice promised to fulfill every need if only I were brave enough to ask. "This is your last chance to come clean before we get absolutely filthy."

Leaning in, I dropped my mouth to his neck and sunk my teeth into the tender flesh between neck muscle and shoulder, pulling back and feeling his skin stretch while his cock twitched against my thigh. His fingers dug deeper, massaging the soft tissue of my ass and hips while he methodically rubbed his erection against me.

"Come on, PenPen, just tell me you want me," he breathed against my temple. "Admit you want me. Admit you never want me to forget you again and you'll do anything I want to keep my memories strong. You said on the couch yesterday that you weren't going to push me away anymore."

"Y-you remember that?" I stammered. Pulling on my sweater, I fought to get it over his head. One arm at a time, he loosened his grip on me just enough to get the sweater free, and I had an unobstructed view of the glorious body underneath. Diving in tongue and teeth first, I pulled his man nipple into my mouth, raking my teeth along his pec and sucking.

"Penny..." he moaned, wrapping a fist around a bundle of my hair and tugging my head back, exposing the column of my throat under a feral gaze. "Are you going to stop running away from me?"

"I-I want to..."

"Are you going to stop being scared?" He punctuated the question with another roll of his hips that rubbed my core against his thigh.

"But..."

"I'll give you everything... if you tell me... Tell me you want me forever."

My mouth opened, ready to offer him anything he wanted if he'd bury himself inside me.

"Artemis!" Someone was pounding on the door. Every bang of their fist jarring me back to reality. The reality that all of this was wrong and Artemis had a woman at the door, one he'd likely called to take care of the beast he couldn't stomach letting me feed.

"Open the door, asshole! I know you're in there!"

No amount of water and soap could make me feel clean.

Especially not his soap, in his shower, where everything smelled like him.

Before Artie could speak a word to the woman on the other side of the door, I'd retreated into the bathroom at lightning speed. With the door locked and the shower running, I'd had a minor meltdown on the bathroom rug. My skin burned from his touch and nothing made sense without his hands all over me except...

My head dropped against the fiberglass wall, banging it gently and willing the universe to put itself right. My life was a mess, but it had order. Everyone who was permanent had a box and a label.

Artie was my friend.

He'd always been hot.

He'd always been sexually charged and inscrutable.

But there was a line we didn't cross.

Sex was not on the neatly labeled card attached to the identity box.

But it could be... Except that really wasn't enough.

Not anymore.

I shut off the water, grabbed a towel, and concentrated on a dress from my meager wardrobe. The full skirt, cinched waist and color block design beneath a mocked neckline to cover the little love bites Artie had left behind. My fingers touched the air, feeling the soft fabric, while my eyes saw the colors, the contrast, flowing over my curves and hugging every spot the mean girls called disgusting.

My eyes opened, and I was wearing the dress, braless and... I wiggled my nether regions.

Yup, I had not brought myself any underwear. I could not for the life of me picture which pairs were clean or even what the unclean pairs looked like. Without an image to grasp, there was a possibility my magic would shoplift someone else's underwear, and no way was I getting a magical levy over underwear.

Nope, if I was going down, it was going to be for murder.

Whose was as mysterious as the run-down street just beyond the town center. I considered again that neither Grim nor Artie could perceive it and no one at the table last night had felt any semblance of recollection of my memories. Grim was not generally subject to the magic of man, easily seeing through glamours and identifying shifters.

"Why couldn't you see the street, buddy?" I asked him and his eyebrows moved slightly, wondering the same question. "And how did I show everyone what they couldn't see in real life? How did I knock down a few dozen people? And what the hell is with those dreams?"

The last pulled me up short.

I hadn't given much thought to the dreams, but they always came when I fell asleep near Artemis. Were they his memories? Were they a projection of my own inner demons?

"Should I have told my mom about the dreams and the burn?" I asked him and he sneezed at me. A gesture I usually took to mean yes, but this time it sounded like he was laughing at the idea.

"Right... Tough witches don't need family, sex, money or a home," I told my reflection, wishing that I had eyeliner and lip gloss to put on as armor against the world. "Hex it all! We got this!"

I punctuated my pep talk with a fist pump in the air that even Grim, laying guard by the door, turned away from in shame.

"Don't give me that. Do you know how hard it is to give yourself a pep talk as an adult? You already know the world is garbage, and you still have to go out and live in it. Adulthood is the biggest scam since the rabbit in a hat magic trick, and cheese is too expensive."

My canine companion perked up at the mention of cheese and I couldn't say I blamed him. Next to coffee and fluffy blankets, nothing was better than cheese.

Well, and dogs, but his place in my world was never in question.

"Yeah, I agree. We'll stop at the store on our way into work."

Grim moved from the bathroom door, and I pulled it open, taking inventory of the hallway. It was empty, the spot I'd nearly come on Artie's leg as innocuous as the rest of the space. Empty cups in hand, I put on my best "fuck with me and get genital warts" face, striding down the hallway with all the confidence a woman about to default on her student loans and not wearing any underwear could fake.

Which was a rather impressive amount, given the sinking sensation that replaced it at the female laugh floating in from the kitchen. It was melodic, wind chimes in a summer breeze, and Artie's responding chuckle was genuine.

He's not mad she's here, I thought, trying to regroup. I needed to take the cups to the kitchen where, if I was lucky, there would also be more coffee.

I also needed to run the hell away from here and wait for the apocalypse.

"Penny?" Artie called and my eyes snapped to his face where it peeked out of the kitchen. "Where are you going?"

He stared at the cups in my hands.

His cups in my hands.

And his teeth marks on your neck, but I'd covered those up.

"Why?" He looked down at the woman's clothing in his hands that he'd clearly replaced with the jeans and T-shirt he now wore. With a long inhale, Artie breathed in the scent of the whole house and his eyes went wide with surprise. "How...?"

Artie looked toward Naomi, who raised an eyebrow at me while she took a dainty sip of coffee.

"Please tell me you didn't forget me again. I wasn't in the shower that long!" I waved a hand toward them, acknowledging as I did that I was still holding his dishes.

His face scrunched up and he smelled the clothing, a sensory memory stronger than any other method of recall. I could see the moment everything came back, wicked filth playing out across his facial features like a dirty puppet show.

"I remember... and I repeat, where are you going?"

"Just... I have work." I tried to head toward the door, but a look from Nay sent my feet into the kitchen. Refilling my coffee and the cup of water, I dropped into an empty seat between the pair of them. "But I guess it can wait."

"Wise choice. If I had to run after you, there would be bloodshed," Naomi warned, and I waved off her words. I'd have stayed to explain just to erase the looks of confusion and lust from Artie's eyes without her warning.

Well, the confusion at any rate.

I couldn't keep doing this to him.

When he pressed my clothes back to his face, I watched Nay's nose kick into high gear. She scented the air around us and grabbed the collar of my dress, pulling it down.

"I can't believe you'd cover those up. Some of my best work," he beamed proudly while Naomi snickered into her hand. Releasing the collar of my dress, she sat back and looked between us.

"Did you seal the deal this time? I've been smelling your lust for two days now and it would bring me great joy to compare notes on his cock," she smirked when I blushed, but Artie preened with all the plumage of a male peacock.

"We did not..." I sighed with a little too much longing. "And I haven't seen his manhood in the flesh. Just in my head while showering... twice."

His eyes flashed a deeper citrine, something shifting just below the surface, an agitated expression of annoyance... but more. It had a tinge of salty cranberries and left a burnt taste in my mouth.

Jealousy - the word flashed in my head with warning bells and whistles.

"Careful, Peep. You're toying with a real monster." His simmering words did vicious things to my lady parts, and I tried to cross my legs at the onslaught.

He still noticed.

"Insatiable little lamb," he purred.

Gripping my coffee mug, I took a long two-handed drink and tried to think of something, anything, to stop the scalding lava bubbling between my legs.

"Enough, Artemis, we have bigger problems than Penelope's skanky nether regions," Naomi came to my rescue, but not before another sniff. "Damn though... you got it bad. Why are you toying with her so hard?"

"I don't know how to stop," he admitted, and I cocked my head to the side. "You make me feel out of control. Like I'd rip apart the world to be near you... and then all I want to do is be closer. Unfortunately, I flirt like... well, like a guy who's never had to work that hard at flirting."

"It really doesn't matter, though, does it?" I sighed, looking at Artemis. "No matter how close we get, how close we come, you always pull away. You don't want this, do you?"

"Not until we can figure out how to stop me from forgetting," his response, just soft enough for me to hear. "Do you know what it's like to get so close to something you want only to lose it again? Not just the opportunity, but all of it? I had you in my arms for hours yesterday and then it's all gone..."

I nodded slowly, knowing that even though it wasn't the same I'd lost the same thing he had.

"It feels like having parts of you ripped away slowly and the empty spaces never fill, no matter what else is happening in life. I'm a curse, Artie. Don't you get it? Remembering me, being stuck in my orbit, it'll ruin your life. But you're happy, right? I remember that I wanted you to be happy... you look happy!"

"It still feels hollow. You leave a hole in my life every time I'm away from you. It's not until I'm with you I can even breathe without the weight of loss trying to crush me. You aren't a curse, you're my oxygen. Please, don't leave me to suffocate."

I reached out and took his hand, squeezing it tightly.

"What happens when you try to undo it?" Naomi asked and I looked at her with slowly coloring cheeks. "You never tried, did you? Even after we talked yesterday, you didn't try?"

Silence filled the room. Not even the coffee maker dared to drip and break the fragile crystal of quiet that stretched between us. One move and it would all shatter, either ripping us to shreds with its jagged edges, or thawing the wall between us.

"No... I didn't think... I mean, we spent so much time together... why would I need to?"

Grim shifted and put his head in my lap, letting out a soft whimper.

Glancing at the clock over the stove, I winced at the hour.

"Sorry bud," I said, picturing the stainless-steel dish, fresh and clean, on my kitchenette sink. Focusing on the light, the image, every angle, I brought it to me filled with dog kibble from Grim's bag beside my desk. Placing it in front of him, I chanced a look at the rest of the table.

Naomi was staring me down, waiting for me to confess that I was too selfish to take back what I'd done. Artie was pensive, likely reconciling the pain in his life with the mirrored absence in my own.

"I never wanted to hurt you. I thought I was doing the right thing," I whispered, and he nodded but didn't speak. The tickle of impending tears threatened to spill over, and I wasn't sure if they started to fall I'd ever be able to stop them. "I also thought spending so much time together would make a difference."

"Try to take it back," Naomi spoke, reminding us both with a start that we weren't alone in the kitchen. "Remove the charm."

I sagged back in my chair, trying to remember the words I'd spoken all those years ago.

Nothing materialized besides wanting him to be happy and carry my love, even when he no longer knew who I was.

"We might have to do this the hard way..." I said, looking at my hand on top of his. He flipped his palm up, lacing our fingers together. Tracing the back of his hand with my thumb, I wondered if I could distract him enough to skip the part where I proved I wasn't really *that* good at magic. His heat seeped into my palm and through my whole body, filling me with warmth.

"Penny," Artie warned, and I let out a sigh while a slow smirk spread on his lips.

"Shh... working," I whispered, eyes closed. "Also it's involuntary. At this point, I'm not even sure you're not doing it on purpose."

Through our joined hands, I reached into him. Inky shadows

lurched through the space, a powerful struggle and a larger threat. The bear and the horned creature slipped around me like smoke, touching and caressing bits of my mind while I searched him for the small part of my magic I'd left behind.

Everywhere I went, my essence was flanked by his shadows. I wanted to feel scared or threatened, but wherever they touched the lavender haze I saw sifting through his energy, the shadows quieted. In place of the restless energy was a need, raw and powerful, that slipped between my legs and around my neck, clinging to every part of me with the feathered kisses of a lover.

Lover, the shadows repeated back, leading me farther in until a matching light glowed faintly in the distance. I pulled it toward me, attempting to manually uncast a spell made by words I couldn't remember.

The lavender light resisted, weighed down and trapped. As I got closer, two butterflies floated around it, the opalescent sky worm twinning its flight pattern with the obsidian counterpart somehow incapable of touching each other.

They were held apart by my magic and whatever had formed around it, a cage of shifting images that vibrated at a frequency so high it rendered them invisible. Concentrating, I tried to pick just one, squinting and blinking to try and get it into focus. Moving closer and closer, I started to make out a pale shadow cloaked in fire, and then I was falling.

Fire lashed at my skin, the impenetrable black ascended, and a strangled scream died on my lips at the glistening teeth in a hinged rock reaching up, cackling, stretching to devour my essence.

A warm nudge on my leg, followed by another and I felt Grim beneath my other hand. He was real, his love pulling me out to face the trapped magic. Reaching one last time, I could swear it was crying for help.

Letting go, I left a new spot of lavender to comfort his shadows before sliding back out the way I'd gone in, an angry howl from the near invisible crack that lay just beyond the light.

Eyes opening, I studied the man before me and the woman who watched us.

"I can't undo it." I shook my head, trying to make sense of what I'd seen. "Something grew around it... the spell is part of you... or trapped by something or someone else. I'm sorry. How do you feel?"

I released my fingers, but Artie's grip held firm.

"I feel like you're not telling me everything. But with what you've said, there's only one solution," he whispered, sending another shot of liquid lava to my core and a ball of anxiety into my gut. "You can't go anywhere without me until you can reverse the spell."

"What if I can't?" I asked, looking at my pale flesh contrasting against his darker skin tone and trying not to think too hard about how amazing those hands had felt exploring my body.

I swallowed hard when he forced my chin up with his other hand. When our eyes locked, I gasped at the predator looking back.

Beside it, I was defenseless, a tasty morsel that could never get away.

"Then you'll be with me forever."

TWENTY

It was a long walk to my office from Artie's townhouse.

"Our townhouse," Artie corrected, and I snapped my head toward him. "You didn't say anything, it's just written on your face. It's our townhouse. You and me, we're in this together and that is our home."

"What about my…?" I trailed off at his raised eyebrow and let out a sigh. "Fine. I'll move my stuff to your townhouse until we can reverse the spell."

"What stuff, PenPen? You aren't even wearing underwear," he scoffed, a little too loud. A group of teenage girls snickered and made faces in my direction. "Also, you're moving in forever because sleeping in your office can't be good for your back."

"Would you keep it down? I live here, you know," I hissed, but he just laughed and slid an arm around my waist, fingers toying with the hem of my dress. When his first finger grazed my inner thigh, I screamed slightly and shoved him away.

"Public, damnit!"

The group of girls carried on with a game of hopscotch in front of one of the last townhouses on the outer edge of town. I'd always hated this section of town and its never-ending goal of being exactly like something it wasn't. All of the residences were identical, reminiscent of the brick and metal brownstones in movies about New York. Six stairs with a wrought iron handle leading to a maroon front door with a brass knocker.

It had to be brass, since iron would have been discriminatory against fae... though I suspected a few of the town's more "Witches Only" members had made their knockers iron.

People are such assholes.

We crossed the invisible boundary between the residential and commercial parts of town. Ahead of us, Huckleberry Hollow was just waking up. Shopkeepers were rolling up the shades on their windows and steam announced the day's cooking had begun in every food establishment.

Including Naomi's, as she'd left us shortly after the failed spell reversal, with a last reminder to be at Sue's coven meeting tonight, *or else.*

She'd put the address in my phone with a reminder, following it up with an entry in Artie's phone when she realized mine was one more fall away from being a paperweight.

"Let's get you some breakfast. You're always cranky before breakfast," the half-demon offered, and I stubbornly crossed my arms.

"I am not! I'm always cranky before coffee. I'm also always cranky when someone puts my personal business on blast for all the Hollow to hear. Could you..."

The press of his mouth against mine cut off my tirade. Faster than I could process, the man had wrapped an arm around my waist, pulled me against him and delivered a breath stealing kiss.

Mouth still open, his tongue slid easily inside. Tasting like coffee and minty toothpaste, the same as me, I wasn't sure where I ended and he began. Blood rushed to my head, making me lightheaded and a little drunk on the feel of his lips.

A little drunk on him.

When he pulled away a moment later, forehead pressed against mine, all the fight had leaked out of me.

"Are you ready to be nice, little Peep?" He asked softly. I nodded, brushing our noses together. "Good girl."

I shivered despite myself; the praise doing decidedly wicked things to my body. I'd never known about my praise kink until he stumbled upon it yesterday and now all I wanted was him to tell me I was a good girl and give me my reward.

This is so fucked up...

"Now..." He took a step back, bringing my hand with him and lacing our fingers together. "Obviously, you need more coffee. Do you want pastries or sandwiches?"

I stared down at our joined hands.

"Since when do we just... do casual kissing and hand holding?" I asked, more for my benefit than his. "Did I miss a conversation where we define the parameters of this?"

"We don't need parameters. If we have a feeling, we do the feeling. Just roll with it and pick your breakfast, cranky no underpants. I don't abide by the rules of hungry witches."

"Sandwiches. I hate sugar breakfast, it gives me jitters and starvation the whole day. Sugar is delicious, but sometimes you need bacon... and cheese!"

We were walking hand in hand toward a series of restaurants. The facades were the same as they were when we were in high school, frozen in time like Main Street USA in Disneyland but with drastically less magic...

Except our magic is real...

The thought hit me and floated away when the first resident tossed a scornful sneer in my direction. Then another... and another... It reminded me of the first day of school, when all the kids I'd never met immediately moved away upon hearing my name.

It was like being The Boy Who Lived in reverse.

I was The Girl Who Would Death.

Never mind the poor grammar we hadn't yet learned.

"Good morning, Artemis!" Yasmin trilled, gliding over on toothpick stilettos that would shatter my ankle into a million pieces. If not for her hideous personality, I would say she is pretty. Soft blonde hair, pale blue eyes. She was a poster child for the Aryan Nation that had invaded Northern Idaho in the 1990s.

"I was wondering if you could help me with a project? My husband is out of town and he told me to make sure that I was taking care of myself. Unfortunately, I have this itch…"

Moaning on the last word, her back arched while she wedged her way between our joined hands, shoving me until I let go to avoid being body slammed into a light pole. Her neon yellow nails scraped down his arm… marking him.

The pale red marks faded quickly, but I'd still seen them and it could not stand.

My magic surged to the surface, possessive and violent.

Nobody marks what's mine!

The primal scream inside my head burst from my lips with a fury that carried on the wind.

"Do not touch him!"

Wind whipped around me, snarling my hair and hers while Artemis stood rooted and immobile. His body caressed by the same wind that threatened to blow the rest of us away. My anger bubbled up and the howling wind reached a fever pitch that nearly knocked the much smaller woman off her impractical shoes.

"Excuse you, but your weak ass magic…" Yasmin puffed out her chest, the air shimmering around her.

Grim sneezed.

I sneezed.

Artie sneezed.

Nothing else happened.

"Ha!" The villain of my formative years declared in victory while I exchanged looks with my two favorite unrelated males. As quickly as it had risen, my anger and revenge were gone. Looking down, I saw Artemis's finger grazing the back of my hand, every negative emotion leaving through that point of contact.

Since when can he do that??

"How do you like them berries?!?!" Yasmin shouted, and I looked back at her.

"Ha what? What berries?" I asked, and Artie tilted his head in support of my question. The wind had calmed, and in its place a cool breeze that tickled the hair tied at the base of my neck. It was the same sensation radiating from the single point of contact between me and Artie.

"Ha, you don't even know because you probably don't own a mirror but..."

Her face fell when she saw the three of us just standing there. I checked my hands and legs, not seeing any boils or rashes... I still wasn't wearing underwear, so obviously she couldn't give me a wedgie. My feet didn't feel like they had grown a fungus, and my hair was always a disaster, so that wasn't exactly magic.

"Ugh... never mind. Come on Artie, we need to get out of here before her loser-ness wears off on you and you become broke, unloved and scarred," she sniffed at the exposed corner of my burn. "Burn yourself cooking? Or do you even bother heating food before you shove it in your face hole?"

Scorn and judgment played out on her face, but no satisfaction at the sight of an injury I'd credited to her for fifteen years. It was both disappointing and a massive relief.

It wasn't her...

Artemis looked at me, rage behind his eyes that would have incinerated a weaker woman... or a less stupid one if Yasmin's vacant expression was any indication of how much time she spent aware of the world around her.

"Well... there goes that hypothesis," I said, darting my gaze between her and my arm. My fake boyfriend, who was once again behaving as though all of this was real, caught on immediately. "Didn't you promise me cheese and bacon?"

Artie chuckled at Yasmin's immediate scowl.

"I believe I did. And coffee..."

Sidestepping the irate former prom queen, he wrapped his arms around my waist and rested his chin on my shoulder. Pressing us against each other from pelvis to shoulder, I tried not to rub myself against him.

While I'd never been particularly feline, the urge to rub my scent all over him was strong.

My scent and... other things.

His arms stiffened, and I didn't need to confirm that my scent was exactly what he'd gotten.

"Anyway... not nice seeing you. Hope to never do it again... give my insincere-est regards to your mother," I chattered, backing away so that my ass was practically glued to Artie's cock region... not that I was thinking about that.

Nope, I had to remain in control of my scent, or my underwear wouldn't be the only piece of clothing I was no longer wearing.

"This isn't over, you fat psychotic..."

Artemis let out a threatening growl and Yasmin shut her mouth, eyes wide in shock as she realized the demon bear wasn't on her team. Whether she still believed I'd enchanted him to feel protective of me or had somehow been cured of that delusion was anyone's guess.

"You can't growl at me! I own this town!" She took a step back, and then another, when he let out a snort of derision. "Don't you know who I am?"

Her exclamations were like a broken record, continually skipping over any real threat and relying exclusively on name and status to see her through.

"I can buy and sell this town, Yasmin. Get out of my face," he snapped, and I tried not to applaud outwardly when she turned around and half-ran, half stomped up the road in a huff.

"Goddess, I hate her," I muttered, turning at the sound of my name.

"Penny!" Naomi called, coming out of Gnomewich with a brown paper bag. "I was going to help you take out the trash, but it looks like you beat me to it. I'm so proud of you! Your prize!"

She held out the bag with a faux bow and threw in a Middle Ages English accent for fun.

"Bacon, egg and cheese sandwich, milady."

I took the bag with a curtsey, and then an awkwardly enthusiastic hug when she produced a very large coffee. Since I was wearing a man as a backpack, he also had to hug her. Then slobbery kisses from Grim, payment for the smell of bacon I was sure she put in there for him.

"Yes, there's extra bacon in there for you," she told Grim, confirming my suspicions and planting a kiss on his nose. Eyeing my crotch area, I saw her give a small sniff and then roll her eyes. "Put some damn underpants on, woman! Short people have eyes too and I don't want to explain to my wife how I saw another woman's cooter!"

I crossed my legs and gave her an apologetic look.

"Sorry..." I squirmed in Artie's arms, but after a hiss of breath, he clamped his arms around me to keep me steady. "What?"

Something prodded my lower back, and I sucked in a breath of my own.

"And for you," Nay continued, as though we hadn't just been nearly fornicating in public. She held out a second bag that looked a little heavier. "A breakfast burrito with extra fungus and guacamole."

The half-bear licked his lips.

I contemplated barfing.

"You would ruin guacamole with 'shrooms? What is wrong with..." Her eyes cut to me, narrow slits that threatened to take back my sandwich. "People who don't appreciate good culinary masterpieces by amazing chefs with incredible business savvy and..."

"You're laying it on a little thick," she smirked, but I knew she appreciated the compliment... at least the parts that were true.

Everyone knows there's nothing *fun* about being force-fed *fungus*.

"You should probably head to your office; I think you have customers."

Her tone was conspiratorial, and I looked between her and the man behind me before finally braving a glance at my psychiatric practice.

A line of potential patients congregated near the door, clutching insurance cards. From this distance, none of them looked mentally disturbed. At least half were wearing cheer uniforms and the preppy attire of the socially accepted.

"Why don't they have boils and hooked noses?" I wondered aloud, curious if my spell had failed... and if it had, would the spell on Artie go away on its own too?

It hasn't yet...

Miracles could happen.

"They must be patients!" Artie beamed, so excited that I nearly toppled over when he started moving that direction while still attached to me. "Come on! We're going to help people today!"

Panicking, I looked back over my shoulder at Naomi, who simply blew me a kiss and called out, "I'm sure you'll be brilliant at helping people. But you still need underwear!"

TWENTY-ONE

PENELOPE

Google's search bar featured dancing circles that reminded me the Olympics were coming, while I typed *Is there a justifiable homicide in Idaho?*

There were 200 pages of results and none of them answered my question, so I tried again.

Can I legally murder someone in Idaho?

Scanning the results, I tried not to hear Artemis in the other room. The first batch of young women had filled out the paperwork, submitted their copays, and used the hour to ogle and preen before the almighty Artemis Nita-Nusi.

How *this* many people knew about hockey when this town didn't even have an ice rink was beyond me. They'd all appeared with jerseys and selfie sticks, making duck faces and heavy-handed passes at the male specimen occupying my reception desk.

A desk which now housed a computer monitor I have no bank charges for but looks too new to have "fallen off the back of a truck". New technology that also somehow had every bit of software a medical practice needed, including real scheduling software, a medical coding program to make sure I got paid, and a patient chart database that had security up and out the wazoo...

A place I was uncertain on the benefit of securing, but my wazoo was officially wearing underwear, so I'd accomplished one thing today... not that it was clean anymore.

Artemis's innate ability to send arousal coursing through my veins and to the very end of every nerve hadn't dwindled. Even now, his voice floating down the hall was enough to have my lady engine humming to life.

And his voice never stopped talking.

The gaggle of females had been replaced by yet another, slightly older, group that included a few out of the closet young men. All of them armed with questions and pleas for information about a life on the outside. Though not that far away, few of them thought they'd ever get to see more than the farthest boundaries of the Hollow.

Which would have made them perfect candidates for psychiatric services, but no one wanted to talk to me. A situation that turned out to be for the best as I fought to keep my jealous revenge magic under control.

Instead, Artie kept entertaining a steady stream of paying visitors with a steady stream of chatter. He talked about the things he loved, like movies and books. Told them about the supernatural league and resurfacing memories about puberty with a succubus demon half and a best friend who gave him his first kiss.

A story which elicited a few too many "oooohs" every time he told it.

The more time we spent together, the more he remembered and, as he shared with them about our life together, the ache in my chest grew stronger.

For years, I could pretend the memories were a dream. An imagined past with the boy who grew into a man filled with magic fingers and kisses. While no one else knew I was part of his life, we were a secret fairytale that belonged only to me.

Now he was sharing our story with the world and in it, I found the pieces of my heart and soul I'd buried in the wilderness as I made my escape. Every fresh memory that he solidified as loving and wonderful from a new perspective was a dagger into the careful narrative I'd built my life around.

He was proving that I wasn't meant to be alone.

Showing the world that I was loveable.

Bringing positivity and energy into a life that had been bleak and robotic.

All of my crumbling reality narrated to the soundtrack of gasping coos from his adoring fans.

Worst soundtrack ever.

I was fairly certain that charging for his company was insurance fraud. Artemis had neither training nor skills to help the neuro spicy and magically afflicted, so he was just providing nothing more than entertainment for the low rate of $200 an hour, like a sex worker, but with pants on.

But since it was Artemis and the patients committing the fraud, I was fairly certain the IRS wasn't coming for me, and I couldn't afford to turn away paying clients.

Magical and mind-numbing alike, the bean counters wouldn't pin these beans on me. So long as I didn't run out there screaming or send their insurance companies a thank you note for the money I hadn't earned, I would be fine... financially, anyway.

Psychologically, I was in trouble.

Every ten minutes like clockwork, actual clockwork since he used a timer, Artie would walk into my office and spend exactly five minutes, I *also* set a timer, in physical and auditory contact with me until I kicked him out and a new batch of young ladies and gentlemen arrived to entertain and be entertained by him until the timers went off again.

It would be so easy to love him.

The man was lovable.

His gentle touches, the little gestures like bringing me coffee and making sure I drank water. Telling me memories of us that even I hadn't remembered but were imprinted forever in my mind as a reminder that what existed between us was real.

Our friendship, however damaged, was real.

And the fact I could crush it by leaving the room for even a few minutes and send the whole foundation of us crumbling into nothing was too much.

We needed to be separated before either of us turned a corner we couldn't walk back from.

Except that corner was squarely in my rearview mirror and I no longer knew if I could let him go.

I switched back to Googling legal penalties for permanent solutions to temporary problems.

Do you really want him to forget you again? The part of me that had longed for friendship and connection whispered into the dirty slideshow my lizard hindbrain had on repeat. She was down to ride that man into the depths of hell, all else be damned.

But could you let him go after?

A soft knock interrupted my scrolling of the results for *Are lobotomies invasive procedures?*

"It's the next door..." I started, giving directions to the bathroom. It was the only question asked of me today by anyone other than Artie. My eyes went to the woman in my door frame. She was a little younger than the groups who'd been coming in, maybe 12 or 13, and dressed in jeans and an oversized hoodie. Bright grey eyes peered through oversized glasses, and she clutched a book to her chest with my business card held out between two fingers.

"I'm sorry?" Her soft voice was the most calming sound I'd heard today.

"You aren't looking for the bathroom?"

"No, I..." she glanced down the hall and then dropped her voice even lower. "I need to talk to someone..."

Her sleeve slid up, and I saw the edges of a plastic hospital bracelet on her wrist.

"Sure, come on in," I said, gesturing toward the chair in my office. She wasn't holding a clipboard, but I could see small red indents in her fingers from tightly gripping a pen for too long. A blinking icon on my computer drew my attention, and I clicked it to see the scanned intake forms.

The man was efficient, and a killer admin. If the supernatural league ever kicked him out, I could definitely hire him to manage my paperwork... assuming I could afford him.

I gave my undivided attention to the girl in front of me, letting her speak in her own time.

I'd had one of those bracelets at her age, too, and no one had known what to say then. But everything they had said made it worse.

"Your card was in my bag at the…" she glanced toward the open door and lowered her voice again. "Hospital"

I waved at the door and a shimmering veil filled the space.

"Privacy screen," I explained when she just stared at it. "I can't close the door, long story, but no one can hear what's happening in here."

A braying laugh carried down the hallway and we both winced.

"It only works one way, sadly. In my adolescent years, I needed to hear impending danger… not important."

I heard Artie's footsteps as he made his way up the hall. Leaning against the frame, he peered into the room, running a single finger along the magical barrier. Instead of fighting, he caressed the magic. I felt his caress across the room and into the center of my being.

Shuddering, I looked at the patient, who was also watching, wondering what to do next.

"How long is he going to do that?" My patient asked, and I shifted uncomfortably as I scanned her intake papers. Maddison Yates was 13, the child of a witch and a human, born outside of town and her family emigrated inside the boundaries when she started showing magical powers.

"Five minutes, then he'll go back out into the lobby," I answered, coming up short at the "reason for visit" box. She was sent to the hospital after experiencing vivid hallucinations, disorientation and sudden thoughts of self-harm.

"Can you describe the supposed hallucinations?" I asked, then winced. "Sorry, I'm a good psychiatrist, but a crappy socializer. Why don't you start where you're most comfortable, Maddison? We'll get to the interrogation after."

My patient tilted her head to the side and offered me a genuine smile that lit up her whole face. The hunched shoulders of her hoodie relaxed, and I got a sinking feeling that I was the first person to question the diagnosis.

"You can call me Maddy," she said, and I nodded my agreement at her chosen name. "You don't believe it was a hallucination, do you?"

I smiled at her and shrugged.

"Depends on where you were and what you'd eaten before it occurred. If you did drugs, maybe. But I'm leaning heavily toward not likely. If you don't mind me telling you what to do instead of leading you there like they teach in med school, start with the beginning of the timeline and end with your arrival at the Hellscape... I mean... Hospital."

Nodding, Maddy took a moment to compose her thoughts. Adjusting her glasses and setting down the book she'd been clutching, the young woman wiped her palms on her jeans and made eye contact with the space above my left ear to begin.

"I wasn't born here. My mom moved us just outside of town about four years ago and everything had seemed... normal in an off-center kind of way. The other kids wouldn't really talk to me, the curse of being an outsider, but some other non-Hollow kids moved outside of town and eventually we all became friends with one another and a small band of half-shifter kids who lived between the hollow and the pack lands. Last year, when I turned 13, I noticed something weird. About the town, the residents, the... energy? Like, something was drawing the magic out of all the residents, and they all seemed... sick isn't the right word, but I don't have a better one. The other kids in my group felt something off, but most of them are shifters or magical beings in their own right, so they feel magic differently. A few weeks ago, I turned 14. It's the age my mom told me my full magic would come in and the second it did, nothing looked right anymore."

She swallowed a little, looking around a little lost.

Opening the fridge beneath my desk and pulling out a water bottle, I handed it to Grim. Sending it to her by magic would have been easier, but I didn't want to startle her. Grim gave me a meaningful gaze, looking between us to let me know he thought the same as I did.

This would not be a hallucination, and it wasn't going to be news.

Grim carried the water bottle to the girl, cradling it in his teeth until he sat beside her. Maddy took the bottle, cracking the lid and taking a long drink while she absently stroked his flat head.

Another benefit of canine waiters: stress relief. He should totally count as a tax deduction.

"From the corner of my eyes, I kept catching movement that would be gone when I looked at it. Areas of town seemed to redirect me, I guess, like they always had, but I was aware of it. When I started fighting the sensation of redirection, something... sinister moved in. All the sharp corners and edges became clearer. I felt compelled to walk in front of moving cars... My heart felt like I was constantly sprinting."

Maddy paused, taking a drink of water. Her hand shaking slightly as she went to set it down, the crinkling bottle spurned Grim into action. He used his head to brace her arm, guiding it safely back to the table and then hefting his oversized head into her lap.

"I told my mom. She went to the Council. I don't know what was said or how, but I ended up in the hospital. A doctor would come by once a day with a potion for me to drink, but..." she shifted nervously, eyeing the privacy screen. "But I never did. I was packing up to break out when your card appeared with my socks in the patient bag. Then the pandemonium covered my escape."

My mind was whirring as it attempted to process what she had told me.

"What did the doctor look like?" I asked, wondering how I could make him suffer.

"Blonde hair, kind of like the guys in the band JT was in before he brought sexy back. You gave him neon yellow warts and a bouncy butt... it was pretty great. Some friends on the street level sent me a video."

I nodded while she laughed. It was a small, almost sad sound, that once again took me back to another time in my life.

A sadder time.

Before Artie... I glanced at the door, staring at the man leaning against the frame, watching me. I knew he couldn't hear us, but he still made a T-Swift heart hand in my direction. With one last meaningful look, he went back toward my lobby to a loud cheer from whoever waited there.

"It wasn't that bad... no one hurt me," Maddy said, almost to herself.

"You're rationalizing to make a difficult situation bearable. Don't give them an out," I sighed, and she looked at me with a head tilt that Grim shared, both encouraging me to explain and over share. "They don't deserve to get away with it."

Too many events she described mirrored my own. Not just from growing up, but these past few days as well. It was all eerily familiar.

"I think he believed in the diagnosis... "

Her scrunched face suggesting that of the two of us, she was likely the more compassionate person. But I needed to be sure it was real, that she wasn't planted or...

Geez, I'm paranoid..

I reached out into the room, wanting to touch her magic and get a sense of it, but Grim sneezed lightly and I looked at him, aware of the prolonged silence. I switched back to the patient and tried to get back on track.

"Where is your mom? What did she say when you got home from the hospital?" I asked, not sure where to go from here without parental input. Grim was right. I couldn't search her energy without permission. It was an unwritten rule. A rule that maybe should have been written... but the only paper I had was a prescription pad.

I couldn't ask her for permission, either. Because minors were like women. We're technically people, but we weren't allowed to make decisions about our lives, or our bodies, because of some papers written by geriatric white dudes.

"She's in the lobby with the hockey guy..." Maddy chewed on the inside of her cheek, eyeing the privacy screen again. "When I got home, she was surprised to see me. She'd thought I was at a sleepover at a friend's house. She had no recollection of going to the council, of me being in the hospital... it was all just... gone."

TWENTY-TWO

PENELOPE

My phone chimed with an incoming message from my mom.

"Finally!" I sighed, grabbing the device and opening my messages... and then squinting through the cracks in the screen to read her response. "Errrabada hoopla unicorn?"

Grim lifted his head and blinked blearily at me.

In the hall, Artemis was wrapping up his last celebrity meet and greet for the day and a few of the stragglers were getting clingy.

"How are we going to break this spell so I can go to work alone again?" I asked Grim. His eyes went wide, eyebrows moving imperceptibly in time to the steady tap of his tail on the cushioned dog bed. "You don't get it. I'm not used to this much togetherness. Eventually, he'll get tired of me. And then what? I have to get this close so he can leave me again?"

"I will not get tired of you, Peep," Artie said, strolling into the room and setting the office keys on my desk. "Stop freaking out about stuff that isn't going to happen. We have all the time in the world to figure this out. We're in this together."

"You don't know that. What happens when your demon half needs to feed?" I asked, watching him stalk around my desk to the chair I was sitting in. He spun it around, slowing on the second pass to lean down, hands resting on the arms of my chair.

Our noses were centimeters from one another, his breath a cinnamon swirl I wanted to taste.

"Well... he seems to like you. Guess we'll have to come to an agreement about how best to manage that," he rubbed his nose against mine, a derivation of the Inuit kunik. After a day of gentle touches and affectionate caressing with tension relieving massage, it felt... tame.

Boring.

Unsatisfying.

"That's not what you said this morning," I countered, petulance outweighing pride per usual.

"I lied."

I jutted my chin forward until his lips brushed against mine, the contact all the motivation I needed. Stealing a quick kiss, I rolled my chair away before I could give into *all* of my urges.

Some of which might be felonies considering the enormous window behind Artie with a group of teen girls, cameras at the ready.

"That new window, besides being crooked, doesn't hold a privacy spell. I need to talk to my mom," I announced, standing from the chair and forcing him upright. "And you... need to not bend over near windows. Mrs. Theremin is going to have a heart attack."

He turned around to see our town's septuagenarian widow. The woman was leaning on her walker, eyes half glazed over, licking her lips and gumming her tongue. If her hands weren't firmly gripping the aluminum rails of her walking aid, I had a feeling I wouldn't be the only one on the verge of exhibitionism and public indecency.

"Did she just mouth 'that's going in the spank bank'?" He asked, taking two big steps back from the window and drawing the blinds closed.

"Probably. I heard she's been hitting the horny goat weed pretty hard recently. So you might have options if I'm unavailable," I snickered into my hand as I knelt beside my plastic tub of clothes. Though I had two tubs and five pairs of shoes, there was no order from which to easily find or select an outfit. While the mock neck dress worked for... well work, it wasn't something I'd wear to visit my mother.

Especially not when I planned to grill her about whether or not she remembered sending me to the psych ward of a hospital when I was 12. For the third time since I was home, I had to lament the lack of chain mail and ruby crusted swords in my wardrobe.

I really need to invest in 15th Century Armor...

"We should take these to our house," Artie said, easily hefting one bin while I rummaged through the other. He nudged me away from the second bin, my hands still holding two articles of clothing, popped the lid on and stacked it on top of the other. Both easily balanced on a single arm.

Goddess, help me, that's hot... if I ever need to move, he'll save me hours.

"Can't right now, I have to go see my mom and demand answers."

"What fun," he intoned sarcastically. "We can take these home and go there after."

"You know, if you were a Golden Retriever shifter instead of a bear shifter, I could just add a bed for you on the floor next to Grim and I wouldn't have to move out of my office," I commented, trying to de-sexy the sexy man holding nearly everything I owned in one hand. "Then you would look all cute and happy following me around. People might talk to me just to get to pet you."

"I already look cute and happy following you around," he answered, giving me the full body once over that sent goosebumps shivering over every inch of my skin. "And if you're a good girl, I'll let you pet me. Now, let's go, PenPen. You can hang up your clothes like a civilized person and then we'll visit your mother if you really want to."

"I don't want to visit her. I don't want to be civilized," I said, taking off my dress and tossing it at his head. I pulled on the pair of jeans and a sweater, the neckline revealing a few of the marks Artie had left along my clavicle this morning.

I was baiting him on purpose, and I felt like a goddess when he answered me in a heated tone.

"What do you want to be?"

I let my eyes take the long way up Artie's legs, admiring the way his slacks showcased his thick muscular thighs and curved ass while keeping his junk discreetly covered in... whatever state matched that tone.

By the time I got to the tattoos on his forearm, the man was vibrating with a need that reverberated back against my own. With a slow, methodical swipe of my tongue, I licked my lip just as our eyes locked.

"I want to be feral, Artie," I purred, relishing the heady scent that hit me just before he dropped the totes and wrapped his hand around my neck. Leading me backwards, Artemis pinned me to the wall, pressing his hips against mine while his hand added just enough pressure to make my lips tingle.

"Careful, little Bo Peep," he hummed, lips meeting my jaw while the hand at my throat shifted to cup the base of my skull. "You don't have any sheep. Just a very hungry bear and we can't go all the way until you promise me I can remember it tomorrow."

Rocking back on his heels, the bear shoved his hips against mine. Through both of our jeans, I felt him—rock hard and ready to deliver.

"I didn't ask you to be gentle, Artemis. I said I want to be feral," I punctuated the statement by wrapping both arms around his neck and jumping on him, legs wrapping around his waist so that our good spots lined up *juuuust* right.

Our mouths crushed together. Every tender moment ripped away in a greedy rush of lips and teeth. His hands kneaded the flesh at my backside while I took advantage of their preoccupation to relieve him of his shirt. My mouth left his long enough to get it over his head before we were back at it, tongues fighting for dominance and taking no prisoners as we pillaged and plundered the other.

My back slammed into the wall, head protected from impact by the hands that slid up my ribs, fingers leaving scorching hot trails, until my sweater joined Artie's shirt on the floor.

"Cold!" I squeaked, my naked back against the plaster wall.

"Not for long," he snarled, rocking his hips again so that his cock brushed against my clit through the fabric of our jeans.

I let out a moan, and he did it again, fingers gripping my love handles to use, as their name implied.

"Beg me, Penelope," he rocked us again, the pressure building despite the lack of contact. "Beg me to fuck you with my fingers, my tongue... I want to feel you cum all over me."

A pitiful moan was all that came out.

"Beg. Me." He growled, and I tried to form words.

"Artie I..."

Two sharp raps on the door frame preceded a very dignified throat clear.

"Penelope, I sincerely hope this isn't the reason you brought me here."

"Mom!" I squeaked, pressing my chest against Artie's, covering my breasts while he laughed under me. The subtle jostling being a decidedly inappropriate sensation for this situation.

"I didn't invite you here!"

"I told you I was coming over," she sighed. "Did you even read my message?"

"Not exactly... my phone is slightly illegible." I slid down Artemis, swinging my legs to the ground and turning away to keep my mom from seeing the shabby state of my bra. Taking a couple deep breaths, I tried to slow my heart rate from a lust induced stroke back down to being in a room with my mother... a whole different form of stroke.

I thunked my head against the wall, wondering how I managed to be constantly stuck between a rock and a hard place.

A hand slid between my head and the wall, gripping my chin and pulling it back. Neck stretched toward him, Artie gave me a brow raise of warning.

I was apparently not supposed to be damaging the contents of my brain box.

I rolled my eyes at him, and he tightened his grip, dragging me backwards. When I was once again almost touching him, my sweater dropped over my head and he pulled it firmly between us.

Teeth almost grazing my ear, he whispered, "This isn't over, but roll your eyes at me again and I'll show you what happens to bad girls who don't follow directions."

Taking a giant step back, Artemis grabbed his own shirt from the floor and pulled it on while I considered cursing my mother and praying to the Goddess for him to take it back off.

"Penelope!" I flinched and turned back to the tall blonde. "You need to focus. What was so urgent?"

Taking a deep breath, I centered myself and counted to ten.

Then again, because ten was a little too close to how many inches might be lingering just behind that zipper. A thought that wasn't helping and...

"Penny," Artemis warned, and I bit back a sigh.

"Right. Mom. Do you want something to drink?"

She was still standing in the doorway. Her black skirt suit looked custom tailored, featuring a modest knee length pencil skirt that would be hell if you had thighs that touch. Underneath, she wore a white button down with red stripes and a scarf tie knotted to the side like an ascot that sat beneath her collar.

Crossing to my desk, I pulled a couple bottles of water out of the mini fridge under my desk, tossing one at Artemis. He easily caught it, but my mom declined the one pointed in her direction.

"I'll take coffee if you have it," she said primly, and I scoffed at the implication that I would ever run out. Tossing another bottle to Artemis, he poured it into the drip maker while I stared at the woman in front of me.

"Tell me about my psychiatric hospitalization."

"Your... what?" She sputtered, but her eyes wouldn't meet mine.

Like Grim when he had something in his mouth that I would take away if he showed it to me. Walking to the plastic container in the corner, I took a scoop of food out and waited for her to give into the silence while giving Grim dinner.

She didn't fill the silence.

"Easy way or hard way, mom. Dad isn't the only one with ways of making people talk," I warned, and she glared daggers at me from the doorway she'd yet to enter all the way.

"Don't threaten me, Penelope. I brought you into this world and I can take you back out," she held up a single manicured finger. The short almond shape would have been more threatening if it weren't a somber, and perfectly appropriate DMV beige.

The coffee maker signaled its completion, and Artemis prepared three paper cups of coffee. All three with lids, a social cue that this wasn't meant to take long, and we'd be leaving soon.

Joke's on him.

"Then tell me about when I was 12, and they locked me up on the fourth floor for hallucinations and..." I tried to remember if they'd ascribed self-harm and disorientation to my history or if hallucinations had been enough to hold me in the first year of the new century. "Maybe it had just been hallucinations then..."

Beneath the porcelain mask of perfection, I watched my mom's jaw clench and unclench. Back at her side, my mom's fingers were tapping against her thigh, beating a silent tattoo to the rhythm of her own anxiety.

She'd yet to take a single drink of her coffee and I drained mine in three gulps, gesturing to Artemis for another. Like a gifted bartender, he obliged to hit me again.

"I have all night mom," I said in my best parental voice... a deeply uncomfortable sound I was unprepared to find in my repertoire. Before she could speak, Artie's phone and mine let out a series of reminder sounds, and I checked the clock. "Scratch that. I have thirty minutes. And if I'm late to this coven meeting, Naomi will cut me off of the quesadilla list."

"What coven? That new one outside of town?" My mom asked, looking between the half-demon and her daughter. She finally took a drink of her coffee while I killed the one Artie had prepared for himself.

"Yes. Don't change the subject, mom. You didn't know about the abandoned street before last night, did you?" I asked, deciding I might need to start with a different tack to lead into the whole *why did you let your daughter get locked up* thing.

"Not exactly," she huffed out a breath and finally entered my office. Sitting primly on the edge of the armchair, she crossed her legs at the ankles, showcasing T-strap heels in a boring beige color that almost perfectly matched her skin tone.

In the growing silence, I tapped my wrist to egg her on. Instead of speaking, she took another long, pointed drink of coffee. Setting it on the floor beside her foot, she spoke, a reminder that, yet again, I was on her timetable and she was running the show.

"You are impossible. I didn't know about the street, when I saw your memories though... I recognized the timeline. You didn't come to me or the Council about what you'd seen. The hallucinations were an accusation lodged against you by Yasmin and her mother. You had tried to defend yourself against an attack by her... something about torn homework or a library book. You were accused of imagining things and sent to speak with someone... it was before this private practice was in place, so it must have been someone in the hospital. They declared you unstable, the early stages of your magic manifesting a dangerous image that compromised your mental stability," her even, emotionless cadence was as much a gut punch as the words she spoke.

"So you let them take me?"

My voice didn't break, and I was secretly proud of myself for matching her indifference.

"Of course I didn't let them take you! I knew better than to trust the Council. But I couldn't stop them," she snapped, the first crack in a mask I thought impenetrable.

"Why not? You're a witch! You're a member of one of the most powerful magical lines! Didn't you always tell me that Marino magic was unmatched? Isn't that why you didn't change your name? So everyone would know just how much power you wield?"

"No, I don't," she breathed the words like a secret I wasn't meant to know.

"You don't what?" I asked, but beside me, Artemis was having a revelation and I looked between the pair of them. "Someone clue me in."

"She doesn't have power," Artemis said, and I stared at him. "That's the secret jealousy and longing that takes over whenever you see your child. You don't have the same magical strength."

My mom nodded, staring at the hands balled in her lap.

"How do you know?" I asked Artemis, and he tilted his head in my direction.

"Demon magic. I've... I've never been able to use it before, but these past few days, when I'm with you... It's the magic demons take into soul deals. We can see the biggest weaknesses and desires in humans. We use it to convince them to trade us their life force for that which they desire most. Except..."

He took a long, deep breath, and my mom stiffened. Her eyes snapped to him, anger lashing out at him in icy waves that coated the air in a bitter spice that clung to my airway.

"I don't want to harm my daughter, Artemis. None of this is because I want to steal what is hers." She looked in my direction, truth creasing the lines of her face. A silent apology passed between us and my breath stuck in my chest.

"Before you were born, the area was growing. It was growing and the people coming here weren't safe... they came with their bigotry and their narrow-minded beliefs. There wasn't much to do but wait it out. Except... two years before you were born, there was an attack on the Hollow."

My mom began rubbing her temples, face in her palms. Muffled words still drifted out of hands fighting to keep them in.

"A deal was struck. We gave our magic to the Council, bound ourselves to the land, and they would be powerful enough to make the Hollow disappear. We wouldn't be on maps, we wouldn't be visible no matter who or what came looking for us, the Council alone capable of reversing the magic. But it was a lie." She sat back, hands at her side with palms up. "All of it was a lie. The threat hadn't found us, but something else did. Something else that wanted magic or blood in exchange for immortality for the Council. They sold out all the residents for themselves and manipulated everyone into believing that continuing the pattern was the only way for us to survive."

"So, my magic... why isn't it affected? What does this have to do with the parts of town no one can find?"

My head was swimming. I couldn't piece everything together, but it was all starting to make sense.

"Because you left before the first Blood Moon after your 18th birthday. The ceremony always happens on the blood moon, but your magic isn't yours to give until you turn eighteen... how or why, no one knows. They tried taking it from young witches earlier, but it can't be done. Everyone who stays must pay in blood and forfeit their bond to the earth for the perceived safety offered by the Council. But after that first blood moon, you have a choice. It's why you had to go that night, the night of the new moon. You needed to leave," she sniffed and reached for a tissue.

"How did you know I was planning to leave?" I asked, wondering if I had said something to anyone besides Artie before I left. "Why have you been giving Artie shit for not knowing I was going?"

"I thought he would go with you. I didn't know about the Alpha command." She tossed the tissue into the can while I looked back at Artemis. "I thought he would protect you, even without a bear. My power to protect you was gone, but he still could have."

"What alpha command? You said nothing about an alpha command. You said..." I struggled to bring back that night. My face scrunched in concentration; I fought the fog of time and rose-colored memory. "You said to wait a couple of days. That you wanted to tell me something but couldn't. Not yet... Do you remember?"

Head shaking, Artemis closed his eyes.

"If I'd known you'd leave without him, I might have waited," my mom said, standing up and smoothing her skirt.

"Waited on what?" I asked, studying her face. With a quick flick of her eyes, she looked at my arm.

Just a millisecond, but it was all I needed.

"You..." I started, but Artemis wasn't using his words. The man leapt forward and just as my mom screamed, I threw magic at him. Trapping him just millimeters from my mom. Claws and teeth bared, he fought my magic while the older woman stood perfectly still.

"What are you doing?" I shouted at her, sweating with the effort of holding back my best friend.

Artemis was fighting me, demanding blood retribution on my behalf, and I was losing my grip against his beast.

My mom glanced at me, still frozen in confused horror.

"What-"

"Pen-" Artemis roared, cutting her off.

"Don't talk! Just run!" I screamed, watching her heel disappear through the doorway just as I fell to my knees, letting Artie go free.

TWENTY-FOUR

Anxiety slowed my feet as I shuffled down an unfamiliar street, weighed down by thoughts and memories. My hands hadn't stopped shaking, my energy wiped out from trying to prevent a homicide. Instead of heading home to dive headfirst into a quart of ice cream, home being a relative term since we had been at my office before I left and I technically still lived there on paper, I was off to a coven meeting. A group of strangers gathered together for... whatever covens do... drink wine hopefully.

None of them would know about blood moons, magical leeching, or the scar on my arm from my mother. My own freaking mother had scarred me forever, and she didn't even feel bad.

I couldn't even process the truth or the betrayal.

Couldn't link my past and present reality to a future or I would scream until the world ended.

Not that the world was all that great. It was, in fact, a shitty world that was forcing me to be wearing shoes and pants while processing trauma without the aid of liquor or ice cream.

Goddess, I needed ice cream.

I had very little experience with covens, so whether or not they'd be able to help me upon arrival was an unknown, but I was damn sure ice cream would make me feel better.

Though my time in college had been better than my time in high school, I struggled to connect with other witches. Shifters were easier to befriend, but I was constantly waiting for them to find the same defects that kept people from wanting to be my friends back home. Any friend I made had to be kept at arm's length, including my roommate.

She'd been a witch from the east coast, socially well-adjusted with emotional maturity and intelligence. Her found-family coven had welcomed me into their meetings, but they were similarly unafflicted with enough emotional baggage to sink a submarine. It made spell casting with Louise and her group a little harder than I cared to admit, since petty vengeance wasn't on their to-do lists.

Strolling along the sidewalk, I tried to psych myself up to sit in a room with other witches and pretend to be normal. Studying the more nontraditional dwellings sitting on the right side of the street, I wondered how someone came to live out here. None of it conformed or matched the stylized architecture of downtown. Everything was still orderly, but somehow freer.

Open.

There was a whole chunk of forest behind the houses on the right that I'd never explored. Beneath the waxing gibbous moon, light glinted off of the needles in tall conifers, a breeze sending the fallen leaves dancing along the pavement before they retreated into the shadowy woods, their flaming colors swallowed by the canopy of trees. Unfamiliar magic floated out, the same path the leaves traveled but in reverse, bringing instead a hint of fae magic and sprinkling of woodland nymph, a subtle reminder that Naomi lived here and more than witches moved in the night.

Partway down the street, the air shifted. Like coming up from underwater, I could suddenly breathe easier. An invisible weight fell from my shoulders and the pressure in my ears cleared to allow the spirited singing of insects to fill the night air.

Turning on the spot, I looked back.

The center of town was invisible amid the maze of houses. On this side of the barrier, every home looked unique, the townhouses sporting arbitrary awnings and porch decorations that challenged the uniformity and singular mindset enforced by the council.

I stared at the small space between where I stood and where I'd crossed over. Small tendrils of warmth seemed to push me away, disguising the uniformity on the other side with a physical warning to keep out.

Grim's nose worked incessantly. He sniffed toward the barrier and let out a soft growl at the empty air. Raising his hackles, Grim inched away from the barrier.

"I think we've left town," I murmured, shaking off the unsettled feeling and continuing forward to the fourth townhouse on the left.

While its neighbors felt empty, Sue's house emanated warmth and life. I could sense the bright magic inside, carrying me closer until I had grasped the metal knocker and banged it against the door, an unbidden plea for sanctuary and community.

Dramatic much, Quasi-modo? But it had been a long day, so I let myself be dramatic... at least on the inside.

Before the knocker had even settled again, the door was pulled open by a short woman with a silver bob. She was twice my age, half my height and based on the no-nonsense look in her eyes, unlikely to be on board with petty revenge magic or mutational spells that gave assholes exploding hemorrhoids.

"You must be... what the hell is that?"

I followed her gaze over my shoulder to where Artie was floating in a magical bubble four feet off the ground. It was a shimmering purple and unlike physically holding him back, containing him didn't rob me of energy I didn't have. It wasn't strictly necessary. His rage went down after she was out of sight. But there was a chance, always a chance, he'd go after her.

And like before, I needed a break.

But I couldn't leave him, couldn't risk him forgetting again.

Love is the worst, I grumbled internally.

Unfortunately, this was definitely love and I wasn't sure it was just the love for my best friend anymore.

"It's my concession to murder. Not mine, or his, but murder none-theless. I did a lot of Googling today and it's definitely illegal. Murder, not the bubble." We watched him bouncing around the purple sphere like it was his own personal bounce house. He rolled along the side, dropping to his knees and then back to his very firm ass. The snug jeans were slowly getting lower and lower.... Heat flooded my face and made a steady path south, lighting up my sensitive nipples and reintroducing the throbbing ache between my legs that got stronger by the hour. "That, unfortunately, is legal... though it hardly seems natural for a man to look that hot."

A low whistle set my skin on edge, and I turned back to see a younger witch, pointed hat on her head with a pair of blinking eyes just above a weird metal rod over her left ear. Her gaze was squarely planted on Artie's exposed ass, a bit of her tongue poking out, chest rising and falling rapidly.

My energy built, an involuntary reaction that I was too weak to control. A vibrating current crackled between my fingers while I zeroed in on every potential weakness to target. My possessive need empow-ering me to destroy her and protect what's mine.

I had no strength left to deny it.

Artemis is mine.

"Lucille!" the older woman snapped. The younger witch took her time responding to Sue, hesitant to look away from Artie's bubble. Her tongue peeked out farther, and then got sucked in with her breath when realization smacked her in the face. Without a mirror, I couldn't be sure what she saw, but it sent her scur-rying back inside, disappearing amongst the hodgepodge of furniture.

"I can see why Naomi insisted you come..." the coven host let her eyes travel my length and took another assessing glance at Artie.

My magic swirled around me, ready to fight. Without a target, I started vibrating, and the world spun on a new axis. The woman before me blurred, my bones shaking under my skin, as I tried to get myself back under control.

Darkness snuck into the edges of my vision, the cackling voice from the woods calling to me... a seductive mix of mockery and summoning, while every sharp edge came into sharper relief. The shadow inside me trying to crawl back to the greater shadow of town and drag me with it.

A furry head nudged my hand, and I jumped. The veil of foreboding receded, my building magic rushing out of my mouth in a startled scream, shooting out into the night like a firework that illuminated several blocks. Blinking, I looked down at a Doberman whose head stopped a few inches shorter than Grim's.

I didn't know who he was, but he might have saved my life.

"Hi." I crouched down to ruffle the dogs' ears and plant a kiss on his nose. Grim made a disgruntled mumble, sending doggy death glares from where he stood guard beside Artie's bubble. It was a job he had not been assigned but took very seriously. "Well, come here then. I think his murder impulse has passed."

My voice cracked, words catching on the raw edges while my hands continued quaking.

What the hell was that?

You were about to go nuclear because another woman was appreciating Artie.

My Artie, something deep and primal reminded me.

Sweat broke out at my hairline and I squeezed my eyes shut, balancing on the balls of my feet and reciting the alphabet in Latin. An alternative to counting breaths, it was both more distracting and impossible to accomplish.

The only Latin I knew was how to sing "Old McDonald had a Farm" and the Pledge of Allegiance.

Rising slowly, I gave the dog one last pat and then faced the woman in the doorway.

"I'm sorry... Unfortunately, you've caught me at a bad time," my professional voice held steady, the mask of calm above a raging storm.

Grim whimpered, forcing me to turn around again. He was looking up at Artemis, who'd gone still, smoldering in radiating waves of violence. Instead of bouncing, Artie watched me, brow furrowed, looking dangerous and ready to fight... again.

"What's wrong?" I asked, first Grim and then the man himself. On the inside, I was demanding to know if he was the only one allowed to have a tantrum of unexplained homicidal tendencies. If he really thought I could hold it together with everything I'd been through, then he was dumber than every man on the planet combined.

But for once, my thoughts stayed inside my head.

However, the woman at the door answered with insight, taking my shaking hand in hers and trying to hold it steady.

"I take it there is more than just a memory spell at play?" She spoke with the eloquence of a lecturer, a soft accent in her voice that I couldn't place. Nodding, I sank to the stairs and waited for the tremors to stop. "Care to explain it or should I ask your familiar, as he seems to be the most mentally stable at the moment?"

The Doberman came up, resting his angular head on my shoulder as the first tear fell.

"I'm sorry... It wasn't on purpose... I... I'm not... I think I'm broken and need to be locked away from people at this point? At least people who want Artie."

I looked between her and the man in the bubble. He was now standing with his arms crossed, brooding. A chunk of hair had worked its way loose from his hair leather, draping over one glowing cognac eye. The sleeves of his flannel shirt were rolled up to reveal bulging forearms and that intricate mural of ink that seemed to reflect the shimmer of magic that surrounded my man-shaped shadow.

In the shadows cast between street lamps, he was a punk rock wet dream and I had to turn away. My stomach was flip flopping between lust and nausea, but I was pretty sure the urge to vomit was winning.

Extending my hand for the Doberman's paw, I introduced myself.

"Penny," I said to the dog, who placed his pads against my palm and looked toward the witch in the doorway. Her assessing gaze was discomforting, like standing in front of a room and waiting to be judged.

Nodding once, she decided and took a step to the side.

"He's Max and I'm Sue. Please come in, bring both your familiar and your man—no bubble," she warned with an extended index finger. "I do not believe you are broken, but there are shadows swirling in your heart. I do not know yet what to make of it, but you may experience some discomfort upon entry."

"Shadows?" I asked, hanging my head in shame. "And discomfort? More discomfort than this?"

Sue didn't say more, and my aching throat declined to fill the silence.

Turning back to the two males, I waved my hand and popped Artie's bubble, slowly lowering him back to earth. Grim licked Artemis's palm, the man responding by giving the dog a head scratch. Exchanging looks, the men seemed to reach an agreement before approaching me, attempting to keep quiet and refrain from sudden movements.

In the silence they left, I could hear Lucille telling the others about my magical blip while Sue warned them not to look at Artemis too much until we lifted the curse.

It was unclear if the curse being referenced was the magic with Artie's memory or me. I wanted to believe they'd help, that they could help, but a larger part expected them to behave like everyone else.

Scornful, dismissive and scared.

If my mother was willing to hurt me to make me go away, why wouldn't they want the same thing?

"You aren't broken," Artie said, taking my arm and pulling me to my feet. "I fucked up. This... was my fault. But..."

"But nothing, Artemis. Just... nothing," I leaned against the rail. His lava touch adding to the turmoil in my intestines. I parsed through words and feelings until the weight bowed my spine. I couldn't stand anymore, sagging until I was six inches shorter with my head against my chest, dripping tears onto the walk.

"Penny..."

"Enough," Sue said, having returned to the doorway. "You've said enough. Go inside."

The air shifted as he moved away, following her instructions without question. Two pointed snouts took his place, nudging my cheeks and love handles until I had enough strength to stand.

"Sorry, again," I told Sue, not daring to look at her.

"You have no reason to be sorry. Come inside, you'll feel better," she said, offering me a hand. Upright and damp with tears and puppy kisses, I looked down at the three-person pep squad.

"Thank you," I whispered to all of them, but only Sue answered with a hesitant smile.

"Don't thank me yet..."

I took her hand, stumbling as she pulled me through the doorway. A blood-curdling scream ripped through the night as a violent spirit was pulled out of my chest to fade into the moonlight. Its shadow rejoining the larger one looming over the town.

TWENTY-FIVE

PENELOPE

"What the fuck was that!" Artie shouted, appearing beside me where I sagged between Grim and the entryway wall. "What did you do to her?"

"Artemis, you need to stop immediately, or I will put you in a bubble myself. Give Penelope a moment and we will speak," Sue instructed. Whatever look she gave was enough to have the angry mixed shifter stomping away. The angry clomp of his boots vibrated against my nerve endings, each stamping foot fall causing my overwrought body to flinch.

"Stop being petulant, Artemis!" She called after him and I almost laughed. When the action threatened to come out as a sob, I remained silent. Sliding to the floor and wrapping my arms around my legs, I pressed my forehead to my knees and tried to block out the light, sounds and smells that filled every corner of Sue's house. "Men... cause all the damage they want, but then make a fuss when someone gets hurt and there's no one to retaliate against."

"Eat this," she said, coming over and poking a hand into my face fortress. Accepting whatever was in her hand without opening my eyes, wondering if I could eat it out of her palm or if that was crossing the line between abnormal and straitjackets. Since it was a single bite, I released one arm from around my legs and popped it into my mouth. Chewing slowly around the lump in my throat and the acidity rising in my belly, it would be a miracle if I managed to swallow.

The dark chocolate shell crunched between my teeth, freeing the oozy filling to slide down my throat and calm the rising bile. The sugar on my gums settled some of my nerves, a new revelation to the column of positives for the candy.

Sue returned and handed me a large slice of cheese and a partial glass of wine.

"Grim has indicated I shouldn't give you too much of this. Apparently, you have a history of avoidance and wine is your vehicle of choice, but I'm afraid the protection spells on my doorway tend to leave entrants with passengers a little on edge... so please try to keep your wits about you."

My eyes rolled to the tattletale canine who was laying across my leg, white Grinchy toe paws crossed on the opposite side. His gaze bounced between my eyes and the doorway through which Artie must have disappeared, reminding me that there were consequences to spending too much time in the hall.

"Thank you," I said, accepting the partial glass and cheese. Sipping a little and taking a large bite of what might have been Gouda, I slowly rose with the support of the wall, displacing my familiar to the floor. Shoving his butt in the air, he did a big stretch and then shook, jingling the tags on his collar.

"I suppose I should get back to Artemis before he forgets me."

"You don't sound like you object to the idea," Sue said, studying my face.

I tossed back the rest of my wineglass and handed her the empty.

"It would be easier... or I guess it would have been. We've spent too much time together these past few days... I don't know if I could lose him again." Sighing, I looked toward the opening to the room. Laughter bubbled out of the room, feminine and genuine. Whoever was on the other side was extremely amused by my exuberantly cheerful man... friend.

Man friend.

"I do still need to determine the nature of the shadow I removed from your soul."

I blinked at her, and she reached up to pat my shoulder.

Way up. She was so small, and yet I felt insignificant beside her.

"I think it's part of the town... There's a shadow over the town and it seems to call to a darkness inside me... It might be a place to start," I suggested, and she nodded at me, brow furrowed in concentration. "I'm sorry again. My mom... scarred me fifteen years ago and we found out tonight. He attacked her, but I think there's more we didn't get to learn... Everything is a damn mess."

I swiped at a tear on my cheek while she nodded.

"Go, meet the rest of the coven. I'll be along shortly, but do not attack anyone for hitting on Artemis, please. He's an attractive man and the pheromone-based response to him is not intentional."

Hunching my shoulders. to my ears, I entered the room, staring at my shoes. Artemis was in an armchair toward the outer edge and I went that direction, sitting on the floor in front of him beside Lucille. Picking at the skin around my fingernails, I tried to find words that would seamlessly integrate me into their social group. With none coming to mind, I switched to calculating how many people I would have to trip over to run away.

"I don't recommend it," Lucille whispered, the blinking eyes on her hat moving toward the outer rim. A small possum crawled out onto the metal rod, wrapped its tail around twice and arched down to stare at me from a dangling post. "Despite her stern demeanor, she's way nicer than anyone outside the Coven of Misfits about unexplained attachment magic. Trust me."

My head tilted, the possum mirroring my movement, to the amusement of Lucille and Artie.

"I had *run away* face my first time here too... actually, most of us did. Andrea and Sue, they kind of run this coven like the Island of Misfit toys. They love having us here, but they know it's not healthy to have magical maladies and *not* work on them. It's like magic therapy, but I don't think anyone is expected to leave... I hope not anyway. I heard this town is full of assholes and I really need a place to go where people aren't judgy... or at least less judgy. Did you know the whole town bullied a girl for eighteen years? Like all the kids in the school and the adults, until she fled? I heard it was because of a tarot reading... like they thought she was dangerous because of a card. I heard she snapped and lives in the woods, drinking rainwater and eating tree bark..."

Artie snickered from the armchair behind me, and I huffed out a breath.

"I didn't reject civilization, but I went to med school... Penelope Ophelia Odenberry, aka Death," I held out my hand and the woman went completely pale, all chatter around the room ceased, reminding me I was in a room of strangers. I switched from looking exclusively at Lucille to making eye contact with each of the other dozen or so women in the room, preparing to apologize for existing. "My initials spell POO, but I would prefer Death over Poo if we're passing out nicknames—"

A dozen sets of eyes blinked at me and I tried to swallow a lump in my throat, but my muscles felt paralyzed. I was already screwing this up.

"Sorry, hi, you can call me Penny? I'm not having a great week for magic and emotional trauma, so probably a bad look to meet me now. But I've never killed anyone... well, some spiders, but they scare the shit out of me."

Staring at my hands, I went back to picking at the skin. It wasn't quite a callous, but the edge was a little tougher and I wondered if it had a name. Grim nudged my shoulder, and I gave his ears a ruffle. "This is Grim. He's not from here... but he goes where I goes... I mean go..."

Artemis cleared his throat, and I sighed.

It's like being in AA... except I'm the only one people think is unstable and going to snap.

"Right, so... This is Artemis Nita-Nusi. His father is the alpha of the Pacific Northwest pack and liaison between the pack and the Kootenai people. There's a memory spell where he can't remember me or anything we did together if we spend too much time away from each other, *too much* being relative and poorly defined. You can look at him... What happened outside and at the sandwich shop the other day... Actually, that second one was involuntary and directly because of him, but more specifically who was touching him. Outside... I just got some really..."

I hung my head in shame while Lucille threw an arm around me.

"Don't worry about it. We heard what you said, and I'd have lost it too. Magic isn't easy for me. Actually, magic isn't easy for a lot of us, but I have the least control. Late bloomer, like super late, and it's only been a couple of years since I've had it. I turned Tempe into a statue when we first met... sorry again," she said to a brunette across the room who waved her off.

"I have a winery and a cave with a dragon shifter who can't leave. It was kind of nice to be a stone for a while. What sucks is owning a winery and being named after a wine and inheriting a damn moody cursed dragon shifter and...," she took a very long drink of wine and looked at the rest of the room. "And a lot of things, but that's neither here nor there. If I recall, you're the new psychiatrist in town. I get you're going through a lot right now, but in the future, do you think you'll have openings?"

"Nothing but openings..." I tried not to wince at the overwhelming sympathy that filled a room full of faces. "I've never actually seen a patient since moving here and considering a bunch of people used their insurance to pay me for Artie's company today, I might be going to prison. I didn't want to move back here, and I wasn't planning on staying, so maybe prison won't be that bad."

Scraping skin flakes from my lip, I worked my teeth along my mouth.

"I think prison is the least of your problems, what with your mom, the council..." Artie interrupted.

"Shut up!"

"Don't you think they should know?" He countered. "They could help you!"

"You aren't supposed to dump on people you just met. It freaks them out."

"If you don't want to freak people out, why are you making that face?"

"Why would anyone care about my face when yours is always right there?"

Irritated, I stuck my tongue out at him, wishing I could hit him without causing a scene.

He responded by licking his lips slowly, intentionally giving a flash of teeth. His pink, wet tongue left a shiny trail along his lips.

My breath stuck in my throat, heat coloring my cheeks and working its way lower and lower, until the underwear in my pants was damp and everything got a little blurry. My eyes shut as the pulse in my chest thundered in time with the pulse in my clit, waves of arousal crashing against me. Clenching my fists, I dug my nails into my thighs and waited for the lust wave to pass and hoping if I climaxed I wasn't obvious about it.

"Holy shit…"

My eyelids peeled open to see Naomi and two other women scenting the air while everyone else fanned themselves, pink cheeked and breathless. Two other women, eyes dilated black, looked at me like I'd just fed them for a year.

"I might have been hasty in denying you more than a half glass of wine…" Sue said, as flushed as everyone else in the room. "And I think Artie should come help me with it."

My once best friend shifted, trying to disguise the erection that popped up when his plan to toy with me backfired. One long arm draped across his lap, throat working to produce words that wouldn't hint to the rest of the room that he had a raging boner ruining the fit of his jeans.

"I won't ask twice, Artemis," Sue warned, and he stood up, eliciting more than one snicker from the gathering of women.

"Ms. Sue," he tried not to smirk as more than one snicker turned into a gasp of surprise and… I couldn't think about the *and*.

I took several more moments to talk myself down from jealousy and destruction, and when Grim bumped his head against my triceps, I peeked out of one eye to check for bloodshed.

"Right, well," a woman in her sixties wearing glasses collected herself to address the group. Her hair was greying at the temples, the rest a chestnut brown, draping down her shoulder over a knit shawl.

"Welcome, Penelope."

"Th-th- thanks," I stammered out, tongue sticking to the roof of my Mojave Desert mouth. The woman on my left passed me a plastic water bottle that I drained in four gulps. Lucille took the empty bottle and replaced it with her glass of white wine that I drained in one gulp, following up my ragged inhale with a loud burp that seemed to set the world right. "I think I'm good now."

Andrea nodded and looked at the group.

"We usually set intentions for the week and troubleshoot spells... recharge our collective energy..." The collected group started shifting, the stupor wearing off to hear the second Woman of the Coven. Whether or not that was her official title didn't make it any less valid as I watched everyone turn to her with respect. "But I think, intentionally or not, Ms. Penelope and Mr. Artemis have given us a boost that makes the second part moot. Does anyone have anything to discuss?"

Every head shook, and I tilted my own, looking at Grim.

Did we do accidental magic? I mouthed at him, and he shook his head, letting out a sneeze of assurance. Sagging inwardly, I attempted to relax before remembering someone had stopped my spell in Naomi's shop yesterday.

Please let them be in this group.

Hesitating, I raised my hand like a kindergartner trying out the motion for the first time.

"Ms. Penelope, this isn't school."

"R-right... I..." Letting out a breath, I focused my energy on the words and not how stupid I felt asking them. "Was... was one of you at Gnomewich the other day?"

Tempe gave me a little head incline.

"Oh, good... You stopped my spell? Did you... feel anything similar to whatever... this was?"

The winery owner chewed on her cheek, reflecting.

"I stopped the tentacles trying to crush that woman, and I saw the magic coming from you... but now... I don't know if that was you. This... tonight... it feels different. I've never felt anything like that before... at least... not since," she looked from me to somewhere over my left ear and the instant hardening of my nipples told me exactly who was there.

"If it wasn't my magic, what was it?" I asked, at the same time Artemis asked.

"Not since what? When did you last feel it?"

"I don't know what it was… But if you had a shadow, it would explain the variation in flavor."

"Yes, I think whatever clung to you has been manipulating your mind and your magic. I can't predict whether or not it will rejoin you tonight, but I can offer some protections. Do you feel different?" Andrea took over answering for Tempe and I tried to conduct a self-assessment.

Except with Artemis in the room, the only thing I could sense was him. His location, his heat… it was the only part of the room that felt occupied.

"I don't…" I tried again, my heartbeat rising as I asked myself to feel. "I feel less weighed down, but mostly I feel like…"

My eyes drifted to Artemis, Sue, and Tempe, nodding in understanding.

"The last time I felt that kind of magic and power was the last full moon before my grandma passed away, severing her mate bond."

"Mate bond?" I swallowed hard, noting with horror that no one was looking at me directly anymore. I'd become a freak even in the misfit coven and the dread I'd been expecting finally realized itself.

"Does this mean I'm dying, or that Artemis is exuding mate hormones and I'm getting caught up in them? I know the mating time is coming… Is it just projection?"

Tempe looked between me and the man who lingered just beyond the periphery of my vision triangle, choosing her words carefully. In the end, Sue saved her from explaining.

"I believe the mate pheromones you are feeling are not displaced or discharged energy. You and Artemis are fated mates."

"We can't be mates! I'm not a shifter… I'm not… We're not… Wouldn't we have known before now??"

My palms were sweating, and the pressure in my ears made soft pops. Short gasping wheezes ricocheted through my chest cavity and the room rose a thousand degrees. Laying all the way flat, I stared at the mural on Sue's ceiling and tried not to pass out under the bright lights bursting in front of my eyes.

"I'm afraid your memory spell may have impacted the order of events some. I'm also to understand you left before he turned nineteen, by two weeks, so he would not have been able to mark you." Her speculation offering me sympathy I wasn't sure I deserved.

"I've seen him since then, though!" I sat up, holding onto the glimmer of hope that I wouldn't ruin Artie's life. "If he didn't know or mark me, then…"

"Please, listen. Regardless of the hows and whys, you have larger problems than a sudden mate," she interrupted my rambling, and I quieted. Laying back flat on the floor and bracing for something traumatic, like news he had a child or seven other mates he'd neglected to tell me about. It might be better if he has more and doesn't need me.

I was way too defective to be a mate.

"As your *one* true mate, you must seal the bond before the blood moon fades to harvest. Unfortunately, you cannot bond unless he can remember you, so you must reverse the spell to seal the bond."

"Great! How in the Hecate do I do that?"

"That is presently unclear. But if you don't…" she trailed off, wringing her hands.

"What? What will happen? We'll never see each other again?" My chest squeezed with anxiety.

Losing him forever would be too much.

"No. If you don't seal the bond, one of you will die."

TWENTY-SIX

PENELOPE

The walk home was silent.

Grim's clicking claws on the sidewalk, evening insects singing their farewell to the day, sounds I normally took for granted were magnified in the growing chasm of wordless panic that settled between me and Artemis.

Fated mates, the words rattled around my head in a rapidly accelerating game of ping-pong.

Fated mates destined to die because of a fifteen-year-old spell.

My brain ping-pong machine just hit a new high score.

Only one of you.

If only one of us had to die, I'd give my life to save his.

But would you give him your heart forever?

I didn't have an answer.

He deserved better. Someone who could go out into the world without attracting an angry mob. If we stayed here, I'd spend the rest of my life under the thumb of the town council, Yasmine, and her family.

Not to mention my mother.

There was always the possibility of leaving. We could run away, start over somewhere that no one knew about the Hollow, the Council, or tarot cards.

What about everyone else?

Could I turn my back on everyone to make sure we didn't die?

Possibly die. Nothing in magic is guaranteed and there was no precedent.

At least not that we've found yet...

I'm not sure where that last thought came from. We'd been at Sue's house and then walking. When the hell would we have even looked?

It's a figure of speech!

It was not, but arguing with my brain had never gotten me anywhere, so I let it go.

We were only two blocks from Sue's, walking up the neat steps of a modern townhouse in blacks and greys. There were no colors, no inviting fire or warmth, just a sinking dread that once inside the dam would break and the scream lodged in my throat would finally burst out and consume everything in an explosive pain.

Because no matter how this ended, it was going to hurt.

Artie unlocked the front door, shuffling in and flipping on the hall light switch as he and Grim moved aside for me to enter. Artie silently removed his shoes at the door, tucking them into the wooden rack that had likely been purchased by the same interior decorator who'd chosen the rest of the neutral but natural colors.

Despite the empty, sterile feel of the space, it was comforting. The air still held his scent, and mine, from this morning.

"I'm going to take a shower," I mumbled, walking down the hall.

My brain was still screaming when I shuffled into the bathroom. It switched from screaming to berating me when I grabbed the door and turned to shut it. Everything went still and quiet beside a large hand attached to a larger man blocking the frame.

He looked older than he had an hour ago. Much closer to 34 than his bouncy personality and miraculous body would lead you to believe. I looked over my shoulder into the mirror and decided I looked the same amount of old I had earlier.

Probably because the only part of me that bounced was the over-weight tits and fat pouches I'd carried for years.

"What is it?" I asked, searching his face for some sign that this was a mistake, a new coven member hazing and everyone would pop out and shout *gotcha*.

"I didn't know," he whispered. "I'm supposed to know... but I didn't. We were in the kitchen, and I got the impression Sue was trying to figure out how long we could be apart before my memory faded. If it was just visual or smell and sound would do the trick... then you said or thought something and..."

I nodded along, wondering how she'd made her deduction. Wondering if I should have tested the parameters or done something before this morning... Maybe I could have prevented all of this.

If fate decided this, what the hell could you have done?

It was the clearest thought I'd had since I'd landed on my ass in front of the man a few days ago.

Two days ago.

Within two days, we'd become literally bonded to each other.

Until death do we part.

Which might be sooner rather than later.

I waited for the panic to set in, but in its place I found only resignation and dread

"But... It's been 15 years. Why now?"

"The moon, I think," he answered, both of us looking toward our feet. "Something to do with the moon. But no one thought I had a mate, so no one told me how it works... Well, except my dad."

Turning away, I pulled back the shower curtain and started the shower. Water thundered against the tub, and I held my hand under the tap, expecting the cold water would give me the answers I hadn't found on land. Almost instantly, the water went from cool to scalding. With a small squeal, I yanked back my now red palm, waving it around to stop the burning, and smacked my hand against the shower wall.

"Fuck!" I shouted, pulling away to cradle the limb to my chest and stepping back. My heel caught on the edge of the bath rug and folded it under, trapping my shoe under the weight resting on my other foot. I was trapped and started swaying backward, arms windmilling at my side like little chicken wings—too scared of hitting anything to risk extending them outward.

I knew my ass was going to hit the tile, deciding to give in and let the momentum win. Bracing for impact, I squeezed my eyes shut and tensed every muscle against a collision with an unyielding surface at gravitational speed.

Except the impact never came.

Instead, a warm, and relatively softer surface, pressed against my back. Artie's thick arms wrapped around my torso, his long inhale tickling the skin at my neck and sending goose bumps from my scalp down to my toes.

"You OK?" He whispered against my scalp and I shook in denial. The simple question felt loaded in the aftermath of the day's revelations.

"No. Are you?"

"Yeah... No... I don't know..." He shifted his gaze from mine. "But if we want to know what's going on, I think my dad might know and maybe your mom, but I still want to rip out her throat. He's been dropping hints and... I think he might be holding something back..."

The mention of Alpha Kuruk turned the pleasurable goose bumps into a shudder of anxiety. Dinner near the alpha had been enough to reaffirm everything I had already thought about the man–he didn't like me, and he didn't want me near his son. If he found out we were...

"Do you think the alpha command he'd issued was about you being my mate? Do you think he knew?"

Artie stiffened in my arms, the new thought an unwelcome addition to our conversation.

"We'll go ask him."

Forcing myself to step away from Artie, I removed my size 13 boots and tucked them beside the sink, painfully aware of how undainty they were. Pulling the ponytail holder from my wrist, I gathered my unruly curls and bound them in a pile on top of my head.

"You'll have to tell me what he says. Now, shower?" I asked, hoping he'd realize I needed privacy without making me ask him to leave.

Artie shook his head slowly, denying me the space and privacy to rationalize our connection as nothing more than friendship. Creased brows and soft lips fading into a wicked smirk.

"First, you're coming with me, PenPen. You're coming with me everywhere," he advanced on me as he spoke, sending electricity cackling through the air.

"What if I have to pee?"

He powered on like I had said nothing. Apparently we both knew bodily functions weren't a deal breaker.

"Second, until we know the limits of this spell, you aren't leaving my sight. And since you're my mate, I get to see…"

He grabbed the hem of my baggy sweater and pulled it over my head, taking a sharp inhale when he discovered I'd ditched my bra while he was in the bubble.

I looked down, noting the smattering of freckles and clearly excited nipples jutting out of my heavy ass breasts. Beneath that was the swell of my belly, slightly concealed by the waistband of leggings ending in the just visible pink-toed socks I'd had on under my boots. My body wasn't dainty, delicate, or firm. It was also ill-suited for viewing in the harsh bathroom lighting, a fact I faced every morning, but his prolonged silence set my hackles on edge.

It wasn't perfect, but it'd survived, damnit! And almost all of it worked properly.

"Problem, Artemis?" I demanded, crossing my arms under my breasts and jutting my chin out to stare him down, but the man wasn't looking at my face.

"Fuck me, PenPen…" he growled, hands clenching and unclenching around my sweater. His eyes shifted colors between their normal milk chocolate, swirling citrine and a startling goldenrod with almond-shaped pupils. The mesmerizing kaleidoscope almost drowned out his follow-up question.

"When the hell did you take off your bra?"

"Is that really what you want to ask?" I'd meant to sound accusatory, but in the steamed-up bathroom surrounded by his smell, my voice was small.

Desperate.

Needy.

"No. I want to ask if you're ready to be devoured, Peep," he said, prowling toward me. "You're the queen of the sheep, my Little Bo Peep. The only one who could tame the beast… But now, you belong to him, babe. And he's done playing nice."

A switch had been flipped. All thoughts of mates and secrets evaporated under the scorching promise of pleasure.

"Wow... did you practice that cheesy rhyme in the mirror?" I taunted, pretending his ridiculous predator routine hadn't made me wet.

My sweater hit the floor seconds before his hands were on me, stealing the rest of my scathing dialogue.

Pinching my nipple, his left hand massaging the heavy flesh of my right breast, lifting it to his mouth, daring me to say no. I lost myself in the swirling colors of his eyes, defying his assumption that I was a meek little prey.

If he wanted me to submit, he'd have to fight for it.

Artie's warm tongue flicked the rose pink, sensitive peak, and a greedy moan escaped my throat. Challenging him to do more.

It was all the encouragement Artie needed to suck the rest of my nipple into his mouth, twirling his tongue around the right while his fingers worked the left. Pinching and suckling at the peaks until the sensitive flesh was oversensitive and raw.

"You're mine, Peep," he breathed against my skin. "I own you."

My objections lodged in my throat, Artie's teeth scraping against my battered teats, pulling me back to him, back to the moment.

Artie pushed me back until my ass hit the counter. Without breaking the seal of his mouth, he dropped both hands to my waist and lifted me onto the cool marble. Using his leverage, he shoved me backward until my head rested on the towel hanging by the sink.

Artie's mouth switched to the other nipple, his hands kneading my waist and working the waistband of my leggings.

The sensation was overwhelming, my brain barely registering when my leggings disappeared, and the freezing tile stung the back of my thighs. Steam swirled around us, the shower's hot water supply as steady and unending as the arousal pooling at my entrance. Writhing, I inched my hips closer to the visible bulge behind Artie's zipper, rubbing it against my core and demanding he do more than suck me like a calf.

His cock twitched in his pants, moving just a fraction closer to the promised land. My hands sought his hips, ankles locking above his perfect ass to force him closer.

Rotating his hips, Artie kept his pants zipper out of my reach. Matching the rhythmic circles of his pelvis to the assault his mouth was lavishing on my breasts.

Sliding my hands up his chest, stroking the ridges and plains until he smacked me away. I found the knot of hair at his crown and wound my finger around it, pulling at the roots.

Dragging his mouth away from my tits, I pulled his face to mine, crushing our lips together. His taste was heaven, the smoky hints of cheese and wine dancing with the taste of *him*.

He was my drug. There was no hesitation, his tongue probing and tasting every inch of my mouth with the same curious plundering that he'd used against my chest.

My free hand traveled back to his chest, slipping beneath his T-shirt to stroke the ridge of his abs, moving up to his pecs and pinching the nipple at the same time I nipped his lip. A menacing laugh rumbled between his chest and mine, a reminder not to poke the bear.

I bit him again.

Artie's mouth left mine, nipping his way up my jaw to take a hard bite of my earlobe, his rough tongue licking away the sting. Distracted, I missed his hands slipping into my panties, one up each leg, his knuckles trailing roughly on the soft flesh where he fisted the material between openings.

The loud tearing of fabric was lost in a whispered curse pressed against my ear.

"I'm starving, Penny. And your porridge is juuust right."

I wanted to laugh, but his face disappeared. Dragging my hand that was trapped in his hair, it traveled down, down, down to where it landed between my spread thighs. I tried snapping my legs closed, but he sank his teeth into my leg, blocking my retreat. Using muscular shoulders that shoved defensemen out of his way on the ice, he widened the gap to an almost painful angle that let an icy breeze caress my soaking wet slit while he inhaled my scent.

"Fuck me," he muttered before his mouth was on my opening. With one long lick from my channel to my clit, Artie savored every drop that poured out of me, but I needed more. I squirmed and writhed against him, his fingers digging into my hips to hold my lady V against his face, enjoying the sight as much as he'd enjoyed his first taste, but I wasn't here to be appreciated.

Pulling on his tangle of hair, I brought him to my clit and sighed when his mouth went to work. His tongue alternated between drawing circles around the opening and flicking against my nub; groaning against my sensitive flesh, adding vibration to the pleasure and sending me higher.

"You taste fucking incredible."

He let loose another growl against my core and dove back in, a drowned man tasting the air.

My grip tightened in his hair, pulling against his scalp and sliding my hips forward to give him better access. While he moved in a figure eight, I tried to suffocate him, grinding myself against his face and still needing more.

With a chuckle, he dipped his tongue into my channel. Shuddering in pleasure, I flexed and fluttered, trying to get even more.

One of his hands released my hip and smacked my pussy, forcing me to cry out and release his head. Seizing the opportunity, he made even more space for himself between my legs.

"Oh Goddess," I screamed, and he sank two fingers into me, pumping hard while his mouth sealed around my clit and sucked until I fell apart while staring into the swirling mosaic of his gaze.

Shaking and clenching my walls around his fingers, I screamed his name to the rhythm of his continued attention while he sucked me through orgasm. Before it could fade, another one built on its heels, an excruciating pleasure that set my nerves on end. Another wave followed the first, and I came again while he laughed against my core, grazing his teeth on the spent flesh.

The laugh resonated around the room, around my brain, and sent me spiraling to the edge of a third peak while his tongue and fingers latched on. The claws of a predator capturing its prey, I was powerless to fight the rising urgency of his feeding.

Another wave built, my whole body aching, shivering in between pain and pleasure.

It was too much.

My fingers tightened in his hair, using a burst of magic to drag his glistening face away just as the third crest hit and I screamed myself hoarse. Artie refused to pull back, my magic dragging at the edges of his form, fighting with such limited energy I was convinced my death was imminent. The towel under my head slid out of its rack, my sweat slick flesh sliding on the smooth countertop.

One last burst of magic sent him back just enough for the almond-shaped pupils to dial back into chocolate orbs. His sudden step back removed my anchor. I slid around, gripping the metal ring to stay on the counter while all of my bones were liquified into nothing.

The cheap fixture gave out, and I tumbled off the edge of the counter, landing hard on a bath mat beside Artie who'd been too slow to save me.

"Fuck, are you OK?" He tried to reach for me, but I scuttled away like a drunk crab on rubber limbs. I was terrified that if he touched me again, my body would rip apart, forced to ride another wave of pleasure.

And I hadn't even seen his cock yet.

He let out a laugh, and I tried to kick him.

"Oh, little Peep, always fighting," he sighed, moving over to crouch beside me. In a smooth display of strength and grace, he scooped me up and set me down in the shower. Plugging the tub, he turned off the shower in favor of the tap to fill the basin, squirting a little shower gel in to make it foam. "Let's get you cleaned up, dirty girl. I have big plans for you."

My brain said, *show me how big,* but my eyes were heavy, and my chattering teeth couldn't make words. Vision fading under the weight of magic, orgasms, and mates, the weight of sleep edged in with the soothing water lapping against my aching and sensitive flesh.

"Don't sleep, little Peep, there's more left to do and say," he warned, but the words muddled into a hum that sent me under.

CHAPTER

TWENTY-SEVEN

PENELOPE

The freezing wind howled, carrying pine, and the low hum of magic.

I stood in the clearing, facing off against the pale woman, but she wasn't alone. All around us, the trees were haunted by dead energy and foreboding shadows.

Above the trees hung the pale orb of a harvest moon. The residual crimson from the blood moon faded into the early morning gold.

Artic was gone, the ground where he'd been before a scorched mark.

"Only one could live," she cackled, her voice no stronger than the wind that carried it to me. "Did you think it would be you?"

My feet were rooted into the earth, not that I seemed capable of moving any part of me. Stunned and trapped, my existence felt heavy and hopeless. Without my mate, without anyone to love me, I wasn't strong enough to carry myself.

"She didn't even love you and still you pine for the woman some imaginary goddess said would be yours forever," a man spoke, walking out of the woods to stand beside the demon.

Of course I love you, I screamed into his head, but never out loud.

"Bring her back!" I shouted, but I didn't sound like me. My gaze *dropped to my hands, Artie's hands. "Bring her back or I swear to the goddess..."*

The growl ripped through my chest and cut the night sky with a million shards of sadness.

Four more men joined the first, all wearing black robes. The last dragging a man on the end of a chain. When they were all assembled, the man looked up, and I met the eyes of the alpha, bloodied and beaten but defiant as he held his head high.

"No! You took me! No!" I screamed, but the sound was carried away on the wind.

No!

"No!" I screamed; my heart was racing. Something heavy weighed me down, and I fought. Shoving and screaming, throwing my fist into the air until it connected with something warm.

"Ow, fuck, PenPen! It's just a dream. Shhh..."

Artie's hand stroked my hair, his scent enveloping me even as my body felt like it had been hit by a bus. Every limb felt heavy, my eyelids refused to open, and I couldn't be bothered to protest when Artie lifted me onto his chest.

"Uuhnn," I groaned, but that was far too much work to do again.

"Coffee is brewing," he answered, and I wondered how he knew what I wanted. "Don't make that face. You always want coffee and I want to not be castrated. Ergo, coffee is brewing."

I snorted at his use of "ergo". It was so whimsically archaic and I wondered about his life in the league.

My mouth opened to ask him, but I couldn't get any words out around the lead weight of my jaw. My jaw, my arms, my everything felt like it weighed a million pounds and my bones were jellified lead that no longer offered any structural support.

The only thing that felt solid was the chest of the man I was lying on.

He did this to me!

My brain screamed, but it's not like I could be mad at him.

You don't come that hard and regret it.

Artie's fingers threaded through my hair, sliding out against the knots while he rubbed my scalp. The relaxed, intimate gesture would have had me bolting out of bed under normal circumstances, but everything still felt too heavy to move.

Maybe just this once, it's OK to cuddle.

"I'm sorry about last night," Artie whispered.

There must have been something wrong in my brain because who the hell apologizes for...

He regrets touching me... I tensed, needing to move away. It was the very thing I'd tried to guard myself against. The reason for the memory spell and never being around the morning after.

A tear slid down my cheek without permission. I was too tired to know why I was crying and not tired enough to sleep through this rejection.

This would be so much easier with coffee... or chocolate. Maybe cheese.

Who can't process their emotions easier with cheese?

"Hey, why are you crying? Did I hurt you?" His hand left my hair to run up and down my arms and legs, checking for injuries.

I didn't know a simple apology could rip a hole into my heart, but I knew he'd never find it feeling me up.

"PenPen, I need you to speak now. Where does it hurt?" His whisper had turned into a sonorous plea, cracking at the end.

"You didn't hurt me physically, Artie. Calm down," I managed, wishing I had coffee for this. "Just tell me how much you think last night was a mistake and it'll never happen again, so we can get this over with. I thought you said you wanted me. That if I promised not to push you away we could... but whatever. Just bring me coffee before politely asking me to get out of your bed so you can get on with your life. I'm sorry about the spell, but I never thought you'd change your mind about l-lo-"

I hiccupped on the words, bringing a pause to my verbal proclamation of love.

Curse me. Love sucks.

My eyes were still closed, but his feverish energy changed from anxiety to confusion. It coated the back of my throat, like blue Slurpee—familiar but not identifiable.

"You think I'm... fuck, PenPen, what the hell? I love you." He shifted again, hauling my dead weight back over his naked chest and wrapping his arms around me like a vise. "I'm so not fucking sorry for making you come all over my face. I'd fucking shove my head between your legs again this second if I could... Was that all that memory spell was? A way to keep me from... you know that's dumb as fuck, right? Also, in case you missed it, you're stuck with me. For fucking ever, you're mine. I'm sorry I lost control. Nothing tastes as good as you do, absolutely nothing, and I took too much."

"You... love me?" I sobbed, and he shook his head.

"You already knew that, Peep. You know what you do to me, you've felt it, haven't you?"

I felt something twitch against my hip and I was suddenly VERY aware that Artie wasn't wearing anything besides boxers. His cock twitched again, and my mouth watered in want.

"No, stop that," he scolded, and I let out a sad mewl of protest. "You need to keep resting and listen because we have a bad habit of ignoring tough conversations when sex is on the brain."

My hand wandered closer to the cock I wanted in my henhouse, but his arms tightened like a vise over my shoulders.

"Took too much what?" I asked, not really listening. My body had gone from terrified and restrained to horny teenager in a millisecond, and I was relieved I might die at the harvest moon.

The hormonal whiplash was brutal, and I was not cut out to be Artie's THOT.

I was also not cut out to stay on top of the latest slang and acronyms.

I'm getting too old for this shit.

"Penny, I don't have control of my demon succubus around you," he warned, and my fingers stopped inching closer to his dick. Angling my head toward where I thought his face was, I tried to pay attention. "Or even my bear. They all fucking want to claim you, force you to admit and submit that you belong to us."

"What do you mean?"

On an exhale, his breath ruffled my hair, sending the tendrils sliding across my face and renewing the intimate feeling of his hands in my hair.

His hands loosened, fingers drawing shapes on the skin at my lower back.

"I mean that... That part of me that feeds on the pleasure of others can't be too long without a ready supply of willing partners to feed me. But I've never lost control before... Not until you. Your pussy is a fucking drug, Peep. I could have feasted on you until I killed you. And based on the fact you still haven't opened your eyes..."

His voice was tinny and far away, neck working to swallow beneath me.

I searched for something to say, but the grey matter floating around my skull had melted with my bones and I wasn't sure either was coming back.

A slight jostling preceded the sound of scratching scruff on a calloused palm and it did deeply uncomfortable things to my nether regions. Who knew beard scruff on hands was so damn sexy?

"Not to be that guy, but what a way to go..." I was wet just at the memory, and he tensed beneath me. It was too obvious he caught my scent by the twitch of his dick against my hip and I was suddenly wide awake, if still too exhausted to be more than a pillow princess.

"Don't go there, Peep. We can't... not until we get some answers... or like... sex bear spray for if I go too far."

"Fine. If you won't give me another orgasm, please give me coffee..." My half-opened eyes caught sight of the red tree through his raindrop strewn window.

The dark, moonlit tree outside his window.

"What time is it? Why is there coffee brewing before the sun is even up?" I demanded, noting how good Artie looked when he climbed out of bed. He was, however, somehow less attractive than he'd been before I realized he'd woken me up before the ass crack of dawn.

He didn't wake you up, you had a nightmare.

One that you've been having some variation of since he came back.

"It's four. If you're going to be back in time for work, we need to get going." He opened the closet and pulled out a pair of jeans that quickly covered his checkerboard boxers. A T-shirt and flannel followed the pants, sending him from bedroom beauty to man meat on the street.

All thoughts of asking about the nightmare vanished when my clothes appeared in his hands.

"Back from where?" I asked, watching in wonder as he threw a bra, undies, jeans and a sweater out onto the bed for me. "And how are my clothes here?"

"Your clothes are here because you live here," he scoffed.

"You were in a bubble! How did you get them here?" I clarified and his face fell slightly at the reminder of yet another time he lost control.

"I called in a favor from an old friend. They moved it while we were at the coven meeting. Also, I got you a new phone. It's on the nightstand and your old one has been recycled."

"What old friend?" I glared at him, knowing that aside from me, most of his "old friends" were past lovers. Glancing at the new phone, I considered its possibilities as a projectile, but probably I should just use it and be grateful.

"You're so cute when you're jealous... They are ace and have zero interest in me or my beast." He strolled over and kissed me. "Now, we have to head out to the pack lands to see my dad."

My jaw worked like a hooked fish, words escaping me to explain all the offensive parts of that sentence, starting with calling me cute and ending with the fact he thought I was going anywhere near the pack lands.

Artie's nose appeared several millimeters away from mine, smiling eyes holding a wicked gleam.

"Close your mouth, love. It's too tempting to stick my cock in it."

I both wanted to kiss him and punch him... and suck him off until his face was as tired as mine and I could force him to do my bidding. His smirk faded into liquid heat, a head shake preceding a chaste kiss as he moved out of my airspace.

"Get dressed and I'll give you coffee."

"Give me coffee and I won't hex you sideways with oozing pustules on your balls," I snarled, left high and not-so-dry. "Also, don't let people into my office. Patient confidentiality rules still apply to doctors without patients!"

Hell hath no fury like a witch deprived of both coffee and cock.

"They are a lawyer, specifically mine, so attorney client privilege.

Goddess, you're so testy…" he laughed, bounding out of the room to do my bidding while Grim appeared to supervise my wardrobe change. He nosed at the sweater and let out a sneeze of disapproval.

"Yeah, I know, but he means well," I sighed, standing up and wandering into his oversized closet to see all my clothes hanging neatly amid his suits and flannels. Compared to the delicate fabric and designer labels, my clothes looked shabby and cheap. "He can do better, Grim."

The familiar whimpered in disagreement and I tried not to disagree with his disagreement because it was early and I was tired.

Also, he was usually right.

I hung up the Star Trek cosplay sweater and pulled out a vegan cashmere one that featured smirking pumpkins, also replacing the jeans he'd picked with hunter green trousers. His choice in undergarments seemed reasonable, and I walked out of the closet in search of deodorant and a toothbrush.

Nearly colliding headlong into Artie, holding a steaming mug of coffee.

"Bless you," I sighed, putting my face into the cup and tilting to drink without having to accept the mug from his oversized, magic finger wielding mitts.

He let out a masculine chuckle that would have made me blush if I wasn't face down in a mug of coffee. When the liquid level dropped below the minimum threshold for assisted drinking, I came up for air with a satisfied gasp.

My tongue flicked against my upper lip right as my eyes clashed with Artie's.

His chocolate irises had disappeared in dilated pupils and his clenched jaw mirroring clenched palms at war with the arousal probing the exit is his jeans. Through his labored breathing, his chest rose and fell, jostling my precious elixir.

"Hey! Watch the coffee," I warned, taking the cup from him and wishing for all coffee cups to have lids. He never broke eye contact with whatever had caught his attention, gazing at something over my left shoulder.

Wrapping my lips around the edge of the mug, I looked over my shoulder and saw a bathroom. In line with my body was a fully lit mirror, reflecting my rotund hips sans underwear, beneath the hem of the too tight T-shirt Artie had placed on me at some point during the night.

The shirt ending just above the finger shaped bruises he'd also put on me, but those... those I remembered like a mushroom flashback.

The sight did things to me.

His mark on my skin was like an aphrodisiac and I nearly dropped my coffee, my clothes, my life, to beg for more.

Nothing is more important than coffee!

It was the first rational thought I'd had that morning and I said a silent prayer of thanks to the Goddess that I hadn't abandoned all my priorities for a man.

A hot, fun, kind man, but come on.

Coffee.

Greedily chugging the liquid in the mug, I gave him a full frontal... of my backside. The frigid tile bit at the soles of my feet, cooling me from the bottom up while I finished the coffee and set the empty mug on the counter with my change of clothes.

"Pen-" Artie rasped before clearing his throat and trying again. "Penny, we should..."

I pulled off his shirt and threw it at his face. With his brief diversion, I pulled on my "Fluff Off" angry kitten undies, my bra, and had the sweater over my head by the time he'd stopped inhaling my scent on his shirt.

"Son of a witch's tit, you bastard!" I spat, looking at the wide square neckline in the mirror.

"Well..." He sauntered into the bathroom, scooping my hair to the side for the full effect of his handiwork. "Maybe..."

"Maybe you have to find me another sweater, Bitey McNibble Face!" I reached for the coffee mug, enraged further to find it empty.

And defensive as hell that the marks on my neck and collarbone were wetting the fresh underwear I'd put on.

This man is hell on my hormones and *my laundry.*

"You know you like it," he breathed against my neck, sucking in air along the surface from the sensitive bone behind my ear to my clavicle. Eyes meeting mine in the mirror, his tongue flicked out and brushed the skin just below my right ear. The air cooled his lick right before his lips pulled back and he sunk his teeth into my skin.

"Artie," I screamed, panting and breathless as his tongue flicked at the spot a second time. A tickle to cover the sting and another red mark joined the small collection of love bites he'd left on my torso. He scraped his teeth back up the curve of my neck until his lips were once again at my ear.

"Smells like you need new panties to go with your new sweater, Peep."

Goddess help me, I had a feeling this wasn't the only pair I'd have to change today.

"You suck!"

TWENTY-EIGHT

PENELOPE

It was ten minutes to the pack lands boundaries and an hour to where the alpha lived.

The Pacific Northwest pack consisted of dozens of different shifter species, from predator to prey and creatures that only existed in folklore. Against the laws of nature, they'd been forced to band together to survive.

Like coyotes venturing into a new subdivision in the California desert where no concessions had been made to house or preserve the habitat.

The pack land included the whole of the upper Idaho stick into Canada, then followed the Western border down into the Northeast corner of Oregon. It was only a fraction of the land they'd had before and, like the coyotes, were forced to either hide or be cut down for a problem they didn't create.

History has a way of revealing who the real villains are and, in my bid to be free of the Hollow, I'd come to know more than I wanted to about the tragedy that shaped not only northern Idaho, but the westward movement of the European descendants.

Manifest Destiny, throughout the 1800s, stole most of America from the indigenous peoples. First pushing them west and then back east until only the least fertile parts of the country were left to them, and then the settlers salted that. Instead of being free, the Native Americans were given sections of their own country following decades of brutal treatment at the hands of religious groups who thought that living with the land was the same as aligning with the devil.

For all their talk of freedom from religious persecution, European immigrants loved to tell people how they should live their lives and then punish them for not doing what they said.

Essentially persecuting them, religiously.

Shifters, hoping to stay under the radar, had buried their nature under a smooth veneer of assimilation. Blending into the lumber and mining towns with little to-do, they kept to themselves and went camping often. The smaller shifter communities grouped together, but mostly, they were all able to continue on with their lives despite the harassment of Western religion and its all too eager followers.

Until the 1990s came along and destroyed the area forever.

I was too young to remember the Ruby Ridge incident, but I remembered the fear.

White nationalism was seeking a place to take root and an area as remote as Northern Idaho had been the place to do it. Once politically neutral, alt-right zealots flooded the area, looking to "escape the city" even as they built chain businesses and suburbs to the detriment of the local culture and industry.

As the "white is might and might be right" crowd surged, the magic in the area suffered. Huckleberry Hollow closed itself to visitors in the early 80s. Initially, the shifters hadn't been so lucky.

A few too many natives had discovered their packs and grown indifferent to the supernatural walking among them. The packs grew bold and stopped hiding their secrets.

I remember the first shifter hunt.

Smoke had lingered in the air for weeks after. The charred remnants of homes and forested dens smoldering in a sickening reminder of what it meant to be different. Savage cries of violence mingled with pained pleas for humanity, even as their lives were cast aside as worthless by those who thought they were better.

The Goddess wept, her torrential rains soaking the area and washing away the remnants of what had been. Splintered and alone, the shifters had been facing certain death until Alpha Axel had emerged. A wolf shifter who was raised on the reservation, he sought out the huddled populations and urged them to join together. Forming the largest shifter pack in the west, he built a community that didn't aim to blend– they hid.

Five years into creating his pack, the alpha's son fell in love with the daughter of an evangelist leader. No one knew how they met or who she was until, one fateful night, the couple left.

They disappeared under the shadowless new moon.

In the morning, daughter missing, Mr. Evangelist made a crocodile tear-filled plea. In his heartless, hate filled speech, he called for the head of anyone he deemed "other". He blamed the Natives, the immigrants and the monsters who lurked in the shadows. Evangelist and skinhead followers gobbled it up with all the fervor seen at a Star Wars first-viewing trailer release. An all-consuming perverse energy gathered, a single spark igniting a wildfire.

Before he could get his crusade off the ground, Alpha Axel made a deal with the Hollow's Council.

He'd give his life in payment for his son's choice if the Council would make everyone forget. Forget shifters, forget witches, forget all of it–his bloodshed, a binding covenant that would protect the shifter pack forever. With the deal in place, he gave himself to the evangelist cult, and both men died that day, taking the memory with them.

In the wake of his sacrifice, the pack lost direction. An alpha was needed to keep the peace between animals not meant to live together and without that strength, fights began to threaten the very thing Axel had given his life for.

Battered and damaged after a similar hunt in the south, Alpha Kuruk and his son stumbled in with a small band of refugees. With a quick wit and aggressive response to descension, the bear shifter quickly won the allegiance of the pack.

An allegiance that was passed on to Artie.

My trip down memory lane ended as we entered the city border of pack lands, and the first members spotted the man beside me. Without breaking stride or derailing activities, they all turned to him with exposed necks, showing submission and fidelity to the son of the pack alpha.

A son clenching his hands on the steering wheel as he drove. Despite slowing down now that we reached the main populous, he avoided eye contact whenever possible.

"Fuck, I forgot how much I hate this," Artie mumbled. I stared at his profile as he nodded to a group of little girls playing jump rope who'd paused to show respect. They were too young to have known who he was personally. Most of the residents we'd passed would have met him and watched him grow from aimless teen to adult athlete, but the younger generation knew him as their alpha heir, and I began to wonder what it would mean for him to live here... forever.

"Hate being acknowledged or hate feeling like people adore you, oh famous hockey player, man," I teased, but my joke fell flat on his furrowed brow and rigid back.

My easy going best friend was not in a laughing mood.

"You know it's all fake, right?"

Artie navigated his homeland without the aid of a map or digital direction. Several members of the pack nodded to me as well and I shifted in my seat, wondering what they knew.

They couldn't possibly know you're mated. It's just because you're with their alpha.

"What's fake?" I asked, looking closely at the buildings and people for signs of magical interference.

"The submission," Artie said, turning left onto a narrow road with a muddy shoulder that pressed against a collection of conifers. "You know, there's a reason I went to Public School while the rest of the shifters stayed on the pack lands. At least in the beginning."

Eyes squinted shut, I worked to remember a time I'd intentionally tried to forget.

Artie had certainly been a unique sight in our school, but we must have had other students from the pack. There had been several kids from the reservation, the Kootenai people having a link to the land and magic that continues to produce some of the strongest witches in the area. With Artie's people, we'd also gained a few new witches from the south who'd gotten caught up in the fight and lost their homes.

"I can see what you're thinking, and no. When we first moved here, there weren't any shifters at the witch school. None besides me." He didn't look at me as he spoke, but I could sense the discomfort. "The day they discovered I didn't have a bear, I wasn't welcome. The assumption was that if I couldn't shift, I couldn't possibly take part in shifter related education. I was like Rudolf the fucking red-nosed reindeer, no one wanted to play with me. It was the first thing everyone agreed on after Alpha Axel died."

"Why didn't you ever tell me?" I asked, reaching for his hand. It was resting on his thigh and I pulled it into my lap, squeezing it lightly.

"Because..." he trailed off as he parked the car in front of the pack house. He hung his head, not looking at me or the house. Spine curved over the steering wheel, he wasn't the object of adoration or confidence... he was the same as me.

Broken and lost, the child nobody wanted.

"Because why?" I asked again, not willing to let him off the hook. Not after he knew every unsavory detail of my life in the Hollow.

"Because I wanted you to like me, PenPen," he sighed. Finally looking over, I met his angsty gaze and fought between my conflicting needs to laugh at his foolishness and kiss away his sadness.

"You know what they say about people in glass houses," I offered with a shrug. Squeezing his hand one last time, I let it go. "But I get it. If I could have kept you from knowing I was Death, I would have. The fact that you knew and were my friend anyway, though... that was worth more than anything I could have hoped for at the time."

"Would you have wanted to be friends if you knew I was more unwelcome in my home than you were in yours?" He asked, eyes pleading for the lonely teenager he'd once been.

"I'll always be your friend, Artemis. And I always would have been. Admittedly, the truth might have made me like you more, but even if you were Glinda to my Elphaba, I'd have clung to your kindness. The problem with being an outcast isn't that everyone hates you. It's that they all hate you and you secretly wish they wouldn't." I leaned over and gave him a quick hug before returning to my side of the car. "It would be easier to not care. But caring what other people think is what makes us human."

"And keeps your practice in business with anxiety and depression?" He joked, and I nodded.

"As long as you're strong enough to hear it, there's always someone who needs you to listen," I thought of Maddy as I spoke and looked out toward the road. "My patient yesterday was a lot like me. She's even friends with another shifter who doesn't shift, but they live on the outer edge. Sounds like you paved the way for more shifters to go to school in the Hollow."

Artie scoffed at me, and I gave him an eyebrow raise.

"The pack didn't have a choice. The only way to survive was to allow relations with other magical creatures... and those people are still not given full pack privileges if they can't shift."

Chewing my cheek, I wondered if it was truth or projection on his part.

"Must be the illusion of progress, then. It's so much different here than the last time I came out."

"What are you talking about? I never brought you out here." Artie looked at the street for himself as though it would trigger a memory he hadn't gotten back yet. "I don't think."

"I came out on my own. A few days before I left, I'd come out to bring your birthday present for the surprise party they were throwing for you... I don't think I was supposed to know about it. Alpha Kuruk was so mad when he found me on the doorstep. Your dad wouldn't take the gift from me, told me to leave you alone and that you'd be better off if we never met." I shook out the tension building in my shoulders as I spoke. Years later, the memory hit hard as it had the first time.

"What the fuck?" He shouted, reaching for the car door handle.

"Stop, listen," I said, grabbing his arm and holding on to keep him in the car. "Before you go off, just listen. I told him that our friendship was your choice to continue, but I wouldn't stand in the way of your future if that was his concern. Instead, he said something about the daughter of the moon returning to the elements to keep the balance. He said something similar to you too, when you came home. You were arguing about someone, turned out to be me, but you were arguing about the future..."

Alpha Kuruk opened the front door, filling the whole entryway with his frame and power. Around us, pack members going about their day flinched and scurried away as fast as possible.

By the time we opened the car doors and got out, there was no one left in the area.

"Penelope," he said, not looking at his son. Despite the crackle of power, he remained unmoved on the wide porch in front of the house.

"Welcome to your new home, *luna*."

Acid dripped from his every syllable. I was too unnerved to speak.

Artemis and I stood on either side of the car, watching the man clench his jaw and swallow with his arms crossed over his broad chest. Something about the man was off. He and Artie resembled each other normally, the russet skin tone and black hair showcasing angled jaws and chocolate brown eyes.

In this moment, however, the man on the porch didn't look at all like my best friend.

He looked feral, like he was about to...

"Artie, get in!" I shouted, climbing back into the car.

"Wha-" he started just before the gigantic bear leapt off the porch, landing in front of the car in a snarling display of teeth. He let out a roar and began to lumber closer. There wasn't time. I pulled Artemis into the car using magic and stabbed the engine button with my fingers.

The half-demon finally came to, throwing the car in reverse and sending gravel flying as he backed away from the house. Before he could switch to drive, the front door filled again. The car moved forward while I watched the pale woman with dark hair float off the porch in a char-coal dress, stroking the bear, who screamed in anger until they both disappeared in the rearview mirror of the car.

"What the fuck was that?" Artemis shouted, pulling over to the shoulder after the pack house was no longer in view.

Hand shaking, I pulled out the phone Artie gave me and launched my lunar tracking app.

Waxing gibbous, 96%.

"The full moon will begin tonight... and it's the start of a blood moon."

TWENTY-NINE

PENELOPE

"What do we do now?" Artemis asked, parking his sedan behind his townhouse.

The hour drive back had been silent, punctuated only by the snores of Grim in the back seat and Artie's phone exploding with incoming calls and messages. Mostly social media alerts from his publicist, some texts from unmarked numbers that seemed drastically less serious than being attacked by the man's father... and there had been two calls from that father that went to voicemail.

Though he hadn't left a verbal message, he'd certainly sent one.

On the long drive back, I'd tried to find the words to explain my fear. Tried to tell him the woman with his dad had been plaguing my dreams and if my dreams were the future... She was going to torture us both.

Please don't let them be the future.

"I guess..."

The clock said it was 6 AM. Too early for me to go to work and too late to go back to bed.

"Do you know who that lady was?" I asked and Artie looked at me, brows furrowed. "The one on the porch with your dad? Pale, dark hair... kind of looked wispy?"

"There was no one there... just my dad... as a bear..." Artie scrubbed both of his hands over his face. My best friend had aged ten years on a single round-trip car ride. "He fucking knew you were my mate, too! He knew, and he said nothing... just turned into a bear and came after us..."

Prying his hands from his face, I pulled him over the center console and wrapped my arms around him. In the back seat, Grim wriggled forward to rest his head across both of our shoulders.

"Should we get some breakfast?"

Grim's butt wiggled at the mention of his second favorite word. The shaking of his body shook the car, his whiskers tickling our cheeks.

When his cold, wet nose ended up in my ear, I squealed in protest and pushed him away.

"Haven't my ears been attacked enough?"

Clamping my hands over my head, biceps on my ears, I hunched my shoulders up to conceal everything from attack. The suction marks protesting as the muscles and skin bunched and drew attention to the broken blood vessels.

Unfortunately, it left everything else exposed.

"Get her!" Artie shouted, digging his fingers into my torso and tickling me. Joining in, Grim put his paws on the center console and wedged his head between my arm and face, licking anything and everything not covered by clothing.

"No! Stop! I yield!" I gasped, curling in and trying to defend my torso. Neither stopped until I was a wheezing, slobber coated mess with tears streaming down my face. When my airway finally opened and my eyes were free of tears, I was half naked from squirming and mostly on top of Artie.

"We have to stop meeting like this," I joked, but his salacious orbs weren't giving off joking energy.

"Come on..." I wriggled my shirt back down and climbed to my side of the car. "Lets get breakfast. I'm starving and Grim is starving and you would know you were starving if you weren't threatening to eat me with your eyes right now."

Gripping my chin, he pulled my face to his. Our lips brushed, and I let out a small gasp when his teeth took their place. Slipping his tongue in my mouth, he slid it along mine while his hand slithered up my shirt and under my bra in a heartbeat.

With a single flick of my nipple, I forgot all about food.

"Artie..." I gasped, preparing to dive back in when a shiny wet nose worked its way between us.

Then a third tongue intruded. I'd definitely seen Grim licking the white spot on his skunk-butt with that tongue, so I hauled myself back and clamped my mouth shut. Artie must have known the same because when I was back on my side of the car, his clamped shut jaw was getting a tongue bath from my familiar.

"Grim said no sidelining breakfast," I translated, pulling his collar to get his giant head away from Artie's face. The beast resisted, forcing me to strain my inexperienced muscles and grunt out instructions.

"Get over here or you'll have to wait for him to take another shower."

Relenting, I got my dog back into his seat while my best friend struggled to breathe without getting dog slobber in his mouth. In Artie's bathroom was a pouch of facial wipes, probably put there by the property rental people. I pictured the white package with flowers, and it appeared in my hand. Peeling back the tab, I handed him a damp towelette, and he swiped his mouth. I handed him another, and he cleared his eyes.

The third one he took himself and swiped inside his nostrils.

"You feed him salmon, don't you?"

I sniffed Grim's lolling tongue.

"Maybe? Dunno. You ready to go now?"

He collected all the towelettes in a ball and stuffed the pouch in his glove box.

"Yeah..." He opened the car door and climbed out, letting Grim exit from his side while I righted my clothes before exiting mine.

By the time all three of us were outside of the car, it was 630.

"Where to?" I asked, starting down the alley. Before I made it two steps, a large hand slipped into mine and I looked up at the man I was supposed to spend my life with.

My heart thumped in my chest, uncertain if it was affection or anxiety clawing its way up my throat. Wind gusted down the alley as we reached its mouth, carrying a bone rattling chill that drew clouds over the sun. I shivered against the cold and Artie wrapped his arms around me, taking hold of Grim's leash that I didn't recall clipping on.

"Let's hit up Gnomewich," he offered, leading us out of the alley and down the first street toward town. "I don't think Grim will tolerate waiting for us to get kicked out of a dozen establishments before realizing it's the only place that will let you inside and give you food."

"Hardy har har," I huffed, but he wasn't wrong.

The wind kicked up even more as we continued down the street. My hair battered my face, sticking to the tears streaming down my cheeks from the frigid air in my eyes. Artemis held me closer, but the cold seeped through him and the thin clothing I wore, until my teeth could do nothing but chatter.

To stay alive, I warmed myself with a revenge plot.

"One day… I don't know when, but one day, I will find a way to get back at Yasmin. I'll take every business she owns and I won't keep her from eating there, I'm going to let her in but refuse to let her use utensils so she has to eat everything with her fingers and every chair she sits in turns into a high chair and… what the hell is that?"

Standing on the corner beside Gnomewich was a short, gleaming, man ass with a kilt hiked up in the strong wind. The red hair coating the globes matched the crop on top of his head and neither seemed the least bit concerned he was bare-assed on a street corner in broad-ish daylight.

"Penny!" Sue called, waving to me from beside him. The short man turned and…

"Oh, my dog!" I yelped, slapping my hands over my eyes before I could get the full frontal of my father's contribution to my origin story. "Oh my goddess, what in the hell did I do in a past life to deserve this?"

"Pen-eh! Dun jus' stan' 'thar! Git outta the street!"

His voice was as strong as the wind holding his kilt aloft, and I wasn't moving until he fixed the weighted pouch to cover his divining rod.

"Pen-eh!" my dad hollered again. "Ar'emis! Make er move!"

Correctly sensing he was the weak link, my dad's words spurned Artie into forcing me forward while I stubbornly dug my heels in.

"Nu uh. I am not going over there until he covers his junk. If I see my dad's man parts, trust me when I say that I will join a convent and never be willingly near another penis again. Ever. Do you understand?" I informed Artie, who was now carrying me across the street.

"Mr. Odenberry, your dingleberries are showing and your daughter is scarred," Artie laughed, and I aimed a knee toward where I thought his own twig and berries might be.

But like Yukon Cornelius, I got nuttin.

"She'll be eh lot mor'n' t'at if she do'n get a move on! Get inside, all a ya!" He ordered, leading us inside... or into traffic.

I still wasn't opening my eyes.

When the shop door opened and the bells chimed, I was hit with the smell of cheese, bacon, garlic, and flaky dough.

"Yum..." I moaned and Artie stiffened beneath me.

"Don't make that sound after I was looking at your dad's junk, PenPen," he stage-whispered, and I cackled. The loud braying echoed around the room and I chanced opening my salt crusted eyes to face Sue, my dad and Naomi with grim expressions.

"What's wrong? Did someone die?" I asked, trying to lighten the mood. No one's expression broke, and I felt the heavy weight of dread settling on my chest.

"Yer ma din' come home last night."

I blinked at Naomi and waited for her to say "Psych!" or "Bazinga", but the group facing me remained stoic.

"Run that by me again?" I queried, sitting down heavily in the nearest chair. It was too much, too early, and I wasn't ready to have another anvil lobbed on my head.

"And do it after I've had more coffee, bacon and Grim gets his breakfast. Because my mom is a mentally competent adult and you are all acting like she's a child who wandered off at the zoo."

Naomi already had a cup ready for me, passing me the semi-sweet pink tinged coffee in an off-black mug. Up close, my dad was visibly shaken. All of his movements were trembling jerks, and he stumbled over every bit of furniture within his gravitational orbit.

Sue took a seat across from me, eyeing the older man and running through her memory banks for a solution. My dad had grown up on the shores and deep within the belly of Loch Ness, a mer-person with a siren song was not meant to look lost. He'd carried with him an air of content authority my whole life, and it was discomforting to see him struggle with disorientation.

For all his disinclination to give up his Scottish accent and "don the devil's trousers", the man had never been a fish out of water... pun intended.

"Dad, why don't you take Grim to my office and get him some food?" I asked, trying not to let the anxiety he exuded filter into my brain. Arran Odenberry was a pillar of strength in all areas of life, but at this moment, he needed direction.

So I'd offered him a lighthouse... named Grim.

"Ye, I can do 'at," he nodded, looking toward Grim, who picked up his own leash and passed it to my dad with his teeth. My furry best friend gave me a look, promising to keep the man safe, before leading him back out into the wind battering the side of the building.

Artie fashioned his own mug of coffee and leaned against the counter, letting the silence in the room build to the harsh melody of the wind, waiting for someone to break it.

"Breakfast," Naomi said, walking into the room laden down with plates of breakfast burritos and potatoes. She had a small plate with a short stack of bacon left after delivering everyone food, searching the floor for the intended recipient.

"He took my dad to the office. I got it," I said, looking at the meat and picturing it on my desk amid the calendar and knickknacks. When the plate left her hand, I gave her an apologetic smile. "Promise to bring your plate back."

"It was paper, just recycle it," she sighed, settling into another chair at the table. Of the three of us, I was the only one cramped with my knees at my ears in the foot-high chairs. Taking a huge bite of burrito and another drink of coffee, I waited for one of the other women to pick up where my dad had left off.

"Your mother went to your office yesterday evening," Sue began, pausing to take a drink of her own coffee. "And after a confrontation with Artemis, she ran from your office at your urging."

A low growl rumbled from Artie's chest, a reminder of why she'd needed to run.

"Cool it, Yogi," I sighed, acting like the most violence he could muster was stealing picnic baskets. "Or I'll send you across the street to help my dad."

"It's bullshit, Pen. Why the hell are you so calm about your mom scarring you? For fucking ever?" He added, and I swallowed the sarcastic quip with another huge bite of cheese and bacon in a tortilla. His gesture toward my arm drew Naomi's attention, but she couldn't see the mark through my sweater. I got the impression under normal circumstances she'd have taken off my sweater to get another look, needing to see it again with the added information of who had placed it there. It hadn't changed since yesterday morning, but she refrained for the sake of keeping Artemis beneath the threshold of rampaging bear.

"It's been a weird bunch of days, Artemis. I'm feeling generous and accepting of everything. You'd do well to remember I didn't have a mental breakdown about being told I had a mate, or your dad turning into a bear to attack us, my inability to keep my panties dry in your presence, or the increasingly disturbing dreams of a winter death in the summer solstice clearing..."

I bit back a curse when everyone stared at me.

That last part was meant to be an inside thought, and I'd screwed up saying it out loud.

"You've dreamed of your death?" Sue asked, scrutinizing me behind half-moon spectacles I hadn't yet fully appreciated.

I chewed my food more slowly, hoping the wind storm would steal the ceiling. Or my dad would come back and flash the room.

"You are stalling," Sue interrupted my mental wish list, and I puffed out a breath. I drank my coffee and considered pretending to be deaf to get out of answering.

"How long have you been having these dreams?"

My eyes darted in Artie's direction, noticing him watching me.

"It's just a dream. There's nothing to tell," I hedged, not ready to explain the woman beside the alpha on the porch and her prominence in my dreams.

Not ready to explain that they started with my growing bond to Artie and hinted that the harvest moon would bring about my death.

It's not winter, there's no snow, so it could be a different harvest moon.

"What's going on with my mother?"

Grim led my father back into the shop, the greasy bacon crumbles on his chin, a good sign he'd gotten his meaty treat from Naomi with no issues. For his part, my dad looked slightly better for having taken a time out to feed my furry monster, but the lost expression at the corner of his eyes still lingered.

"Yer mu'er sent me a message last night," my dad answered. He'd taken a mug of coffee from Artie and a plate of Full English from Naomi, finally settling into a chair at the neighboring table. "Said she'd made a mistake an' it was time she did som'in to make it right."

"Can I see the message?" I asked, reaching out a hand for his phone. My fingers brushed along his arm and the static energy zapped me backwards. A sharp inhale beside me and a quick glance at her confirmed Sue had seen and felt it, too. Her hand joined mine, pressing against the barrier that kept my dad just out of both of our grasps.

"Wha' are you lot on abou'?" He asked, giving us side eye as we tried to touch him and couldn't. Instead of fighting the barrier, I reached out with my own essence, and sampled the energy coating him like royal icing. It was sweet, laid with affection, and a crisp, refreshing cucumber essence. As soon as that taste swam around me, the barrier yielded, and my hand fell on his furry arm.

Beside me, Sue remained unable to penetrate the protective barrier placed by my mom.

"I thought my mom traded her magic to the Council with everyone else," I wondered out loud.

"Of course she did," he said, still staring at my hand. "All wi'ches have ta in order ta keep the town alive. Ba she ne'er trusted those men, so before sh' joined, she put a protection spell on all a' us. Ye's sister and bru'er got one, too."

"But I thought she made the deal before we were born?"

"You ev all people know yeh don' need to have magic to use it," he scoffed, and I nodded, wondering if she'd put it in a charm or something more permanent. "Tho' I dunno how she knew how many kids we'd have."

"Do I?" I asked, Sue reaching out to touch my arm, coming into immediate contact with me. Artemis and Naomi each had a turn, the former going last and keeping as little space between our skin as possible without losing clothes. Hands sliding over the small span of neck that peaked out of my sweater, he aimed to distract us both from what was headed quickly down the path of serious conversation. The warm contact sent my heart into overdrive, hammering against my chest.

"Why didn't she protect Penny?" He demanded, and I squeezed his hand in warning.

"She ha'," he answered, shaking his head. "But when sh' was sent ta the hospital, she came back without it. She came back without most of the magic an' yer ma thought that meant you were safe. But then 'e showed up and... I dun' mean to agree with her method, but yer mum knew at the rate you and Artemis were going, if she didn't get you out of here, you'd be forced ta take the Council oath. They planned on forcin' ye at the summer solstice festival."

"How can they force me? I thought it could only be done under the full blood moon?" I looked between him and the rest of those assembled. None of them were sure how the bonding ceremony worked, and none of them had ever wanted to find out.

"Cuz if they waited tha' long, Artemis would have turned 19 firs' and been able to claim ye as his mate. Once boun' ta'gether, ye couldn't join the Council cause, and their power breaks. Yer all trapped, witches and shifters, by the Council bond to the land and both groups. When the two of you join t'gether ou'side er tha', it creates a new link, a stronger one, that will rip away the need for the Council. They'll lose all their power and everyone will be free."

My phone buzzed, and I tried to process while reading the incoming text from my mom.

Mom: I'm sorry, Penelope. I can't stop them. It's your turn. Take Artie and run.

Outside, a firecracker snapped, and the building shuddered before going black. The door rattling under Naomi's lock and Sue's protection; I took hold of Artie's hand. Grim's head in my lap. Wrapping my fingers around his collar, I thought of the safest place I could imagine.

To the woods, I breathed, winking all of us out of the room just as the first Council member stormed into Nay's shop.

THIRTY-ONE

Beneath me, the earth was cold and wet.

The howling wind was dampened by the towering trees I could smell but not yet see. My eyes had decided to stop working. As had most of my limbs and the other generally mobile parts of my body.

Too much big magic my brain supplied, but it didn't have a solution for how to get off the ground. As far as places to crash land, though, I wasn't complaining.

Beside me, Grim snuffled under my arm and warmed the left half of my body. In my mind I stroked his fur, but in reality, I was just laying there.

As inert as any other rock in the woods.

Which woods, I wasn't sure. I could no longer sense the town. Its boundary growing more and more solid every time I passed through it. What was once a semipermeable field was turning into a border wall that fought to keep people in, as much as it worked to keep others out.

Somewhere to my right, something larger than Grim moved. Artemis gave a small grunt, and his hand joined mine, fingers interlocking with mine while I lay there, burnt out and broken.

"Where are we?" He asked. I twitched my hand minutely, my half-dead version of shrugging. "Hey Sanka, ye dead mon?"

I laughed at his use of a quote from *Cool Runnings*, one of my all-time favorite movies. The meaning behind the title, peace be the journey, was a personal goal I'd never made progress on.

"I haven't been awake long enough to do this much magic," I whined, promptly regretting the wasted energy. Moving myself through space and time was hard... moving myself and a dog and a huge-ish man was enough to send me back to bed.

"What the fuck happened?"

"Phone," I said, hoping it was still in or near my hand. The half bear man settled beside me, patting my pockets and then lifting my hip to pull the device out from under me. It wasn't locked, so I heard the phone click open with a swooshing noise and wondered if somewhere there was a person whose job it was to choose the haptic tone on mobile devices.

"Awfully wordy for a warning," he scoffed, hateful undertones seeping into his words. To his credit, the man could hold a grudge. Nothing my mom did would make him happy.

Despite my petty nature, people usually had to cross me more than once for it to stick.

"If she'd just texted me to run, I'd have asked follow-up questions. I think it was just wordy enough," I countered, thinking back to all the misinterpretations and inflections I'd added to someone else's words over the years. "Remember that time you texted me a picture of your finger?"

"And you thought it was my dick?" He laughed, and I nodded, most likely getting extra dirt and mud in my hair. His laughter paused and then renewed double. "I should have been fucking insulted."

"What do you want from me? I'd never seen one before and you managed to crop out all the ridges and bumps that would make me think 'finger'."

"But it was still the width of a finger!"

He emphasized his point by waggling the aforementioned digit in front of my eyelids. The sun winked around his wiggling finger, and I wondered if his cock was two or three digits wide... Two had felt good, three would feel...

"What are you thinking?" Artie's words fought their way out in a pinched tone. A reminder that when I spent too much time thinking about his dick, his tongue or his fingers... "Penny!"

"Sorry. I'm sorry. I was just thinking about Krull the Warrior King," I cackled inwardly at my own movie reference joke.

"Krull? Not Princess Sophia?"

"Only if I want to lose you in ten days," I chuckled, using the movie's title to bring the conversation home. "Do you think it's weird that we use movie lines to deflect from the reality of our lives falling apart?"

"Probably. But I think as long as we avoid *Brave* and any other movies with mother and bear issues, we'll probably make it a few more hours without having complete mental breakdowns," he offered, and I flopped my hand in his direction in a backhand slap. He grabbed hold and kissed my palm, lacing our fingers together again.

"We'd make it longer with coffee," I sighed, thinking about the cup I hadn't quite finished at Gnomewich. "I hope they're all OK and no one poured out my coffee."

"Well, at least you know what two things to be concerned about," he tugged my hand, pulling my torso into his lap. My hair fanned out and I could feel him removing twigs and dirt from the tangled mass of curls. In the open air amid the evergreen trees, I could still smell the faint scent of ash. Out here, though, instead of a slow burning catastrophe, Artie smelled like a campfire on a frosty night under the stars.

Everything about Artemis felt like home.

I opened my eyes and saw him studying my face, a visceral need pulling at something deep in my belly. Trying not to overthink it, I reached out the hand not clasped in his, taking hold of the loose tangles that escaped from his bun, pulling on them until he brought his face to mine. Eyes drifting closed, I let the warmth from his lips take the chill out of mine.

His lips stroked mine, deepening with a dip of his tongue into my mouth with languid desire. Releasing my hand, he slid his freed fingers gently along my rib cage. Everywhere he touched came to life, heat and fire chasing away the fatigue while his tongue chased away my fears and resistance.

Whatever we were, it was real, and I couldn't fight it forever.

"I want you," I whispered against his mouth, returning my lips to his before he could object or break the spell surrounding us. The honesty tore a hole in the wall I'd built around my heart, his tongue tasting the words as he searched for more in the space I'd given him.

Instead of declaring he felt the same, he slid his hand under my sweater. Stroking up my muffin top and the soft rolls of flesh that sat beneath my bra, he massaged them, letting me know he craved every part of me, before pushing up my bra to flick my nipples. The hand in my hair spun, the thick locks wrapped around his fist so he could angle my head, the sharp bite in my scalp adding to the pleasure.

"Artie," I whispered, his face pulling back a fraction. We stared at one another, a million words passing unspoken in the chilly morning air.

The sharp call of a gull from somewhere above us broke the spell, and we looked up to see the white and grey bird circling to the west. Silhouetted by the rising sun, I wondered how sea gulls developed such a sleek figure and lengthy wingspan, eating nothing but garbage.

As his call faded, another sound filtered through the trees.

Cars, voices, a too loud radio... the sounds of a city floated in and I startled upright. Artemis pulled my shirt back down, the massive boner that had been prodding my back plainly visible and achingly painful.

"I can help you with that," I whispered, wiggling my brows at him after checking the trees still concealed us and we weren't near a school.

No need to get on another population's shit list.

"Not happening," he sighed, scooping me up into his arms and holding me close. "When you finally touch this cock, it's going to be buried so deep inside your pussy that you'll never want anyone but me again. Which sounds really fucking great because I might never take it out of you again."

My mouth watered, as did my pussy, and I let out an aggrieved moan when he put me down. Once again proving that his self-control was unmatched.

Unmatched and undoubtedly his most annoying quality.

"You're trying to kill me," I whined and Grim butted his head against my leg, holding his leash out to me.

Accepting the leather leash, I let him lead me.

"Are we just following Grim?" Artie asked, slipping his hand back into mine while I tried not to picture where those fingers could be if the man weren't basically a robot.

"My brain is fried. I'd follow you if you offered to lead, but he seems like the only one of us with a plan."

Grim sneezed, a warning that Artemis had better stick with that plan or there'd be hell to pay.

Or a gnat flew up his nose... it was hard to tell in the woods.

Towering hemlock and Douglas firs gave way to scrub brush and other ground plants until we were standing on a manicured lawn. Silhouetted by two mountain peaks, we'd arrived on a plateau in their valley.

Grim's nose hadn't stopped with the rest of us, scenting the air toward a Smurf-blue building at the edge of a dirt road with small stands of trees near open gravel lots. A vault toilet beside a wooden cork board were the first clues we were in on government protected land, the parking lots suggesting it wanted people to come here.

Presumably to make them go blind looking at the horrendous blue paint job.

"Who the hell paints a building that color?" I muttered, shielding my eyes to make out the Lego block standing before us with equilateral toppers. Artemis remained silent, and I looked at him, curious why he wasn't laughing at my obviously hilarious joke.

Instead of fixating on the blue building, he'd locked in on a white one sitting beside it. From the rear, it looked like just another box with one key difference.

Jutting out of the highest peak was a thin cross.

An image tickled in my mind. A memory of something in a brochure or pamphlet...

"Cataldo Mission," Artie muttered, looking an odd mix of awed and angry.

"The oldest building still standing in Idaho?" I asked, searching the foundation for the same cracks clear and present in the religion which founded it. "Why the hell are we here?"

Beside me, Artemis remained fixated on the mission while, below us, Grim let out a soft whine, taking us a few steps closer.

"I don't think it's open, buddy," I told him, crouching down to check his paws. Behind us, a woman spoke in a voice worn by age and over-exposure to the elements.

"It can be opened, but it won't have the answers you need... I'm the one who brought you here."

Artemis and I turned to see a short woman with salt and pepper hair braided in two bunches on proud shoulders, covered by flannel. Her weathered skin matched Artie's, but she withheld her smile juxtaposed to the way Artie easily shared his with the world.

"Why?" I asked, not sure why my usually talkative and socially competent companion was not saving me from public mockery. His stiff jaw worked under pinched eyebrows creasing his forehead. I looked between the pair, noting the similarities in the set of their eyes, the graceful slope of each nose...

"Are you..."

"Abeque is my grandmother... On my mother's side."

THIRTY-TWO

ARTEMIS'S MOTHER WAS A DEMON.

It was knowledge I possessed, but not something I'd ever endeavored to visualize. Demonology wasn't taught in the Hollow, or anywhere else that I was aware of, and everything I knew had been taught to me by Artie.

Standing here, now, I wish it had been more.

The shadow of the cross formed a line between grandmother and son, the arms of the symbol poking into the space between them. Divided by religion, if only symbolically, the span of the cross's arms attempting to measure the gap without offering a bridge.

Unfortunately for them, the world's most awkward human was standing there, and she was worse with bridges than God.

The only thing I knew about awkward silences was how to fill them.... Awkwardly.

"So... You're a demon and you hang out at a church?"

Grim gave me the "what the hell is wrong with you" look I reserved for people who ate mushrooms and started their day without the aid of caffeine.

I don't know how to fix awkward, it's where I live.

I tried to mentally shout at him while the older woman stared at me.

"I am not a demon," she conceded, deciding I wasn't going to take the question back, and it was better answered than not. "But I hold the lineage. As did Halona, my daughter, and this young man's mother."

I nodded, chewing my cheek and trying to understand the difference between being something and holding its lineage. The simple solution was that it made her feel better to distance herself from the label, but I got the impression she was the demon equivalent of a non-magic offspring in a magical lineage.

"I can see that you don't understand. Please come with me," she said, gesturing to the space between Artemis and Grim. Letting her take the lead, we followed her to the mission.

Though the landscaping was well-maintained, divots on the lawn threatened my ankles. The shoes I'd chosen for a car ride followed by work were ill-suited for an outdoor adventure, but I was still too weak to attempt any magic to replace them.

At a small door on the side of the mission, Abeque inserted a key that had been clipped to the belt loop of her jeans. Unlocking the door, she swung it inward; the door creaking only slightly before it settled.

"You likely have heard of the 'black robe' prophecy, where the Natives here are recorded as saying they wanted the Jesuits to come out here. What year and who escapes me, but the point is that it was many years before the actual visitation by the Jesuits. The land is referred to as 'where the old ones walked', the original tribe Schitsu'umsh renamed Coeur d'Alene tribe by French traders and included most of the Idaho curve, parts of Washington and parts of Montana. Like many stories, ours was swept into the white narrative as our people were ripped from their homes to labor in boarding schools under the guise of religious protection and curiosity."

We'd entered the main floor of the mission. Above us was the stained Huckleberry wood vaulted ceiling. A curving altar carved out space in the front beneath a domed ceiling decorated to resemble a globe without land masses. A large organ in shades of blue and red sat in the center beneath a portrait of what may have been Jesus, though white and wearing robes covered several European religious iconography images.

The irony of all ironies considering Jesus was a middle Eastern Jewish man who roamed the desert.

If he'd been born "white", he'd have spent his life red with sunburn and died of skin cancer long before crucifixion.

Instead of entering the room fully, Abeque led us through a seam in the wall. Hidden by decorative patterning, it was invisible to the naked eye.

"This mission was built by the Schitsu'umsh people, to the specifications of the emissaries, but there was more to protect than the knowledge of a religion they did not seek," she explained, leading us down a set of stone steps by the light of a keychain flashlight. "Here, we hold the truth."

At the bottom of the steps, she moved to the side. Angling her light toward the wall, I saw the industrial light switch just before she switched it on and illuminated another world.

Gracing every wall were hieroglyphs and translated oral history written in a language not even my magic knew. The exposed bulbs were harsh, an afterthought added to a space not meant to be seen.

"The black robes prophesied were not the Jesuits, but a warning of a rift between worlds. This world contains inherent magic, linked to the elements and the life it creates. Many magical beings can cross here, make a home for themselves, and become a part of the natural order. Demons are not inherently evil, but they cannot become part of the natural order," Abeque advised, leading us to a dim corner of the room.

In these images, small human shaped figures brought gifts to another shape with curved horns. Whether these were offerings or payment was unclear, but the shadows escaping each, their items fallen beside them and scattered to the bottom of the image, suggested that they were not enough. Whatever request they had made left them hollow at the foot of the horned figure with an eternal light at his back.

"Human greed gave them a power they couldn't control. Many returned home, scared to harm that which did not belong to them, but others... like humans, others craved the power and infamy. They wanted to test the boundaries of humanity and did so by offering material goods for the life force energy of the people they encountered."

She took a long breath, not quite making eye contact with the myriad of images that told a story the white Catholics had neglected.

"We did not let those few speak for the many. Instead, ambassadors seeking to restore the balance joined forces with the tribe and worked to right wrongs. I am one descendant of that partnership, but my daughters—"

Artemis shifted beside me, and I squeezed his hand. A promise that nothing we learned could change how I felt about him.

"My daughters came because I was weak. I couldn't have a child and in exchange for a pregnancy, I gave up my powers to protect this world. Halona, to the horror of her father, was loving. She left these mountains and sought a life of her own, void of the trauma and responsibility that came with this lineage, mine and her father's. I lost her for years, but without my protection, this area grew under the shadow of hate and violence. The demon half attracted humans that sought to harm humans and witches, using each group to manipulate the other until she reached the ultimate power deal."

A single portrait hung in a place of prominence.

The equivalent of a picture posted to a dartboard. The woman stood in infamy amid abstract threats from the past.

"Unfortunately, she used the human threat of violence to bring about a treaty with the witches. A council that operated outside the laws of nature and threw off the balance. They sucked the magic from the land and the people until the elements strangled in their hold. To save itself, nature used magic to bring about a return to balance-cutting off that diseased limb until it dies out on its own."

"The Council made a deal with an evil demon and now they hold power that will kill everyone?" I asked, not really surprised as I stared at the portrait. Her jet-black hair and snow pale skin hadn't changed. Neither had the piercing look of violence that glared back at me from slightly sunken eyes. "Why didn't you call for backup? Whoever... passed onto you the whozamawhatzit?"

I wished I was better with genetics and inherited traits, but my specialty was brains.

"Because I'd already passed it on to my offspring. Recalling Halona was not possible, she'd passed away giving birth to Artemis," Abeque spoke, looking at Artemis like a priceless sculpture she dared not touch. "Without her, there was no light to counter the darkness. Balance was lost, and it cost the former alpha his life to restore it, but in exchange, he bound the pack to the same fate as the witches. Their intertwined fates linked like the ni which created them."

"Ni? Like yin and yang? The principle of inseparable and contradictory opposites? For every darkness there is a light and balance is the piece of the other in the whole?" I stared at her, puzzle pieces shuffling in my mind and failing to form an image. Her knowing look was a discouraging reminder that she didn't believe I'd piece it together on my own. "If your daughter was the light, who is the dark?"

My eyes darted to the image, and I looked at the woman, trying to calculate her age and coming up short with her sunken eyes.

Sunken, but familiar…

I moved closer until my nose was brushing the canvas.

"The dark was her twin sister, Chepi, the ghost haunting my choice. She cursed this land until a new balance was born." She looked at Artemis, the beacon of sunshine in a cloudy sky. "A light."

Her eyes met mine, apology in the crease between her eyes.

"And a dark."

Artemis stared at her, looking at me as though he was the only one who saw beneath the darkness in my heart to the light I hid.

The light that shone for only him with love I feared more than death.

"Until there is a singular dark to balance the light, everyone suffers."

"Someone has to die?" I croaked out, the room getting smaller.

"Unfortunately, it comes down to either you or her. One force of darkness needs to be eliminated in order for the balance to return."

"You want someone to kill your daughter… or me?"

"Not someone, Penelope. One of you will have to choose her own death."

THIRTY-THREE

PENELOPE

The heaviness in my chest remained long after we said goodbye to Abeque.

During our time underground, the sun had risen and brought with it tourists and schoolchildren. Wide-brimmed hats and fanny packs on every cargo shorts and polo clad man beside an overdressed woman hell-bent on maintaining an impossible beauty standard for an afternoon with her family.

If she had a choice, I imagine she'd scream, but I wasn't sure she knew what the future looked like in a world where she never stood up and screamed enough.

I knew, though.

Standing up and giving up my life would save everyone, but Abeque couldn't tell me how. Only that the time would come.

Artemis turned off the rental car's radio. I didn't want to talk, and I didn't want to sit in silence, so I'd played DJ and blasted every Linkin Park and Taylor Swift song stored in my phone without questioning how either ended up there.

"I won't let anyone hurt you."

It was the fourth time Artemis had said the exact same phrase, hence the very loud music. After a half-hour walk to a rental car dealership and two hours of whatever sorcery he'd done to secure the vehicle, we'd driven north to formulate a plan and find a place to rest. In two and a half hours we'd been through Meteora and Hybrid Theory twice, and the Folklore / Evermore duology. The lyricism and melodies saying all the words in my heart that couldn't fall from my lips.

He parked the rental car in front of a resort with a collection of vacation cabins at the edge of the Hollow. It was a popular spot among the supernatural, hidden away enough to be safe without having to keep a lid on any normies they might be related to.

The perfect vacation spot for a blended family.

"It doesn't have to be you," he stated, his sixth time making the same claim. On a normal day, I would have asked him the last time he had a CT scan, because he was clearly in broken record mode.

Tonight, I couldn't bring myself to speak.

Staring up at the cabin through the windshield, I wondered whose idea it was to build a log cabin hotel. At two stories, it was hardly rustic beyond the design and seclusion offered by the tall stand of trees sitting around us in a semicircle.

"I've never been on vacation," I said, my voice cracking from hours of singing too loud. It hadn't drowned out the thoughts, but it made them harder to hear.

"Doesn't your dad have to go back to Scotland every year?"

"Yeah... but he always had to go alone. We couldn't leave," I sighed, and his face scrunched in remembrance. "I hope when this is over, she goes with him and gets to see the world... also a tiny bit of hope that she gets kicked in the shin by a leprechaun and tail slapped by Nessie, but..."

I trailed off.

Artemis reached over, his palm cupping my chin as he pulled me to him and brushed a soft kiss on my lips.

"Penny, your mom has already seen the world. She lived a whole life before you were born, before she came here. It's your turn to live," he spoke with his forehead against mine. Another intimate gesture that slipped through my stomach like a bucket of worms.

He didn't want to acknowledge the reality that only one of us would give up our life for balance, and it wouldn't be his aunt. Grim nudged his head under my arm and I stroked his fur, deciding the time for hard truths could come later.

"Are we going in?" I asked.

"Yeah, let me run in and grab the key. See if you can find the energy to summon us clothes." He kissed me again, letting his mouth linger. I smiled despite myself, the easy affection reminding me there was more than one way to get your mind off death. I let my hand slide into his lap and squeeze his inner thigh.

"You never learn, do you?" He growled, pulling me closer. "Don't. Poke. The. Bear."

Our lips crushed together, his teeth scraping against my lip before pulling away.

Stupefied, aroused, and bereft of an outlet, I let out a small whimper.

"Technically, I squeezed. I didn't poke."

His laughter carried him out of the car door and up the steps while I stroked Grim's fur in the quiet car. With shifting eyebrows, he quietly informed me that I was making a huge mistake, becoming close to Artemis. That strengthening this bond was more dangerous than returning to Huckleberry Hollow without a plan.

Grim sneezed, shooting slobber and snot all over my neck and the side of my face.

"Ew! Fine! Damnit," I used my palm to squeegee the liquid from my face. "You're so touchy about me putting words in your eyebrows. Geez! Can't you, just this once, let me ruin my life and happiness for the sake of a trauma response?"

An enormous head butted into my chin, and I sighed, wrapping my arms around him.

"Yeah, yeah. Love," I muttered, taking out my cell phone. A string of messages had come in when we emerged from the basement. All of them assuring me that everyone was fine but warned us not to come back. The Council was unstable and on the warpath.

They probably know that you and Artie are the only barriers between them and life ever after.

If I weren't around, Artie would be safe... wouldn't he?

Grim let out a whimper and I shook off the rabbit hole of thoughts I was spiraling into.

Opening Nay's thread, I typed a quick message.

Me: We're ok, but we need clothes. Do you think you can get into the townhouse without drawing suspicion?

Naomi: Do you think you could have answered hours ago before I baked six years of bread in a single day?

Guilt hunched my shoulders.

Me: Sorry, Nay. We ended up near Coeur d'Alene... it wasn't good.

Naomi: It wasn't good here either. Yes, I can get to the clothes. How are they getting to you? You have to be about to fall over.

Performing a self-assessment, I measured my energy and capacity for both magic and life.

Me: Yeah, probably. If you put it in a bag and send me a picture of the bag, I can probably manage. We're not too far.

Naomi: Don't say more. There's no telling what the Council will do. Give me a few minutes. If I fail, use DoorDash for clothes, idiot.

Me: Please also put Grim food, Grim dishes and a chew toy in another bag.

Naomi: Way ahead of you, asshole.

Beneath her message was a JPEG with an overstuffed tote filled with Grim's necessities. It was sitting on the desk in her office and I suspected she'd collected his things earlier, knowing I'd need them for my new life on the run from the Council... Not that I had any intention of running.

Those assholes were going down... somehow.

Re-reading her message, I smiled at her terms of endearment, though I was pretty sure there wasn't anyone out here to sell me clothes, much less deliver them. A normal person might think idiot and asshole were insulting, but for Nay, it was the same as calling me sweetie or bestie.

But better because traditional affection made me uncomfortable. My eyes drifted closed, and I held the image of Grim's bag in my mind, feeling the air shift as the bag arrived carrying the smell of rosemary bread and bacon.

"You ready?"

I jumped out of my skin, smacking my head on the chicken stick above the car door.

"Shit, are you OK?"

Artemis had appeared and opened my car door without a sound. His roving hands caressed my face, checking for lumps, bumps, and bruises. Swatting his hands away, I rubbed my head, looking up and up into his backlit profile and pale brown eyes. My friendly affection gave way to an insatiable yearning.

"Yes..." I squeaked, his hooded eyes flashing sex while his nose worked. Before he could reach for me, Grim let out a warning bark and our eyes snapped to an approaching figure in khaki and flannel.

"Sir! We had a cancellation for one of the cabins if you're still interested," the young man called out, waving a metal key on a green plastic tag. As he got closer, the bright yellow 7 on the tag caught the nearly full moon in the night sky, reflecting it in a thousand directions.

Cabin number seven, seven visible phases of the moon...

Seven hours until the first glimpse of the rising blood moon.

Watching Artemis take the key from the young man, I wondered which prophecy was more alarming: being fated to mate my best friend or destined to die to save the town, Artie and everyone else.

When he turned back to me, eyes alight with humor and affection, both futures faded into an abstract concept that didn't seem as daunting. Bounding toward me was the most perfect man and whether or not he was mine forever or mine for now, I was tired of not having him.

All of him.

He slowed as I climbed out of the car, grabbing Grim's bag from the seat and letting him out through the back door. The dog shook hard, sending his fur scattering and leash whipping against the side of the car.

Artemis took hold of my chin, tilting my face to the side. I tried to lean closer to steal a kiss, but he held me firmly at arm's length, humor dancing in his eyes.

"What's on your neck?"

Brow furrowing, I reached up and swiped across my cheek. My hand came away wet and slimy, my gaze dropping to the wide-eyed culprit at my feet, tail thumping gently against the dirt under his paws.

"Your sneezle juice is on my face," I told him, and he wagged his tail harder. "Ugh, let's just go."

Shaking Artie's hand off my face, I let my cheeks burn as embarrassment erased my resolve to be a sex goddess. Nothing puts the clamps down on potential sexy times like being covered in dog snot, drool and probably fur.

"Hey!" Artemis called, reappearing beside me, taking my hand and kissing my forehead. "Where are you going?"

Tucking my arm under his, the half-shifter reeled me in like a fish until I was plastered to his side.

"To the room," I said, climbing the porch of the large cabin themed hotel. My heavy feet caught on the ledge, but my human appendage kept me upright.

My feet may have given up, but gravity was no match for the boundless energy of my best friend turned walking stick.

"We aren't staying in there," he said, redirecting me behind the building.

At the base of the semicircle of trees was a semicircle of cabins. There were seven total, each about the size of a storage shed, but secluded from one another by the ground cover of mid-growth forest plants. Artemis veered us left, and we went to the smallest cabin in the line. It was set back a little farther from the well-worn path, a metal stove pipe poking up for either a pellet stove or an oven.

We took the two steps up, Artie opening the door and standing back to let Grim enter first, gesturing for me to follow the fluffy tail held aloft, bouncing back and forth in perfect symmetry.

My furry metronome with the fluffy butt.

Two steps into the room, my shin collided with the wooden corner of an end table. The sharp edge broke the skin and sticky blood dribbled down my leg.

"Damn it!" I swore, grabbing my shin and hopping on one foot in the other direction.

The back of my knee hit against a new object and I fell backward onto a softer surface that bounced. A bare overhead bulb flicked on and I blinked back the bursting lights dancing on my retina.

"How did you hurt yourself in two steps?" Artie laughed, then sucked in a breath at the growing reddish brown smudge on the leg of my pants. His hands went to my waist, undoing my pants and pulling them off my legs before I could register what was happening. Artie's hands ran up my leg, sliding his hand up my calf, face inches from where it had been the night before.

This time he was on the verge of panic instead of threatening to eat me.

Oh, how the mighty have fallen.

"It's not deep, you're just a bleeder," he commented, rising from a crouch and taking my pants through a tiny door off the side of the room. His large frame was still partially outside the room when he ran the water and reappeared with a wet washcloth.

Kneeling between my legs again, he lifted my leg onto his shoulder, carefully wiping away the blood while his other hand rested on my inner thigh.

My airway constricted, the position of his hands and face far more distracting than the minor cut on my shin. With a last swipe of the towel, he pressed his lips to my injury and met my gaze.

"Since you were such a good patient, I feel like you deserve a lollipop... but I don't have one."

His eyes peered at me from above my mound, my leg on his shoulder and the hand resting both too close and too far from the land of happy, fun times.

Not that the slippery cascade in my slit cared.

"Maybe I can give you a different kind of treat."

Sliding my leg off his shoulder, Artie dragged my hips to the edge of the bed. His nose trailing up my inner thigh followed by his tongue, eyes locked with mine. With a flash of teeth, he nipped at the skin just below the crease in my legs, his fingers sliding into my underwear to part my folds.

"So fucking wet," he murmured, swirling around my entrance before retreating and sucking two glistening fingers in his mouth. My whole body trembled and my head swam, silently begging for more.

Grim let out a whine and started barking at us, killing the moment. On instinct, my legs snapped closed, and I bolted up from what turned out to be a bed.

Struggling to gain my balance, I staggered in place until I got my bearings and stayed upright.

"Maybe I should take a shower. Check out the other bed... hopefully it's bigger than this one for you," I said, edging my way toward the bathroom door, halting when he let out a sharp laugh. I watched his crooked smile bloom across perfect teeth.

If he keeps this up, I'm going to start growing mushrooms down there.

"What's funny?" I asked, looking down at my rainbow unicorn underwear. "You picked these!"

My phone pinged a message, the image of a bag from Nay, but I was too on edge to bring it here. My stomach lurched, and I didn't know if it was butterflies or nausea, but it didn't feel great when the room kept shifting in and out of focus.

I searched the room for the source of his amusement as he rolled onto the balls of his feet and stalked closer. My back ran into the wall, his hand slipping between the hard surface and my head. Looming over me, he slowly folded his arm until his mouth was at my ear and I was certain my inner thigh looked like Niagara Falls just from his proximity.

"There's only one bed, Peep."

THIRTY-FOUR

PENELOPE

"J-just one?" I stammered, his lips trailing from my ear down my neck.

"Yup," he answered, nipping my collar bone.

Grim let out another bark and I let out a shaky breath.

"We should f-feed..."

Artie's hands went up my shirt, and I forgot how speaking works.

"He can wait."

Grim let out a low growl and head-butted Artie, who puffed all the air from his chest onto my neck. Chills raced down my arm, my nipples at full attention threatening to shred the bra I was wearing.

"Saved by the bell, little Peep," he said with one last lingering kiss at the base of my neck. "But I have all night."

Sweet cheese and crackers. I was so screwed.

"Not yet, little witch," he smirked. "But soon."

I stared at him wide-eyed.

"Since when can you read minds?" I hissed, searching the room for listening devices like it was a state secret.

"You didn't keep that one as an inside thought, little mate."

Placing a kiss on my nose, Artie shifted one foot to the right, opening the canvas bag of canine supplies. There were two stainless steel dishes, and I took them from his hands to the small sink beside a microwave on a freestanding cabinet.

My shoulder collided with a lamp, my feet catching on the corner of a rug until I stumbled into the kitchenette.

It was a sorry excuse for a kitchenette, but there was a coffeemaker in the corner, so I elected not to put that opinion on Yelp. Placing the first bowl in the sink basin, I turned the tap on and filled it with cool water. Artemis moved in behind me, taking the second bowl and filling it with a scoop of dog food from the bag. With a small chuckle, he pulled out a plastic bag of crumbled bacon strips and sprinkled some on top of the food.

"Naomi spoils you," I said to the dog, setting down both dishes and angling back toward the bathroom. "I'm just going to…"

Artie intercepted my escape trajectory and handed me the phone. Three new messages from Naomi.

Two pictures, the bag of clothing and a paper bag labeled "dinner" in the one word text beneath it.

"Ugh, she spoils us too."

Sending a quick thank you, I studied the pictures on my phone and then looked around the room for a place to deliver the items. My foot caught on the base of the bed, and I face planted into the mattress. It was too springy to be considered soft, but my proprioception had the world spinning like it was New Orleans at Mardi Gras.

"Ow," I breathed into the top blanket that felt like sandpaper on my skin and smelled like sawdust. When the waves of nausea subsided and the world maintained a lateral axis, I chanced tilting my head to the side.

"I think I'm dying," I said to Grim, but he kept his tail pointed up in my direction while he searched the empty bowl for more food. Artemis appeared beside the bed, looking down at me with concern. His face kept losing focus, disappearing at the edges between something larger and something sharper.

"What's wrong?" His hand went to my forehead, checking for a fever… or he had weird kinks and one of them was foreheads. Aside from being clammy, I didn't feel warm.

"I think…" I pressed a finger into my temple and rubbed at it. "I think I might need to be carried into the shower."

Effortlessly, Artemis scooped me into his arms and carried me three steps to the open door of the bathroom. He set me on the toilet lid and ran the water to fill the tub, checking the temperature while holding me up. Unlike his multitasking prowess, my bones had given up the gambit, and I was a pile of over-cooked pasta trying not to barf.

"What happened, Penny?" Artie asked, pulling my sweater off and unhooking my bra. It was neither erotic nor sensual. His hands moving efficiently until I was completely naked and being placed in the warm water. He gently stroked the liquid over me, making sure every inch of me was rinsed.

"I don't know," I whispered, letting the warm water soak into my skin and rinse away the sticky sweat film on my skin. Grim tried to wedge his way into the tiny bathroom stall, but there wasn't room for him. "I don't think I can bring the bag or the food here."

"Don't worry about that," he said, stroking my hair back into the water. Squeezing a few pumps of soap from the dispenser, he trailed his hands up my legs. Scrubbing the left and then the right, he kept going until his hands were cleaning between my legs. The gentle strokes were not meant to be sensual, but as soon as his fingers touched me there, I was slick with more than just water and bubbles.

"Artie," I pleaded, not sure what exactly I wanted but knowing that only he could give it to me. "Please, touch me."

I felt his hand disappear briefly. The rustle of fabric, the metal click of a belt buckle, and two thumps of his shoes hitting the ground. He slid a hand under my shoulders, pushing me upright before the water level rose and I was resting against a wall of heated flesh.

"Just relax, PenPen," he said with his cheek beside my ear. Citrus, ash, and sage filled the space, and I heard the release of the soap dispenser just before he went back to work. His legs bracketed either side of my ribs, the movements of his arms rocking me gently as the pain behind my eyes ebbed.

Artemis slid his magic hands under my breasts and up my neck. Using the warm water to rinse my face, he placed soft kisses on my temple, then my cheek, until my head tilted so our lips met.

It was a gentle meeting, the soft affection was one of the harder aspects of us for me to accept. His mouth matching the languid movements of his hands as he continued to wash away the day that clung to my body and heart. I swiped my tongue at the seam of his lips, requesting entry so I could taste more of him. Our tongues swirled together, his hand twirling my aching nipples in the same pattern while the warm water chilled on the exposed skin.

At my lower back, I felt his erection press against me, ready and willing to be of service. My hand folded behind my back to stroke him. Gliding from the base to his tip, I pumped him in my fist and delighted in the sharp hiss that slipped through his lips. His hand drifted lower, parting my folds and running a finger along the seam, spreading my arousal up to my clit before adding a touch of pressure.

It wasn't enough; I arched my back, pushing his hand on to my clit. My own hand moving more erratically behind my back at the growing pressure in my pussy. Beneath my back, Artie's hips thrust into my hand, his cock throbbing under my touch.

Two fingers entered my channel, and I cried out. The instant satisfaction at being filled was outweighed by the driving need to make him feel like I did.

Make him feel like I could shatter his world with pleasure and give him what no one else ever could. We both pumped harder, racing each other to climax, his palm on my clit, fingers buried inside me until he curled them forward and I shattered.

Screaming his name, my grip tightened around his cock and with two more thrusts, I felt his release as it shot out along my back. Panting, we rode out our orgasms, milking the other for every last drop of ecstasy.

Arms wrapping around me, Artemis held me to his chest. I rolled over like a manatee and burrowed into the tattoo on his chest, licking a droplet of water off the nose of the bear.

"Don't leave me, OK?" I asked, a yawn slipping out as I snuggled against him. "Please, don't ever leave me."

"I love you too much to ever leave you, PenPen. You're mine, forever," he growled into my ear and I fell asleep in the tub, sated, warm and, for the first time in my memory, happy. Safe knowing that Artie wouldn't let me drown.

THIRTY-FIVE

I WAS NO LONGER TETHERED TO THE PHYSICAL WORLD.

Beneath me, a horned bear screamed in agony and I felt my heart ripped to shreds at the sound. From up here, the snow-covered trees were no longer the pillars that held up the sky. Their roots held everything together, their branches dancing with the wind while the snow took refuge amidst their branches.

Only fire dared to challenge the power of the trees and once it ripped through and fell apart, the trees were reborn. The same ashes from their predecessors nurturing in the new round of life.

Below me, I watched a controlled burn.

The wind carried a demon bear toward the woman. Council members stood, the faux forest without life or purpose. Their forms were nothing. If I could, I would pull them all into the earth and return their life force energy to the closed system of life.

The law of thermodynamics is never more prevalent than when something has held onto its matter longer than the reaction intended, a defilement of the natural entropy.

A few tremors shook the upper branches. A black bird cawed and took flight. I watched the bear charge the first figure and saw a ripple of movement amid the black robe statues.

Something clawed its way from the soft earth beneath their feet, an invisible force pulling one man under. First his feet, then his legs. In a matter of seconds, a council member was consumed by the earth and the neighboring trees grew slightly taller.

Return them to the earth...

"Eat this please."

I felt something pressed against my lips, and they parted without question. Chewing slowly, the strawberry burst in my mouth and I swallowed greedily until it was gone and I opened my mouth for another.

"Nope, sit up to eat so you don't choke," the male voice warned, and I snorted. Struggling to re-inhabit my limbs, I shimmied and flopped until I could slide one eye open and stare at the naked male specimen holding a fruit and veggie plate.

"Human charcuterie board?" I propositioned him, even as I accepted the plate without ordering him to lie down. Stuffing two cucumber slices into my mouth, I felt the bed dip under Grim's weight as he climbed up beside me. A single lamp was the only light in an otherwise inky space. None of the windows offered me a concept of time, the moon completely hidden in the dense night.

"It's a little after midnight... Sue said you needed to eat something," Artie said, shifting a little to pass me a bottle of water so he could slide in beside me with his own plate. I nodded and continued to graze eagerly, putting small stacks of mismatched snacks together and eating them without regard for proper chewing protocol.

"Slow down or you'll choke," Artie warned, trying to put his hand between me and a bite larger than my mouth.

I bit him instead.

"That's what she said," I laughed and stuffed the cucumber berry sandwich in my mouth. Absently, I pet Grim and tried not to think about my dream. It was different this time, no feelings of being powerless, no sense of dread, just a weightless sense of purpose.

I'd been one with nature, and she was glorious.

"Speaking of what she said, I think..." his cheeks turned a light pink and my mouth fell open.

"You can blush?" I bounced on the bed with a shimmy of glee. "I didn't know you could blush! This has to be good. You've told me about three-ways in explicit detail and not so much as a twinge, but you're blushing! Ooh, I need my phone... Where's my phone? This must be documented!"

My hands searched the bed, completely clueless where the phone might be since I passed out. One found Artie's thigh, and searched for that, squeezing under the sheet draped across his lap. Gently pinching the left side, then the right, effectively making him squirm. Powerless with a plate full of food, I remembered our tub time.

As fast as he'd undressed me, I ripped back the sheet to see... boxer briefs.

"What? Boooo!" I complained, pulling his sheet back over the thick ridge in his underpants. My desire to make eye-contact with the one-eyed snake stymied by two square feet of fabric. "Ugh, carry on. You were thinking?"

Flopping back against the pillows, I picked up the water bottle and drank half of it in a single swallow. The pillows were flat and some of the water dribbled from the corner of my mouth, traveling down my breast.

Artie followed the drops with his eyes, their color shifting between his own, the cognac I'd associated with his bear, and the almond shape that went with his demon. It was satisfying to see his appreciation, more satisfying to see the sheet in his lap twitch.

At least I'm not blue balling it alone.

"You... uhh..." Artie cleared his throat, an effort to regain a train of thought derailed by my failed wildlife expedition for trouser snakes. I passed him the bottle of water and he finished the rest, exchanging it for the plate in his hand. There were three cucumbers left, and I ate them, leaving him the gross melon that hadn't been in my own mix.

He laughed, scrunching the bottle into a small plastic ball and tossing it in the blue recycling can under the counter. Though it was only two feet away, I considered clapping in approval of his athletic prowess.

"You and melon," he shook his head. Taking back his plate, he scooped the cantaloupe into his mouth and then stacked our plates and set them on the counter. Leaning back against his own pillow, he slid an arm under me and effortlessly rolled me over to lie on his chest, holding me there so he could speak.

Apparently, there was going to be more blushing, and I was in a time out.

"I was thinking," he cleared his throat again, and I considered my proximity to his soft belly for tickling... except it wasn't soft. It was hard. A master artist having sculpted the abs of Adonis right above his belt and I regretted not using my tongue to count them while I had the chance.

I'll have more chances... if I make them.

"No! Stop it!" He clapped his hands over my eyes, my naked legs squirming for friction.

"I was thinking we needed to figure out how to seal the mate bond," he declared, and I stilled in his arms. Was he proposing that we... "I can't be the first half-shifter with a mate. I've been doing some research and put out some calls for help... But I think..."

My heart pounded in my chest.

He wants to be my mate.

He wants us to be bonded.

"I think it will help keep you safe," he finished, and my stomach dropped out.

He's just being nice.

"The mate bond is pretty strong. I think it will give you some of my shifter strength and..." I wiggled away from him as he talked. I stood up and stretched, my joints popping loudly in my mind, covering up his words. "I mean, if we can figure out a way to make it happen, shouldn't we try?"

I shrugged and made the sluggish walk to the bathroom, turning on the light. My blood-stained pants had been cleaned and hung to dry on the towel bar. My sweater, underwear and bra were neatly folded on top of the toilet tank and two toothbrushes with a small tube of paste rested on the counter. Clean dry towels were stacked on the shelf above the toilet and all evidence of our time together was erased.

While I slept, he'd managed to get food, toiletries and do laundry.

"What's wrong?" Artemis asked, behind me but not touching.

"Nothing," I said, stepping into the bathroom and reaching for the door. "I just need to..." I gestured to the toilet and his brows scrunched together in the mirror.

"No," he said, hand on the door to stop it from closing. "No, it's not nothing. Something is wrong. What is it?"

"Just... if you had a choice, would you pick me? Of all the people in the world you could and have had, could you settle for just one? If my life and yours weren't on the line, would you still want to be bonded to me? Forever?"

"You heard Sue and my dad, you're my mate," he dodged my question. "I think even your mom fucking knew."

"Artie, I don't give a shit about the mate bond. And neither do you. The physical attraction can be chalked up to the bond, but what about love, Artie? Do you love me enough to bind us together forever?"

"I love you more than anything, Peep." He swore.

"Enough to be forever?"

I met his reflection head-on and saw the hesitation. The moment of uncertainty and I moved him away from the door with magic.

"That's what I thought. There's no divorce for the mate bond. You can't change your mind and if you're not sure, I don't want it. I'm pretty hard to kill, Artemis. Don't saddle yourself with me out of nobility or a sense of responsibility. I can take care of myself, and everyone else, even if it means I die." I shut the door on his montage of facial expressions and turned on the sink to pee and cry without him hearing.

"Penny, please," Artemis knocked on the door and I shook off the vestiges of sadness. I'd lost track of time, unaware of how long I'd been sitting on the toilet, but the numbness and tingling in my legs suggested whatever number I came up with might need to be doubled.

Standing, I flushed the toilet, washed my hands and turned off the sink. Red-rimmed eyes stared back at me and I swiped some cold water on my cheeks.

Flinging open the door, I stepped out and gestured him in.

"All yours," I gave a half bow, unsure what exactly I was going for besides weird and awkward.

Not that either of those require much effort.

"Penny," he started, but I was already summoning the bag of clothing. Opening the top, I found sweatpants and a hoodie that I pulled on without bothering to mess with the whole undergarment thing.

"I need to take Grim out. You should be fine to use the facilities," I said, keeping my back to him and the rest of the room. My large fur ball hopped off the bed, slinking toward the door with leg stretches and a yawn, shaking himself and then holding steady for me to attach his leash. "I'll try to keep my time outside to a minimum."

Tugging open the door, I exited into the night and took a long inhale. Amid the trees, Artie's scent cleared from my nose and I was able to breathe without being reminded of the pain, the life I could never have,

Grim led us off the porch, sniffing the stairs and the trees. He lifted his leg on a few short plants but continued into the center of the semi-circle. Taking two abrupt turns, he sat down and stared up. Following his lead, I tilted my head back to stare at the sky.

Above us, the moon was as bright as the sun. It was still the normal light yellowish blue, somehow more beautiful than any I'd seen before. We were far enough from all major cities that there was no light pollu-tion, and I swayed in time to the tall trees as I shifted focus to stare at the stars beside it.

A cabin door opened, but I held still with Grim, trying to find my guiding star through this mess.

"There," Artemis whispered, and I sighed lightly when his hand landed on my lower back. His touch added to the peace of the night sky despite everything. "You see, the Big Dipper?" He tilted my head lower to the horizon, down from the north star.

"From the bottom left, there are three stars, one behind it and two to the front. Those are her back paws." His finger trailed down the hori-zon, but I couldn't see the stars.

"Whose paws?" I asked, still trying to find the stars as I leaned into him, trying to get the same perspective he had. He was only a couple of inches taller than me, but I always felt small standing beside him despite my easily hundred pound advantage.

His presence and energy looming larger than any metric I could fathom.

"Ursa Major," he continued, pointing along the bottom of the dipper. "Then there are two stars, one coming off the top and the other off of the bottom, reaching a point right there."

I closed my eyes, no longer looking. Rationally, Ursa Major would not be visible this time of year after ten. The moon said we were closing in on two in the morning, but listening to Artie talk about the stars soothed my heartache.

Whatever the future held, he was still mine. My best friend.

I wasn't going to throw him away, even though I couldn't be his mate.

"You're not looking at the sky," he murmured, arms wrapping around my waist and swaying back and forth. A dance to the music of the wind in the trees.

"I can't see her," I admitted, Grim leaning against my leg and joining the dance.

"Most people can't, outside of the summer months. But I always know where she is," he spoke next to my ear. Open and honest, with no pretense, the Artemis of my childhood. "Zeus is said to have an affair with Callisto, and Hera turned her into a bear. One day, the son of Callisto and Zeus, Arcas, was out hunting and nearly killed her. Zeus threw them into the sky to keep them with him forever. It is said that while Selene is the goddess of the wolf shifters, Callisto is ours. A beautiful nymph and huntress, fighting and loving in the night sky."

I nodded, wondering how I'd never known this before.

"Real bears, really any pack of animal species, don't have alphas. It was just a numbering system used to catalog chicken hierarchy. But Zeus, father of so many, wanted to rule it all despite his weak and inconsequential nature. So, he made the male of the shifter species alpha, an attempt to affront nature and the natural matriarchy of the animal world."

"Zeus was kind of a philandering cunt nugget, wasn't he?" I muttered and Artie shook behind me with laughter, the lightest moment between us since I'd tried to invade his southern borders. "I mean, is there any woman in Greek mythology he didn't fuck and then fuck over?"

"Like many men, he thinks that jealousy and limitless procreation give him power over those who are stronger than him. I'm not one to cast stones at sexual insatiability, but it's certainly telling that humans are the only species who haven't learned the power and superiority of the feminine. I'm not sure I believe in all the mythology, but if I were to pick it apart, I'd bet Zeus was created by men. The genuine power, the real history, is a council of goddesses."

It was a thought that made me smile. I'd always felt Zeus was superfluous whenever I was forced to engage with history or mythology. Toxic

masculinity littered our history, a destructive force that wanted to domi-
nate others for the power they could never have.

For all their boisterous words, men could not create.

So, they'd spent centuries telling those who could what they would
and would not allow.

"Bears don't naturally form families. They can live near each other,
form alliances and friendships, but the true bear would not mate. His
hierarchy is determined by size. The largest bear in an area becomes the
dominant bear, known for posturing and looking tough in front of the
other bears. He has no leadership skills, familial instincts or territory to
defend. He's just big and grouchy."

The similarities between the dominant bear and myself were a little
too many. He may have been intending to describe himself, to explain
his fears and hesitations, but all I saw was myself: standing alone,
fighting off the world in the hopes that everyone would think I was too
big and bad to get too close to.

"I'm scared I'll be a bad mate," he confessed. "But I would never let
that fear stop me from doing whatever it takes to save you. So maybe we
aren't ready to get married or be the forever kind of love in stories, but I
will love you forever."

It was as unsettling as the rest of the day had been, and the bone
weariness from earlier returned. I shivered as the cold seeped into my
stockinged feet. Artemis gave me one last squeeze and led me back inside
by the hand, Grim trotting behind us.

Indoors, Artie had started a fire in the pellet stove and put another
blanket on the bed.

Stripping off my sweatpants and hoodie, I pulled on undies and a
large T-shirt with a dinosaur on it. Laying the damp socks in front of the
pellet stove, I stared at the bed and its singular surface.

"Should we... build a pillow wall?" I asked, not sure how we would
fit on a full-sized bed together at all, much less without touching.

"Penny..." he set his clothes in front of the pellet stove, not sure
whether to look at me or the bed when he spoke. "You are such a pain in
the ass. Build whatever walls you want, but like I've done every time
before, I'm just going to knock them down again tomorrow. Because we
both know that no matter what stupid shit I do, you love me more than

you will ever say out loud. And you already know I love you, even if you take every opportunity to prove you're unlovable."

I stared at him as he crossed his arms, wearing only boxers, waiting for me to make a move. It had been a long day, and though I was exhausted, sad, and probably facing my own mortality, I loved him.

And he loved me.

And we'd definitely done far more intimate things than this.

It just felt... different this time. Knowing what I did, sober, made agreeing to this feel like an admission of love and devotion that neither of us was ready for.

Were we?

"Ugh, you're so annoying," I huffed, climbing into bed and pulling the covers to my chin. Instead of building a pillow wall, I just laid there, fuming at his too accurate assessment of my personal propensity to run away from intimacy. "But for the record, I was unconscious when we went to bed last night, so it's not like I had a chance to over think and be weird about it. Same with being wasted the night before. And the whole coitus interruptus thing is... I don't know. Pheromones."

"Well, at least you know what you're doing. Admitting you have a problem is half the battle."

The bed dipped, Artemis sliding in beside me to lie on his side. Head propped on one arm as he stared down at me with a crooked smile.

"The only problem I have is your stupid, smug face and perfect body. Now go to sleep."

Using a single finger, he rubbed the crease between my eyes.

"You keep that up, your face will freeze that way," he teased, laying down on his back. Just like earlier, he slid his arm under me and rolled me onto his chest. With his other hand, he turned off the light, leaving only the fire to light the room in a warm glow. The dancing flames played games with the shadows; a puppet show without a plot.

If only real life were as random.

"Tell me a story, Peep." He asked, and I shook my head.

"No way. You tell me a story."

"I told you one outside!"

"Fine... but I'm not telling you a bed-time story because you're a cocky pain in the ass,"

"I'm glad you're thinking about my cock and my ass," he smirked in the darkness, and I rolled my eyes. A smile snuck across my face, and I hoped he couldn't see it. Despite myself, I was definitely thinking about his cock... and his ass.

"What did you get me for my birthday?" Artie asked beneath me and I tilted my chin to watch him study the dancing firelight. He must have sensed my confusion because he clarified. "For my 19th birthday... what did you get me?"

"Oh..." I tried not to squirm. "It... well..."

"Do you still have it?"

Nodding, I closed my eyes and pictured the gift where I'd left it in the bottom drawer of my dresser at my parents' house. The paper was covered in little rainbows, a light blue background making the whole package bright and happy.

The gift appeared on the bed beside him, and I felt my eyes droop.

Too much magic... you are out of sync with nature.

Rustling paper by my head, and then a sudden intake of breath, let me know when the pendant on a simple leather cord was in his hand. In my periphery, the opalescent stone bear danced in the firelight and shone with the same light and energy as the man, made with magic from both of us and meant to bind us together no matter the distance. Carved out of the chest near the front paw was a small heart, beneath which on one side was a tiny inscription that I didn't know if he could read in the low light without a magnifying glass.

You Are My Heart,
I will always be with you.

I woke up wrapped around Artemis, boa constrictor style. My head smashed into his chest with a small puddle of drool I'd feel bad about if it weren't on Artie. One of my legs was threaded between his, my lady V pressed against his thigh above which my hand was fisted around the waistband of his shorts.

"Sorry," I muttered, releasing his pants and trying to convince my pussy she did not, in fact, want to rub her scent on his leg to mark her territory.

Artemis was already awake, one hand running through my hair while the other rubbed the stone bear he was wearing around his neck. At my apology, he set the bear back on his chest and squeezed the thick flesh at my hips, bringing me closer.

I tried not to dry hump his leg with the added pressure, but it was harder than it should have been.

"Any dreams?" he asked, looking down at me.

"For my life? Not really," I joked, rolling to the side and off my human heating pad. It felt the same as opening a pizza box and finding it empty—hungry and a little depressed.

"Not what I meant," he grumped, poking me in the ribs. Yelping, I rolled off the edge of the bed and stretched. "I meant *the* dreams…"

"Not this time."

Plodding across the room, I went to the tiny coffee maker. At some point last night Artie must have put the water and grounds into it, because I needed only to flip the big red switch on and we were in business.

Grabbing my sweats, I ducked into the bathroom to relieve myself and brush my teeth. Swiping on some deodorant, I exited the bathroom and grabbed Grim's leash. Despite the circumstances and location, my autopilot was fully functional.

Bemused, Artemis watched me stick my feet in the nearest pair of shoes and wander outside. My familiar didn't follow, anticipating my screech of suffering and hasty retreat. Grim gave me the doggy equivalent of a mocking laugh as I searched the bag Naomi packed for a hat, sunglasses... anything to protect me from the flaming ball of gas. Finding a ball cap that was probably not mine, I stuffed it on my head and tried again.

Under the bill of my cap, the sun was still a massive dick, but he couldn't cook my eyeballs like soft-boiled eggs. Grim meandered off the porch, circling the back of the cabin and then weaving in and out of trees until he found the perfect spot to do his business.

Conveniently near a pet waste disposal caddy, because he was the best boy.

Empty and sniffed out, we went back into the cabin where Artemis was still lounging topless in bed, playing with his necklace. The room smelled like us both, and when he looked at me, there was only a flicker of uncertainty before he smiled.

I would not be smiling before coffee.

I released Grim, who took up my former bed space, and checked the coffee maker to see how it was progressing.

It was not progressing at all.

"What the hell?" I shouted, lifting the lid and seeing the same water and dry grounds as before. Flipping the switch back and forth, I bit back tears when nothing happened. "No! Please, not today!"

I begged the machine, saying kind, loving words while I flipped the switch.

"You are such a good coffee maker! You can do it! Pretty please? Give me satisfaction and you'll want for nothing!"

I was fairly certain I could afford to be a coffee maker's sugar daddy.

On the 18th toggle, the button turned bright orange, and the appliance burbled to life.

"Oh, thank the goddess," I sighed and turned into Artie, who was standing there pointing at the wall with a cord poking out of it. I followed the cord up to the coffeemaker, staring back at him. "What?"

"Nothing." He pulled me in for a hug and I leaned into it. "I think we should go on a date."

"Hmm…" I said into his chest, inhaling his scent and then wondering if I could rub his abs with… "Wait, what?"

I stepped back and bumped into the bed. My foot landed in Grim's water dish, sloshing liquid all over the floor. Grabbing a towel hanging in the kitchen, I lost balance and tumbled onto the bed, taking the towel and the small metal ring it had been hanging on with me. The displaced metal clattered on the ground, scaring Grim, who shot up and jumped on my chest, pinning me down while the room settled from my recent gravitational storm.

The coffee maker beeped and while I tried to relocate the large black dog off my chest, Artemis prepared two cups of coffee. I got Grim moved to beside me after Artie had prepped both cups and was extending one out for me to take. Hesitating, I reached out a hand to take it, worried it was a trap of some kind.

"Drink. We'll talk after."

Keeping one eye on him, I took a long drink, letting my eyes close to savor the greatest magic to spawn from people who randomly put things in their mouths. When I removed the cup from my lips, it was sadly empty.

"What kind of cup is this?" I wondered, splaying my hand beside it to discover it was the same size as my palm. "What the hell? This is a shot glass. Who gives people coffee shot glasses?"

Artie plucked the cup from my hand and started refilling it.

"We're going on a date." He didn't make it sound optional this time. "Since it's already after noon, I think now would be a good time."

"Do we have to? You've already seen me naked and I'm not good at the whole..." I gestured to the outside world. "That."

I took my mug back and drained it a second time. The liquid was not as hot as a normal coffee maker would brew, but it had been moderately broken until I wished it back to life, so I tried not being too judgmental.

Coffee makers were sensitive like that.

"I think we do," he said, casually sipping the tiny cup I worried was his first and that meant I had to give him a chance at a second before I killed the pot. "Maybe not a full-on normal dinner and a movie date, but I think we need to spend some time together outside of the Hollow. Where we can both just be people... I think all the mate bond sex energy is throwing us off from just... being us."

"That sounds terrible. You know I hate being people," I grumbled. Artemis gave me the rest of the coffee and I perked immediately.

I knew it was a bribe, but some things are worth dating for.

"Fine, we can be a people... but I'm not putting pants on for this."

NOT ONLY WAS I wearing pants, but we were outside in the sunshine.

"Who really enjoys picnics?" I complained for the fourth time and he stuck a grape in my mouth. Handing me a glass of wine, I tried not to spill while reclining slightly on the outdoor blanket. "I mean ants do, but in Guatemala, they carry away feces so I don't think we should model our life choices after..."

Another grape was placed in my mouth.

In front of us, the desolate beach was the perfect venue for Grim to jump in and out of the lake, waves gently crashing into the sandy shoreline. He pounced at the water as it came in, running away when it wanted revenge in the form of soaking through his fur coat.

The temperatures remained freezing. No other humans had ventured out to the lakeshore, and we were alone on the sand watching him play. Beside me was a large bag filled to the brim with random foods Artemis had grabbed from the grocery store to assemble this romantic outing.

"I used to come here a lot," Artie said, his words strong despite the wind and crashing waves. "Back in junior high school, when we thought you couldn't leave the town or the forest, I used to come here and wish you were with me. I'd think about all the places we could go if you weren't trapped. I'd write out lists, places from back home I wanted to show you and places I hadn't been to yet but saw in books or movies."

I took a drink of wine and listened to him, Grim returning to the blanket to lie down with us.

"When we got to high school and learned your boundaries were a little wider than just town, I kept making plans to bring you here. Wanted to show you the place, show you the list..." he reached into his back pocket and pulled out a small spiral-bound notebook. I took it from his outstretched hand, flipping through the pages. Some destinations had only a paragraph, others had pages and pages of stories. Some were places he'd only read about, others places he'd lived, but all of them written as a tour guide for a woman he wished were with him.

"Even after you left, when I couldn't remember who I was making this book for, I kept making it. There was a hole in my life, a counterpart I wanted every day to share stories with and be near. I know who I've been over time, the playboy and the fun story people bring out at parties about that famous alpha they fucked one time. It wasn't always just about survival and feeding, Penny, I enjoyed it. But I always knew you were missing. What I didn't know, until last night when you gave this to me," he pulled out his opalescent bear, fingers tracing the inscription I knew to be there. "Was whether or not I was part of your heart, part of your life, even when I was gone."

"You were always a part of me, Artemis. That necklace... I'd found a spell one day in the woods. It takes a bit of magic from two people and binds them together, creating a link so you're always connected. I made it so that when we went our own ways, you could always have a part of us with you. That if you missed me, you could hold it and it would tug on the line to call me home... Because when I was younger, and even now, where you are has always felt like home." I stared out at the water. "I thought about you every day."

"You asked if I wanted to be your mate forever." He took a deep breath, and I held mine. "I didn't hesitate because I don't want to be with you. I hesitated because I was worried you didn't want to be with me. Not forever. And that if I told you the truth, you'd freak out. You are not known for being emotionally mature, Peep."

Gulping the rest of my wine, I reached for his hand, pulling him toward me. If I'd been good with words, I'd have spoken them, but I knew whatever I said would come out wrong.

He was also spot on about my emotional immaturity.

"Penny, I..." he started, but I crushed my mouth to his. Trying to tell him with my actions the words I couldn't speak. Pushing him back onto the blanket, I straddled his hips to kiss him deeper, pinning him where his cock was in line with my entrance but not touching. I hovered over him, fingers linked together above his head, our kisses growing more feverish and desperate.

With grace and speed, he flipped us over and trapped both my hands in one of his above my head. Rubbing himself against me through both our pants, I nearly cried out at his cold fingers slipping into my sweater and pinching my nipple through the thin bra I'd put on.

"What do you want, Penny?" He asked against my jaw, teeth and lips, giving equal affection to my tender flesh. My earlobe disappeared into his mouth, and I arched up into his hips, begging for more while his teeth left little nibbles on my neck. Lips and tongue working lower and lower until he bit my left nipple through my clothes, pinching the right at the same time.

A wave of liquid heat poured from my opening, soaking my underwear.

"I want forever, Artie," I gasped and pulled back hard on his hair. When our eyes met, I tried to show him every feeling in my heart. "I want to feel your mark on me forever."

"My naughty little sheep, you like it rough," he murmured against my abdomen, the sweater I was wearing shoved up to my neck. His hands and lips continued to work my breasts through the bra until I was shaking with need.

"Artie, please. I need you," I begged, my hips rubbing faster against the ridge in his jeans. "I need your cock. Please?"

"I don't have a condom," he groaned, looking like he might cry. "You'll have to wait."

"Witch," I reminded him. "I don't wait for anything."

His low growl was my only response before he had my pants pulled down, the first two fingers buried deep in the liquid heat he drew from me like air. In a flash, the easy-going man was replaced with his demon half.

A demanding, controlling, and aggressive beast who would pull everything he wanted from my body.

"Scream my name, Penny," he ordered, as I fought to take my hands back from him. "Scream for me."

"Fuck me, Artemis," I demanded, looking up at him through my lust filled gaze while his fingers kept working me over. Two inside, his thumb on my clit, I was aroused, angry and violently in need of release. "Fuck me hard and don't stop."

It was all he needed, flipping me onto all fours. His fingers continued while his other hand undid his jeans. I stared at him over my shoulder, shoving backward into his hands as I held my breath for a look at his cock.

My tongue darted out against my lips, wetting them and wishing I could lick the little bead of pre-cum off his tip. It was thick, the ridge at the top sliding down into a smooth velvet length.

Holding my breath, I watched him remove his fingers and suck my arousal off each one. Catching each drop before it could drip down his hand, while the other came down hard on my ass cheek with a smack.

His cock slid in then, filling me completely to the brim.

Another hand slapped my ass and I let out a mewl, rocking on my knees to make him move.

"Naughty girl, do you like my cock?" He asked, reaching around to circle my clit and refusing to give an inch of relief to my desperate pussy that wanted to feel him, hard and ferocious, like the look he'd given me last night.

His hand came down a third time.

"Answer me, Penny," his fingers pinched the nub on my front, and I shattered, my walls fluttering around his cock as I screamed his name. On the final pulse of my quivering channel, he pulled himself almost completely out and slammed home again.

Then again, his hands fisted in the heavy rolls at my hips.

"Fuck me, Artemis," I screamed, and he went to town. Pounding into me at a pace faster than any I'd had before. The ridge of his cock hit my G-spot just right over and over again.

"Artie, I..." I gasped, fingers digging into the blanket.

"Don't fucking come until I say you can," he warned, picking up the tempo. My breathing was ragged, the building pressure threatening to burst as I held onto the rising tide, threatening to split me in half as the crest grew higher and higher.

"Fuck, now Peep!" he gasped, and I shattered around him. Hand around my throat, he pulled me up to ride out his orgasm, mouth and lips at my neck until his teeth sank deep into my skin, the pain bringing on another wave of release. His hot come coating my insides with a second orgasm, and we both shattered in spasming waves of pleasure that shook the ground beneath us. The wind subsided, and the waves stilled, everything settling into a satiated purr with the orgasm still rolling through me. Artie tilted to the side, pulling me on top of him to catch my breath, laying out on the blanket. His hands tangled in my hair, dragging my face up for another blistering kiss.

"We should go back to the cabin," he breathed, his cock already hardening again. "You are hours from done, and I just remembered everything I've wanted to do to you... for years."

"What do you mean, 'you remember'?" I wheezed, still trembling from my release.

"Everything, Peep. I fucking remember everything."

Six orgasms later, I was gasping in bed beside Artie. My whole body was aquiver from my latest release while my heart hadn't slowed in five hours.

"If I die, please put 'fucked to death' on my tombstone," I panted. "I'd like my death to make people as uncomfortable as I did in life."

After our exhibitionist beach stunt, Grim was pointedly facing a wall with paws on his ears. If I'd had any energy or strength, I'd have given him a sound bubble... but everything I had was spilled on the mattress, the side table, and the bathroom sink.

Artie popped up from between my legs, forearm swiping across his face with the biggest pussy-eating grin I'd ever seen.

"Deal," he chuckled, spreading out on the mattress beside me. "Now that I've had dinner, should I get us a pizza?"

"Probably more than one... and feed Grim. Also, I need water, and wine... and cheese."

I ran out of breath to continue my list, still seeing stars. My limbs ached from being folded into new positions, my thighs raw from beard burn, and my knees just a little red from being fucked on the beach.

"So demanding, my queen," he joked, dropping a kiss on my cheek and strutting into the bathroom. He caught me looking in the mirror and gave a wink. "You are insatiable."

I tried to look innocent, but it was a lie. Watching his ass was almost as good a view as the sight of his cock buried deep inside me.

"And I'm wet again," I muttered, standing up and trying to walk like a sober person. Grim gave me a look that showed he approved of my choices, but not having to witness them. As though I hadn't been woken up on more than one occasion by him aggressively going to town licking himself.

Staring out the small window in the kitchenette, I watched the setting sun. Long shadows dragged along the ground, a reminder that winter was approaching. In my dreams, snow had rested on the trees in the clearing. I had some time before I needed to worry about that future.

A bigger concern was the blood moon, set to rise in a few hours. There was no way to predict the harvest moon, no way to know when the deadline was for us to seal the bond.

If we even could.

Alpha Kuruk seemed to think the harvest moon would follow the blood moon this time. At least that's why he'd summoned Artie home, but how would he know?

My research had netted very little. There was no recorded history of a shifter, even a half one, not knowing their mate on sight. Records showed the blood moon made the bond stronger, a powerful time to be with other shifters and find your other half. References to the harvest moon were sparse and Artie's reference to '*when the moon children walk among man the same as night*' was not recorded anywhere in the history of magic.

But it was still the reason he'd been called home.

"What are you thinking about?"

Artemis had appeared behind me, freshly showered with minty fresh breath. I leaned into his embrace, trying not to get too excited at the feel of his man-meat brushing my leg.

"I was wondering why your dad needed you here to take your place in the pack now..." The feeling in my chest was hard to explain. "Same with my mom... it's starting to..."

"Feel like a trap?" He finished, and I nodded. "I've been wondering that, too. When pressed why he wanted me to 'take my place in the pack', he'd gotten upset and cagey. Like he wasn't... himself."

"Meanwhile, my mom had my siblings move out of the Hollow, but she arranged for me to come back and have a job... one that implies I can't leave. Almost hedging in case... but then you..."

Rubbing my temples, I felt a low grade migraine starting behind my eye.

"Maybe we should eat before you do so much heavy thinking," Artie suggested. "Go grab a shower. I'll get the food."

I nodded, not sure my brain would work right pre-pizza anyway, and shuffled off to the bathroom.

Emerging from the bathroom, I tried not to look more sore and exhausted than I'd been going in. After jumping immediately into the stream, I'd seen the early stages of bruising on various parts of my body and decided that mirrors were the enemy at the moment.

Whether I'd be freaked out or turned on was a toss up and I was too tired to be either.

In the time it had taken me to wash, Artie had gotten three pizzas, a large salad and iced coffee delivered. He'd also fed Grim, changed out the sheets with the aid of hotel staff, and cleared the trash. Though we were closer to a city than I'd initially thought, it was still impressive he'd accomplished it in under thirty minutes.

I made a mental note to give him a tip later.

But since I was broke, his tip was going to have to be more service oriented.

"How did you do this all so fast?" I asked, settling into the bed beside him where all the food was set up, not bothering with clothes. My first iced coffee was already gone, consumed as mysteriously as it had appeared.

"I started ordering the food before my shower... the rest is just perks of being me," he said with a wink. I deadpanned disgust, taking an aggressive bite of pizza that left sauce dripping down my chin and toppings spilling onto my boob shelf.

All thoughts of anger evaporated, the melted cheese and olives bringing an extra pleasure that rivaled two of the eight orgasms Artie had given me.

They'd all been good… but so was pizza.

"Don't make that sound, Peep, unless it's on my cock," he warned, but I could barely hear him over the disappearance of another slice of pizza. Piling green leaves on my plate, I devoured the salad with the same satisfaction I'd sucked his cock an hour ago; amazed that the bland crunch water tasted so good.

"So good," I said around another mouthful of pizza, this one sausage and… who the hell knew what else? I just knew there were no fungi or pineapple. I was no longer concerned with naming the flavors. I just wanted them in my mouth.

"Shit," he laughed, leaning over to kiss my head and swipe my chin with a napkin that I personally felt was pointless. The rate at which condiments were falling onto my body made using a napkin more wasteful than helpful. "Watching you eat should not be this hot."

"Is you fault," I said in my native dialect, food in mouth. "You should know be'er than to make me do that much cardio without a snack break!"

"Sorry," he responded, laughing harder. "Remember senior year when your mom was trying to make you diet and forced you to go without eating for 6 hours?"

"Intermittent hexing fasting, yes," I grumbled, not at all a fan of whichever trending influencer gave her that dumbass idea. If I ever learned that witch's name, they were going to get genital warts and pink eye.

"And you led a siege on the cafeteria? They started screaming about Death and gave you a half chocolate cake, three wheels of cheese and an apple," he was laughing so hard, tears were streaming out of his eyes, and I joined his merriment.

Some things were only funny in retrospect.

"Ugh, I had the worst stomach ache for second period. Then they tried to call my mom on me." Our laughter died out as we remembered what came next. Yasmine had her friends give me a pig snout and tail, cursing every word I said to come out as honks and snorts. "At least now I know why my mom had done nothing to help me."

I pushed the pizza box away from me, no longer hungry.

"I'm going to..." I stood up, looking for something to wipe off my skin so I could don pajamas. There was a stack of napkins beside my "Dinosnore" shirt, and I quickly swiped off the sauce to pull it on.

Artie was on me in a second, his thumb and forefinger gripping my chin.

"Look at me, Peep," he ordered, but I couldn't do it. Not after that... It was more than humiliating. What they'd done had given me a compulsive fear of being without food and, worse, letting people know I had it. I was willing to fight for anyone taunted about their weight or size, cursing them into next Tuesday.

But I wasn't willing to fight for myself.

"Now, Penelope. Don't make me ask you again."

I shot him a look, deadly and defiant.

"You don't own me, Artemis," I growled. His knee bent, parting my legs while his second hand stole the shirt I'd just put on, throwing it across the room.

"No? I don't own this pussy?"

His hand stroked my seam, reminding me I hadn't put on underwear when his finger probed my entrance. Immediately, my body flooded with heat and I lost my words.

"This," he said softly, loosening his grip on my face to trail down the extra skin under my arm. Bringing it to his lips, he laid a soft kiss on the spot. "I own this."

His lips went to my collarbone and down to that little extra pudge above my breasts that made wearing bras uncomfortable.

"This is mine too."

His head slid under my arm to the spot at my back where it bunched. Artemis gave it a quick nip, followed by a kiss. I was once again bucking for friction on his upper thigh as the man who'd just spent hours ravaging my body sucked and kissed all the areas I'd been told were problems.

My muffin top was massaged and kissed.

As was my inner thigh, my stomach, my back... he kissed all of it until I was somewhere between crying and screaming his name.

"All of you is mine, Peep. And I love all of it."

He sucked one hard peak into his mouth. Pinching the other between his fingers, alternating back and forth until just his breath on either would send me over the edge. Swiping a finger along my folds, he placed them against his nose.

"I love the way you smell."

Sucking off my arousal, he returned his hand between my legs, lazily milking every drop from me.

Knowing there would always be more.

"I love how wet you are for me."

Artemis leaned in and captured my lips, giving me soft, loving kisses to the same rhythm as the strokes of his finger.

I bucked against his hand, needing more. Needing the intensity and the pain, instead he picked me up and laid me gently down on the bed. Stacking the pizza boxes, he moved them out of the way and turned off the light.

Outside, the over-bright full moon cast a red glow around us while his hands and lips stroked and coaxed me into a soft orgasm, the feathered edges sending shivers to the tips of my toes.

"And this," Artie whispered against my ear, shuffling to remove his pants and line up his cock at my entrance. "This is yours. All of me is yours."

His thick length slid in while his mouth delivered feathery kisses on my mouth, my eyes... anywhere he could reach while delivering long, slow strokes deep inside me. The next orgasm built. I could feel him tense and knew he was getting closer.

I leaned into his ear and whispered, the full red moon lighting my lips.

"And I love all of you."

Our orgasms hit at the same time, his teeth sinking into my neck while my own itchy gums ordered me to do the same.

Under the light of the blood moon, I felt the mate bond snap into place with the taste of blood and magic flowing between us.

Outside the window, the first snowflakes fell.

THIRTY-NINE

ARTEMIS

Sunlight poured through the open curtain, and I blinked away the spots of light that burst into my vision. Penny was wrapped around my body like a baby koala, her soft snores and snarled hair from the relaxing scene I'd waited years to wake up to.

Years I spent unable to see or hear the woman who'd become my whole fucking world.

Carefully, I slid my hand under the thick tangle of hair and moved it aside.

My mark sat on the curve of her neck. A constellation to rival Ursa Major in beauty. I wanted to run my tongue along every dent, curve and freckle in her skin.

Mine.

The sound reverberated pleasantly in my head.

Grim appeared beside me, his cold nose catching my ribs.

"Shit, OK. No wonder your mom's always crabby," I half laughed as I shifted out from under Peep, dropping a quick kiss on her forehead. It had seemed possible I might lose her so many times, possible that I'd fuck it all up. She was too scared of being hurt and rejected, too scared of being unlovable to let love in.

But she was here.

And she was mine.

As was the massive dog tippy tapping by the door, his bushy tail up to show the heart-shaped white spot on his butt. Though he wasn't a shifter, the animal was as bonded and linked to my woman as I was.

So naturally, I served as his surrogate human.

Clipping on his leash, I took him outside. A thin layer of snow lay on the ground, the low morning light making it a gray blanket instead of the brilliant prism it'd be in a few hours. I followed the dog around the corner, noting once again that Grim had a strange way of choosing his spots. Sniffing at every shrub and tree and then peeing on rocks and buildings.

Made me wonder if the plants talked to him the way they talked to Peep's mom.

"Excuse me?" A man called out, and I turned toward the main hotel, watching Grim scent the air. His hackles went up. A stegosaurus with black fur.

"Can I help you?" I asked, putting myself between the newcomer and the canine. To our left was the cabin and to the right was the forest. Keeping my eyes on both, I let Grim watch our backs.

"My family and I were staying over there, but our car died. Can you maybe give me a ride into town to get a battery?"

The man looked like every other white person, a sea of nonsense that rarely varied in more than name. Some version of would-be survivalist who claimed to want less government while actively supporting discrimination against women, natives and wild animals.

Though I'd left to play in the league, I'd stayed on top of the area. I knew what type of man I'd find out here and I didn't want him anywhere near my woman or her dog.

He was also a damn liar because I'd rented every cabin out here last night, so no one would hear Peep scream my name while I fucked her into oblivion.

"Afraid I have somewhere to be, but they have a phone up in the main house," I advised, moving away from the man and back toward the cabin where my mate was sleeping. Grim made noises behind me, a reminder that he was here to protect and defend.

But if anything happened to the chunky dog, Peep would murder me.

Ahead of us, the man in khakis hesitated, his mask slipping for only a moment, to give us a flash of all black eyes.

The only forewarning I had to brace myself.

The creature launched forward, his obsidian eyes sparkling above skin faded into near translucence.

Without the glamour, I recognized the demon as great Uncle Asmodeus, my grandfather's brother, and another demon of the dark. I lowered my head and braced my feet on the ground. Claws elongated out of each of his fingers, a transition that telegraphed his moves before he lunged at my throat.

Too fucking slow.

I dropped to the ground, his claws slicing the air above me. It shimmered purple, the dog behind me sinking his teeth into the man's leg. Asmodeus let loose a screech, claws dragging the air toward Grim, who flung his giant head toward a tree, releasing the attacker at the height of the arc so his back slammed into the tree with a sickening snap.

A flash of red and the scent of sulfur filled the air, and what should have been a broken, bloody corpse turned to ash. I smiled at the dog, who just shook himself and bared his teeth, vision locked in behind me.

The ironic slow clap pulled a growl from both of us, and I turned away from my ally to see what else was coming.

We'd squared off toward my mother's twin, the woman's patronizing claps continuing long after a normal person would stop.

"You should work on your dramatic timing," I bellowed, checking that Grim was behind me. "Any performer will tell you that the slow clap beat is a three-count."

"Should you be brazen when I hold the life of your family in my hand?" She extended a fraying rope, ending in a noose around my father's neck. Face bloody, eye swollen shut, he remained stoic in the face of captivity. Every one of his actions from the past weeks, and possibly years, coming together.

He hadn't been an especially loving man, but he'd certainly hadn't been as much of a prick before we'd moved to Idaho.

"I see you've sealed the bond with the witch," she nodded toward my neck and I fought the urge to rub a sore spot. If Penny had marked me, I'd have to wait to appreciate it. "That'll make this next part harder for you."

"What can I say? I like it hard?" I shot off, falling into the easy-going persona that carried me through hard times. "Show me what you got."

"Perhaps I should start with something easier and kill your lucky Penny." Chepi turned toward our cabin and took a single step.

Snarling, Grim and I stood side by side between my aunt and our Penelope.

"Touch her and die," I snapped. My dad's eyes widened, but he didn't speak. I could feel his bear just under the surface, but I couldn't tell who he was working for.

"I won't have to," she laughed at us. "I had your dad bring you home to get Ms. Penelope. She created quite the challenge with that little spell. Couldn't be sure she'd come for you if she thought you'd simply forgotten her. Who'd have thought sex on the beach cures problems?"

"Alcoholics," I spat, pissed that she'd somehow been privy to our fucking.

No one was allowed to hear Peep scream but me.

The Council appeared, taking posts behind and around Chepi. Their presence enraged me, and I readied myself to rip them to shreds.

Behind Grim, I heard the ash reform into my great uncle. An unfortunate drawback to fighting the immortal–with an unlimited power source, they could be removed, but it wouldn't stop them from returning. Usually they needed to collect souls, but this group was being fed all the magic in the Hollow.

Fuckers.

"Come with us, Artemis, and your dad lives. Fight and he'll be dead where he stands." She made the statement like a carnival barker, the candy-coated lies that any of the games she peddled were fair. My dad was dead the second she got that noose around his neck. "If she doesn't come for you, you die. But I promise you that your dad will live if you do."

"Why should I believe you?"

"Because I'm family," she laughed, the council braying alongside her.

"Why make me go with you?" I demanded.

"I told you, we need your Penny." Her voice was growing more agitated.

"Why do we have to leave at all? Fight me here, and let's end this," I growled and Grim sneezed his agreement beside me.

"Why are you asking so many questions?" She snapped, the Council taking a step toward us. Her anger gave away my answer. Location was everything. If I could keep us here...

"Come with us or your dad dies, and I drag you there. The only way he lives is if you shut up and come with us, insolent man-child."

The Council shifted, all of them looking up slightly toward the harvest moon.

When the moon children walk among man the same as night.... My dad's words mixed with Penny's, Abeque's and Mistletonia's. I finally understood, and it was worse than living in the dark. The veil had thinned between our worlds. He wasn't talking about the mate bond; he was talking about sacrificing Peep to the other world and my aunt had used him and her mom to make it happen.

"Son of a bitch."

We needed more time for the curtain to close... but would it be better to keep them here or take them away from Peep?

I needed to stall.

"Is it because we aren't in the Hollow, or because we're too far from the rift?"

Her curled lip was the confirmation I needed.

Penny's death was only useful if it happened where the power could be taken. That was what Abeque had meant about the darkness needing to be returned to restore balance. Penny couldn't just give up her life. She needed to surrender it to the rift for the energy to be restored.

"Shut up and come with us or I will kill your father!" Her hand yanked the rope. My dad falling to all fours with the resignation of someone who knew they would die. But whether he'd been coerced or joined her willingly, most of this was his fault.

"You're so full of shit," I muttered, looking down at Grim. The dog wasn't the best person to ask for advice, but there weren't any other options. His drawn eyebrows advised against going, but also didn't offer an alternative. Probably because he was a fucking dog.

He sneezed at me and I laughed, a dry quip without words. Gesturing to Grim, I made a deal with a demon, hoping Peep slept through their timeline and we'd deal with it later.

Dealing with shit later was my specialty.

"Fuck it. Fine, I'll go, but he stays."

My aunt rolled her eyes, looking so much like my grandmother.

"Like I care about a dog," she scoffed.

"Like you care about anything," I shot back, leading Grim back to the cabin.

Muttering quietly, I said a prayer for peace. Speaking to nature and asking her to sow love where there is hatred and give hope to Penelope in place of despair.

Also, if it wasn't too much trouble, to send these fuckwads back to where they came from and reconnect the Hollow to the natural order.

I opened the door, whispering to Grim as I slipped off the bear necklace and placed it on his neck.

"Don't let her find me, dude. Cool Runnings."

Peace be the journey.

WE WERE GATHERED in a clearing just outside of town.

The smell of beechwood and strawberries hung in the air. Spent campfires filled the circle in the shape of a pentagram, crushed and dried flowers caught on branches and leaves. Leftovers from the summer solstice celebration despite nearly 6 months since its time.

"Now what?" I asked Chepi.

Beside her, my dad was on his knees. Serving as pet bear to my mother's evil twin.

"Now you shut up and appreciate the silence," she snapped, and I laughed despite myself. Bouncing on the balls of my feet, I felt like I was about to take the ice in a championship game. I didn't know when they'd call me up, but I knew my time was coming and I had to be ready.

"I'm always ready."

Above us, the harvest moon hovered. A ghost of the full moon from the night before and a reminder that day and night each have their time, but true magic happens when neither is bound to the laws of man.

True magic... The words stuck in my head, and I felt her like the energy signature of the bear that I'd worn around my neck.

Penelope was in the woods, her magic caressing my essence just out of reach.

"No!" I shouted as the first bolt of pain shot through my chest. "Don't fucking do this!"

My words disappeared in a roar, my hands transforming into paws. Around the clearing, every person became smaller. I grew in height and in size, but I was still tethered to the ground by an invisible cage that leached my essence when I fought. It matched what Penny had whispered in her sleep, the impenetrable cage of evil that held her magic inside of me.

Held it like a lifeline to the world I wanted to live in.

I wasn't the light and the cage holding her magic was the fucking darkness that tricked the world into sending Peep to her grave. My family used me as damn bait and when she died, only evil would remain. Her magic, caged inside me, was to hide my nature. The shadow on her at the coven meeting was mine.

I was the darkness, just borrowing her light.

"No!" I shouted again, my beautiful pale love bursting into the clearing with scratches and smears of blood dripping down her naked arms and legs. The earth having taken what little it could and sending the rest off to fucking die.

"Run!"

"Let him go!" Penny shouted, facing Chepi without a drop of fear or hesitation. "Let him go and I will let you take me. I've seen the truth, and it's time, but no more blood can be shed."

"Don't do it!" My roars weren't words. Her eyes darted to mine, and I saw something terrifying.

This was her dream.

She'd always known what our future would be, and this was a sacrifice she would make. Trading her life for the assholes in the Hollow who wouldn't lift a finger to save her. I watched the woman I love clench her fists, releasing her tension while all the droplets of her blood pooled and were pulled into the ground.

"Tell him you love him then!" She shouted, and Penny looked me in the eye, mouthing the words.

I love you; you are my heart. I will always be with you.

A rumbling howl filled the sky, my heart ripping into a million pieces when my aunt threw a glowing dagger through the air that lodged in Penny's heart.

A burst of purple light, and she was gone.

FORTY

ARTEMIS

The moment the air cleared, I charged.

My lumbering bear didn't have any of the muscle or control I needed, but I went for her throat. Surprise mixed with confusion crossed her face. My teeth sank into the soft flesh of her half-human form and ripped it out. A gargled cry slipped out, and she was dust.

I clawed the rope from my dad's neck, the frayed twine an optical illusion for a demonic stranglehold ripping at his skin until the sparkling blood was consumed by the jet black cord. My uncle came at both of us, and I handed my dad the lead end of his own rope, willing him to take it and do something my paws couldn't manage.

Rising with the strength of our people, both magic and not, he spun around to challenge the man who would never be family. Charging forward, he was above, beyond, and behind the man before either of us could blink. The rope reappeared, wrapped around Asmodeus's neck and bit at the paper-thin pelt, sucking at my dad's essence to rip through his uncle. The rope snapped, and my uncle's head separated to land on the ground beside his body.

"Let's go, son," my dad spoke, nodding at the tree line where the rest of Chepi's minions waited in the shadows.

Grim bounded up beside me, dropping my opalescent bear on the ground and barking at the Council members in the tree line. His barks startled them, catching them off guard while the sky itself joined the fight.

As I watched, tree roots rose, snaring the ankle of a council member. He fought the grip, but the land beneath him opened up and pulled him underground. Each tree grew brighter while the remaining black robes cried out in pain.

A snow pile fell from a conifer, landing on another of the black robes, and pulled him with the frozen water back into nature. His scream barely registered before it was drowned out with a rush of air.

Wind carried off a third, while the piercing sunshine that followed the snow incinerated the fourth like an ant under a microscope.

The fifth stood, changing shape and form to be Chepi. Her re-birth hosted by the last of her followers.

"You think you can defeat me, Bear? You are nothing!" She wailed.

A chant started in the surrounding space, one hundred witches speaking together.

"Restore the balance, set nature right. Return to her realm, this eater of light."

Smudging sage wafted with them. New coven members joined with long-time residents, some nymphs and shifters mixed in. All of them lending their voices with lit bundles of sage and heartfelt intent. The air held its breath and listened, charged with the magic of a hundred unified voices.

"Restore the balance, set nature right. Return to her realm, this eater of light."

The demon shrank before me, my form returning to its own amid the residents of Huckleberry Hollow.

"Restore the balance, set nature right. Return to her realm, this eater of light," I joined in, standing beside Grim and Sue, Max on her other side.

Chepi stood frozen, unmoved by the spell.

We needed to believe it.

I pictured Penelope, her smile and love for everything but mush-rooms and cantaloupe.

Penelope who wanted to free the town so everyone else could see the world.

Who loved crappy movies and needed affection but was too fucking awkward to ask for it.

My mate, who gave her life to save me.

On the ground, my opalescent bear glowed white hot. Its light expanded into the foliage on the ground, reflected in the snow and on the horrified pale skin of my aunt. Every face rose to the sky, chanting into the sun with a single purpose-to bring back the balance. When the wind kicked up and trees chattered their branches, the earth listened.

"Return to her realm, this eater of light!" We shouted, tears streaming down my face.

With an ear-splitting scream, Chepi burned into ash that blew away on a gentle breeze.

At my feet, the bear continued to shine. Grim pawing at the ground, looking back up at me. A tear running down my cheek fell on the bear. I picked it up, placing it around my neck.

The weight landed on my heart, pulling from my chest the strangling darkness. I could feel her light, her magic, filling my chest and the air. Around the clearing, the ground shimmered, droplets of red and branches from the forest gathered together just out of sight.

I read the inscription again.

You are my heart. I will always be with you.

Gripping the necklace, I let another tear fall and whispered.

"If you're always with me, please, come back to me. Please?"

I begged her magic within the bear, the bits of my own I'd give a thousand times over if I could hold her one last time. My family was the reason for the imbalance. Why did she have to pay?

The trees shimmered, and nature exhaled. The thick band that wrapped around the town fell away and we all took a collective breath. Ahead of me, a naked woman stepped out of the tree line. Her red hair snarled with leaves and branches, as her face stretched in a victorious grin.

"I knew we could do it."

"Penelope."

I ran to her, the woman meeting me halfway until she took a flying leap and collided into my chest, legs wrapped around me. My arms held her tight, the smell of citrus and lavender clinging to her like sunshine and peace.

"You shouldn't have come here, you know that, right?"

She shook her head.

"I had to come here. It was in the prophecy, and it was always going to happen. It was the only way we would ever be free."

"This town doesn't deserve you," I said, shaking my head and burying my face in her hair.

"I didn't do it for the town, Artie," she whispered against my neck. My heart swelled in my chest even as I wanted to punish her with a reddened ass and far too many orgasms.

"You still..." Her teeth sank into my neck, sending waves of pain and pleasure stampeding through my bloodstream. "You need to stop being a pain in the ass."

"You need to stop telling me what to do."

My fingers slid up her thighs to the soaking wet pussy I'd eat daily until Calisto called me home.

"I think I can change your mind," I growled, feeling her gasp as my finger slid between her folds. She smacked me and hissed something about *public*. "Why are you naked?"

"I love you, but that was so fucking dumb," she whispered into my ear, pressing feverish lips into my neck. "I died... Kind of. The necklace and my blood on the plants bound me to the earth, while the mate bond bound me to you. I had to become nature in order to control it and destroy the council, but only you could tether me to this plane and bring me back. Apparently, I set this whole thing in motion when I made that necklace. And I just thought it was cute."

She rolled her eyes and then looked down at my member, probing her belly.

"Why the hell are you naked?"

"I turned into a bear, GoldiLocks." A crowd had gathered, listening and staring slightly. Jealousy rose between us at all the people looking at what was ours, so I made the executive decision to be done with all of it. "And I'm going to take you home and fucking eat you."

Swinging her in a circle for all the town to see, I threw her on my back and took off into the woods. Smell and familiarity leading me back to my townhouse, where I'd finally be home.

With her.

"Everywhere you are is home, Artie."

You got that fucking right.

FORTY-ONE

PENELOPE – THREE MONTHS LATER

"Will you slow down!" I shouted at the man leading me up the street at breakneck speeds. "I'm an indoor cat! We don't run!"

Artemis simply laughed, continuing to pull me forward until we arrived, breathless, at the winter solstice festival. The once invisible streets alive, the business owners who'd refused to make a deal with the Council, could finally come home.

Why they would want to was a mystery, considering it still looked like the middle of nowhere, but people in glass houses and rocks or whatever.

With numerous residents freshly returned, the celebration had grown even larger. This year, the festival was being held from the center of town out to the woods. Nearly every street dressed to the nines, yule trees and lights in every window. Vendors had set up booths up and down nearly every street, selling Hollow merch to witches and magical beings from around the world.

Again... Why people would want to visit here was similarly mysterious. But since no one wanted to kill me, I didn't ask too many questions and simply appreciated the thriving economy of our town and my psychiatric practice with its new receptionist-Lucille.

Current and returning residents credited me with being their savior, but Sue, Andrea, Tempe, Naomi, and the rest of the coven had been the ones to gather the witches and other magical beings. They had put out the call and drawn on the magic I returned to the land with my temporary death. Still, everyone wanted to thank me with physical affection, my least favorite form of gratitude unless it was from Artie.

So, I endured a lot of awkward hugs because Artie told me it was what normal people did.

Like a lot, and I went home every night smelling of strangers and weird colognes that may or may not be drugs.

In the non-magical world, people who acted and smelled like that were on drugs.

"Shouldn't we be headed to the airport?" I asked Artie, checking my watch to see there were only two hours left until we were three hours from departure on an international flight. I'd read a hundred different websites about how many hours early one should arrive and while I could probably bibbity bobbity us there faster, I wanted to experience air travel and adventure.

I wanted to have a real adventure that wouldn't potentially kill me.

My first.

"Calm down, worry wart, there's just one thing you need to see first."

He kept pulling me up streets and alleys, everyone we passed waving and smiling.

It was unnerving.

When the Council had disappeared, many former business owners came out against Yasmin. She'd used illegal means to purchase them under market value, a fact that wouldn't stand now that everyone had their magic back. The banks and magical IRS had levied and foreclosed on most of the buildings, allowing them to be resold and revamped.

Giving the town a kitschy makeover that was both cute and disgusting except for the dog bakery.

Grim and I were pretty excited about the dog bakery.

Gnomewhich had also gotten a much needed facelift, and an officially published not-so-secret menu. Naomi had kept the name, letting her wife and kids paper mâché a new gnome statue at the front which occasionally flipped people off, as it did right now to a waif in heels passing out pamphlets to elect her mayor and "Make the Hollow Great Again."

The gnome started giving her crotch chops, and she shouted louder until Naomi chased her away with a broom.

I thought my Offensive Gesture Gnome was inspired and since it only insulted Yasmin and her stiletto sisters who kept trying to rally for a return to the old ways, no one really cared. Unfortunately, the number of teenagers attempting to replicate the magic meant I was going to need to work on being a "responsible adult"... eventually.

Until they actually figure out how to do it, I could plead the fifth on knowing that they're trying.

The harder change to make had been at the hospital. My mom was on the board, but it was also filled with men who had grown accustomed to doing things a certain way. After a series of meetings and staff surveys, the old dudes still refused to budge, so she brought in my dad. Whether he convinced them to surrender with the sight of his twig and berries or siren song was now part of Hollow lore, but it worked nevertheless.

The hospital staff was free of their prom hell, non-witches finally allowed to practice as doctors and non-medically trained doctors being relegated to mop bucket duty.

Only the mop buckets and only for vomit.

It would have been insulting to the custodial staff to give those frauds the same pay and responsibility as actual skilled workers.

It was still a hellscape, but it was getting better. And while I was of the *burn it to the ground and start over again* mentality, most sane people thought progress, however small, meant there was hope for change and salvation.

"Come on! Where are we..." he stopped in front of my office. It still said I was a psycho, but I'd long since decided to give up the manhunt for the sign painter. If the world wanted a little madness, I wanted to watch it burn... at least I did before coffee.

Afterward, it was probably safe from burning. I knew where the water came from.

Assembled in front of the building was my new coven, my family, Naomi and her family, Alpha Kuruk and Maddy.

"What's going on?" I asked, looking from each smiling face back to Artie.

Who was on his knee beside me.

"Dude, we went over this. You can't eat me out in public," I hissed, and his wide smile turned a touch wicked. "Also, I have underwear on this time!"

"That's for later. This," he pulled a ring pop out of his pocket and the ring he'd given me in front of the coffee shop three months ago. "Is for now. Will you marry me?"

"What? But... mate bond. We're kind of already married," I protested, even though my heart soared, and I took the candy ring. "I mean yes, but..."

Pulling off the wrapper, I stuck it in my mouth and looked down at Artie suggestively. Artemis slid the proper ring on my finger, though the one in my mouth was far tastier, and didn't take the bait. It fit as perfect as it had before, a reminder that it was mine.

That it had always been mine.

Rising, we faced the assembled friends and family together and I tried not to explode with joy at the sight. At the center were Sue and Andrea, flanked by Grim and Max, holding a spell book.

I have people.

"It's more for them, but I thought... if we're going to see the world, I'd like the normies to know you're mine too," he said, pulling my candy ring out of my mouth and replacing it with his tongue.

The kiss was passionate, friendly, and fast.

A promise of more to come.

"OK, but if you want me to wear both my rings in public, you'll need to buy more... probably in bulk."

He pulled another one out of his pocket, handing it over.

"I always have what you need in my pants."

About the Author

Noelle Rider is a fiction author writing romance with plus-sized female leads and their furry friends. She is one of two authors under the Perry Dog Publishing Imprint, a one woman, two dog operation in Idaho... for now. My dogs are Perry and Padfoot, the furry beasts shown above. They are well-loved character inspiration in all things written and business.

If you are interested in joining my newsletter, please subscribe on my website, PerryDogPublishing.com

You will receive A Bite in Afghanistan, the prequel to the Sharp Investigations Series, as a thank-you for joining. I only have one newsletter for mental health reasons, so both romance and mystery are on there! If you only want one in your inbox, follow Perry Dog Publishing on all socials to stay on top of the latest news... and pet pics.

www.ingramcontent.com/pod-product-compliance
Lightning Source LLC
Chambersburg PA
CBHW070553310726
48982CB00011B/1574/J